FRENCH CO[...
BOO[...

Christophe

CHRISTINE PERRY

Acknowledgements

Thank you for being there.

Steph Mason, Lorraine Campbell, Donna Quinlan, Alistair Quinlan, and most of all, my favourite secret detective.

One

⁓

WOW, SHE JUST LOVED the snow. It was as if an impressionist painter up in heaven had picked up his brush and was happily dabbing dots of light all over the place for her to run through. She looked up at the highlights it was making on the Wellington Arch. Beautiful, London is so beautiful when it is white. She jogged on the spot while she waited for the lights to change, and looked down at her feet. The melted snow had mixed with the dirt on the pavement. Well, it was beautiful until people got their feet in it, then it was more like a mucky trail from a coal mine in a Gulag.

The lights changed and she crossed over into Hyde Park. It was even more stunning in the park. It glittered and shimmered, just like a Christmas card. And everyone was happy, you could see it in their faces. Even if the stock market crashed they wouldn't get down, because hey, it would be a white Christmas.

She looked around nervously as she ran. Just a few other hard core enthusiasts out today. They smiled at each other and said good morning - if they had the breath.

Mostly they were happy because of the snow. They were also just a little bit smug that they'd beaten the sofa into submission, and lowered their heart attack risk.

She turned further into the Park and headed towards the Serpentine. It would be frozen this morning. The poor ducks would have to waddle over it to find open water. She watched the clouds of her hot breath as they pumped out, turning the falling snowflakes to rain. She forced herself to concentrate.

'Happy, happy, happy,' she muttered, as her feet hit the ground. 'He'll soon be home, soon be home, soon be home.' She kept the chant going in time with her running pace. It was the only way she could stop herself getting stuck in mind loops. And when Christophe was away she could turn into a mind loop world champion overnight. She'd start the day with it all under control. By coffee time, she'd already done a 'I wonder what Christophe is up to' mind loop. By teatime he'd be 'flirting with someone', and by bedtime he was 'fighting them off' from every corner of the planet.

She deftly dodged a jogger coming the other way. Get a grip on yourself, woman! Christophe does not have affairs. It is not in his nature. And in the highly unlikely event that he did have an accidental lapse, due to a fatal attraction type female spiking his drink, surely you could forgive and forget. Nope, much more likely that raging jealousy would make me lose all sense of proportion, and I'd take the nearest pair of scissors and cut my nose off to spite my face.

Honestly, why do you do this to yourself? There is no way he is cheating on you. Opportunity does not equal action. So he's in meetings with a load of financial whizz women, but that doesn't make it a done deal. Just because you are a dyscalculic maths disaster, does not mean he's automatically eyeing up every Mensa female within a five mile radius. And even if he is, he won't do anything about it, because he always does the right thing, he's famous for it.

She tapped herself gently on her forehead, to try and get some focus. Think about good things, on Jean-Claude, on Christophe, on how amazing life is. You are so lucky! She smiled, thinking back to those first days with the eccentric old fashion designer. The moment that Jean-Claude had first seen her, he'd said, '*Julia ma cherie*, you can hide everything with good clothes and a beautiful face, but you must stop biting your nails.' He'd squeezed her hand affectionately as if he'd known her for a lot longer than the last thirty seconds. Then there was the icing on the cake, he'd brought Christophe into her life.

She lifted her head and smiled brightly at a jogger coming the other way, then went cold with shock. Slim build, pale skinned, red haired, male. She shot across the other side of the path at speed. Her heart started racing wildly. It wasn't Girault, but it could have been.

She switched to sprinting. She needed to reassure herself that she could run fast enough to get away from anyone and everyone. After a full two minute sprint, she slowed to a gentle jog on the path next to the Serpentine. Head down and panting, she gradually got her breath back and looked up across the lake. The ice was melting and the ducks were moving across it very carefully. She concentrated on watching them, and it calmed her. She laughed as one slid off to the side and almost fell over. They deftly plopped into the water one by one. She thought she saw a reflection in the water of someone standing behind her. When she swung around to look. There was no one there.

Honestly I really do need to get a grip. Girault is

probably lying in a ditch somewhere on the other side of the world. And I have to stop giving him so much head space. Why Do I let that sicko keep getting into my head? He's just a sadistic closet psychopath, only without the closet. She shivered at the thought of those thieving light hands. He had a seriously weird way of leaving the left little fingernail to grow long. He told people it was because he was a French aristocrat and that's what they did.

She jogged on the spot at the fork in the Serpentine path, and looked around. She hesitated. Never run the same route for more than two days in a row, Christophe had said. She looked again for a redhead. No need to hit the panic attack button, unless he actually appeared. She breathed deeply, took a whiff of Christophe's aftershave bottle that she kept in her pocket, and managed to make the switch from thinking bad things to thinking good things.

Only one more day to go and he would be home and she could cash in the marathon running for marathon sex. She smiled to herself and felt that wonderful ache down there. Definitely looking forward to a bit of that!

Funny how sex worked really. You could go for years with less sex drive than a woolly mammoth frozen in the Arctic. Then, ka-ching! In comes the sexual lottery winning ticket from left field. Julia's therapist had spent years trying to treat Julia's frigidity. Nothing had worked. In the end it had all been cured by the sensuality of a good man with a pleasant smell. And Christophe did smell good, always - even when he was sweating from a serious game of squashing every opponent he met on the court. She wondered if that was why they called it squash.

She deftly stuck her tongue out to taste a snowflake. Unfortunately, they were both away so much that they were getting less and less time together. Talk about ships that passed in the night.

She headed out of the park and waited for the lights to change. The time it took was exactly the amount needed for her to get into another mind loop. Congratulations, she said to herself. You've spent most of the run, mulling over being attacked by Girault and being suspicious about what Christophe is up to. Bad move, definitely a bad move. She started slapping her forehead, again.

'Stop it! Stop it. Just stop it,' she shouted. Sensing she was not alone, she swung round to see a couple of people in dark hooded jackets. They stood with their heads down, avoiding her gaze. She stared at them for a moment trying to decide if it was because they were embarrassed or because they were henchmen preparing to chloroform her and drag her off to Girault.

The taller one slowly lifted his head. She felt her heart do a cardio workout all on its own. She caught her breath. No, please no… Then gave a huge sigh of relief. The man, a complete stranger, stared at her in alarm. He was more scared than she was. He quickly lowered his gaze.

Get a grip on yourself. Jaime Girault is not here. The man in the hoodie looked at her again, his face even more alarmed. She realised she had clenched her fists and raised them ready for a fight. She quickly lowered them.

'Oh. Sorry. Really sorry. Didn't mean to worry you. When I was shouting stop it, I meant me, stop it. Not you. You are fine. You're not doing anything. It's me.'

The other, even skinnier one, didn't look at her, but pulled the man further away.

The lights changed. Julia had never seen two people sprint across a road quite so determinedly. You'd think they were after the last flight out of Armageddon. She was so busy looking at them, she ran straight into the traffic light post.

'Ouch! Ouch' she said clutching her head.

The two people after the Armageddon flight ran even faster.

'Christ!' she said, still gripping her head and muttering. 'Great, that's just great. Now I'm going to have a humongous bruise on my forehead. Excellent addition to my welcome home, seduction routine.'

She started to feel dizzy, and the guilty traffic light post was dancing to psychedelic club lights in her head.

It was just typical of how things were when Christophe was away. Somehow her comfortable, stable life collapsed like a volcanic crater about to do a Pompei rerun. She wondered if she was somehow subconsciously triggering it. The PTSD therapist had said it might happen. That she would crave the excitement of an adrenaline rush.

She jogged on, towards Eaton Square, looking in the shop windows as she drifted past. Dresses threaded with real gold. Hum, oh, so tempting. No, not today, credit cards are so high, they've probably landed on the Moon. She could try and kid herself that it was her dyscalculia, but the truth was she just loved beautiful things.

She jogged past one more tempting window display and stopped abruptly. Nestled between a red sequin dress and a diamond necklace, was a big card asking for donations for the Helping Hand homeless charity. Their charity. Good one Christophe. He was amazing – a gentle reminder about getting our perspectives right. Her eye caught something reflected in the shop window and her heart started racing. There they were again, behind her, the two people in the hooded jackets. She swung around to speak to them.

There was no one there.

***

Back at the flat, she went straight to the bathroom and started hunting through the drawer, looking for the arnica. It was too late for ice but maybe the arnica would do it. She found the tube, squirted some on her hand and gently rubbed it over the large red golf ball that had appeared smack in the middle of her forehead.

Her head and her hand started burning. She picked up the arnica gel and read the label. Hell, she'd put the deep heat muscle rub on. She dived over to the sink, and tried to wash it off. Too late. The golf ball had gone so red it was more like an airport landing light.

'Great, that's just great,' she muttered as she stripped off her jogging gear. By the time Christophe gets back tomorrow, it will probably be bright blue. I'll look like I've been cross bred with a Cyclops.

She set the water to steaming hot, and fished around in the complimentary shampoos they'd accumulated. She felt guilty. Look at all this plastic. She was most definitely developing a conscience. It was like a bird tweeting in her head.

Christophe had managed to get his wealth and conscience working together in perfect harmony but she hadn't cracked it yet. Hers were more like a dysfunctional family. Cain and Abel to be precise. At work she'd be all fired up, doing a brilliant job selling Jean-Claude's clothes for tons of money. Then she'd walk out of the door into Kensington and within two minutes, she'd see people struggling in doorways on the streets. So of course she'd give away all her cash. Then, she'd feel depressed because it reminded her of when she'd been down and out. And she had been. Not quite hell but near enough to pat Cerberus on one of his heads. So, then she'd get upset that she couldn't help everyone in the World. The devious mind loop would tell her that she needed to be careful, because one never knew what was around the corner, and she could easily end up back in a kennel with Cerberus. And before you could say Jack and Jones, she'd be doing obsessive compulsive retail therapy. You'd hear her credit card limit being broken like Concorde breaking the sound barrier. And then she'd feel guilty about spending so much money while the world was starving. So she'd head back to work, even though it was after hours. And she'd work her butt off, because then she could feel as if she deserved her nice life. And the next day, Jean-Claude would find her snoring on the sofa in the fitting room, using the bubble wrap as a duvet.

***

Poor Jean-Claude. He was feeling as fed up as she'd ever seen him. His worst nightmare was about to come true. It was only a couple of months to the Oscars and he didn't have an Oscar dress to design. And as far as he was concerned that was the kiss of death.

'Julia, if I don't have an Oscar dress, I might as well design straightjackets or motorcycle helmets.' he'd said, in tears. 'I will be nothing.'

He did have an Oscar dress to design but the elderly actress had died on him. Julia had rushed around trying to conjure up the nearest pair of long legs with an Oscar nomination, but there was nothing doing. Everyone was already organised. He was so sad and she could feel his sadness. It went much deeper than a problem over a dress. They both knew that their time together was coming to an end. Only neither of them knew how it was going to end and neither of them seemed to have the guts to tell the other one.

She stepped out of the shower and towelled herself dry.

Maybe she should resign. If Christophe did too, they could do lots of worthwhile things together. Or something more exciting. Even better, something more dangerous!

Her thoughts of battling with Christophe through the jungle while being chased by a jaguar they were trying to save from extinction, were interrupted by the phone.

'Hi. Is that Madame de Flaubert?' asked a gravelly voice.

'Yes. Well, no. Well, sort of.'

The deep voice laughed. 'Well Madame 'sort of' de Flaubert. Is Christophe there?'

'Sorry. He's away on business.'

'Oh. This is Simon Chapman at the gallery. I'm hoping he can lend us his two Breton School paintings for an exhibition.'

'Well, he'll be back tomorrow, I'm sure...'

'Get him to call me as soon as possible please.'

'I'm sure he'll deal with it as soon as he's back.'

'It's more urgent than that. Do you have a mobile number for him? I've only got this number.'

'Hang on. I'll see if I can find it.'

She scrambled around looking for her mobile and got the number up on screen. She kept repeating it, but was nervous that she would fluff it. She hesitated. Was it 5 2 7 or 2 5 7? She could hear Chapman talking to someone in the background. He sounded very annoyed. That did it, she was bound to give him the wrong number and quite frankly he wasn't exactly oozing patience and charm. No. He could wait until Christophe got back. She cut him off. It rang again, so she ignored it, and listened when it switched to take a message.

'Simon Chapman here. It seems we got cut off accidentally and Mrs 'not quite' de Flaubert has disappeared into thin air, like Cinderella at midnight. Let me know as soon as possible, Christophe, about the paintings.'

Interesting. The man with no patience thinks himself a bit of a Prince Charming.

The phone playback kicked in again and she listened to earlier messages while she tidied up. There were three other messages from him. You could hear the increasing anxiety. By the third message his boxers were well and truly in a twist. She bet they were flamboyant silk Versace Baroques. He sounded like a Versace kind of guy.

She looked over at the Chapman painting. She loved it. It was one of the best Breton impressionist paintings in the world. When you went up close, it was a massive mess of psychedelic blotches and splodges that you'd think a finger painting three year old must have done. When you stood back it transformed into a beautiful landscape where the light flickered between the frosty fields and the icy water. Pretty clever technique the impressionists had. Sort of painting with concussion.

She hoped Christophe didn't lend it out, because they'd have to put something else there and he might put the black hole back up. The art negotiator had raved about the black hole being a wonderful example of the rainbow shades of red, through to blue, that can hide themselves in black. But a black hole is a black hole when it's hanging on your sitting room wall. Sometimes just for fun, she'd turn it upside down to see if Christophe noticed. He never did. In the end she'd managed to convince him to swap it for the Chapman and she'd stuck the black hole in the downstairs loo. She told the art negotiator that it matched the other black hole - the one where goldfish go when they die. The art negotiator smiled, nervously. He was worried his commission was going to go the same way as the goldfish.

Christophe had laughed with her indulgently. Then after the art advisor left, he got really mad. So they'd had a row, and then fantastic sex when they made up. So, she supposed having art you don't like does serve a purpose after all.

***

She tried to get hold of Christophe but he didn't answer, so she went to bed. The heating had made the room hot and stuffy so she opened the window. The wind was getting up speed and it blew the curtains around so they rustled against the carpet. The moonlight, deformed by bizarre cloud formations, created monstrous shadows on the floor. She got up and shut the window. They really should invent non-eerie moonlight. She imagined someone jumping out from behind the curtains or hands shooting out from under the bed to grab her. Only one thing for it, jump from the window into the bed. It was a huge leap. She made it in one, settled down comfortably and pulled the duvet up under her chin. Zut, she'd forgotten to put the alarm on again. Maybe she should get up and go and put it on. No. Too scary getting out of bed. She kept the bedside light on. Very childish. But then again, not everyone had a Girault in their life. And you didn't have to be a child to be bloody scared of him.

If Christophe was there she was never scared at all. Moonlight against rolling clouds was really romantic. A howling wind would have made them snuggle deeper under the duvet together. It was not so much howling now, as taunting her with an excruciating whistle, like it was trying to call in a pack of thirsty bloodhounds. She grabbed the ear plugs next to the bed and her hand hovered over the sleeping tablets. If I take them I'll wake up groggy and miserable. If I don't, I'll never sleep and the bags under my eyes will be big enough to take a full Royal wardrobe. After ten minutes of mind racing with her hand going backwards and forwards, she gave in and took one.

She fell asleep quickly, clutching Christophe's pillow like a baby with a comfort blanket. She didn't hear the sound of the bottom lock pins on the door being manipulated with the tension wrench. Nor did she notice the very slim, long fingered hand slip through the letterbox and open the top lock. The two people that had been watching her earlier in the day, crept along the hallway into the lounge.

Two

JULIA WOKE UP STILL clutching the pillow and jumped out of bed with extra urgency because she'd overslept. She wandered around slurping her coffee and grabbing clothes, vaguely trying to disguise the mess in cupboards so that Hilda wouldn't be too mad with her. Hilda rang the doorbell as she was reading a message from Christophe.

'Couldn't get my key in the bottom lock again,' she said, tutting as Julia opened the door. 'And what's all these bits on the carpet?'

Julia looked down at the tiny bits of wood near the base of the door mat. 'Don't know. Maybe we've got mice again.'

'Yes, well you wouldn't have if you didn't leave food out all the time. You should get some poison.'

'I couldn't possibly poison them, Hilda, they are sweet and they are God's creatures just as we are.'

'Humph.' she replied. 'And so are them cows what's skins made them boots you're wearing. Thought you'd be up earlier today.' she continued, 'Given that Mr Christophe's comin 'ome.' Julia wandered into the sitting room. She kissed a message from Christophe.

'I've made coffee if you want some Hilda,' she shouted back to her.

She could hear her grumbling about making herself some instant thanks very much, that filter stuff really did her tummy no good at all and she'd be up for a week with all that caffeine. She then heard the crash as she opened the dishwasher.

'Oops. Sorry Hilda' she shouted, remembering that she'd stacked it like the leaning tower of Pisa. She sneaked off into the bedroom to read her message again.

She loved Christophe's messages. He wrote them by hand, on the hotel stationery, took a picture and sent it to her. Then when he got home, he gave them to her and she kept them in a little box, tied up with ribbons. He said that in years to come he wanted their grandchildren to have a bundle of their love letters to read.

Tried to video call, hoping to catch you naked but you didn't pick up so thought you must be asleep. I love and miss you so much. Can't wait to get home. If all goes well, I'll be air bound tomorrow. I left a message for Simon Chapman at the gallery that he can take the paintings as soon as he likes. He knows the routine re: insurance and security etc. I have a big surprise for you – besides the one in my boxer shorts that is. C xx

Honestly any more of that and she'd have to go out for another marathon run.

She sighed. Only about ten hours to go. She wasn't even near ready to leave when Jean-Claude called.

'Julia you always do this, always. You never come early like you say.'

Jean-Claude I'm sorry. I'll be there soon. I was just on

my way out of the door.' She lied.

'I need things for today. I need a model, I need shoes and hair and many, many more things. You do not understand how important this is for me.'

Hilda was just walking past with a pile of dirty laundry and Julia gestured to her to hang on a minute. 'I know, really I do understand, Jean-Claude.' Julia grabbed the corner of one of the shirts and took in a good whiff of the remains of Christophe's smell for sustenance. His aftershave mixed with the smell of him was so much better than pure aftershave. Imagine if I could bottle it. That's an idea. Custom made perfume. Your partner's smell with a dash of *Eau Sauvage*. Hilda tutted and Jean-Claude carried on, getting more and more distressed.

'No. No, you cannot possibly understand how it is for me. You have your life all very nice Julia and I have so many, many more problems...'

'I know you do Jean-Claude, really I do.' She muttered. She felt sad, and guilty, knowing she was going to resign. Knowing she was going to desert him.

The doorbell rang, she stretched across with the phone, tripped over the carpet edge and accidentally cut Jean Claude off. That was not going to help their relationship at all.

Two men in brown overalls stood armed with large art cases, so big you could hide a dead body in them.

'Mrs de Flaubert?' The taller one thrust a card under her nose for her to look at, like it was a warrant card and she was under arrest. 'We're from the Impressionist Gallery. We've come for the Baudoin and the Chapman.' That was a relief, it was the paintings that were under arrest. Julia glanced at it, not really paying attention.

'They're in here,' she said and led them through into the sitting room.

'If you could just sign here Madam. Got to have the paperwork signed. Insurance and everything.'

'Oh, yes, of course.' Julia took the paperwork. She noticed two armed security guards in uniform were standing by the open door. They weren't interested in her, they were watching up and down the street.

'Good morning,' she said to them.

The younger one turned very quickly, smiled at her and then went back to looking down the street.

The two men in brown overalls took the paintings down and propped them up against the wall. They wrapped the Baudoin in special art protection material. Then put it into one of the cases.

'Gosh that's very well organised,' said Julia.

'It's the new system,' said the elderly man. 'Every painting has its own padded, tailor made case.'

'Looks a bit like a coffin,' said Julia as she handed back the papers that he'd given her. There seemed to be an absolute mountain of them. He tore the top copy off each and gave them to her. She stood looking at her phone messages while they came back for the Chapman. She watched them seal it in its own case and had a sinking feeling.

'I'm going to miss it,' she said, smiling as she put the papers on the telephone table.

They looked at her surprised.

'Well you know, I like it.'

'Oh yes of course. It's very nice.'

Julia followed them out and closed the door. She fumbled around for her keys. Maybe she would lock Hilda in good and proper, just to prove her point. She couldn't get her key in the top lock. She was so late already and Jean-Claude would be climbing the walls. She'd call the security company from the office and get them to call round and have a look.

***

Jean-Claude was in the downstairs fitting rooms. He was pinning masses of blue satin fabric on a model who Julia didn't know.

'Sorry I'm late and sorry I cut you off.'

Jean-Claude didn't look up.

'It was an accident, Jean Claude!' she insisted.

Still he did not look up. He huffed and puffed instead.

'Some gallery people were at the door. It's been crazy with Christophe away.' She placed her hand gently on his shoulder. Finally, he looked up and it was safe to give him a hug. He hugged her back and kissed her on the cheeks affectionately, then his face changed.

'Sit down Julia,' he muttered nervously

Julia was confused. Jean-Claude was never nervous. He took the fabric off the model and then shooed her away. He swung round on her.

'I am very sorry, *chérie*,' he said, clearly not sorry at all. 'You are sacked.'

Julia stood up horrified.

'What?' OK, so she was late and she couldn't get an actress for the Oscar dress, but sacked! He couldn't sack her. Her instant reaction was to counter attack.

'You can't sack me. Christophe finances your design company. You can't sack me.'

'*OUI. Si*. I can.'

'No, you CAN'T.'

'I can. I have a new sponsor. I do not need your Christophe's money. She is my sponsor and she wants my dress for the Oscars.'

Julia crossed her arms defiantly. 'So why am I sacked?'

'Because she doesn't like you.'

'She who Jean-Claude? Who is *she*?'

Jean-Claude was looking down intently at the edging of the blue fabric he was holding.

'No one. No one you really know.'

'Huh.' Julia started pacing up and down the fitting room. 'No one I know? Then how does she know to say that she doesn't like me, eh Jean-Claude?'

'OK then she does know you.' he said shrugging. 'She knows you because she had a nice affair with Christophe before you stole him.'

'What do you mean, stole him? You were the one that was trying to set me up with him! I didn't even like him at first. You were the one who sent me off down to his house in Provence. You didn't tell me it was his house because you knew I wouldn't go if you did!'

Jean-Claude pouted sulkily.

'And!' Julia continued, 'What was it you said?' she narrowed her eyebrows together as if deep in thought. 'Oh yes. I remember. Our self-destructive tendencies were supposed to give us something in common, not lead to the annihilation of both of us. I am pretty sure that's what you said. So no Jean-Claude I did not steal him!'

She paced up and down the room glaring at Jean-Claude. How could he? How could he sack her because of an ex of Christophe's. Then she twigged it. She dropped her bag on the floor with a loud thud and started pointing her finger at Jean-Claude.

'It's that French actress isn't it? It's Sophie 'please let me take my clothes off in this film' Petrarch isn't it?'

Jean-Claude found the blue fabric very interesting again. He shrugged. 'Maybe yes, maybe no.'

'Yes, it is, Jean-Claude. How could you? Honestly, how could you? You are so fickle.'

He turned around and glared at her, very red in the face. 'Because if I do not have my Oscar dress, I will fail as a designer. I will be a failure.'

The tears welled up in Julia's eyes. 'And what about a friend Jean-Claude? What about failing as a friend?'

'Huh.' he said pointing his finger at her. 'You want me to feel guilty. But I do not feel guilty, and you Julia, are a big hypocrite. I know you are going to resign. Maybe not today, maybe not tomorrow, but soon. You want a nice life with Christophe and I am not important anymore!'

Julia stood open mouthed, then picked up her bag and stormed off.

'I will clear my desk Jean-Claude. But think about it carefully. Sophie Petrarch is hardly going to be a good advertisement for your clothes is she? Because she never bloody well keeps them on for long enough!'

***

Julia sighed with relief as the taxi drew up outside the house. It had been far worse than she'd expected. Deep down she knew, and Jean-Claude knew, it was the right thing for both of them, but it hadn't made it any easier. They had both gone on the defensive hiding their feelings behind a brick wall of stubbornness. He was like a father to her and she knew he felt the same but the split was all too raw and upsetting for both of them. She knew it would calm down, and it would be OK eventually, but for the moment they both needed to lick their wounds.

It had taken her precisely one hour to clear her desk and then she'd set off to get some retail therapy. She struggled up the stairs with the shopping bags in her arms, went into the kitchen and put the bags on the table. Hilda had left her a note.

Dear Julia. I've had an extra go all round because I don't want Mr Christophe to think you're slovenly. I have put that bottle you told me to in the freezer. Don't leave it too long or it will EXPLODE!

Julia wrote back on the note. *Mr Christophe knows I'm slovenly but please don't call me that because it upsets me and when I get upset, I become even more slovenly. And I never explode champagne bottles, it is sacrilege.'*

She put the shopping in the fridge and started singing as loudly as possible. *'Tonight's the night. Everything's all right, Oh I love you babe, 'ain't nobody 'gonna stop us now.'* She'd read that if you sang louder, you had more chance of singing in tune. It wasn't true.

What was she going to wear? She pulled the sleek little black number out of the bag. No, the dresses were not good. It had to be something small and sexy, that was quick and easy to get off. Even the underwear would take too long. A flannel perhaps? No. She'd have to sit in the bath for ages. If he was delayed, she'd have to keep topping up the hot water and she'd end up red and wrinkled like a sun-dried tomato. A hat? Why not? She went into the bedroom, got undressed and put on her favourite 'Breakfast at Tiffany's' hat. The enormous wide brim flopped so low it hid the whole of the top of her face halfway down her nose. She pranced around naked, straightening the sheets on the bed. She fluffed up the pillows that Hilda had already expertly fluffed. She was so excited. It felt as if he'd been away for years, not a week.

She was singing so loudly that she didn't hear the door open. She jumped out of her skin when a voice behind her said, 'Wow, nice hat. Were you thinking of going somewhere Julia Connors?'

Julia spun round. 'My God Christophe you know if you creep up on me like that, you never know what my PTSD could cause!'

She launched herself from the bed right into his arms. 'Thank heavens you're home.'

Christophe nuzzled his face into her neck and hair.

'Mm you smell so good, so nice, so familiar, so ... um sexy.'

'Mm you too. You smell so ... so ... there. I've decided you're not allowed to go away for any longer than the time that the sheets smell of you. This time was too long.'

'I'm back earlier or haven't you noticed?'

'Not early enough,' said Julia.

He pulled her down gently onto the bed.

'I had to make some manic connections to get to New York in time to get the earlier flight.'

Julia removed his jacket and began to unbutton the front of his shirt.

'In that case, I'd better make it up to you, Monsieur de Flaubert.'

Julia noted that his mouth tasted ever so slightly of champagne and smoked salmon. She looked deep into his tawny eyes. 'What big gold flecks you've got in your eyes Monsieur de Flaubert,' she said.

'All the better to keep you in the rich style to which you've become accustomed Mademoiselle Connors.' he answered, slipping the hat from her head.

***

They were lying in bed snuggled up like spoons. Christophe snored gently into Julia's hair. The background

25

hum of the morning rush hour traffic was almost soothing. Occasionally she heard the closing of a door in a nearby house or the sound of a desperate dog, barking happily as it finally got taken for its walk. Christophe continued to snore. She could understand he was exhausted and jet lagged but she was so bored waiting for him to wake up. She'd already woken him up once in the middle of the night.

'Are you asleep?' she asked loudly, knowing full well he was.

Silence.

'But are you really, really asleep?' she asked again, nudging him gently.

Silence.

'Because if you're not there's lots of things I want to ask you.'

Silence. Slightly bigger nudge.

'I mean are you really, really, really, asleep?

'Yes I am.'

'Good. Well I've decided I want to give up work. I want to do something more worthwhile.' Bit of a porky pie, she thought to herself. No, not really a lie, more of a pork scratching, because I was itching to resign anyway.

'And either you're away or I'm away at fashion shows, and we don't seem to spend any time together.' she said. 'Anyway it's pretty shameful making as much money as you do. We could do something better together, organise charity things. Save the world.'

'Julia I'm exhausted. I haven't slept for about three days.'

'Well that's what I'm talking about. If you didn't go away so much you wouldn't be so tired, would you?'

'Is there any reason, Julia Connors, why you are the

only person in the world who does not sleep after making love?'

Julia looked suspicious. 'You can't possibly know that unless you have slept with every other woman in the world.'

'Fair point.'

'I think it's because I wasted so much time before, you know. I was always pretending to be asleep so that I didn't have to do it, because I didn't like it. Now with you, I do like it, so there's no point in sleeping. It's much better to stay awake and do it again. Otherwise I'm not going to get my life quota, am I?'

Christophe put the pillow over his head and groaned. He sat up suddenly.

'What do you mean? It's shameful making as much money as I do?'

'Well isn't it? You've already got enough to feed the world on Fortnum's picnic hampers.'

'I don't, actually. Even the cheapest hamper costs...'

'OK. OK. Please don't talk numbers, you know how it freaks me out.'

He pulled her down gently, so that her head rested on his chest.

'I know it's not easy, but you really do have to work this life, money, conscience balance out, my darling. What do you think we do with the money we make?'

'Err, buy paintings?'

Christophe looked horrified. 'Buy paintings? Is that the first thing you think of?'

'Well and lend them to galleries and give money to businesses.'

'Yes, and finance scholarships for arts students and organise placement of charity money so that it works the best way for the charity, and build schools in Africa, and Bangladesh and invest in a whole portfolio of green issues. And while I am negotiating my own deals, I get a percentage put into those charities too.'

'Oh.'

'And financing a rehabilitation centre, the centres for the homeless that your crazy Scottish mates run. Not to mention financing Jean-Claude's affair which I have to point out is running at a massive loss. It currently constitutes quite a large sum, whilst employing very few people and doing very little for unemployment and not doing a great deal for the world as a whole.'

'Ah, yes, I hadn't thought of that..'

'But the most important thing is, when you see someone who needs help, help them if you can but don't beat yourself up because for every person you see on the street that needs help, there are thousands more that we are able to help and are helping through the work we do. It just isn't so obvious because it is not right in front of your eyes.' He rolled over and pinned her to the bed. 'So, my answer, my darling. 'He kissed her gently on the lips. ' about giving up work is…' He kissed her again. 'Yes if you marry me.'

'Oh.' Julia felt the sickness knot tangling itself up in her stomach. She wriggled out from underneath him.

'It's not very nice, you know, to say no to me absolutely every time.' he shook his head sadly.

'But it only takes me to say yes once and I'll have to go through with it because a promise is a promise. Anyway I can't because I've got nuptaphobia.'

Christophe shook his head in disbelief. 'You've got what?'

'Nuptaphobia.'

'There is no such thing.'

'I looked it up. Anuptaphobia is scared of not getting married. So I figure nuptaphobia has to be a word and it must be scared of getting married. And that's what I've got.

'Well my nuptaphobic, dyscalculic, PTSD love, never let it be said that I do not embrace neurodivergence.' He sighed dramatically, took her hand and she sat down on the bed next to him.

'Well maybe it's not a phobia but I just know that if we don't get married then everything will be alright and that we'll stay together out of love. It's kind of an instinct.'

'So, if you're not nuptaphobic, you are rejecting me cruelly by saying no to me every time I ask you. I'm not going to ask you any more. Next time you can ask me.'

'It's only when people get married that all the problems start. Look at all the great love affairs that lasted. They had some great impediment to them marrying and they stayed in love forever because they had to fight to be together.'

Christophe looked disbelieving. 'Like who?'

'Like Nelson and Lady Hamilton and like Anthony and Cleopatra.'

'That's only hearsay. And as a matter of fact, Cleopatra was actually screwing Caesar at the same time, so I hardly think you can count that.'

'History is not big on ruby weddings is it? And look at Richard Burton and Elizabeth Taylor. They tried it tons of times each and every time they were married to somebody else their love flourished, and every time they were married to each other it was a complete flop. If that's not proof, I don't know what is.'

He picked up a book to read.

'OK, I don't want to marry you any more. I give up. You would be a terrible person to marry anyway. You are far too stubborn and argumentative and fly off following any old instinct or intuition without a second thought. And you turn into a disaster magnet every time I go away. So what was it this time?' he asked, looking her straight in the eyes. 'Apart from the obvious one which is that large blue lump on your forehead that you have tried to disguise with make-up.'

Julia sighed. 'Attractive isn't it. I ran into a traffic light post.'

Christophe gently ran his fingers over the lump to check it. 'Because?' he asked. 'You ran into a traffic light because?.'

'Well, you know, panic attack, I thought two people were following me and turned around not concentrating and ran into the traffic light post.'

'Hum,' he kissed it better. 'Anything else I should know about?'

'Nothing. Nothing else. I resent that I really do.' She hit him with the pillow, then paused for a second. This was as good a time as any.

'OK. So I did have a slight altercation with an over-running bath, but it's nothing that can't be fixed. It's so complicated when you're away. My PTSD is far worse and there's no sex to take my mind off it. So I have to go for these enormously long runs.'

She hit him again with the pillow. He hit her back with his and the fight got so out of hand they didn't hear the front door intercom buzzing for quite a while.

'I'll get it,' said Julia, slinging on a bathrobe that did nothing to hide the long, tanned legs and barely covered the curve of her bottom.

'No, you won't,' said Christophe, wrapping a towel around his waist. 'Not looking like that.'

She looked at Christophe's dark tousled hair and

muscular torso above the towel.

'Yes, I will.' she replied, going to grab the door. 'It might be a woman. Or a gay man.' Or even a straight man, she thought to herself. If she was a straight man, she was certain one look at him would flip her.

'Mm jealous,' grinned Christophe. He followed her down the stairs and watched her as she headed towards the front door. She really did not have enough clothes on to answer the door in his opinion.

'I still can't believe you've got through a whole week, without any major disaster at all. I've been thinking about this running in the park. I worry about you being out early in the mornings on your own. Girault is still out there.'

'You know I can run really fast, you needn't worry so much.'

'I doubt you can run faster than a bullet.'

'That is not helpful.'

'Sorry. You're right. How about we get a dog? We could make it a guide dog for the blind then you might not run into any more traffic light posts.' He wandered off into the kitchen, his voice fading slightly. 'There's an added advantage too,' he said, shouting back down the hall from around the kitchen door. 'Then when I come back from my trips, if the dog wags its tail friendly to any strange men, I'll know it knows them and you've been unfaithful to me.'

'Very funny,' said Julia. 'I've never heard of a dog being called as an expert witness in a court of law, not even in America.'

'Are you kidding?! In America dogs have their own attorneys.'

Christophe watched Julia open the front door, appreciating the pleasant way the line between her tan and the curve of her bottom just peeped out from the bottom of the bathrobe.

'You have a suspicious mind,' she called back to him.

Two men in brown overalls stood at the door. The younger one blushed seeing Julia in just a bathrobe. The older man smiled apologetically, and pushed a card into Julia's hand. Two security guards with guns stood outside the front door looking up and down the street. Before they even spoke, Julia had a sinking sense of déjà vu.

'Chapman Impressionist's gallery. We've come to collect the Chapman and Baudoin paintings.'

Three

INSPECTOR DENTON FROM THE Scotland Yard Arts and Antiques unit shook Christophe's hand. He was a very unassuming elderly man who seemed to have years of detective work etched on his face. Julia liked him immediately. A shorter, middle-aged man was bending down behind Denton, looking at the door hinges and frame.

'May I introduce my colleague, *Inspecteur* Guillemain from the OCBC, our equivalent unit in France,' said Denton, 'we will be working this case together.'

There was an embarrassed pause as *Inspecteur* Guillemain did not acknowledge them but took his time to look more at the floor and door. Inspector Denton smiled at them apologetically. Eventually, Guillemain stood up, shaking his head and tutting unnecessarily. He and Christophe glared at each other. No introductions needed there.

'Guillemain,' said Christophe, nodding disparagingly.

'De Flaubert,' replied Guillemain, equally disparagingly.

'Ah, you've met before?' asked Inspector Denton,

surprised. 'Inspector Guillemain didn't mention it.'

'No, he wouldn't,' replied Christophe. 'We've been acquainted for years, though.'

'Oh?' asked Denton, with raised eyebrows.

'Yes. Monsieur de Flaubert is always meddling in affairs of art.' replied Guillemain, puffing out his chest like a bantam cock.

'And Inspector Guillemain always seems to be around when disaster strikes,' retorted Christophe.

Ouch, thought Julia.

'Let me get this right Guillemain,' said Christophe. 'You just happened to be in London when my Breton School paintings were stolen. What an extraordinary coincidence.'

'The Chapman Gallery asked me to come over in an advisory capacity. They have been worried about the Breton school paintings for a while. They have suddenly become very popular on the black market. I'm advising them on security.'

'Well you've obviously done a terrible job,' replied Christophe, leaving them all gasping. 'Perhaps I can sue you if I don't get my paintings back.'

Inspector Denton, stepped in to calm things down.

'Could we sit down, do you think Mr de Flaubert?'

Denton and Guillemain sat on the sofa that Christophe offered them. He and Julia sat down in the two chairs opposite.

'Can you tell us what they looked like Miss Connors?' asked Inspector Denton.

'Well they looked just like the two that came today. Same overalls and they had identity cards. I didn't really look at their faces. They had similar security guards in uniform with them. I was expecting the gallery people and

I had somebody on the phone.'

She glanced across at Christophe who was looking at the blank spaces on the wall, as if he was expecting some spiritual graffiti from beyond the grave to appear in explanation.

He turned back around and looked at the policeman, without really listening.

'They were insured of course, Mr de Flaubert?' asked Inspector Denton.

'Sorry? What did you say? Christophe looked more than a little exhausted.

'Insurance?'

'Oh, yes. Of course. The Chapman was insured for its market value. The Baudoin doesn't have any worth, just a couple of thousand for its curiosity value, because he was Chapman's friend. But it does have great sentimental value.'

'Oh?' asked Inspector Denton, making notes.

'It was a present from my god-daughter, Françoise.'

The ticking of the clock and the sound of the rain against the window seemed to enhance the silence rather than break it.

'I'd like to get things a bit clearer, for the paperwork. You're not married?' asked Inspector Denton.

'No.' replied Christophe, not looking at Julia.

'Civil partnership?'

'No'

Guillemain stood up, and started strutting around. Without conferring with Denton first, he took over, and directed his attention at Julia.

'So, in actual fact, Miss Connors signed away two very valuable works of art that did not belong to her,' he said, with the air of a man who thinks he's already solved the case.

'Very odd Miss Connors, that the gallery people accepted that you sign for the removal of the paintings. You could have been anybody.'

'Well no.' Julia shuffled uncomfortably in her chair. She could feel the first wave of a panic attack starting to rise. 'Christophe had said that they were coming, so I didn't think twice about it.'

'What are your own personal financial circumstances Miss Connors?'

'Well. Normal, I suppose. Christophe does all of that. I have a salary from the Vasin fashion company and apart from that, well I live here, obviously.'

'You have no assets of your own?'

'I have no idea,' Julia, answered. She stared angrily at Guillemain.

'No inheritance or private income?'

'Look I told you. I don't know. Ask Christophe.'

Guillemain ignored her comment.

'No shares?' asked Guillemain, still staring at her. He made note of her agitation. She was visibly shaking.

'No!'

She shifted in the chair and clenched her fists. She quickly unclenched them and sat on them, hoping it would stop her leaping up and giving Guillemain a piece of her mind. Christophe had noticed the clenched fists and shook his head at her, just as Guillemain looked up from his notepad. Guillemain had seen the look between them and decided to push his provocation further.

'No pension?'

Pension, thought Julia. Just how old does the guy think I am? I am *so* going to plant him one.

'Let me get this right. De Flaubert has complete control over your finances. Very unusual in this day and age.'

'Are you trying to insinuate something, Guillemain?' demanded Christophe.

'No. I'm doing my job de Flaubert. Finding the motive. Financial and personal relationship problems such as coercive control are clear motives.'

'What?' 'You can't be serious?'

'We'll see de Flaubert.'

'You should be looking at where the paintings might have gone.' Christophe stared coldly at Guillemain. 'You more than anybody should know there is a massive traffic of valuable art into private collections and collectors pick out the artist and the painting they want before they even steal it. Once they've decided on it, they will stop at nothing to get it. Why don't you look into that before you start worrying about Julia's pension plan?'

Guillemain did not look Christophe in the eye, but continued to stare threateningly at Julia.

'I'm well aware of that de Flaubert.' He added.

Christophe ran his hands through his hair exasperated. 'Well,' he said. 'Why aren't you looking into where they could have got hold of the Chapman Gallery identification, the uniforms and the paperwork. Presumably they would also have needed to have fake security guard uniforms too.'

'I was just coming to that,' said Guillemain. 'Where exactly did you leave the papers that you say you signed Miss Connors.'

Julia could feel her heart beating frantically and knew that her fight or flight mode was peaking. She was fairly sure flight was not going to come out on top.

'I told you. On the table by the front door. When they came back for the Chapman, they were there. Maybe they took them. Maybe I didn't react because I had a concussion at the time because I ran into a traffic light post.'

'Oh dear,' said Guillemain.

You didn't have to be a fraud squad detective to pick up on the false sincerity.

Guillemain started to pace up and down, and read out his notes, mechanically.

'Let's get this right, Miss Connors. You have no substantial personal income, large credit card debts from our reports and you have recently been sacked from your job with the French fashion designer Jean-Claude Vasin.'

Julia's jaw dropped. How the hell did he know that?

Christophe threw her an enquiring look that both Guillemain and Denton noticed.

'Oh you didn't know that de Flaubert?' said Guillemain. He continued reading from his notes before Christophe could answer. 'And seeing the small pieces of wood by the door, obvious evidence of an attempted break in, you forgot to call the security company.' He added a further note reading it as he wrote '…possibly due to concussion sustained by ... running ... into … traffic light ... post.' He turned the page and carried on. 'You then let the thieves walk into the house and take the paintings, before finally giving them back their false or stolen paperwork. We don't know which it is because we don't have the paperwork to check.' He threw her a cynical smile. '*Mon Dieu*, with help like that I'm surprised de Flaubert has any paintings left at all.'

'I think that is quite enough Guillemain,' said Christophe, jumping to his feet.

'Look de Flaubert. It's time you shut up and let me do my job. This kind of thing always has help on the inside and Miss Connors is showing serious signs of aggression and defensiveness.'

'You are such an idiot Guillemain! Julia suffers from

dyscalculia, that's why she's nervous. You mention anything to do with money or numbers and she virtually throws up. Your interrogation techniques are tantamount to abuse.'

'Well why didn't you, or her, point that out!'

'Because we're not the bloody fraud squad detectives Guillemain, you are!'

The phone rang before Christophe could finish his tirade.'

'Hello Simon,' said Christophe. 'No, we haven't. Guillemain and the UK police are here. I don't expect there could have been a mix up at your end and the paintings were collected early or went to another gallery, maybe the Paris one or New York?'

Silence for a moment.

'No. Well it was wishful thinking'

Christophe hung up.

'Simon you said?' asked inspector Denton. 'Would that be Simon Chapman?'

'Yes. He is the artist's grandson. He's in charge of the Chapman galleries and all the authentication procedures of any of William Chapman's works. But then I imagine you already know that.'

Inspector Denton nodded. 'Yes, I do. I also know him, on a professional level. Are you a personal friend of his too?'

'Yes. I'm surprised that Inspector Guillemain didn't mention it.'

'Not relevant,' said Guillemain, snapping his notebook closed. 'I'll take a look around,' he said to Denton and headed towards the hallway.

'Dammit, Guillemain. You really have no manners. This is mine and Julia's home, you might want to ask before you go nosing around.'

'Hum, he's rather old school I think,' said Denton, smiling reassuringly after Guillemain disappeared.

'You don't say. Do many police officers still use pencils and paper?'

'Not many,' said Denton, smiling. 'Some do. It seems to help them concentrate their thoughts and they don't like modern technology changes.'

'And you? Where do you stand on that?'

'Well I have rather a good memory and I've never been terribly fond of making notes. I am quite happy with modern technology, but I confess I am also rather partial to pen and paper.' He smiled kindly. 'Now then, Mr de Flaubert, why don't we indulge Inspector Guillemain and let him have full reign for a few moments while you tell me how you know the Chapman family'

'Well, we all grew up together, even Inspecteur Guillemain. Simon and I went to the same school and I would spend much of my holiday time in Brittany with him and a few other friends. One of those friends was also Baudoin's grandson as it happens. We would spend most of our time hanging out in all the places where they painted. It was quite something. As I said, the Baudoin painting had no worth but the scene is a familiar one of those childhood days when I used to go to Brittany. That's why it is so special to me.'

Julia, much calmer since Guillemain had left the room, stood up and put her arms around him.

'Christophe I am so sorry. It's all my fault.'

Christophe hugged her back.

'Don't be silly. It could just as easily have happened if I'd been here.'

Guillemain came back into the room and Inspector Denton stood up as if they were about to leave, but

Guillemain had other ideas.

'I want Miss Connors to immediately present herself at the station to look through the Interpol pictures of all known art criminals. I want to know when you last upped the insurance policy for the Chapman as well as the names of any individuals, companies or museums that have made offers for the Chapman in the past. I want access to both yours and Miss Connors financial records de Flaubert, and a full breakdown of any insurance claims that you have previously made for works of art.'

'What?' said Christophe.

'Inspector Guillemain,' said Denton, exasperated. 'As the theft took place in London, this case is officially under my jurisdiction, so if you don't mind, I'll take it from here.' He turned to Christophe.

'It would be useful if Miss Connors could look through a few photos. Your personal financial information is not necessary at the moment. If we need to, we can access any insurance claims information directly. We will be speaking to Mr Chapman again, to see if we can ascertain how the thieves could have obtained the identification, and the overalls, or at least copies of them. I'm sure Inspector Guillemain didn't mean to imply that Miss Connors was involved, but of course it has been known that when a relationship is bad, one of the parties decides to take the financial maintenance problem into their own hands.'

'Thank you, Inspector Denton,' replied Christophe tight lipped as he showed them to the door. 'It was not the money that was the insult, it was his insinuation that the relationship might be bad.'

Guillemain turned sharply on Christophe.

'De Flaubert. She has a large bruise on the front of her head, which she claims is due to the fact that she ran into a traffic light post. There are many false explanations for bruising on women and children. Running into a traffic light post is quite creative.'

Julia looked horrified. 'You can't think that Christophe ... Surely you don't think ...'

'I don't think anything' replied Guillemain. 'I am basing my assessment on knowledge of de Flaubert's previous violent behaviour.'

'What??!!'

'Oh?' asked Inspector Denton, surprised.

'Unbelievable. You really are Guillemain.' said Christophe.

'Do you have previous form of violence to women?' asked Denton.

Christophe glared at Guillemain.

'Do I Guillemain? Do I?'

'Well not that has been proven… but…'

Denton sighed, shaking his head. 'Then I suggest we stick to facts and get back to the point of the missing works of art.'

'Exactly,' said Christophe. 'Inspector Guillemain has clearly dedicated a lot of energy to investigating both Julia and myself, as well as dragging up old student pranks from the depths of his bitter paranoid mind. Shame he hasn't put the same energy into finding the stolen paintings.'

Christophe turned back to Denton and smiled. 'Well thank you inspector for your help and please notify me the moment you have any leads.' He glared at Guillemain again.

'And for your information I do NOT hit women.'

'Of course not,' said Denton. He turned and smiled kindly at Julia. 'I hope you have had that head injury checked by a doctor. Good day Miss Connors.'

'Good day,' said Julia, smiling with relief that they were going.

Then she thought about it. Good Day? Very inappropriate. Police officers really should be banned from using that particular nicety. What the hell had been good about it?

Four

CHRISTOPHE WENT BACK INTO the sitting room and stared at the blank wall.

'Well, we'd better put something there.' He went into the loo and came back with the black hole.

Julia stared at him, in disbelief.

'Christophe. I know it's a disaster, and I feel bad enough as it is, but that is really punishing me.'

'No. It isn't. It's the only one that's the right size.'

'Really? The Chapman was a lovely landscape that fitted perfectly, whereas THAT is a black hole the size of Jupiter! It's the only one that you know I can't stand looking at. It's like putting a black armband up there because somebody has died, and every time I come into the lounge I can feel terrible, like we're in mourning and I'm the murderer'

'Julia, you really are exaggerating.'

'I'm not. You're doing it deliberately to punish me and make me feel bad. All that talk in front of the inspector about how it could have happened any time when you were here. It was all just a show in front of him. You do blame me.'

'Look, of course I don't blame you. Here grab hold of the bottom can you? I can't get the hook lined up properly.'

Julia hesitated, then took hold of the bottom.

'OK,' she said, 'but I'm really not happy about it.'

'Well I'm not happy about you giving my paintings away either.' He replied.

Julia let go of the bottom of the picture and he just managed to grab it before it fell on his foot.

'Julia!'

'Hang it up yourself Christophe. You have just confirmed that you do blame me. And you've obviously got such a damn big ego you really don't believe that it would have happened while you were here. Do you?'

'I do NOT have a big ego. But what I do have is a brain that would tell me to check the paperwork thoroughly. And I certainly wouldn't have left it on the side for them to take away with them.'

She stood up feeling angry and very guilty. Lord, she thought to herself. Why does it always happen to me? I really do feel bad. Really bad. On a Judas Iscariot grassing up Jesus scale of bad, a nine point nine. Then using the age-old tactic of the best line of defence is attack, she let rip.

'I had a concussion OK. I was dizzy when I hit my head, and I probably had a concussion. Thanks a bunch for your consideration. Nice of you to be so concerned about me – NOT.'

Christophe put down the picture and pulled his hands through his hair as he stood up and paced the floor. He only ever did it when he was extremely upset and it made her feel even worse.

'No, I don't blame you, but hell Julia. Credit cards sky

high, getting sacked by Jean-Claude and lying to me, telling me you wanted to resign when you'd already been sacked.'

'Jean Claude is always sacking people,' said Julia 'You know that. He never means it. Well not with me anyway, well ...usually. I was going to tell you about it but you'd only just come home...'

'No, you weren't! You told me you wanted to resign even though you'd already been sacked.' Christophe glared at her. 'I don't actually care that you got sacked, but I do care that you lied to me!'

'It wasn't a lie. I did want to give up my job.'

'Don't you think for just once in your life you can admit it when you're wrong? And do you know what's even worse? I've lost the only two paintings that I have any emotional attachment to – and you won't even let me be upset about it.' Christophe said angrily.

Julia grabbed her running shoes from under the sofa. Her eyes were stinging as she tried to hold back the tears. She furiously tried to jam a trainer onto her foot but it had shrunk under Christophe's wrath. Her foot just wouldn't go in. She'd turned into Cinderella's ugly sister overnight and Prince Charming had turned into the Prince of Darkness intent on dispatching her into oblivion through a black hole.

'OK.' she said, sniffing. 'So be angry. But be angry at them, not at me. Don't you dare take it out on me. It's not fair. Don't you think I feel bad enough as it is?'

'But it's just so typical. Every time I go away something happens. You are just so disaster prone.'

'So, you think I mentally conjure up disaster, do you? You think I charge headlong into traffic light posts just for the fun of it.'

'No. But well, it's always the same when I go away.'

'So, don't go away.'

'I have to go away. International finance is international, not a doorstep salesman you know.'

She tied the laces furiously and stood up determinedly but could only manage to hobble towards the door because the back of the trainer was bent inside.

'Yes, well I want a doorstep relationship not an international one. I'm going out running.'

'What? You've got to be kidding. Running?' asked Christophe. His disbelief was reinforced by the fact that as she couldn't even walk properly he couldn't see her managing a run. 'You're going out now? But I've only just got back.'

'Yes. Well you're late. If you'd come back yesterday, you'd have been here when they pinched your paintings wouldn't you.'

'No, because following the law of Julia-on-her-own related disasters, if I was here yesterday, they would have pinched them a day earlier.'

'Well look on the positive side. Now you have lots of space on the walls that you can use as a squash court – maybe you can squash your ego.'

She slammed the door as she left, fighting back the tears. That foul inspector Guillemain implying that she had something to do with the whole thing. Then trying to blame Christophe for the bruise on her head, when Christophe would never do anything like that. And now they'd had a row. It was all her fault and she felt awful. Even worse, she hadn't got her music player to stop thinking horrible thoughts. She was going to have to run pretty bloody fast to get away from the sound of her own voice this time.

The snow had turned to mush in the park. The children with their sledges had gone and the trees with their heads bowed, were dripping miserably. They looked like they were drowning their sorrows in sympathy.

That inspector Guillemain was a seriously nasty person if ever there was one. A small-minded, mean spirited man.

And what exactly did he mean about Christophe hitting women? She knew Christophe could get angry but he would never be violent, never. And now she couldn't ask him about it because they'd had a row.

She looked up to the heavens. She didn't often talk to God, except to give him a piece of her mind. She'd decided she'd never really liked him ever since her mother had died, but now seemed like a good time to have a go at him.

'What the hell do you think you're playing at?' she shouted up to the darkening sky. 'I thought we'd got all of this sorted. Don't you think I've had my fair share of hell in this life? It would be really nice if for once you picked on somebody your own size!'

There she felt a bit better now. The running was using up the excess adrenaline and she could feel her mind calming down.

She ran further into the park, winding her way towards the Serpentine and past the gallery. Her mind flipped to the paintings. There had to be some way to make it up to Christophe. She knew it wasn't about the money, it was as he'd said, it was about the sentimental value.

She remembered when Francoise had come with the painting. He had been so touched by the gesture. Then she had an idea. Rochelle! She was an artist. She loved the Breton School. Not only that but she knew Pont Carnac where it had been painted really well. She was sure

Rochelle could do great copies of the paintings. There must be photos somewhere, really detailed ones because they must have had them done for the insurance company. They were always having to do that. There certainly were for the Chapman. Christophe adored Rochelle. She was the only one that he would accept doing the copies. Yes. That's what she'd do. She would talk to Rochelle and make it a surprise for Christophe. It wouldn't make things perfect, but maybe it would help.

The sun came out through a tiny break in the clouds. Its rays shaped multi-coloured arcs of impressionistic light on the Serpentine. Yes, definite benediction for the idea.

***

Julia jogged through the door of the flat singing to herself.

'Red and orange and pink and green, yellow and purple and blue. I can sing a rainbow, sing a rainbow ...'

Christophe appeared in the hallway from the sitting room. He winced at the sound of her voice.

'You're unbelievable. Honestly, singing? How can you sing at a time like this?' he said.

'Oh, Christophe I'm sorry'.

She threw herself into his arms and hugged him.

'I really am so sorry. It's just that I've had this amazing idea. I can't tell you about it yet. It's got to be a surprise. I just want to make it up to you. It really is my fault.'

Julia was expecting some sort of acceptance of her apology, with an apology back, for him being so angry with her. What she actually got was Christophe rubbing his chin and sighing dramatically.

'Well, yes it was, actually, your fault.' he said, leaving her open-mouthed.

'Christophe! How can you? I've apologised. I really do

feel bad, you know. The least you can do is stop sulking.'

He glared at her. 'I am NOT sulking. I am angry and tired and ... I have the right to be angry.'

'OK. You do. You do have the right. But be angry with the robbers, not angry with me. You said yourself that once the collector decides it's what they want they will stop at nothing to get it.'

She caught sight of the black hole through the corner of her eye.

'By the way,' she said. 'The black hole is upside down.'

He burst out laughing.

'You are impossible. I have just lost some cherished paintings. I'm really upset and you don't even have the common decency to let me be miserable about it.'

She grabbed his hand and pulled him towards the bedroom.

'But that's what I've been trying to tell you. I am sorry and I am going to make it up to you. I'm going to cherish you in your favourite way.'

She kissed him passionately on the lips and her hand started to move downwards. He stopped kissing her back, reluctantly, and removed her hand from the very firm bulge that had developed in his trousers.

'Julia I don't think …'

'Darling, I can tell that you are not that angry. In fact, I can feel that you are quite pleased to see me,' she replied, putting her hand back and starting to unzip his trousers.

'Erm, Julia,' warned Christophe gently, in between kisses.

'This must be Madame 'not quite' de Flaubert I presume?' said a deep voice behind her.

Christophe swung Julia around in front of him to hide his very obvious erection. 'Julia, this is Simon,' he said, 'Simon Chapman.'

Julia could feel the full heat effect of the embarrassment. She quickly fanned her face with her hand. 'Gosh. Hello, you'll have to excuse me. I've been on a run so I'm a bit hot and sweaty I'm afraid.'

She took a good look at the man whilst she was still fanning herself. He was wearing a flashy designer tie and Versace suit. His eyes wrinkled around the edges with humour. They were so dark they were almost black and it was hard to see where the pupil ended and the iris began.

He looks just like a feline in the night, amusing itself by playing with its prey, before it pounces, thought Julia.

She then realised that she had been staring.

Simon Chapman ignored her outstretched hand and kissed her on both cheeks French style. 'It's lovely to meet you at last. Christophe's told me all about you but whenever I ask him to bring you over to the gallery he always seems to have an excuse to come alone. I was beginning to think he was deliberately keeping us apart. And now I can see why he keeps you to himself!' Julia blushed even more.

'Hmm,' Christophe muttered to himself. 'Shame I didn't get that dog a few weeks ago.'

'I'm terribly sorry about what's happened, Miss Connors. I feel personally responsible.' said Simon Chapman.

'No, Mr Chapman. I think we've all agreed that it's my fault,' sighed Julia.

'Definitely not,' said Simon Chapman. 'How were you to know? They had our overalls and our ID cards. Either those things were stolen or they must have made copies. If it's anybody's fault it's the Chapman Gallery's.'

Ooh, I like him, thought Julia. She threw Christophe a smug smile and he raised his eyebrows cynically.

'It must have been planned well in advance.' Simon Chapman continued. 'I'm sorry. And this is terrible for the gallery of course. Not at all good for our reputation.'

'Of course,' said Julia. 'I imagine people will be loath to lend their paintings now.'

'Done wonders for the value of the Chapman's though eh Simon? Now everybody is going to want one. And, of course the Chapman galleries have the only available collection,' Christophe added cynically.

'Oh, come on Christophe you know very well that the paintings were worth a fortune before this. It just means that as we suspected, the Chapmans have become interesting to the art underworld and that is extremely worrying security wise. It's going to cost me a fortune in extra security to reassure my clients.'

Julia watched Chapman as he spoke, there was something strangely attractive about him. She couldn't quite put her finger on it. In all the time that she and Christophe had been together she had never found any other man attractive and it came as a bit of a shock.

'Well this is very depressing, especially on an empty stomach,' she said. 'I'm going to rustle up something to eat. Will you join us Mr Chapman?'

'Call me Simon, please,' he said and started to nod. Julia caught Christophe shaking his head at Simon.

'I've got a better idea,' said Christophe, steering Julia away from the kitchen. 'Let's go out and eat, then it'll be ...' he was hunting for a diplomatic word.

Julia waited expectantly. She knew her cooking was terrible, but she wanted to see how Christophe was going to get this information across, without putting her down in front of Chapman.

'We'll… go… to Clarke's Restaurant,' he blurted out suddenly. 'It's a classic 'farm to table' place and it will be really... really...'

They waited expectantly

'Wholesome! Yes, that's the word, wholesome.'

Not bad, thought Julia. I'll let him have that one. She smiled at Simon Chapman.

'Christophe can never resist casting aspersions on my cooking.' she said.

'Oh, I can't believe it's that bad,' he replied diplomatically.

'No, it really is,' said Julia. 'I think the ingredients know that I don't care about them, and they all stick together, and execute a suicide pact.'

'Or,' said Christophe, taking her hand and throwing her one of his mock challenging looks. 'It might just be a clever ruse. If every time she cooks a meal it's awful, then either I'll cook or she'll get invited out to dinner.'

Simon Chapman eyed Julia up and down unashamedly.

'I'm sure she gets invited to dinner all the time and it's got nothing to do with her cooking.'

Julia beamed back at Simon Chapman and returned Christophe's challenging look with interest. She removed her hand from his and headed for the bedroom.

'Just give me a few minutes to shower and change, and I'll be ready,' she said.

Years of working in high fashion had given her the ability to do quick changes and she reappeared ten minutes later in a Chanel mini skirt, Saint Laurent sweater and Ferragamo ankle boots.

'Wow!' said Simon Chapman. 'That really was quick! Very impressive.' It was obvious to everyone that it wasn't only the speed that was impressing him.

'Years of quick changes for the catwalk,' said Julia, smiling.

Christophe grabbed his jacket and handed Julia hers. 'Remind me to stop at the dog rescue centre on the way home.'

Five

~

IT WAS ALREADY GETTING dark by the time they got to the restaurant. The street lights had turned on and the dirty slush on the pavements was beginning to freeze. Only two or three tables were occupied so they chose a table by the window where they could watch the bustle of the street outside. Julia happily watched people rushing in and out of shops, offices and restaurants.

Everybody's on a mission in this city, she thought. Some of them are only small missions, like getting to the station to catch the right train. But others are much more important, fickle missions like getting to the first day of the Harrods sale before anybody else. Then there are the serious missions, like homeless people rushing to a good place to bed down for the night before anyone else gets it. How cold they must be, she thought.

She watched a bus and a taxi jostle for position in the special lane. The bus won, probably because it was advertising faster running shoes.

She loved London but they could do with a bit of a break from it. It was ages since they'd been away on holiday. Yes, they needed to go somewhere where the pace was a bit slower. All this rushing around and flying in and flying out really wasn't good for the soul. They could have a winter holiday and then start working on giving all that money away to charity.

Julia grabbed the glass of Kir Royale that they'd ordered, rather too quickly and took a huge gulp. Cain and Abel were at it again. She turned away from the window to join in the conversation. Christophe and Simon were talking about the paintings and Guillemain's visit.

'Do you know the security Detective Guillemain well?' Julia asked Simon.

'I do. Very well, in fact. He is a distant cousin. Guillemain was my mother's maiden name.'

'So, you're French, not British?'

'Not completely. Sort of quarter American, a quarter British and half French.'

'I don't think Christophe likes Guillemain,' she said, throwing a fake innocent look at Christophe.

Simon laughed. 'No, I'm sure he doesn't. But then not many people do like him. He's a man on a mission. He believes that all major works of art should be in museums and public galleries, and that private collectors should be forbidden to own them. Well that's what he says now, but he hasn't always been like that. He used to be a full on, sell it to the highest bidder, man.'

'That's my main gripe about this new Guillemain,' said Christophe. 'He lacks any kind of understanding of the financial implications. The Museums and Galleries cannot afford many of the paintings, and any art collector worth his salt gives the public access to the works. They agree to lend the paintings for special exhibitions which brings in more revenue for the galleries and museums. So financially speaking, it's a no brainer'. Christophe hesitated. 'Well, unless your masterpiece gets pinched, of course.'

There was a silent moment. It felt like a wake.

Eventually Simon spoke.

'Still, you've got to give Guillemain his due. He is quite an authority on the post impressionists. The Breton School in particular, and he's written a number of books on corruption in the art world.' said Simon.

'I'll give him that,' said Christophe, nodding. 'It's just a shame that he has a chip on his shoulder the size of a giant redwood.'

'Well let's face it, you are a little to blame for that Christophe.'

'Really? What did you do, Christophe?' asked Julia.

'Nothing bad. I was only doing the right thing.' Christophe replied looking down at the menu.

'And?' prompted Julia.

'I'll let Simon tell you about it. Then you won't be able to accuse me of embellishing the story. Or even worse, not telling the whole truth.' he said, smiling at her with a fake innocent look that was more than a match for her own.

Julia looked at Simon who hesitated, not sure if he should tell the story or not. The curiosity in Julia's eyes convinced him.

'A few years back, Guillemain discovered a possible Van Gogh down in Provence on the Lacoste estate.'

Julia couldn't help spurting out her wine in shock. She looked over at Christophe who was concentrating on the menu and hadn't flinched at all.

'You mean Château Lacoste, the Girault place?' she said.

'Ah you know about Christophe's illustrious half-brother,' said Simon.

'Illustrious? I'd hardly call him that.' said Julia. She would have gone further but she felt Christophe squeeze her leg gently under the table. It was a clear sign that he did not want her to say anything about Jaime Girault.

'Oh?' said Simon.

'Julia and I had a little fracas with him a couple of years ago,' said Christophe. 'Not much really, you know what he's like, a bit of a playboy.'

A bit of a playboy, thought Julia. That was a mega understatement. Girault was a perverted drug running psychopath that the police were chasing. Why was everyone pretending differently?

'I don't really know him.' said Simon. 'Only met him once before the Van Gogh incident, and he doesn't seem to have been around much in the art world for ages now. Disappeared completely.'

'He disappeared be... Ouch' Christophe had upped the pressure of his grip on her leg under the table.

'be .. Ouch?' asked Simon.

'Bee,' said Julia, thinking on her feet. She started scratching her leg. 'Unbelievable at this time of year. Think it stung me. But it's fine. I'm very tolerant to pain.' She glared at Christophe.

'Are you sure you're OK' asked Simon. You know you have to take the sting out.'

'No, really it's fine. Probably wasn't even alive when it stung me. You can still get stung by a dead bee, you know. It was probably trapped in my clothes.' She stopped rubbing her leg and took a sip from her wine glass.

'Tell me more about what happened with the Van Gogh? Did Christophe behave very badly?' she asked, 'I'm sure he was terrible.'

Simon laughed. 'No, not really. As he said, he was doing the right thing.'

'Oh' said Julia.

Simon laughed at the obvious disappointment on her face then continued.

'A few years before the painting was found at Lacoste, a possible Van Gogh had been found being used as a door for a chicken coup down near Arles, where the artist often painted. The normal process for any Van Gogh is that it has to be authenticated by the experts from the Van Gogh Museum. It's a pretty lengthy process and can take years of research. The group who found it decided to hold a private auction before the process was finished. I guess they were hoping to get a decent bid for it from people hedging their bets that it would turn out to be a real Van Gogh. In the end a Japanese collector paid quite a few million for it before it had received the full authentication. It was then proven to be a fake.'

'It shouldn't even have gone to private auction,' said Christophe. 'Certainly not before they'd authenticated it.'

'I agree but you know what the Japanese are like for their Van Goghs, especially the sunflowers.'

'True. But that's what's caused such an increase in the number of forgeries over the past ten years. People know that the Japanese will take them, even at the risk of them being forgeries.'

'So, what did Christophe do?' asked Julia.

'He jumped the gun and notified the Van Gogh Museum of the emergence of a possible fake at Lacoste before Guillemain could get his authentication dossier ready. They sent an expert to see it and dismissed it as a fake immediately.'

'Before Guillemain had time to sell it privately to a Japanese collector,' said Christophe.

'If he was going to sell it,' said Simon. 'I don't believe he was Christophe.'

'Even if he wasn't,' said Christophe. 'He's an art expert and he should have known immediately that it was a fake. It wasn't even mentioned in Van Gogh's letters to his brother, Theo.'

'Van Gogh wrote to his brother every day, telling him what he was painting' said Simon to Julia. 'Which means the official Van Gogh catalogue of works is one of the most comprehensive records for any artist that ever lived.'

'So, Inspector Guillemain, had a bit of sunflower-yellow egg on his face,' said Julia.

'Indeed.' said Simon.

'Kindly served up by Christophe.' Added Julia

'It was the right thing to do,' said Christophe. 'Do you think for a second, if it had been the other way around, Guillemain wouldn't have done the same?'

'You're probably right there' said Simon. He leant across to Julia, conspiratorially. 'When it comes to Christophe and cousin Guillemain, as the French say '*c'est physique*'.

'I noticed. But the point is, do you think Guillemain will find the Chapman?' asked Julia.

'It won't be easy,' replied Simon. 'But since that egg on his face, he has become very diligent in his work to the point of being a bit pedantic, to be honest. If anybody can find it, I suspect it's him.'

'I don't think we can rely on it,' replied Christophe. 'I really don't rate him as much as you do, Simon. I think we'll have to do something ourselves.'

'Well we could put the word out that we have a client looking for a Chapman, but in my opinion, they've already got the client. It was very specifically that painting they wanted if you ask me,' said Simon.

'It will be too obvious if you put the word out Simon,'

said Christophe. 'You have a very clean reputation. We need to make contact with someone with a bit of a shadowy past.'

'Or, what if we come up with a fictitious client who is looking for a painting? You have enough contacts Christophe. What about asking around through people you know down in Provence? It would be too obvious doing it here in London or in Brittany. Best not to tell Guillemain though, he really wouldn't approve.'

Christophe's mobile rang just as they were tucking into the hors d'oeuvre and he went outside to talk more discreetly.

'So, you were at school with Christophe?' Julia asked Simon. She watched Christophe pacing up and down as he talked outside. She always found him even more attractive when he was concentrating on his work. It usually led to her trying to distract him and drag him back home to bed. She realised she hadn't heard a word of what Simon Chapman had said.

'Sorry, Simon, we're all a bit distracted over this. What were you saying?'

'That Christophe and I both went to the British American School in Paris.'

'Oh. So you were at school with his friend Bernard too?'

'Bernard Chauvenon, the lawyer. Yes. At the time it was quite the fashion. Wealthy professionals and some of the older bourgeois families decided a bilingual education was the best thing to do. We all went there.'

'Guillemain too?' asked Julia

'No. That's probably another reason they don't get on. Cousin Guillemain's side of the family couldn't afford to send them there. I went along first then Christophe,

Bernard and Petit-Jean Baudoin followed a few years behind me.' He smiled, his black eyes glinting in the candlelight and gestured to his face, 'more grey hair and wrinkles see.'

Julia laughed. 'I know Bernard and his wife Rochelle, but I've never heard Christophe mention Petit-Jean.'

'Strange, they were quite a trio.' said Simon surprised 'They were such a crazy lot. I envied them. They were always up to no good and having a brilliant time.' He pulled a mock boyish disgruntled face. 'I couldn't join in because I am William Chapman's grandson and my father Charles Chapman is a military man. I have always had to behave myself. Family reputation and all that. I used to watch them enviously. Bernard and Petit-Jean were probably a bit worse than Christophe. Well until Petit-Jean decided to drop out completely.'

'Drop Out? Of school?'

'No. Life. Pont Carnac is a bit of a weird place. It has had a rather odd effect on at least three generations of Baudoins. They all ended up going off the rails.'

'In what way?'

'I don't know about the earlier generations. I only know what my grandfather told me about Odilon Baudoin, his friend the painter. But I knew Petit-Jean's father, and I grew up with Petit-Jean. My grandfather claimed they were all 'touched' or 'cursed' and that it led them to do extremely irrational things. I guess these days people would say they carry some kind of risk gene.'

'What did they do?'

'Well, when my grandfather and Odilon Baudoin were painting, they were part of the Breton school – you must stop me if I go on a bit. It's been my life's work and

I am extremely passionate about it.' He held Julia's gaze for just a little too long.

'Not at all,' replied Julia, lowering her gaze. 'Christophe's parents and sister are all dead, and apart from Bernard who is always busy, I don't know anybody else to talk to about when he grew up. His life has been so full of tragedy and he never opens-up about it. I always had the impression there weren't any good times.'

'Oh, there were. I envied them so much. Those three tried everything in life before they came of age. They spent most of their summers in Pont Carnac. Bernard and Christophe were the luckiest because they weren't from the village and didn't have to worry about their reputation. Having said that, Petit-Jean really couldn't care less either. His grandfather had been shot as a collaborator by the resistance and his father died from drink. To be honest even from a very young age, it was almost expected that Petit-Jean would have the same reckless nature. So when they got into trouble, nobody bothered.'

'And you? What about you?'

'Me? I had some serious standards to uphold. Father decorated with a purple heart in the Korean war, and Mayor of Pont Carnac. Grandfather, the great William Chapman was one famous artist and saviour of village history and historical monuments. I had to be squeaky clean. Sadly, no scandal allowed for me. I just had to look on longingly because they were always up to things I'd have loved to have done.'

'Ooh do tell...' said Julia. 'You know Christophe, he's always doing the right thing and it gives you the impression that he never put a foot wrong in his whole life!'

Not to mention the little piece of unproven information of violence to women that Guillemain dropped this morning, she added, silently in her head.

'Perhaps you should ask him about the time they put commercial detergent in the fountain and filled the village with foam.'

'Really? Did he get caught?'

Simon laughed his deep roguish laugh.

'No. Christophe never got caught. Far too wily for that.' Then he laughed even more, at yet another look of disappointment on her face.

'Julia you seem disappointed that he didn't get caught.'

She blushed. 'No, it's that sometimes, you know Christophe, he just …'

'Just..?' prompted Simon. Perhaps things might not be as rosy as he'd imagined in their relationship. And she was definitely sending out signals, although she didn't seem to be aware of it. He found his interest piqued by all sorts of possibilities.

They sat in silence for a second and Julia realised she was being held in that black eyed gaze. She had completely let her guard down. She looked away.

'Enough about Christophe. Tell me all about the Breton School, the paintings and your grandfather.' She said, 'I want to hear all about it from the horse's mouth.'

'Strictly speaking our grandparents weren't impressionists, they were nearer the post-impressionist painters but they painted quite a few years after the first post impressionists, such as Gauguin and Van Gogh. Although, my grandfather did tell me that Baudoin had met Matisse and Monet when he was a child.

Julia looked impressed.

'Impoverished' is a word that is often associated with artists. The post impressionists in particular suffered hugely from a lack of acceptance and couldn't sell their work in the early years. They had to be helped out by members of the family and friends. Even people who sold the artists' materials in shops helped them. Chapman was 'discovered' much later than the other post impressionists and he, Baudoin, Andre and Guillemain were called the Breton School, because they stuck to painting in the Breton area.

'Guillemain? Interrupted Julia. 'As in Detective Guillemain?'

'Yes, indeed. Etienne Guillemain, the artist, was my mother's uncle and Detective Guillemain is a second or third cousin of the artist.'

'Complicated,' said Julia.

'Not really,' Simon replied. In some areas of Brittany, it is best to assume that people are more likely to be related than not. Although that doesn't necessarily mean that they speak to each other.'

'Oh?'

'Yes, the usual stuff, arguments over inheritance, loving another woman's wife, the war and the resistance, Breton independence, the best way to make *moules marinière...*'

'You're kidding?'

'Well about the *moules* yes, but the other things have caused huge rifts in families. The Bretons are really quite hard headed and stubborn.'

'Yes I could see that in Inspector Guillemain. Was your grandfather hard headed?'

'Not at all,' said Simon, smiling. 'He was the American part of me. He was quite the opposite and the only person that could have put up with stubborn old Odilon Baudoin. They had an incredible friendship.'

'So if he was American, how did he end up in Brittany?'

They met when William Chapman was doing his artist's year in France as part of his studies. They got on so well together they even went off and fought with the likes of Hemingway in the Spanish Civil War. My grandfather told me that it was Odilon Baudoin's stubbornness not to leave him that saved his life during the siege of Madrid. And of course, they fell in love with the same woman.'

'Of course,' smiled Julia, 'Your grandmother?'

'Sadly, for my grandfather no, it was Petit-Jean's grandmother. Chapman had the painting success but Baudoin got the girl.'

'That seems fair then. Karmic balance, although their friendship must have been quite strained. Chapman had to see Baudoin with the woman he loved and Baudoin had to see Chapman's success as an artist, never receiving the same recognition.'

'Well it didn't work like that because they were both unknown artists for most of their lives. William just managed to live long enough for the World to discover him.

'Christophe and I both adore the Chapman, that's what makes this all so hard,' said Julia.

'I can imagine,' said Simon. 'I have to say that it is one of my Grandfather's greatest works. That beautiful riverscape in Winter. I jokingly tried to get Christophe to swap it once for a huge landscape painting Chapman did from the top of the Peaks, but he wouldn't, even though mine was worth much more!'

Julia laughed. 'That is quite unusual for Christophe. But I imagine it is because the painting holds such fond memories of happy times for him.'

'Yes. It certainly has strong associations for him, the river in particular.'

'Really, why?'

'The summer skinny dipping.'

'Really?'

'Yes, with none other than the beautiful actress Sophie Petrarch.'

Julia couldn't stifle the tsunami of jealousy that shot up from below, side swiped her heart as it went past, and landed as a furious look on her face. She was certain she must have turned bright green. She gulped down a glass of red wine in an attempt to reset her colour balance.

What was going on? Two days ago, Sophie Petrarch was just a French actress that she vaguely knew of. Now suddenly she was invading Julia's life from all sides. First Jean Claude, now she finds Petrarch and Christophe didn't just have a fling but spent their youth running around Brittany together naked.

Simon Chapman took note of the wine gulping, and smiled to himself, correctly interpreting Julia's discomfort. Sophie did tend to have that effect on other women.

'Pont Carnac is an incredible place. I'm surprised that Christophe hasn't taken you there yet. It really was his second home.'

'Well we keep meaning to go there but you know Christophe, always on the phone, always doing business. Just like Bernard actually. Rochelle and I are thinking of setting up an abandoned wives club.'

'Except that you are not yet married, Mrs 'not quite' de Flaubert.'

Julia took another gulp of her wine and looked up to be caught in that glinting black gaze again.

'And that...' continued Simon, leaning very close to her as he topped up her wine glass. '... makes you still available.'

***

Christophe came back to find his plate had been removed. Julia and Simon had been so engrossed that when the waiter asked if he should clear Christophe's plate they had just nodded.

Christophe stared down at the empty space.

'You know Julia, I think that letting somebody walk off with my *hors d'oeuvres* when I am ravenous is just about the icing on the cake of a day like today,' he said, sarcastically. Then, seeing the lazy predatory look that Simon Chapman was giving Julia, he continued, bitterly. 'They say that trouble comes in threes so what will it be next Simon? Walking off with my future wife?'

Julia choked.

'Sorry,' said Christophe, shaking his head. 'In a bit of a foul mood, understandably, jet-lag, paintings stolen, not been a good day.' He took the last piece of bread from the bread basket and put it to his mouth. 'So, what have you two been talking about? Sorry about the phone call too, think I might have a good contact for the paintings.'

'I was telling Julia about Pont Carnac,' said Simon.

'Yes. So now that I know more about the Chapman's meaning, I can feel really bad,' said Julia.

'I was just about to tell her about the missing panels.'

The phone rang again and Christophe stood up apologetically. 'Might be important,' he said. 'They might have some news. The first forty-eight hours is crucial in this kind of thing.'

'Now we come to the most exciting bit of the whole post impressionist movement,' said Simon as he leant across the table. 'Most of the artists were in financial difficulties. Some had private incomes and tried to help the others. They would buy paintings and materials for them, but it wasn't enough. It was especially difficult for the Breton School. So, to pay for their board and lodging, at the Café Breton, many of them painted the bar panelling. There are four panels in the village museum. Now to the good bit...'

He leaned even further in towards Julia and lowered his voice. She had to move further in herself to hear him. They were so close their noses almost touched. Julia hesitated and then immediately pulled back. What in heaven's name, was she thinking. She could see he was a very adept flirt.

'The good bit?' she asked. Trying to hide the irritation in her voice.

Simon Chapman smiled his charming smile. He was totally unfazed by her pulling away from him.

'Rumour has it that there were another six panels that had been painted by Monet, Chapman, Matisse, Guillemain, Van Gogh and Baudoin.'

'Wow!'

'Yes. Wow indeed.'

'They'd be worth a fortune!'

'Absolutely! It would be one of the greatest art-finds ever, if anyone ever found them. Nearly as good as Tutankhamen's treasure.'

They sat in silence for a moment.

'Except that they don't carry a curse like Tutankhamen. Well not that we know of.' he added.

When Christophe came back, he was disappointed to find that although his entrecôte was still there, it was cold and they'd finished the wine.

The phone rang again and Julia took it out of Christophe's hands and walked off with it before he could grab it back.

Simon Chapman laughed and shook his head in disbelief.

'Well Christophe, I can't believe it. A woman is actually getting the better of you.'

Christophe watched Julia as she headed towards the restaurant door. He gave a look of appreciation of the long legs that were perfectly topped off by the nicest butt he'd ever seen. Yes, she is getting the better of me, he thought. And you can keep your bloody hands off, Chapman.

'No, I'm sorry he couldn't possibly, not for at least two weeks because he'll be on holiday,' said Julia, coming back towards them. Then she switched the phone off.

'That might have been important Julia,' said Christophe, exasperated as she sat down.

'Eat your dinner it's getting cold,' said Julia, 'and we need to get home and pack.

'Pack? Why?'

'Because we are driving to Brittany for a holiday. Even better, we're going to ring Bernard and Rochelle and see if they want to come and meet us there.'

***

Julia started throwing things into a suitcase while Christophe sat on the bed looking exasperated.

'Julia this is crazy. I have only just got back.'

'But that's what makes it even better. Lots of people won't even know you are back and so won't ring and annoy us. And it's going to be Christmas soon, and nobody is going to do any business over Christmas.'

'But I have to stay here, and find my paintings.'

'But they are in Brittany, I know they are.'

'Really Julia? The whole of the London art fraud squad, as well the French OCBC, are out looking for them, but you 'know' they are in Brittany. Why would they be in Brittany? They're paintings, not homing pigeons.'

'Gut reaction, instinct. I really do know they are there.'

'You are so impulsive. Life is not run based on sudden impulses. You run around thinking that this intuition of yours is true or a fact.'

She gave him one of her most endearing looks. 'You have to trust me. They might not be in Brittany, but I know that we have to go there in order to find them. I also know we will find them and get them back.'

'And I suppose you think you are going to find the missing panels too?'

'Well, you never know. We might just look for them at the same time.'

'If they exist.'

'Well Simon thinks they do. And wouldn't he know as his grandfather the great William Chapman painted one of them?'

'Don't you think if anybody was going to find them, then Simon Chapman, or Guillemain the world expert on the Breton School, would have found them by now?'

'Well no. Because they're men.'

'That's incredibly sexist of you, if I may say so.'

'You may say so, but it won't change what I'm thinking.'

'What's that got to do with it, anyway? All I care about is getting back my Baudoin and my Chapman, and personally I do not think charging off to Brittany on some hair brained scheme is the right way to find them.'

'That's the difference between men and women. We feel quite comfortable and happy about our instincts and intuitions and you men don't have any.'

'Once again, sexist,' said Christophe.

Julia hesitated over how many sweaters and coats

they'd need. They took up so much room but then again it was the middle of Winter. She put in as many as she could and then decided she could just throw the others in the car on the back seat.

'Of course it's sexist,' she continued. 'Because men have a phallus and women don't. Men have a brain, connected to a phallus via some kind of telecommunications cable. That's why men invented virtual reality. They don't want to have to cope with the real thing, real emotions and feelings and communication of those feelings. Men have been playing the logic card for so long they don't have any intuition left.'

'That's not true. I have a lot of instinct and intuition. I can sniff out what's going on in any business meeting. Speaking of which I've got meetings, I can't go.

'Don't worry about your meetings, I've cancelled them.' She flung some shirts into the suitcase without folding them.

Christophe stood up exasperated and started taking the shirts back out.

'Julia. Life's not like that.'

'Yes, it is. The whole point of being your own boss like you are, is that you can do what you like. We haven't had a proper holiday for ages and I feel we have to go to Pont Carnac. I'm sure if you ring Bernard and Rochelle they'll come too. We could even pop over and see Françoise at the University in Rennes. It will be wonderful, and we'll get your paintings back at the same time.'

Julia flung the shirts back into the suitcase. The whole thing was a crumpled mass that bulged out of the sides. She had to sit on it to get the lid on. Then she bounced up and down on it with her full weight to try and zip it up.

'I can't believe you're doing that. I am so glad that when I go away, I do my own packing.'

'Doesn't matter,' replied Julia. 'We can get it laundered when we get there.'

'I suppose I should just be grateful that your instincts aren't telling you the paintings are on Mars.'

She jumped up and threw her arms around him. 'I knew you'd come. Maybe you do have some intuition after all.'

He pulled her down on the bed beside him. 'My intuition tells me that if we don't bother to pack anything else at all we've just got time to ...'

They were interrupted by the phone.

They both went to grab it at the same time. Christophe got there first and Julia looked at him exasperated.

'Make the most of it, Christophe, it's your last call, then I'm throwing the mobile in the bin.'

'Don't push your luck. Oh, hello Bernard,' then, slightly tongue in cheek, he said. 'You must be a closet psychic. Julia was just about to ring you.'

Julia pulled a face at him.

'What?' said Christophe.

Julia could see his face turning pale.

'What? When? My God. Okay. We were on our way down there. Yes. We'll see you there.'

Christophe switched off the phone and sat down, quietly on the bed.

'Petit-Jean has had a motorbike accident. He's dead.'

Six

JULIA TOOK IN THE scenery as they sped along the road down towards Pont Carnac. It was early morning and the countryside was covered with a heavy frost and a winter mist hung in the valleys and around the bends of the river floodplains. The slate roofs on the grey granite houses were still white with the frost. It's just like parts of Cornwall or Wales, she thought, eyeing a weird pagan megalith at the side of the road.

Gradually the sun's rays began to burst through the mist and the countryside came alive. The frost began to melt on the houses and the slate began to show different hues of purple, green and blue. The fields became a brighter green as the grass came through and the trees emerged like ethereal beings out of the mists.

Christophe drove in silence. Julia was so in tune with his moods that she knew better than to talk. He'd been so shocked when he'd heard about Petit-Jean. Even so, she couldn't stop herself from fidgeting as they drove along. It was a major challenge for her to stop her thoughts charging through the red traffic light that she'd imposed on herself.

She had so many things she wanted to ask. She wanted to know why she'd never heard him talk about Petit-Jean and why they hadn't spoken for so long. She wanted to know what Guillemain meant about that student prank and hitting women. Most of all she wanted to know all the gory details about Christophe and Sophie Petrarch. Why were they running around naked? Where were they running around naked? What did they do, and was it any good?

She sighed outwardly. Christophe still didn't say anything. It was becoming unbearable. He was deep in his own thoughts and did not want to open up. A lot of men were like that though, she supposed. She wondered if it was genetic – some special little widget tied on their hormones that made them like that. Or maybe their Adam's apple soaked it all up before it could get out. That must be it. Boys that had been conditioned for so long that boys don't cry, men don't cry and they'd swallowed back the tears which over the years swelled up into a massive Adam's apple, blocking a major nerve between their brain and their heart. And that was why men had Adam's apples and women didn't.

Poor Christophe, she hated to see him so upset. She unwittingly gave a sharp intake of breath.

'Are you Okay Julia?' asked Christophe. He looked across at her with concern.

'Don't worry, I'm not going to throw up on the upholstery,' replied Julia. The'd been delayed by twenty four hours and when they'd finally left port, the ferry crossing had been so rough, Julia had spent more time in the bathroom than in the bunk.

'That, is not what I meant,' said Christophe, slightly amused. 'You can't possibly have anything left in there to throw up. Are you sure you're OK?'

'Fine. I'm fine, really,' she said, thinking to herself that Sophie Petrarch won't be when I get my hands on her. She glanced across at him and watched him for a second. Dare I? No not yet. Still not quite ready to talk yet. Christ, I think I'm going to explode if I don't say something soon.

They carried on in silence, until Christophe turned off the main road onto a smaller road to cut cross country towards the next valley.

'I thought we'd stay at the Castle Lodgings,' he said. 'Bernard and Rochelle are going to stay there too.'

'Sounds nice,' she replied. Outwardly she was calm, but inside she was shouting 'eureka!'. Here we go. The question is what order should I organise them in? Maybe I should hide the Sophie Petrarch questions in the middle.

'You'll like it,' he said. He reached across with his hand and squeezed her affectionately on the leg. 'There's no central heating, so we'll freeze to death and have to spend the whole time in bed under the covers to keep warm. They have wonderful open fires in the bedrooms that they light. The walls are so thick that you'd have to use a rock band's speakers for anybody to hear you in another room. So, we can make as much noise as we like.'

'Great,' said Julia. Ka-ching. If he was thinking about sex, this was as good a time as any, and her internal communications traffic light shot fluorescent-green.

'Christophe, tell me about Petit-Jean so that I know him a little, when we go to the funeral.'

Nice, calm, reasonable start, thought Julia, congratulating herself. But before Christophe could reply, she'd put her foot to the floor like she was in a formula one racing thoughts championship.

'And what did Guillemain mean about the student prank? And that being violent to women, thing? And why hadn't you seen Petit-Jean for so long? And how many times did you sleep with Sophie Petrarch? And did you finish the relationship, or did she? How long did it go on for, and what was the sex like?'

Christophe burst out laughing.

'I knew it! You've been mulling that over for the whole of the journey, haven't you?'

'Yes, and if you knew, why didn't you say something?'

'Because I wanted to see how long you could hold out.'

'Christophe, that's terrible! That's like torture.'

'No, it isn't. Well I've only been thinking about it for the last few minutes, to be truthful.. Come on Julia, you know me. I just can't let all my thoughts and feelings out like that. And I feel very bad about Petit-Jean. And…' He pulled the car off the road and turned to look at her. 'Sophie Petrarch is irrelevant.'

'But…'

'No buts! Would you like me to ask about the people you slept with before me, and what it was like?'

Julia shrugged. 'You can if you want to. You know very well that I was frigid and didn't like it at all. And you're the only one I've ever liked having sex with, so ask all you like.'

Christophe took her face in his hands and kissed her. 'OK. If you insist on going down this road. The sex with Sophie was rubbish, awful, and the worst sex I've ever had. Feel better now?'

'Not really, because I don't believe you.' sighed Julia.

'Exactly! Julia, you must have known before you asked, that this is a no solution scenario. If I say it was great, you'll be upset, if I say it was awful, you won't believe me. If I say it was just normal, not good nor bad, you'll ask me what I mean by normal.'

He was right. Why was he always right? And why was she always her own worst-enemy? Probably because she was still carrying a Heathrow terminal full of baggage in her head.

'OK. Let me put it this way.' He looked straight at her so that she knew he was serious. 'I see sex mostly as a pleasurable thing that two people do together because they enjoy it. It's good exercise and great stress relief. I compare it to playing squash, and you only invest a similar amount of emotion as you would playing squash. Then, rarely, sometimes it's only once in a lifetime, you meet someone with whom you don't just have sex, you make love.' He kissed her again, deeply. 'And that, Julia, is you.'

Julia smiled. She could live with that. More than live with it.

'Are we good now?'

'Yes,' she said. Then, hesitated, 'No, well not completely. Because you do get emotional when you play Squash you know you do. You really hate losing.'

'Julia!'

'OK. OK, forget that one,' she said, and Christophe drove off again.

'Next question,' he said.

'Petit-Jean, tell me about Petit-Jean then I won't feel so out of place at the funeral. Simon said his Grandfather thought the Baudoin family was cursed.'

'Did he?'

'Yes, he said they had some kind of rogue high-risk manic gene.'

'I wouldn't say that, but they were all a bit wild. Odilon Baudoin was renowned for rushing off on any old impulse.' he paused for a second. 'Hey maybe you've been channelling him and that's why you made me head off to Brittany.'

'Very funny. As it happens, it is just as well that I had booked the ferry and got everything sorted out because it means you won't miss the funeral.'

'True. Anyway, the business of Odilon Baudoin dragging William Chapman off to join the Spanish civil war and being a hero, saving William Chapman's life is a well known story. As is the business of him collaborating with the Germans and being shot as a traitor by the resistance.'

'Why would he do that if he was such a hero.'

'Breton Independence. Some, not many but a few Bretons believed that the Germans would give them Independence from France after the war.'

'Terrible behaviour.'

'Yes, but it happened in Britain too. Your own King Edward the abdicator was striking deals with Hitler.'

'He is not my King. Why do French people always assume that British people personally own anything bad that Britain or anyone British has ever done? And anyway, I'm only half British, so he is only half mine.'

'Well, you can make up the difference by owning half the bad things the French did then.'

'Great. Two for the price of one. So, tell me about Petit-Jean's father then. What was his wild gene?'

'I'm not sure he had one, or maybe it just manifested itself differently. He was a quiet shy man and very ashamed of his father having been a traitor. I met him a few times. He ran a pharmacy and photographic shop in the village. Sadly, it only took a first taste of Pastis for him to dedicate the rest of his life to drowning his sorrows in an absinthe bottle. He died when Petit-Jean was about fourteen, I guess, more or less.'

'And Petit -Jean?'

Christophe smiled sadly. 'Petit-Jean, where to start on Petit-Jean! He was crazy, brave, devious, witty, stubborn as hell, and one of the most charming heartbreakers you can ever imagine.'

'You had a lot in common then.'

'You think so?'

'Absolutely. You've just described yourself. I'm so glad you didn't drop out like he did and join the commune, otherwise I would never have found you.'

'Dropped out?'

'That's what Simon Chapman said.'

'Well it depends on how you look at things. One summer about fifteen years ago, a lot of students moved into the old farm buildings around the area. You know, looking for a different kind of life and the village has always attracted artisans and a different kind of people. You'd probably think it's something to do with the ley lines or the planets I suppose.'

Julia smiled. 'Well maybe it does …'

'OK. Only joking. Look I won't say anything but just don't get so attracted to it all that you join the commune will you?'

'The commune?'

'Well that's what the locals call it. As far as I've always known it's never been a sect or anything, just a group of free spirits believing in a bit of free love, free speech and self-sufficiency. Call it what you like.'

'Free love? Mmm, it's starting to sound interesting.'

I bet there was, she thought. I bet Sophie Petrarch was very free with it.

'Petit-Jean was a part of the group and he had two or three different girlfriends in the commune and worked selling antiques, arts and crafts, bric-a-brac, dope, anything that provided him with a living. I had heard that he had settled now though, with his girlfriend Charlene who I've never met. Bernard told me they'd been doing up the old Baudoin house in the village.

'How come you never spoke of Petit-Jean before?' asked Julia. She sensed she was on extremely sensitive ground but thought he was in a mellow enough mood to answer. 'If he was such a great friend of you and Bernard? How come I've never met him?'

Christophe hesitated. She thought he was going to tell her and then she felt the tenseness in him and knew he'd clammed up. That's what happens when you prod oysters, trying to extract pearls of wisdom, I should know better.

'One day Julia, maybe I can tell you, but it is not my story to tell. Anyway, it is all over now and Petit-Jean is dead, and I have missed the opportunity to make up a stupid argument.'

Seven

THEY DROVE UP THE hill slowly from the deep valley. The road wound its way up one of the steep sides and suddenly broke out onto a hilltop. Christophe pulled the car off the road and took her hand.

'Come on Miss Connors, this is the best view you'll ever get of Pont Carnac.'

They walked across to the edge of the grass verge and Christophe led her to a gap in the hedge and they pushed their way through across rough ground. The mud clogged to their shoes and the final climb to the top was hard going. Julia breathed deeply, enjoying the bracing air after the long car journey.

'Wow!' she said.

They were right on the edge of a hill looking down into the village which was still wrapped in a mist that seemed to emanate from the river that ran through the middle. The sun shone above them and down into the mist highlighting the rooftops. The exact view of the Chapman painting stood before her. She decided to tease Christophe a little.

'Oh, it's incredible,' she said. 'It seems so familiar.'

Christophe smiled. 'It does, doesn't it. Must be your intuition. That psychic quality that you believe in.'

'It really feels like I've been here before. I just can't think why. I ...'

'Really?' asked Christophe, giving a fake innocent look.

'Yes definitely. I was definitely here in a previous life. I just know it. Maybe I was Breton, or St Cuthbert or something? What do you think?'

'Oh undoubtedly.'

Julia put her arm through his. 'I'm sorry, we shouldn't play games and joke around at a time like this. Not with everything that you are going through. He painted it from here, didn't he? Chapman. That's where I've seen it before.'

Christophe turned and smiled at her in surprise.

'You did like it. You weren't just using it to get rid of the black hole.'

'Christophe! You know I did. I do, I love it. And here it is in front of me.'

They stood in silence, both watching the living painting before them.

'I know you think all this instinct and intuition thing is nonsense Christophe, but I know you'll get the painting back. I know we'll find it. I can feel it in my bones.'

He hugged her to him, even more tightly than usual. 'Maybe.' he said softly. 'Maybe you're right and if you are, I promise to follow every single instinct you ever have.'

'I'll hold you to that, Monsieur.'

'There used to be a cabin somewhere along here. I think it fell down ages ago or got overgrown with bushes and things. Chapman used to come here with Baudoin and they'd spend hours painting. Chapman was obsessed with the light. That's what made him such an incredible painter. Often, he'd do the same scene twenty or thirty times, in all seasons. In rain, snow at sundown, sunrise, just to get all the moods down as fast as he could.'

'Our painting was done in the late afternoon wasn't it? In winter?'

'Yes, when the sun was very white and low in the sky, just as the frost starts to coat everything. I was always convinced that it was near Christmas time. There's a kind of glow to it.' Christophe shrugged his shoulders as if suddenly cold. 'I think, as you would say, somebody has just walked over my grave.'

She put her hand in his, and they walked back towards the car.

'One year I came for Christmas,' he said. 'It was the last year before my mother left. My parents were trying to make a go of it and had gone away together. Bernard's parents were away too, so we both came here to Petit-Jean's. He'd already got two or three different girlfriends on the go. Every year the Chapmans would have a large get together up at the château. We spent the whole night trying to keep all of Petit-Jean's girlfriends in different corners of the room, in case they actually got to talk to each other. I remember, Simon didn't find it at all amusing and neither did his very serious military father, Charles.'

As Julia bent down to go through the gap in the hedge, she moved a branch slightly to one side, then smacked heads with somebody, coming from the other direction.

'Ouch,' she put her head up too soon and got one of the branches of the hedge in her eye.'

'Jeepers, that hurts.' Her eyes stung and filled with water.

The other person was also cursing. Through her

watery eyes, Julia could just make out the petite figure of Rochelle.

'Rochelle, you loony,' she said. They hugged each other warmly.

'Really Julia. You should go through the hedges on the right, like the roads. This is France you know.'

Bernard and Christophe were already squeezing each other's shoulder warmly.

Rochelle and Julia's faces fell, as they simultaneously remembered why they were there.

'Oh Julia. It is so sad. Petit-Jean. And Christophe's paintings too.'

'I know.'

Christophe and Bernard finally let go of each other and Christophe swept Rochelle up into his arms and went straight for the change of subject, knowing Rochelle well.

'Madame Chauvenon, you get smaller every day. You should get Bernard to feed you more.'

Bernard laughed dryly. 'You're kidding! She eats like a Sumo wrestler. It's her highly strung artistic temperament that eats up all the calories.'

'Well that and five children, that all have characters like their father.'

Bernard took Julia's face in his hands and kissed her on both cheeks.

'Julia, *cherie*. Every time I see you, I am amazed how you do it, to keep my terrible friend sane and happy. Nobody has ever done this before. The French will make you a *chevalier d'honneur*.'

Bernard and Christophe looked at each other.

'I'll walk back over there with you Bernard,' said Christophe and Julia instinctively knew that they wanted to be on their own.

Rochelle watched Bernard walk off with Christophe, and Julia saw tears falling down her cheeks.

'This is all so much more terrible than you can imagine,' she said. Then she collapsed into Julia's arms sobbing, more distraught than Julia had ever seen her.

***

Julia followed Christophe to their room up a mediaeval narrow stone spiral staircase. It was very cold and dark. She rubbed her hands together frantically to try and warm them up. The only light came from some small slits in the stone work and a few uplighters on the walls. It was not at all the romantic place that Christophe had described. If they'd been going down instead of up she would have been convinced he'd booked rooms in the dungeon.

'Is this part of the castle?' Julia asked, slightly confused.

'No, they were the original houses attached to the castle where the merchants and clerks associated with the castle would live. We'll walk around the village ramparts later and you'll get a good view of the castle.'

'So is the castle in ruins?'

'No. It was renovated by William Chapman after the war. Simon's father, General Charles Chapman owns it now. It's Simon's country bolthole in France.'

The narrow staircase opened out onto a large landing, and they went through an old oak door and the romance was revealed. They were in an enormous suite with leaded windows across one side. There was a log fire burning in a huge stone fireplace, and the winter sunshine streamed through the windows, making the room at least four or five degrees warmer than the corridor had been. The walls were hung with modern takes on old tapestries and two large sofas were comfortably close to the fire. To the back of the room, a large bed sat on a platform in a natural mediaeval stone alcove.

'Wow! This is amazing,' said Julia

'I thought you'd like it.'

Julia rushed to look out of the window. As she leant out, she could see right across the rooftops of Pont Carnac, an almost completely mediaeval village.

She turned her head, and found herself nose to nose with a large sculpture that was carved out of the cornerstone of the stone wall of the building.

'Ooh. Gargoyle alert. Spooky.' She said, reeling backwards.

Christophe laughed. 'Yes. Very typical of this part of Brittany.'

'I'm guessing it's pretty old,' said Julia looking into the scary pagan eyes of a wolf that transformed into a serpent.

'About the same age as the castle, I imagine. About five or six hundred years probably.'

Julia wandered back over to the fireplace to warm her bottom against the fire and Christophe watched her.

One of the things he'd always loved about her was the complete and utter openness of her beautiful face. Right now, he could almost see the cogs turning as she puzzled over something.

'What are Gargoyles for anyway?' she finally asked.

'They're just drainpipes really. Old drainpipes.'

'So why do you think they make them so frightening?'

'I don't know', said Christophe, smiling to himself. 'But I have a vague feeling you are going to give me a classic Julia Connors take on it.

'Well, now that you mention it,' she said, throwing

him one of her very direct looks. 'I think it's to scare off the young Romeos who try to climb up and deflower the local virgins.'

'An interesting and thoroughly practical use for a Gargoyle. I'd say.' He drew her towards him, his eyes making his intentions perfectly clear. 'And …' he said as he started to remove her jacket. '…excellent news. The perfect deterrent to keep Simon Chapman out of your boudoir.'

Julia put her jacket back on and gave him a knowing smile 'Or you out of Sophie Petrarch's.'

'Ouch! Your barbs, do wound me so.' He fell backwards onto the bed, feigning the pain of a blow to his heart.

There was a knock on the door and Bernard came straight in. He was fumbling to tie a black tie while he spoke. He was very upset.

'Christophe. You've got to get changed. We have to go. The funeral is in half an hour.'

'What? But why so quickly? Who organised it for God's sake?'

'I don't know, and I don't like it. There is some story of Charlene and Petit-Jean's friends from the commune being barred from attending the funeral. They are furious and are putting up a protest outside the church. They are saying that Petit-Jean didn't want a religious funeral. He wanted to be buried in the woods down by the lake.'

'Well they've got a point. He had his own kind of religion.'

'I agree. One thing we know for certain is he didn't want to be cremated. But, as Madame Yvette is next of kin, there's not a lot they can do. I'm guessing she and General Chapman have taken over.'

'Madame Yvette? You mean his Grandmother? Odilon Baudoin's wife?' asked Julia, surprised. 'Goodness is she still alive?'

'Yes,' replied Christophe, grabbing his tie. 'She was very young when she met Odilon Baudoin. A child muse you might say.'

'General Chapman is dictating the order of things as usual,' said Bernard.

'Yes. Or maybe it's Madame Yvette's way of getting back at Petit-Jean. Even after death,' said Christophe, the sadness clear in his voice.

'Isn't that a bit harsh? Asked Julia. 'Won't she be really upset? He's her grandson.'

'Madame Yvette Baudoin is very bitter. She has been like that about her family ever since she had to move in with the Chapmans years ago.'

Christophe could see she was not happy with the short answer, so did a quick business like recap, whilst he tied his tie. 'Odilon Baudoin was executed as a Nazi collaborator, Yvette was pregnant with Petit-Jean's father, penniless and living in the Baudoin house. The villagers harassed her mercilessly so William Chapman and his wife took her in. Yvette never forgave Odilon for what he did. She then drove her son, Petit-Jean's father to drink because of the shame and her hatred for the Baudoin name. Petit-Jean didn't fair much better. To her the Baudoin blood is bad blood.'

Christophe paused. Thoughtful as he tied his shoelaces.

'Maybe Petit-Jean left the Baudoin house to Charlene.'' he said. 'That would really have infuriated them.'

'It would,' Bernard agreed.

'In my opinion Charlene deserves it.' said Christophe. 'She's stood by Petit-Jean for these past few years, no matter what he's done. Yvette abandoned him a long time ago.' And so did I, he thought quietly to himself.

'Perhaps,' said Bernard. 'But you know that won't stand up in court. In France it always goes down the genetic line. Which means the Guillemain family will also have a say.'

Julia glanced at Christophe. His face was set hard and she knew what that meant.

'We'll see about that,' said Christophe as he headed for the door with Bernard.

Hum, thought Julia. Christophe is clearly hell bent on making amends in whatever way he can for not speaking to Petit-Jean for all these years. There is a lot more to this.

She changed quickly and headed off to get Rochelle but she wasn't in their room. After a few false turns through cold, dark mediaeval corridors, several encounters with suits of armour and an unfortunate accident when her coat got caught on a knight's battleaxe sending it clattering to the floor, she finally found her. She was sitting on a cold stone bench up in a top turret, staring bleakly out at the village through one of the arrow slits in the wall. She turned and stared at Julia in a daze. Her eyes were red and what few tears she still had left could be seen in them.

'This is terrible,' Rochelle's voice trembled as she spoke. 'Can you imagine? You can't imagine. We nearly missed the funeral because nobody told us. Bernard and Christophe nearly missed the funeral because they weren't told! And poor Petit-Jean. His Grandmother! How can she do this to him? How can she be so cruel?'

Julia moved forward to try and give her a hug, but Rochelle gently pushed her away.

'Non, Julia, *cherie*. If you are kind to me, I will not be able to hold myself together. Please, just talk to me. Talk to me about anything ... anything to take my mind away from this.'

'OK.' Thought Julia, racking her brains.

'Err…'

She could see Rochelle's large doe eyes, filling with tears again.

'Well …'

'Julia?' asked Rochelle, her voice desperate. 'Please?'

Brainwave thought Julia. Emergency brainwave needed.

Eureka!

'Did you know I've been sacked again?' She gave Rochelle a big beaming smile.

That did the trick! Rochelle was completely wide eyed now. She stood up.

'Sacked? Jean-Claude sacked you?'

'Yep. Definitely and probably for good this time.'

Rochelle took Julia's hand and led the way down the stairs as she continued to chat.

'And is this a good thing?'

'Well no. I'm not sure but maybe yes.'

'You cannot decide?'

'Well. I was going to resign anyway. Because I want to spend more time with Christophe.'

'So, it is good then'

'Yes. But not good, because Jean-Claude has always been like a father to me, and he sacked me.'

'Ah. And will he change his mind? Is this? How do you say? A creative tantrum?'

'Not this time. Because there is somebody else involved.'

'Really? Who?'

'See if you can guess?' Guessing games, that's a good

one, thought Julia. That will keep Rochelle distracted.

Rochelle thought for a moment.

'The terrible Boucher who was so horrible to you before?'

Julia laughed. 'No not her. Someone younger and much more dangerous.'

'A supermodel?'

Julia shook her head. 'Sort of, but not quite.'

After a few moments Rochelle sighed 'OK. I give up,'

'None other than Sophie Petrarch!'

'*Mon dieu*! That is big trouble!'

'I know. So, Jean Claude and I are taking a bit of time out.'

Rochelle smiled. 'Oh dear. Then you had better prepare yourself because Sophie will be here, she …'

'I know. I know Rochelle. She has history with Christophe!'

'She has history with all of them, *chérie*. Petit-Jean, yes, even my Bernard.'

And Rochelle burst into tears again.

This time Julia did hug her, and Rochelle cried all the way to the Church, with Julia's arm around her.

Julia chatted about anything and everything to try and keep her friend afloat.

Eight

THEY ENTERED THE *PLACE DE L'EGLISE,* a large cobbled square with a fountain in the centre and mediaeval stone and half timbered houses on three sides. On the other side there was a gothic church that was so big it looked more like a cathedral. Two crowds had gathered, one at the entrance to the church and the other near the fountain. Julia looked more closely at the group near the fountain. There she was, France's greatest naked export, Sophie Petrarch. She was surrounded by photographers, and she held court as if it was her own press conference and not a funeral at all.

Julia noted the classic Chanel outfit. Nobody has ever done black as well as Chanel does and boy did Sophie Petrarch know it. Well at least she has the decency to have some clothes on for a funeral. She had to admit it, rather begrudgingly, she was stunning. Simon Chapman was with her and he gently pushed the photographers back to make a way through the melee. Chapman and Petrarch gradually made their way to the church and the pack of photographers followed them, keeping a respectful quiet stillness behind them.

Julia turned Rochelle to face her and she took a tissue out of her bag and some eye drops. She handed them to Rochelle who was now sniffing rather than sobbing.

'What's this?'

'Eye drops. They are for allergies but they work really well for red eyes from a good cry.'

'You are such a good friend Julia.' She handed the bottle back. 'Can you do it for me? I can't see.'

Rochelle tilted her head and Julia put the drops in.

'Julia I have to thank you for so many things.' She blinked rapidly to help the drops sink in. 'I know friends shouldn't have secrets but sometimes you can't help it.' She dabbed her cheek with a tissue to mop up the last then opened her eyes really wide. 'Wow that's much better! What's in that?'

'It's a natural remedy, a bit of chamomile.' She put it back in her bag. 'What did you say? About secrets? Is there something you want to tell me?'

'What?' Rochelle, stared over at the entrance to the church, distracted. 'Secrets, no, just me being silly. Come on we have to go and be supportive to Bernard and Christophe. This is going to be so difficult for them.'

The members of the commune were standing at the church entrance. They had organised themselves into two rows facing each other either side of the pathway leading into the church, like a guard of honour or vigil. They were all dressed in brightly coloured long flowing boho clothes which were all different. They cradled their home-made candles over their hearts and were murmuring together, their voices a sad low chant. They were so absorbed in what they were doing that they seemed to be able to completely ignore the people walking past them into the church.

Julia and Rochelle reached the start of the line. The vigil did not react. Rochelle hesitated to go further and took a deep breath. Neither of them wanted to walk down that line. They didn't have a choice. The commune had positioned themselves so well that there was no way of entering the church without going down the aisle of guardians. Julia stepped forward first and felt extremely uncomfortable. It was as if they were running a mental gauntlet of passive-aggression. It ran along the line, like a wave increasing in size as every person they passed added to its energy. Julia kept looking ahead of her, avoiding any eye contact with the guardians. The wave kept par with them and then stopped at the two tall people nearest the entrance to the church. A tall red haired girl and an even taller dark haired man looked up and turned their heads in synchrony, like a pair of siamese cat bookends. They stared hard, blank stares at Julia and Rochelle, without really seeing. Julia felt a huge blast of energy and almost fell backwards as if the wave had peaked, and broken against her. As quickly as it had happened it stopped and a bleak stillness surrounded them.

The tall red haired girl seemed to come out of a trance. She stood proudly, her red hair blazing against the dark olive green of her hat. She had tresses that fell to her waist, pale skin and large dark shadows under extremely beautiful green eyes that were crying, openly, cathartically with no trace of embarrassment. She was proud and defiant. She seemed younger than the others but the ethereal quality made it impossible to tell how old she truly was. Julia felt Rochelle's arm go tense at the sight of the girl. Then, Rochelle suddenly let go of Julia, burst forward and threw herself into the girl's arms.

'Oh Charlene', she sobbed. 'This is terrible.'

Charlene held Rochelle to her and they cried together. Charlene lifted Rochelle's head and turned her face to look upwards into her eyes. She wiped a tear from Rochelle's cheek and spoke calmly but with force.

'Rochelle. Sweet Rochelle. Do not weep for one taken so soon. There will always be karmic retribution for those that have been wronged.'

The other mourner standing opposite Charlene must have been at least two metres tall – and that was without the velvet top hat that he wore. He had shoulder length dark hair and a well-trimmed goatee. He seemed younger even than Charlene, but again, it was difficult to tell. He too stared at Julia and Rochelle, and he certainly didn't need to stare to be intimidating.

He spoke directly to Julia. 'You must tell Madame Yvette. 'Petit-Jean's spirit is with us. And he is angry!!!'

***

As Julia and Rochelle entered the huge church, Bernard rushed up to them and whisked them to one side.

'They were going to start the ceremony using poll bearers from the funeral organiser. It's as we thought, they will not let his friends from the commune into the church. They say they are blasphemers and occultists. So, Charlene and the rest of them are waiting for the end of the ceremony so that they can stop Petit-Jean's body from being taken to the crematorium. Christophe is trying to sort it out.'

Christophe saw them and left the priest that he had been talking to. He covered the length of the church with his long strides in just a few seconds. He looked as if he was moving towards them but at the last moment he diverted off to the side and Julia turned to see why. Sophie Petrarch and Simon Chapman had been manoeuvring forwards from the side pews to get to the front. Christophe kissed Sophie fondly and Julia felt a hot wave of sickness rise up from her solar plexus until she was sure she had turned as green as Charlene's dress.

Simon Chapman threw her an amused look. He proceeded to eye her up and down before inclining his head in acknowledgement as if he was local royalty. She supposed he was. The church was full of people and sensing their antagonism to the commune, she doubted many of them were there for Petit-Jean. They were there for Yvette.

The meeting with Charlene had been the final catharsis that Rochelle had needed and she was now well in control of her emotions. She had seen Julia's face when Christophe kissed Sophie. She linked her arm through Julia's, reassuringly.

'Christophe and Sophie, it is nothing *chérie*. Unless you want to make it a mountain from the mole droppings.'

'Mole hill, Rochelle,' corrected Julia, smiling. She was relieved to see that Rochelle was holding up well.

'Do you think if I married Christophe, it would stop me feeling like this?' she whispered, still watching the intimacy of the body language between Christophe and Sophie. Only people who had history behaved like that.

Rochelle looked confused.

'Like what?'

'You know, jealous when he finds other people attractive.'

'You think marriage stops you both finding other people attractive? *Mon dieu*, It's a piece of paper *cherie*, not a sexual lobotomy.'

Yep. Rochelle was definitely back to her old self.

Christophe came over with Sophie. Julia took a good look at her while she kissed Rochelle on both cheeks.' Not a tear in sight, not even a fake actress one. Simon Chapman took the opportunity to whisper in Julia's ear as he kissed her on both cheeks. 'Such an interesting competition - I mean congregation, don't you think?'

Sophie Petrarch finally deigned to speak to Julia.

'How wonderful to meet you at last.' She said oozing fake sincerity. She looked across at Christophe as she said challengingly, 'So you're the flavour of the month. I'd forgotten what a naughty boy he can be.' Dramatic actress sigh. 'He's always chopping and changing his women as fast as his shirts.'

In your dreams, drama queen, thought Julia. She was about to offer a reply but Sophie had already exited stage left and gone to sit in prime position with Simon at the front.

Christophe turned to Julia and Rochelle.

'That's everything sorted with the priest. He's going to hold things off until we can get some kind of compromise between Yvette and the commune. Let's walk and talk.' They headed back down the aisle towards the entrance. 'You two go to the Baudoin house and Bernard and I will join you there,' said Chrisophe. 'With any luck we'll say our goodbyes to Petit-Jean there, convince Yvette to be reasonable and do the cortège through the village. The commune will be allowed in and the poll bearers will take Petit-Jean into the church. After the church ceremony, Petit-Jean's body will be taken to a place of burial that he would have wished, again, assuming we can get Madame Yvette to agree to it.'

They followed Christophe outside.

'No pressure then!' said Julia.

Christophe kissed her on the cheek. 'I've had worse.' He turned and went over to Charlene. Julia was surprised to see him embrace her and he put his arm around her protectively as he discussed what was happening.

Interesting, thought Julia. Christophe has his arm around another woman and you have no feelings of jealousy whatsoever yet if he'd done that to Sophie Petrarch, you'd have grabbed the nearest communion plate and sliced her head off with it.

Christophe agreed something with Charlene and she turned and nodded to the others in the group and they stopped their chanting.

Christophe addressed them in his clear, friendly but business-like voice.

'I think we all agree that we give Petit-Jean the funeral that he deserves. Some of you know me from our childhood and some of you don't. Petit-Jean was a good friend of mine and I would like us to pay our respects to him as he would have wished. But we also need to respect the wishes of his only living relative, Madame Yvette.'

There were mutterings of disapproval from the commune. Christophe held up his hand to quieten them down.

'Charlene has agreed to the compromise and we will hold the Church ceremony as Madame Yvette has requested. We need four of you to help Bernard and myself as poll bearers and you are all very welcome in the church and at the wake afterwards. It will be held in the Café Breton, Petit-Jean's favourite place.'

Christophe and Bernard went back to the Baudoin house with the car but Rochelle and Julia decided to walk as it wasn't far. It was the first real look that Julia had of the village. She loved it. It was like walking through a film set. A maze of tiny cobbled backstreets wound their way up and down the village and some of them were no wider than a wheelbarrow. The houses were all mediaeval with crooked beams and roofs so slanted they were more like ski jumps. They were so close together that people in opposite houses would have been able to touch each other from the front upper windows as the rooms jutted out over the streets. Rochelle knew all the shortcuts and they got to the Baudoin house before the Christophe and Bernard who had been forced to take the longer, wider road.

The house was one of the few in the village that hadn't been fully renovated. There was a small skip and a pile of rubble near the entrance, left from the work that Petit-Jean and Charlene had been doing. Rochelle led the way down a tiny alley to the side of the house and they went in through an old stone archway and a heavy wooden door that was already open. They entered what must have been the original mediaeval grand hall. It ran the length of the ground floor and you could see right up to the beams at the top of the third floor. Above them, a wide minstrel gallery ran around three sides of the upper floors and doors led off it into smaller rooms. The insides were all clad in the original wood panelling, parts of which had been removed for renovation and other parts had simply fallen off due to rot.

In the centre of the room Petit-Jean was laid out in a simple cheap wooden coffin on special trestles that had been brought in. There were several people already in the room paying their respects.

Rochelle was hesitant.

'We'll wait for Christophe and Bernard before we approach Yvette. I think,' she whispered.

A tall elegant elderly woman stood rigid next to the

foot of the coffin. She stared down into it. She seemed oblivious to everyone else and she had not moved even though the footsteps on the old wooden floorboards were very loud.

Julia looked across at the other people. There were two men, about Christophe and Bernard's age waiting to pay their respects and Julia realised that one of them was detective Guillemain. He nodded to her in recognition. There were more footsteps. Christophe and Bernard had arrived, and this time Yvette looked up. She did not smile and she spoke with an authority that came from age and position in life. It was the authority of someone who was used to people not disagreeing with her.

'Bernard Chauvenon and Christophe de Flaubert. How nice of you to come.'

She turned back and looked into the coffin.

'You were always three, and now you are two.'

Christophe and Bernard nodded solemnly.

'I always wondered why you could not do more. Why you two could go so far in life and not take him with you?' Her words hung in the air.

Christophe and Bernard stood like two school boys who were being berated for not having done their homework.

Julia thought she saw a satisfied look in Guillemain's eyes as he listened to Yvette.

'We did try Madame Yvette, you know we did,' said Bernard.

She nodded understanding, yet defeated.

'I know. I know. And as we all know to our detriment, when a Baudoin has an idea in his head, especially when it is a bad idea, there is nothing anybody can do.' Yvette was now looking at detective Guillemain who was nodding his head in agreement

She gestured with her hand to Christophe and Bernard.

'Say what you have to say to him. Then take him. Take your friend away. Your friends you choose, your family you do not.' She looked at Christophe and Bernard. 'I am his family but I did not choose him, I did not choose this! Her voice cracked slightly, with emotion.

Christophe made a move towards her but she put up her hand to stop him and recovered her composure. She looked him in the eye.

'And I suppose you had better let the rabble into the Church, even though I blame them for this.'

Christophe opened his mouth to say something but again she held up her hand to stop him. Then she smiled cynically in realisation.

'You already have, haven't you young Christophe de Flaubert? Yes, that is typical of you, taking matters into your own hands.' She looked down at the coffin again and sighed.

'I knew it would end like this. Such is the life of a Baudoin. So be it.'

Rochelle took Bernard's hand and they went over to say goodbye. Rochelle, stroked Petit-Jean's head and kissed his cheek. Bernard did the same.

Christophe took Julia's hand in his.

'Julia, I have to say a very special goodbye and I can't do it alone. You know how bad I am at apologising. Will you come with me and stand by my side? I need someone to know, to bear witness that I apologised.'

She approached the coffin slightly in Christophe's shadow. She took a candle just as Christophe did, lit it and placed it by the coffin. She could hear Christophe murmuring but could not make out the words. He leant over, kissed Petit-Jean and stood back to let Julia do the same.

Julia glanced down in the coffin and got the shock of her life. She'd seen him somewhere before.

Nine

YVETTE NODDED TO THE funeral staff and they closed the coffin. She left with Guillemain in the funeral car without saying a word to them. Christophe took Julia's hand and led her outside where Charlene and the rest of the commune had arrived with a horse drawn cart that had been decorated with flowers and local heather. Petit-Jean's coffin was placed in the cart and Charlene and the tall sect leader led the cortège on foot to the Church. Christophe, Bernard, Julia and the others followed them. It was silent apart from the sound of the horse shoes clicking and wheels rolling slowly along the cobbles.

The cart drew up at the church entrance and four of the commune men joined Christophe and Bernard to carry Petit-Jean inside. Yvette was waiting at the entrance and she walked in front of the coffin. You could feel the tension of the commune in the congregation when Yvette entered, but she walked tall, her beautiful face haughty and oblivious to the vibes that were being thrown at her.

The Priest gave a small eulogy, followed by prayers, and then he went over to speak to Yvette. She glanced across at Christophe and hesitated, shaking her head but Christophe held her gaze. You could feel the tension in the air. Finally she nodded, defeated and Christophe let out a huge sigh of relief. The priest gestured that the tall leader of the commune could step up to the lectern.

Julia was surprised at his confidence. He looked as if he could barely be more than eighteen but he stood so tall and composed, he was mesmerising to watch.

'Petit-Jean was our peacemaker.' His deep baritone voice carried all the way to the back of the church, like a Shakespearian actor.

'He was an old soul who had led many lives on this earth and on others. Many of those he had already lived with Charlene.' He smiled down at Charlene. 'They were brought together at the beginning of time.' His voice became even more charismatic and he knew exactly where to put emphasis on his words to create drama. 'Before Adam and Eve, the spirit creators wove their karmic threads together. Petit-Jean and Charlene's spirits were entwined forever, for eternity until this earth and this form of life is no more. In this incarnation they had little time together, but what they had was beautiful. It was an example to us all. They showed us that an all encompassing love can heal the troubles of our souls. We are all given a mission in our lives and we must not weep for his loss because Petit-Jean had done what he needed to do in this incarnation. Yet his spirit is uneasy and he still speaks to us. He has left us an important job to do and we, his true brothers and sisters,' he paused and looked directly at Madame Yvette. 'Will not rest until it is done!'

There was a silence for a moment and then as if a message had passed telepathically through the members of the commune, they put their hands together in the prayer mudra. Their leader lowered his voice to a soothing whisper and led the Buddhist prayer for Petit-Jean's next life.

> *Just as the soft rains fill the streams,*
> *Pour into the rivers and join together in the oceans,*
> *So may the power of every moment of your goodness*
> *Flow forth to awaken and heal all beings,*
> *Those here now, those gone before, those yet to come.*
> *By the power of every moment of your goodness*
> *May your heart's wishes be soon fulfilled*
> *As completely shining as the bright full moon,*
> *As magically as by a wish-fulfilling gem.*
> *By the power of every moment of your goodness*
> *May all dangers be averted and all disease be gone.*
> *May no obstacle come across your way.*
> *May you enjoy fulfillment and long life.*
> *For all in whose heart dwells respect,*
> *Who follow the wisdom and compassion, of the Way,*
> *May your life prosper in the four blessings*
> *Of old age, beauty, happiness, and strength.*

Julia was so enthralled by the leader's voice that she didn't hear Francoise arrive. She felt the girl gently touch her shoulder, and she moved up to make space for her next to Rochelle. Francoise took her mother's hand and wiped away a tear that had started to fall.

'Mama, Papa said you needed me…' then she took her mother in her arms.

Christophe smiled kindly at Françoise, then stood up. It was his turn to say a few words about Petit-Jean. He spoke freely and easily without any notes.

'I'd like to say thank you to you all for coming into the church and for waiting so patiently. None of us really understand what went on here today but the most important thing is that all of those who loved Petit-Jean should be here together to say their goodbyes and to celebrate his life.'

Yvette gave a sharp intake of breath. Christophe looked over at her, sternly. Then he said it again. Directly to her.

'To celebrate his wonderful life, because it *was* a wonderful life.' He turned back to the congregation.

'When we spoke together before the service, I asked you what you remembered most about Petit-Jean. Some of you remembered his ability to whistle louder than anybody else in the village. Some remembered his Far Breton, how it melted in your mouth. Others remembered the way he would chase a chicken for hours until he caught the exact chicken that he wanted and then could not bring himself to slaughter it for dinner.' There was a gentle ripple of laughter. 'In fact, I think the only chicken that ever made a classic Petit-Jean coq au vin was one that died of old age.'

More smiles and laughter.

'But all of you said one thing that rang true and summed up what he meant to you. Once he found Charlene, he was the gentlest, most tranquil person to be around. He was always there to calm situations down, always trying to steer things away from an argument. He hated arguments, he hated aggression, and unfairness. We all know how wild he was when he was young but deep in himself, he had found peace. In Charlene he found his soulmate and a life where he could focus on the things that were important to him and not be disturbed by the struggles and conflicts of the past.'

There was a sudden clicking of heels on the floor at the back of the church. Christophe paused for a moment. A middle aged man had come into the church and was making no effort to walk quietly. He sat down right at the front next to Simon Chapman, Yvette and Sophie. His shoes were very well polished. Julia saw the resemblance to Simon Chapman immediately. The man tapped his walking stick on the floor as a gesture to Christophe to continue, then rested it against the pew.

Christophe frowned at him, then continued.

'For myself. I knew Petit-Jean as a boy. He was a partner in crime for schoolboy pranks. Many a time when I was in trouble for those pranks, few people realised that the quiet brains behind it had been Petit-Jean. We spent such wonderful summers together. My only consolation at his untimely death...' Christophe's voice broke slightly. '... is that ... is that, he had found true happiness with Charlene and a quiet peace here in Pont Carnac close to the people he loved.' Christophe stared at Yvette, who looked away.

Christophe nodded to the organ player and choir master and everyone stood as the music started.

'I believe you have song sheets in front of you and Charlene has asked you all to raise your voices in joy to celebrate the life of Petit-Jean. She knows that he would want us to sing the classic children's Christmas carol, Petit Papa Noel.'

***

As they left the church Julia noticed that the man with the noisy shoes had quickly disappeared. He left a lot more quietly than he arrived. Definitely overly self important and likes to make an entrance. If that's the noise he makes at a funeral, who knows what he'd be like leading the charge of the Light Brigade. She was sure it was Simon Chapman's military father.

They had to wait outside the Café Breton while the owners organised things inside. They'd been at the funeral themselves and hadn't had long to prepare. In normal circumstances they would have stayed closed, but it was for Petit-Jean, so that changed everything. Françoise stood talking to Rochelle while Christophe and Bernard went inside to put down the payment for the wake. Julia thought Françoise looked better than she'd ever seen her. In her second year at University she was now a wonderful tall bright good-looking young woman. Her straight no nonsense glasses just added to her already extremely intelligent look. Julia knew that she was studying something scientific that had to do with marine biology, but had always got lost whenever Françoise tried to explain it to her.

'So how is Uni?' she asked. 'But make it simple because you baffle me every time.'

Françoise flicked her long chestnut hair back from her face and launched into her favourite subject, breathless and at pace.

'Great. Superb. You remember I told you all about the genetic map of all of the different marine species. Well that's what I'm doing my thesis on this year. And guess what, I've entered a competition to go and do a year out in French Polynesia. I'm so excited. You will come and visit me, won't you?'

'You bet! said Julia, imagining those crystal clear lagoons of turquoise water and non-stop sunshine.

'The project's a bit secret because what we're trying to do is identify any mutated genes due to the old radiation fallout of nuclear tests, but what I've done so far is truly amazing. They used to use RFLP analysis- that's restriction fragment length polymorphism- but it was really difficult to discern individual alleles so now PCR has made it all so much easier because we can look at short tandem repeats.'

'Of course,' said Julia, nodding her head.

Françoise stopped and then hesitated before saying sheepishly. 'You don't have any idea what I'm talking about do you Julia?'

Julia laughed. 'Is it really that obvious?'

'Mon dieu! Yes. And don't ever do anything bad because you will never be able to lie your way out of it.'

'I guess I'd better just be a good girl for the rest of my life then.'

'You should stop me when I speed talk at you like that. I get so carried away and I must learn to stop.'

'No,' said Julia. 'You mustn't say that Françoise. I love listening to you even though I don't understand. Your voice is so full of energy and joy because you are so passionate about what you do.'

'Who is passionate?' asked Christophe who'd come back out to join them with Bernard. He put his arm around his god-daughter and gave her a kiss on each cheek. 'Do you have a new special friend?'

'No I was speed talking science at Julia.'

'Ah. Be gentle with her. She prefers her instincts of 'knowing things' rather than hard core science. Don't upset her or she'll make me suffer.'

Françoise laughed. 'It is good for you to suffer, *Tonton*. I believe you would be, what is that English word? Insufferable, that's it, if you did not suffer a little bit.'

Christophe looked at Julia and shook his head, amused.

'What is it about you Julia Connors that you manage to charm the most important people in my life so easily?'

'*Tonton*, I'm so sad about your paintings.' said Françoise. 'You are impossible to buy presents for because you have everything. When I found the Baudoin painting it was like a miracle. Finally something that you don't have but that I knew you would love.'

'I know,' said Christophe. 'It truly was a wonderful present. Don't worry though, Julia knows we are going to get the paintings back.'

'That's brilliant! Do you have a lead, Julia?'

Julia glared at Christophe

'She doesn't but her gut does.'

Françoise turned to Julia, surprised. 'Really? You believe in all that?'

'I do. Some people use their instinct, gut reaction, call it what you like, to great advantage.'

'Not very scientific at all,' said Christophe

'There might be something in it.' said Françoise.

Christophe looked worried.

'I did a lot on the microbiome during my second year. That's the bacteria that live in the gut. We have more bacteria cells in us than our own cells, you know and they don't only live in the gut. And I read that they cured someone of schizophrenia using probiotics. So, the balance of bacterial DNA can even influence the way people think and act.'

'Are you saying there could be a scientific basis behind having a good gut reaction?' Julia asked.

'There could,' said Françoise laughing at the disbelief on Christophe's face. 'Anyway, imagine if Julia was right, *Tonton.*'

'I am imagining exactly that,' said Christophe.

Rochelle and Bernard came to join them.

'Are you going to come into the Café Breton, *cherie*?' Rochelle asked Françoise. We could all have dinner after.'

'I can't Mama. I've got to get back to college. I've got

some DNA duplicating and I'm ready to run the results.'

Bernard Chauvenon smiled dotingly at his eldest daughter and shook his head. 'You do know you cannot legally run people's DNA without their consent *ma biche*.''

Françoise flung her arms around her father. 'Papa! Always the lawyer. I'm running animal DNA. You know, marine mammals, mussels and oysters, and they can't actually sign a consent form even if we give them one.'

'Ah. Yes, of course. Just my legal brain in overdrive as usual.'

'Papa,' she said, hugging him fondly. 'You have to train yourself to stop thinking legal all the time. Not everyone is a law breaker.'

'Well, that has not been my experience so far.'

'Haven't you ever broken the law, Bernard? Not even a tiny bit?' asked Julia, surprised.

'No,' said Bernard.

'You have,' said Rochelle. 'When you drove me to the hospital when I was having Françoise. You were speeding all the way.'

'I wasn't,' said Bernard. 'I told you I was because I thought it would make you feel better and you didn't notice because you were concentrating on breathing through the contractions.'

'That is so you Papa,' said Françoise laughing. She glanced down at her watch. 'Oops, got to go.' She fast tracked kissing everyone goodbye and shot off at high speed.

'That is one very happy young lady,' said Julia as she hooked her arm through Christophe's.

***

The Café Breton was a long thin dark stone building in the middle of the cobbled high street. It had been carved directly out of the stone at the bottom of the castle at one end. The other end had been extended into the street using half timbering that butted up to the other houses. The back of the building went out right under the walls of the castle ramparts into a garden that ran the length of what must have originally been the castle moat. Julia stared in amazement. She was thinking about all the people through the centuries who had been there - everyone from knights and merchants to artists and new age travellers.

The bar was solid oak. It was black with the ages and stains of people resting their drinks and arms on it. There was an enormous stone fireplace which carried the coats of arms of the Pont Carnac family, the original inhabitants of the castle. The tops of all four walls had been decorated with friezes of Breton scenes. Children played in orchards, families gathered apples and women toiled in the fields collecting the buckwheat. In another Julia recognised the distinctive tubular lace headdresses of the traditional Breton costumes.

'I can see why they call it the café Breton,' said Julia.

'It is a beautiful place,' said Rochelle, taking a long deep breath as if trying to absorb it. 'You see the panels at the bottom of the bar where the wood is a different colour to the rest?'

'Yes.'

'That's where the famous panels were. All ten of them. Imagine drinking in here if they were still in place.'

Julia laughed. 'Knowing me I'd probably end up spilling my drink over one of them and leaving it stained for life! When were they taken?'

'I'm not sure. I don't think they were stolen. The story is that during the war they were removed to stop the Nazi's getting hold of them.' Rochelle looked up at the frieze.

'This place is like a cathedral to the Breton School. It's such a shame that they never found the other panels. Imagine a Gauguin, a Van Gogh, a Chapman and a Cezanne all on the same wall!'

'There never was any proof that Van Gogh did paint here Rochelle, it's only here say.' said Christophe, handing them their drinks.

'True. If he did, it would have been way before the Chapman and Baudoin were painted because he would have come with Gauguin, and Gauguin left for Tahiti in 1895.' Rochelle agreed.

'Yes,' said Christophe softly. 'Which reminds me Julia what happened to your intuition on my paintings. Where are they? Where are my beloved Baudoin and Chapman?'

Julia opened her mouth to give a sharp reply but the sadness in his eyes made her stop. He downed his drink and headed over to the bar to get another. Julia watched him go.

'Let it go,' said Rochelle. 'This is very hard for him.' She gestured towards the door. '*Enfin*, Charlene. I was worried she might not come. Christophe would have been so upset.'

Charlene walked the length of the bar without speaking to anyone and came straight up to Julia. She spoke so directly, that Julia was taken aback.

'Christophe is a good man. He has an old soul but he does not acknowledge it. Why did he never speak to Petit-Jean? It broke his heart?'

'Wow, thought Julia. I'm known to wade in full throttle but Charlene is something else. She smiled wryly. 'I don't know Charlene. He has not told me. Did Petit-Jean not tell you?'

'No. He said it was not his secret to tell.'

'That is exactly what Christophe said to me.'

'Well perhaps we can find out?' Charlene suggested. 'Some of us are quite talented at getting others to reveal their secrets.'

'You might be Charlene,' said Julia, but I am not that good.'

'I think you underestimate your psychic abilities' said Charlene. 'Maybe Christophe can tell us, if we approach it together, now that Petit-Jean has passed on?'

'No.' Julia shook her head. 'I don't have any psychic abilities and if the secret was not Petit-Jean's and not Christophe's to tell then Petit-Jean's passing will make no difference at all.'

'Yes,' said Charlene, taking a sip of water. 'Your soul mate will honour that to his grave, as my poor Petit-Jean did.' She drank again, emptying the glass in one go. 'Perhaps it was always my Petit-Jean's destiny to be cruelly taken by them.'

'Charlene,' said the tall sect leader, giving a gentle warning.

'Stefan, thinks I should be more careful,' said Charlene. 'He is a young man but he is descended from the ancient Chicasawba giants so he has one of the oldest souls on the planet. He leads our community and we listen to him.' She smiled an affectionate smile. 'Well I try to listen to him but I do not always succeed. Petit-Jean always listened to him.'

'And what do you say, Stefan, about Petit-Jean and Christophe's fall out?' asked Julia.

'I cannot help you,' he said.

'No, said Charlene he cannot help us in that but he can help us fulfil the mission that Petit-Jean's grandfather left him with.'

The sect leader became more insistent. 'Charlene,

that's enough, you don't know who you can trust.'

Charlene touched his hand reassuringly. 'No. I know that I can trust Christophe.'

She turned to Julia. 'I wonder if I can trust you.'

She took Julia's hand in hers.

At first Julia wanted to take it away but the green eyes held hers and she found she couldn't have drawn away even if she'd wanted to. She flinched. She knew her guard was down, but there was nothing that she could do. It was as if Charlene was looking straight into her soul.

'So much pain,' sighed Charlene. She patted Julia's hand reassuringly. 'But your pain is almost healed.' She removed her hand and looked over at Christophe and then back at Julia. 'Christophe though, his pain lies deep inside. It is hard and unforgiving and was placed there a long time ago. Even before this life. He holds onto it. Such anger, jealousy and frustration. It is like a poison and he trusts no one, not even himself - especially not himself. She put her hand to Julia's chin and cupped it and lifted it slightly like a mother does to a child when she wants to say something important. 'You can help him, Julia. You must help him.'

Julia shook her head in disbelief.

'You can. You are so much stronger than you know.' She turned and looked warily towards the door and then back at Stefan.

'They are coming.'

He nodded and held her hand.

She grasped Julia's with the other.

'Whatever happens, you and Christophe must trust me. I am depending on you. I know that you are good people. Julia, trust your instincts.'

There was a commotion at the entrance to the bar as two gendarmes came in with Inspector Guillemain.

Guillemain nodded to Christophe and Julia but did not smile. He then did his signature move of puffing out his chest, dramatically preparing his audience for what was to come. Julia wondered if he realised how ridiculous he looked. Then with a flamboyant flick of his hand, he gestured for the gendarmes to take hold of Charlene.

'Charlene Madec, you are under arrest for the theft of the Baudoin and Chapman works of art.'

Ten

THEY GOT BACK TO their room late and Christophe sat on the bed. He looked very forlorn. He hadn't said a word on the way home and Julia had learnt to respect that. She'd learnt not to disturb his thoughts. He slowly took off his shirt and tie. Without saying anything, she gently pushed him back so that he lay down. She put a pillow behind his head and took off his shoes. The fire had already been lit and there was a wonderful warm glow in the room.

Julia hung up the shirt and tie and then got undressed herself. She moved around in silence and Christophe obviously did not care for conversation either. She took a tiny bottle of aromatherapy oil from her wash bag and gently began to massage Christophe's shoulders.

'Do you know Julia Connors, I'm getting seriously concerned about you. I think I just saw you hang up a shirt and a dress.'

'I think changes are 'a coming' Monsieur de Flaubert. I can feel it in my bones. Lie on your front and I'll do your back properly.'

He rolled over. 'What's in that? Smells nice.'

'Sandalwood, Lavender and Cedar wood. It's supposed to relax you after stress.'

'Really?' Smells that good, I'd better go out and get some more stress.' He looked up at her, slightly drowsily. Julia thought she saw tears in his eyes.

'Don't change things too much, will you?' he said.

'We can't help change Christophe. We can't stop people dying. We can't change the past, we can only change the way that we look at it. You taught me that.'

She felt the muscles in his neck tighten slightly.

'Just because I tell you that doesn't mean I adhere to it myself you know. I am a great advocate of the 'do as I say 'and not 'do as I do.'

'I really don't believe Charlene and Petit-Jean stole the paintings, you know.'

'I just can't get my head around any of it.' His voice was heavy with tiredness. 'I blame myself completely. If only I hadn't fallen out with him. Maybe they did take the paintings. Maybe he did it for revenge, to get back at me. In which case I deserve it.'

'Christophe, I don't know why you fell out and neither does Charlene because Petit-Jean wouldn't tell her either. It can't be that. I just don't believe they would do that.'

'Well Guillemain says they've got evidence and there's no way they could have arrested Charlene without evidence.'

'Well let's not dwell on it. This has been a terribly sad day.'

She put a bit more oil on her hands and turned him over so that his head rested in her hands and began to gently massage his head.

'I know it will work out, Christophe. I don't know

why but I trust Charlene. Anyway, we should try and focus on the good things we have.'

He let out a long sigh. 'You're right and we do have good things, we really do.'

He became even more drowsy and she could feel the tension leaving his shoulders and arms. His breathing became deep and even. He rolled over half asleep, and the long fingers slipped under the pillow to feel the coolness of the sheets underneath.

'Don't change too much Julia,' he muttered. 'Because I really need you.' And as she leant across to switch off the light, she saw a single tear slip from his eye down onto the pillow.

Julia couldn't sleep yet. She thought about what Charlene had said and watched the flickering flames of the fire reflected on Christophe's bare back. The flames seemed to criss-cross over his spine healing away the exhaustion and stress. She cuddled up beside him, her chest against his strong muscular back. She'd never been needed before. It was always her that had needed Christophe. There was something wonderfully satisfying yet terrifying about it too. It was like being given a heart of pure gold, but oh the weight of it. She pressed herself closer into his back to reassure herself that it was still there, firm, strong and unbreakable.

***

Julia was woken by Christophe throwing open the curtains and the shutters to let the day in.

'Come on.' he said. 'We've got things to do. I agree with you. I don't believe they stole the paintings.'

The fire was just a few coals left smouldering and the room was cold. Julia pulled the duvet further over her.

'What time is it?'

'Seven thirty and we've got to get a move on. I've been thinking about the paintings. And about what Charlene said to you. And what the commune leader said, that Petit-Jean was on some kind of mission given to him by his Grandfather.'

He was prowling around the room like a cat that has seen a mouse's tail disappear, and knows the whole mouse is not far away.

She pulled the pillow over her head to block out the light.

'Christophe. Can't I just wake up a bit first? I'm not really with you yet.'

'You know something. I've no idea what that massage oil was, but it really worked. I just have the feeling that everything will sort itself out somehow.'

'That's great darling. Now can I go back to sleep?'

He lay down next to her. 'I think we should try that massage again and this time I can take advantage of you.'

He pulled the pillow off her head and she looked up at him sleepily. Her hair was ruffled in her face. She blinked rapidly as she tried to unstick her eyes and get them open.

'Do you know that your eyes change colour with your mood? When you're calm, they are pure sky blue. When you're feeling emotional and about to burst into tears they go turquoise like a lagoon.'

Interesting, thought Julia. That massage oil has made Christophe all emotional and touchy feely.

'Now they've gone smoky blue, which means you're pondering your next bit of mischief.'

'Yes,' said Julia 'and after I've had a good cry, they go a sort of bloodshot red around the edges.'

He pushed a lock of hair back from her face. 'When you're feeling horny, they go very dark with hints of violet in the middle.'

'Oh yes? Well let's see if you can read them correctly?'

'Just a little bit of bloodshot because you did in fact have a good cry last night when you thought I was asleep. Now let me see. I think they are starting to go darker. Mmm…' He kissed her gently on the lips. 'I'd say they are definitely showing violet tones.'

It was almost midday before they finally made it out of their room and downstairs. Bernard and Rochelle were already down, sitting in the lounge drinking an aperitif before lunch.

'We thought we'd let you get some peace,' said Rochelle. She jumped up and kissed them both. 'That's why we didn't call you.'

Bernard ordered them a drink and then kissed Julia on the cheek. 'We've had quite a tough time, getting you that peace,' he said. 'Guillemain has been here at least three times, insisting that he talks to you.'

'Bernard was brilliant,' said Rochelle, smiling proudly at him. 'He told Guillemain that he had to get a search warrant if he wanted to wake you!'

'Can't have the pompous ass ruining your day by gloating at his supposed success,' said Bernard.

'Is it a success?' asked Christophe. 'Has he found the paintings?'

'No but he says he has CCTV footage of them stealing the gallery paperwork and uniforms.'

'I don't believe it, Bernard. I know I joke about Julia's gut feeling intuition stuff but this time I agree with her. I just don't believe they stole the paintings. It doesn't make sense. Charlene and Petit-Jean were making a go of it. They were working together doing up the house. He'd finally started to settle.'

'Maybe. But if they've got very clear CCTV it's difficult to refute it.'

'Well I don't care,' said Christophe. 'Even if they did take them, I don't care. I'll just withdraw the accusation and then they can't prosecute Charlene for the paintings. They can only prosecute her for stealing the uniforms for whatever reason she cares to give, a fancy dress ball, whatever.'

Julia, Bernard and Rochelle all looked gobsmacked.

He stood up and gestured to the waiter to come over.

'Have you eaten?' he asked Bernard and Rochelle who shook their heads, still a bit shell shocked.

'Right the *moules mariniere* are on me,' he said. 'I'm starving.'

He smiled at Julia. 'They do excellent moules marinieres here. Then after lunch I am taking Julia to visit the castle. I have no idea why but my gut is telling me that's what we should do.'

Rochelle started laughing. 'Julia what have you done with the real Christophe and how did you replace him so fast.'

'Err, nothing. I mean I …' she looked more closely at Christophe. Crikey, he wasn't even joking.

'You mean you're not even going to go to the gendarmerie and see Guillemain?' asked Bernard.

'No. I'm not. I'm going to send my lawyer to withdraw the accusation of the theft of the paintings, so they will have to let her go.'

'*Oh la!* said Bernard. 'I hope you know what you're doing, Christophe. I want it on record between all of us that I very strongly advise against this.'

***

The entrance to the château was a large square castellated gateway that must once have held a drawbridge. On both sides there were undulating banks that led down to the old moat that was completely dry. Winter pansies covered the tops of the banks and a few snowdrops had already started to raise their heads down in the moat. The castle was stone and built around a central courtyard with different shaped turrets and balustrades. The gruesome gargoyles at each corner of the courtyard seemed a little bit odd and pagan against the rather quaint châteaux feel of the rest of the building.

'It's a bit curious,' said Julia looking up at the main turret that stood out against the blue winter sky. A strange mix of mediaeval and Versailles

'Yes. Chapman refurbished it from lots of parts of stone from various ruined castles and manor houses in France. It took him years. Don't think he managed to pinch anything from Versailles though.'

'Good job otherwise they might have guillotined him.'

I think this must have become his main work of art after he stopped painting.

'Why did he stop painting?'

'Age I guess. Many painters like Monet managed to paint well into their old age, but Chapman got very bad arthritis in his hands quite young. He couldn't manipulate a paintbrush as he wanted. He did try and do a similar thing to Matisse.

'You mean copying him?'

'Well not copying his work. When Matisse was bed

ridden with cancer, he took to doing his famous cut outs. Chapman tried to do the same but the cutting action was even worse for the arthritis and he got frustrated. I remember him sitting huddled up in his wheelchair. He was a tired old man and he ended up very grouchy and bitter.'

'That's so sad.'

'Yes. Very sad. Before he was wheelchair bound, he was always pottering around when we came to see Simon. We used to come here just to bug him really. You know what boys are like. The old man didn't like it too much. Simon was the apple of his eye. He was very fond of him. As for the rest of us, he thought we were a troublesome gang that deliberately left Simon out of things. He more or less tolerated Bernard and me, but Petit-Jean and he were always at loggerheads. Petit-Jean was the most difficult and rebellious of all of us. He would often hide old Chapman's canes so that he couldn't walk. Chapman couldn't hear very well in the end either so it was easy to creep up on him and make him jump. Petit-Jean was always doing that. There might have been a bit of a love hate scenario though. I think Petit-Jean reminded him too much of his friend Odilon Baudoin.

They had come to the archway going through the courtyard. A Japanese tourist group was coming through the other way so Julia and Christophe stood back to let them pass. They all bobbed their heads up and down to say thank you, as they went through, smiling.

Julia started to head towards the left, following the signs for the tourists but Christophe put his arm through hers and led her to a door marked private.

'This way Miss Connors.'

They entered a corridor of rich dark red walls, covered

in Chapman paintings and then passed through to a sitting room. Julia recognised the tall heavy booted man who'd been in the church, as he stood up.

'There you are! I was expecting you earlier.'

'Julia's fault,' said Christophe. 'She was busy falling in love with the castle.'

'Well let's get on with it.'

'I think we should wait for Madame Yvette, don't you?' said Christophe

'Not coming. Told me to handle it,' said General Chapman dismissively,

A secret door opened from behind a bookcase on the opposite side of the room and Simon Chapman walked in.

'Father. Yvette's just coming,' he said

'Changed her mind again, has she?' The disapproval was evident. General Chapman went over to a chair and sat down. 'Well you might as well make the introductions if we have to wait. Christophe hasn't introduced me to his wife.'

'Not his wife, father.' Simon threw Julia his usual lazy smile. 'Not yet. There is still hope for some of us.' Julia shook her head amused at such blatant flirting, right in front of Christophe.

Simon crossed the room shamelessly ignoring Christophe and kissed Julia on both cheeks. He managed to engineer missing her cheeks and getting her on the corner of her lips both times.

'You didn't come to the Café Breton after the funeral yesterday.' said Christophe tersely.

'No. I was busy putting feelers out looking for your paintings. I had an interesting chat with Sophie by the way. As you know, she is quite an art collector herself especially of the Breton school and I thought she might have some ideas. She mentioned that you were kind enough to give her a lift on the bank's private jet so she could get the same connection as you from New York. Very kind of you Christophe.'

Simon Chapman's eyes gleamed with pleasure at Julia who was standing open mouthed.

Realising it was not a good look, she snapped her jaws shut tightly inadvertently making the most awful noise that sounded like a Gestapo officer clicking his heels. Christophe looked at her as if to say 'what?' like he'd done nothing wrong.

Luckily for Christophe Yvette joined them before Julia could say anything.

'Christophe de Flaubert. For what do we owe the pleasure?' She asked, as she put the vase of flowers she was carrying on the table.

Christophe moved forwards and kissed her on the cheek.

'No special reason Madame Yvette. I brought Julia to see the castle.

'I doubt it. You never visit here these days unless there is an underlying reason.'

She turned to Julia. 'Ah yes. I saw you at the funeral and of course Simon told us de Flaubert had yet another new beautiful woman in his life.'

She moved forward and kissed Julia on the cheek. 'Tread carefully my dear, de Flaubert breaks hearts like waves crashing on the rocks.' She turned back to Christophe. 'So out with it, what is it you want?'

'I'd like you to give the Baudoin house to Charlene.'

Julia gave a sharp intake of breath. Wow, that was direct. She knew Christophe didn't beat about the bush but that was seriously up front.

General Chapman stood to attention, prepared for battle.

'And why exactly would she do that de Flaubert?'

'Because Charlene is the nearest thing that Petit-Jean had to family and Madame Yvette does not want nor need the house, nor do you. So, it makes sense to give it to Charlene.'

'Good God. You're out of your mind!' You are aware that they stole your paintings.'

Madame Yvette's face, although emotionless, showed signs of fascination. She'd always had a soft spot for de Flaubert and thought that if anybody could get Petit-Jean on the straight and narrow, it would have been him.

Christophe turned to her.

'Madame Yvette?'

There was a long silence as Yvette thought for a moment. Christophe knew it was better to say nothing, and wait for her to break the silence.

'No. Enough is enough. The Baudoin family is finished. For years I have watched my husband, my son and then my grandson, destroy themselves and all that I love. The house can go. I want no reminder of it, no trace, not even a flicker of a memory of a Baudoin. I don't care if they sell it, bulldoze it or burn it to the ground.'

'I think we both know that it is your guilt that is talking, Madame Yvette. If you had not treated Petit-Jean like the incarnation of the family bad gene, perhaps things would have been different.'

Julia gasped.

General Chapman used his military voice and authority.

'That is enough de Flaubert!'

Yvette's composure broke slightly and she left without a word.

Simon looked at Julia's shocked face and smiled wryly.

'Don't worry Julia, we are all used to Christophe. Christophe was always our resident *sauvage* in Pont Carnac.'

'Well,' said Julia, attempting to be supportive. 'We don't see that side of him very much in England. It must be the Breton air.' She smiled up at Christophe who had a pulse throbbing in his neck. She had no idea whatsoever what was going on in his head. She must have overdosed him on aromatherapy and he'd gone cold turkey or something. Or more likely his feelings of guilt over the argument with Petit-Jean had removed all sense of perspective. The attack on Yvette was harsh.

'De Flaubert and I will discuss this, in private,' said General Chapman. 'Simon, take Julia and show her the castle.'

Simon stood to attention immediately. He theatrically bowed and gave Julia his arm.

'Father I do believe that is the most pleasurable thing you have ever asked me to do.' He nodded to Christophe who frowned.

'Julia can stay. We have no secrets.'

No secrets, Julia thought. No secrets? His fallout with Petit-Jean, Guillemain's comment accusing him of being violent with women and now Sophie Petrarch being on a private jet with him, and him not telling her. She looked down to see if his pants were on fire.

'No really. I'd much rather look around the castle, with Simon, she said, throwing him a frosty smile.

'This way Miss Connors,' said Simon very formally, 'or may I call you Julia as we are such good friends already. Sweetest darling Julia'

She smiled at Christophe provocatively. 'Of course, you can Simon.'

If seething had sound it would have been at substantial decibels as it emanated from Christophe.

Simon led her off with his arm through hers.

'My father and I have the largest collection of Chapmans in the world,' said Simon as he led her through a passageway towards the main castle. 'When my Grandfather renovated the place, he created the perfect exhibition platform for those works of art. The long mediaeval great hall with the minstrel gallery was once used for banquets, and it has become a perfect picture gallery.' He led her through into the main hall where the Japanese tourist group had gathered.'

'Doesn't it bother you having so many people traipsing through your home?'

'Not at all. To be honest these old houses and castles are quite inhospitable. Awful to live in. They are damp and musty, no matter what you do with them. It's good to have people moving through them, helps improve the ambience. We have our private living quarters in a later part of the building on the other side. I like to think of it as the sunny side. And anyway, as Guillemain and Christophe both say, art should be shared with the world not hidden in private collections and this is a good compromise.'

'From what I can tell, that's about the only thing that Christophe and Guillemain do agree on.'

Simon laughed. 'Yes, they have never had an easy relationship.'

'In London, Simon, when Guillemain came to our house with Inspector Denton, he made some comment about Christophe being violent, almost accusing him of being violent to a woman in the past.'

'Hum. Because you had a bruise on your head?'

Julia looked surprised. 'Yes. So Guillemain told you.'

Simon sighed. 'He did tell me yes, but I did notice too.'

'Simon, is there any truth in it?'

Julia stopped and waited for an answer.

Simon hesitated. 'Not that I know of Julia. Nothing was ever proven and the girl in question refused to press charges.'

He saw worry rather than relief on Julia's face and smiled reassuringly, taking her hand again.

'Come on, let me show you the pictures in the private rooms, they are some of my favourites and we rarely put those out on loan.'

They went through a small secret door that was hidden in the wood panelling. Behind it was a long stone tunnel that led downhill.

'This is one of the old castle tunnels that would have been used in battle to take arms, stones and boiling oil up to the top of the castle. There are lots of them but this is the only one that is used. It is the best way to nip back home rather than having to walk around the whole Castle.'

He opened a door into a large sunny sitting room with French windows opening out onto a sunny terrace. A Chapman landscape hung over the large stone fireplace. It was similar to the one that Christophe had lost but it featured a view across the village rather than the river. Julia looked at it. It made her feel sad.

Simon watched Julia's face as she looked at the painting.

'It's very similar to ours,' she said, 'but it's painted earlier, probably in the autumn. The light is not as white.'

'You have a good eye Julia. Very few people would have noticed that. I'm surprised Christophe doesn't involve you more in the art world.

'That's probably because I don't like modern art,' said Julia. 'I'm quite famous for upsetting modern artists, especially the master of the black hole.'

'But he could involve you in more classical art.'

'Christophe would never take the risk of getting me involved. He knows I'd swap the black hole for an impressionist the first chance I got.'

'Seriously Julia. Just as with tea tasters & vignerons having the right taste buds and musicians having the right ears, art experts need a good eye and it is something that cannot be fully taught, they are born with it.'

'Really?'

'Yes. It is a real gift.'

'Well perhaps he'll get me more involved in the future now that I'm no longer working in Fashion.'

'I do hope so. Because then we'd get to work together.'

As she looked up at him, the light caught her eyes, turning them sky blue. She held that black gaze of his and then quickly looked away. What the hell was she doing?

Simon, sensing her unease, returned to a safer topic.

'Chapman was a true impressionist. He painted the same scene many times in different seasons. He was always trying to catch the moment, the light, the true essence of the season. Sometimes you can almost feel the chill of the winter and smell the musty leaves of the Autumn.'

'You clearly have a lot in common with Christophe. He speaks quite lovingly about them too.'

'We have always had very similar tastes, in art, music, wine - and of course women.'

His words hung in the air, and Julia decided to get a grip on herself. He probably means Sophie Petrarch. After all, he was with her too this weekend. Yes, he probably means Sophie Petrarch.

'I'm sorry Julia. It's not very fair to speak to you in this way. You're far too intelligent a woman not to realise that I enjoy playing my little games annoying Christophe. Call it revenge for all those times when I suffered at the hands of Christophe, Bernard and Petit-Jean.'

'Well don't go overboard Simon. Just remember that when you are busy getting him riled, I shall be on the receiving end.'

'The problem is that it's not only a game.' His words hung in the air.

The moment was broken by the sound of raised voices and Julia shook her head. What the hell was she doing? Charles Chapman's Sergeant Major voice barked out orders, as sharply as his shoes had hit the floor in the church.

'I am acting on Yvette's instructions and I will stand no interference from a young upstart like you de Flaubert. She wants to get rid of it once and for all. She is not going to give it to a woman who helped her grandson waste his life.'

Julia braced herself for Christophe's response. It was even worse than she expected. She couldn't hear what he said because he'd progressed from a voice raised in anger to being quietly lethal.

'We have to go back,' said Julia. 'Otherwise there could be pistols at dawn.'

They started to back track but then the force of the argument blew the door open and Christophe appeared.

He grabbed Julia's hand slightly roughly and Julia winced. Then, realising, he smiled hesitantly at her. 'Sorry darling. It's just been one hell of a day. We have outstayed our welcome.'

He nodded good bye to Simon and headed for the door, not even looking back.

Eleven

I HAVE GONE TO *see Charlene with Bernard.*
    Christophe.

'But look at it, Rochelle. Not even 'love' Christophe. Not even a little kiss at the bottom. And it doesn't even say Julia. It just says I have gone to see Charlene. I don't know what's got into him. He was awful at the castle yesterday. Then even worse when we got back. He wouldn't talk and wanted to be left alone. I understand that, but we didn't even have sex which is just not normal. What the hell is going on?'

'Julia *ma belle*, I don't know but I do know this, Christophe is very complicated. He was very close to Petit-Jean at one point, even closer than he is to Bernard.' She sighed. 'We all were.'

'Rochelle, what is it that Christophe isn't telling me?'

Rochelle held her gaze for a moment, hesitated, then dropped her eyes down to do up a button that she'd noticed was undone at the bottom of her shirt.

'I don't know Julia. I just don't know.'

'You don't know? Are you sure about that?'

'Yes I am.'

Which is a huge lie. Rochelle definitely knows something. I will get to the bottom of this one way or another.

'Anyway, you should give him some breathing space. Christophe has lost everyone he has ever loved. When people die the ones that love them grieve in different ways. Some are very angry. Some are guilty. Just leave him a little time. And don't forget he cannot help himself when he is jealous. What happened with his parents, hurt him badly. It's a miracle he's settled at all.'

'But I haven't done anything to make him jealous.'

'Well, what I have seen when you and Simon Chapman are in a room together, will be quite enough to trigger jealousy.'

Julia went on the defensive. 'Well if there really was something between me and Simon Chapman then it is no worse than him and Sophie Petrarch, except that I didn't lie about it. It's so unfair, Rochelle. He has always been able to trust me, but how can I trust him now? All those times he goes away on business, who knows what he might have been up to.' She threw herself on the bed and started to pound the pillow. She didn't know if the pillow represented Christophe, Simon Chapman or herself but whoever it was got a good beating.

Rochelle sat next to her and rubbed her shoulder. 'Listen *cherie*. You and Christophe, it will always be like this. You both have so much fire and so much mistrust. It is part of what draws you together, you understand that in each other.' She stood up and pouted nonchalantly. 'And anyway, these men, they are so stupid Julia. They really don't handle their emotions at all well. Except for one of course, their sex drive. Do you really still have sex every day?'

'Well, usually. Don't you?'

'No. We have five children and we have been together for a long time. We have fights though and that is quite good for the making up afterwards.'

'Well I hope Christophe hurries up and moves on to the making up phase.'

'Everything will be OK, you will see. Unless you are a little in love with Simon Chapman which of course is a little more complicated. But you know you could always take him as a lover for a while until you no longer have the obsession and then everything will be, forgive and forget, no problem.'

Julia sat up abruptly. 'What? I couldn't do that.'

'You know if you manage things well, it is possible to have your cake and eat it too. Or as we say in France, the butter and the money for the butter.' Not very often of course only when it is a very nice piece of cake.'

'Rochelle, that's terrible.'

Rochelle pouted. 'Why?'

'Well it's unfaithful, cheating.'

'Not really. It's in our nature. It's very boring to think that you will only ever sleep with one person for the rest of your life is it not?'

'Well I don't know.'

'No because you are still in the beginning of your relationship. Wait until you get further down the line.

'You mean the seven-year itch?'

'Is that what you call it? I thought this was a thing for eczema. Well now Bernard and I have been together for twenty-one years so we will be getting our sexual eczema soon.'

'But have you Rochelle? Had lovers I mean? You seem so happy with Bernard.'

'Of course, we are happy but if everything is always happy and there are no fights and no challenges life is very boring *n'est-ce-pas*? It only happened twice you know and only a very small thing. Bernard is very forgiving. You know, after the anger and everything.'

'And Bernard, has he?'

'Oh, I don't know. I don't think so but he is a lawyer and he thinks only in justice and fairness and if he did he would never tell me.'

Julia looked at her wide eyed in disbelief

Rochelle continued, 'I look through his things though sometimes to see if I can find things, you know, evidence. Like restaurant bills, perfume and shop receipts or flower receipts. And I always, always check his clothes for *rouge à lèvre*. But I never did find anything, so I think not. Anyway, he doesn't need to be unfaithful. I am an artist and it is part of my artistic temperament. I must feel alive to paint and the thing that makes you feel most alive is sex. There is nothing so good as the sexual tension and the thrill of a little '*aventure*'. That's what I tell him and he forgives me because I always tell him.'

Julia stood open mouthed. 'I can't believe it. You actually tell him?'

'Well of course, otherwise this would not be honest.'

'I am really shocked, Rochelle.'

'Well that's because you are more English in this way and you have so much correctness. It is very common for us French to have lovers.'

'But what do you think Christophe would say? I don't think he would be anything like Bernard.'

Rochelle smiled. 'No, I think not! The tragedy of his

parents' marriage, the terrible mess and the loss of his sister and his horrible half-brother. No, I think you are right. He has seen such destruction and if he ever marries it will be forever, to be faithful and sickness and health and all of the correctness that must go with it. If Christophe marries it will be until death.'

Julia's stomach began to churn. That big M word again.

Rochelle carried on chattering. 'I think this is why he must be so angry with you now. Even a very small look at another man and he is ready to go to battle. It will be good for him to go and think for a while.'

Rochelle jumped up impulsively. 'Come on. See now how our little talk has made you better. I think you are right, *non*? Taking a lover is not a good idea for you. You will have to accept that you are both jealous and will always have fights.'

'Yes!' said Julia, putting the pillow straight. 'And we'll have great sex when we make up.'

Rochelle smiled. '*Alors*, let us go and see what we can do to solve these problems. Come on *ma cher* Julia or should we say Juliette who has her Romeo throwing everything off his balcony.' She gave Julia her hand and pulled her up from the bed.

'Yes. I really do think we should go and collect them from the *Gendarmarie*,' said Julia. 'Christophe is in such a bad mood I fear for Inspector Guillemain's life.'

Rochelle passed Julia her coat. 'We can walk there and I can show you my favourite places. This village is an artist's paradise.'

They took a long cobbled country path to the outskirts of the village.

Julia took in a long deep breath filling her lungs.

'Smell that air! So fresh and full of winter. The air smells different here doesn't it.'

'Well of course, *cherie,* London smells of cars and smoke and beer and restaurants.'

'Here it smells like pure mother nature, not tainted with the smells of the 21st century. '

'The colours are beautiful too,' said Rochelle. 'In late summer it is covered in the dark green of the plants, so very heavy with the weight of the chlorophyll. In spring the green is fresh and transparent when the buds first open.'

'And now,' said Julia, looking around at the stark bare trees against barren fields. 'It is as naked as Sophie Petrarch at a casting.'

'Tch Julia. That is so naughty of you!' Rochelle laughed. 'She has a beautiful body though does she not?'

'I suppose so,' said Julia grudgingly.

Rochelle slipped her arm through Julia's. 'Shall I tell you a secret?'

'Yes, please,' said Julia, hoping it was going to be one of Christophe's.

'Sophie pays a body double, and she pays a very high price because she will not allow that woman to work for anyone else.'

'No?' said Julia. 'You're kidding me!'

'It is true *cherie.* And it is because she has a cellulite bottom and short legs.'

Julia shook her head. 'I can't believe it.'

'OK so maybe her legs aren't so short but her body really is not so good.'

Julia laughed.

'See now how happy I have made you!'

'It's ridiculous but you have!'

'Oh no. We've been so busy talking, I've taken us the

139

wrong way,' said Rochelle, turning down the hill towards the old stream. We're back in the village, look there's the Baudoin house from the back. It borders the edge of the stream. It's the one with the red door.'

'And the 'for sale' sign.' Added Julia.

'Oh la la! It's already for sale. And it's '*en vente a la bougie*', down at the town hall.'

'What's *vente a la bougie*?'

'Auction. They still call it that here and still use the candles. They have to have two candles burn before they can accept the final bid.'

'You're kidding.'

Rochelle laughed. 'No. Really they still do that here. Some modern places use electric lights that they switch on and off, but I am certain that they still use the candles here.'

'Well when does it start?'

'About half an hour.'

'We'd better tell Christophe and Bernard.'

Julia pressed the speed dial as they ran, then slowed down as she realised Rochelle couldn't run as fast. Rochelle was panting when she caught up and Christophe had already answered.

Julia put the phone on loudspeaker.' Just buy it,' said Christophe tersely. 'I want the house for Charlene. I'm tied up here, there's been a slight complication but just buy it Julia for God's sake. No matter what it costs.' He hung up before either of them could reply.

'Nice.' Said Rochelle looking at the sadness in Julia's face. 'Romeo is still throwing his things out then.'

Julia nodded and sighed. Why oh, why was she letting this affect her so much. These days he could upset her so easily.

'Come on,' said Rochelle winking. 'You have just been given carte blanche to spend a lot of money. I am a witness to this and Christophe said, no matter what it costs.

Julia grinned. He did indeed and if anybody needed to be called on to spend money, it had to be her because she was simply the best

***

Julia had to sign some papers and leave a bank deposit cheque in order to even get the right to bid. She thought it was a bit odd, even she knew that leaving signed blank cheques for people was a very dangerous business. Even more so if the person who had to write the amount had dyscalculia.

As they entered the town hall, the starting bell rang. The whole room turned to look at them. There was a lot of mutterings without any attempt to hide the curiosity and, she felt, their discontent.

'Come on,' said Rochelle manoeuvring towards the front. 'Don't worry. They think that we are rich Parisians wanting to steal their heritage from them. Just ignore them.'

'I can see their point. Isn't that what we are doing?'

'No, we're buying it for Charlene, remember.'

There was an old mustiness to the building mixed with the smell of wood polish and tobacco. Rochelle managed to get them almost to the front on the left-hand side and she seemed very pleased with herself.

'Don't let these stubborn old Bretons intimidate you Julia. We have a right to be here.'

'Yes,' whispered Julia, feeling nervous nevertheless. Even though Christophe had said no matter what the cost, it was still numbers. Maybe if she just closed her eyes and kept holding up her number and bid by listening, not looking, it would go better.

'It should go for about sixty thousand,' said Rochelle, 'given the half-finished state it's in.'

'Rochelle, stop talking numbers, this is bad enough as it is.'

'Oh sorry. I forgot. Do you want me to do this for you?'

Julia hesitated. I can do this, I just have to breathe deeply, it doesn't matter how much I'm paying. Christophe doesn't care. I'll be fine. Her mouth was dry and she could feel her heart racing.

'Julia?' asked Rochelle

'No. It's OK. I can do it. I am going to do it myself. But do you have any water? My mouth's really dry.'

'I'll go and get some.' She pushed her way back out through the crowd.

People continued to stare at Julia. She fiddled with her auction number nervously.

The auctioneer came onto the rostrum and started to describe the lot number – in Breton.

Julia looked around for Rochelle but she was already out of view. Surely, they would say it in French?

They didn't.

A small dark-haired man, sitting down to the right of her, started the bidding at thirty thousand euros. There were no other bidders. They probably didn't want to own a house that was full of bad luck and owned by a traitor, thought Julia. She hesitated. The auctioneer lit a candle and Julia knew she only had 30 seconds to make a bid. She flicked her number at the auctioneer. Everyone in the room exclaimed '*mais non!* ' in outrage. Surely this had to be against the law, only giving the details in Breton then so overtly trying to intimidate her. Julia turned to look at the other bidder. He looked very nervous too. He raised the bidding again and threw her a pleading look. He muttered under his breath to the young man sitting next to him who looked like he was probably his son. There was more muttering and disapproving shaking of heads going on from local people in the room as they watched her. It was so intimidating. No, thought Julia. She was not going to let them intimidate her like this. Christophe had said buy it and she was damn well going to buy it. Julia raised the bidding again.

Then he raised it again looking almost near to tears. Julia felt terrible but she'd got to buy it for Charlene. Finally the man bent his head to his son again and shook his head. The auctioneer lit a candle on the rostrum and they all waited. Just before it burnt down, the man decided to bid again. Julia's hand was in the air before the auctioneer could finish speaking and they waited as he lit another candle. This time her opponent didn't put up a fight and when the candle went out, the hammer came down.

Rochelle appeared with a bottle of water. 'Bravo Julia,' said Rochelle. 'These Bretons are not happy with you but Christophe will be. And congratulations, you dealt with your number problem so well, *cherie*.'

Yes, thought Julia. I did. I did it, all by myself.

They turned to leave but it was difficult because hoards of people were pushing and trying to get in and Julia and Rochelle were going against the flow. The auctioneer upped the volume on his microphone and started to describe the next lot, this time in French. It was the house that the painter Odilon Baudoin had lived in.

Julia looked at Rochelle who was standing with her mouth open. 'Oh, *zut* Julia, we have bought the wrong house!'

'We? You mean me!' Bloody hell, thought Julia, that is just typical. I despair. I just can't seem to do anything right. But it wasn't my fault. They only gave the details in Breton. She'd definitely have something to say about that after the auction. And she would get Bernard to write a legal complaint. Honestly!

The room was still getting even more crowded. There were out of towners, journalists, agents and telephone bidders and they were all moving to the front. Luckily Julia and Rochelle had not managed to get too far when they were leaving, so were still quite near the front. This time the auctioneer had two people on the rostrum to help spot bidders, and there were at least two telephone bids. You could feel the excitement in the air.

Julia clutched her auction number and nodded to show that she was interested. The auctioneer looked surprised but made a note. Julia showed her number again. A lot of other people showed their interest and the price started going up in twenty thousand lots. Julia took a sneaky look at the other bidders, they were dropping life flies. Eventually there were only three left. One was a youngish man in a business suit and the other was a phone bidder.

Rochelle whispered to her 'He's bidding for someone else I'm sure.' They watched the guy on his mobile. 'And for some reason that person really wants the house.'

Passers-by had heard or sensed the excitement and were cramming in the doorway. Suddenly there were gasps as the phone bidder put in a bid of one million. The man in the business suit dropped out and the auctioneer looked at Julia. Julia gulped. What would Christophe say? He did say that whatever she did she had to get the house. She raised the bidding again. The phone bidder was talking to his client then he raised it massively to one point three million. Julia had no idea how much to go up by and just wafted her hand in the air. The auctioneer looked surprised.'

'Two million?' he asked Julia for confirmation. There were audible gasps all around. Julia nodded.

The phone bidder hesitated and then shook his head.

The auctioneer lit the candle and watched it burn down. There was a tense silence. Then as the candle burnt to the end he hit the hammer down with great relief and the bell rang for the end of the proceedings.

'Do not seek to ask for whom the bell tolls, it tolls for thee,' said a voice behind her.

Rochelle and Julia both swung round to see Simon Chapman grinning.

'Congratulations, Julia,' he said. 'I'm sure you will be very happy here in Pont Carnac. And I shall be very happy indeed, with her here in Pont Carnac shan't I Rochelle?'

'Oh, I'm certain of it, Simon. Excuse me, I think I had better go and get some fresh air. My knees are wobbling.'

'Christophe will be very pleased, won't he,' said Simon. 'He's very good isn't he letting you spend all his money like that.'

'Simon!' said Julia, embarrassed.

'Sorry. I really am sorry.' He did look contrite. 'How about I help you go through the rest of the proceedings. Let's go to the office. You are going to have to give them two cheques now.

As they approached the office, she saw the man who had bid against her talking angrily on the phone.

'Your client set the ceiling at 1.5 million. I have no right to change it without his authorisation!'

She handed her number with her ID to the auction

145

clerk and they started to prepare the papers. While they waited, Simon leant over and whispered in her ear.

'It doesn't really matter who pays for the house, Julia. Just make sure it's the right man that carries you over the threshold.'

Julia shook her head at him in despair. 'That's enough Simon, really!'

'Or, should I say thresholds in the plural. I'm curious. Why did you buy the other house? Are you intending to take over the whole village?'

'No -err -' Julia blushed..

'Oh.' Realisation dawned on Simon. 'You got the wrong house!' He started laughing. 'My you really are high maintenance.'

'Well they should have given the description in French, not just in Breton. That was very unfair and probably illegal too.'

'Possibly,' said Simon, nodding. The thing is, it was because the whole village wanted old man Riou to be able to buy it for his grandson.'

'Well it's still out of order, that kind of protectionist stuff.'

'Actually, young Riou lost his wife when she gave birth to their twins two months ago and the house belonged to numerous cousins. The ownership couldn't be sorted out and the only way was to put it for auction and all the people in the village and hereabouts agreed not to bid because otherwise it would make poor Riou homeless with his two tiny babies, one of which has a terminal illness …the maximum he could go to was forty thousand. But of course, you were not to know that.' said Simon looking very serious.

'Oh no.' That's terrible. I feel terrible. She signed all

the papers and handed over the cheques and Simon guided her out through a side door.

'Better to go this way I think. We don't want you being heckled by furious villagers.'

They walked along an alley way and came out into a small village square, just down the road from the auction house and ran right into the poor homeless single father. He was lifting one of his twins out of the pram. He looked so young to have two babies.

She felt terrible. She had to do something about it.

She went rushing over to him.

'I'm sorry. So very sorry. I didn't know. I thought it was the Baudoin house. You can have it. I will sell it to you for whatever you can manage.' Actually no, you can just have it. I will give it to you. I am so very sorry.'

The young man looked at Simon, confused. Simon nodded reassuringly. '*C'est vrai,*' he said And suddenly they were all shaking her hand and kissing her and thanking her.

Eventually she managed to escape and walk down the road with Simon, to find Rochelle.

'So now you are a local hero, Julia.'

'I hope that was true Simon, what you said about the family.'

'Well most of it was. Apart from the terminal illness, I made that bit up.'

Bernard appeared in a large BMW just as they caught up with Rochelle. Simon waved to Bernard but disappeared very quickly.

Bernard told them to jump in because he was taking them to the police station.

Blimey the fraud squad works quickly here, thought Julia. I've only just signed the cheque.

'Christophe is not happy at all. There have been some

problems with him dropping the charges against Charlene.' said Bernard. 'Did you manage to get the Baudoin house?'

'Yes,' they replied in unison.

'Good that will make him feel a bit better. How much did you pay?'

They replied in unison again.

'Two million.'

'That will not make him feel better!

***

Guillemain was in a heated discussion with Christophe. They could hear them before they even got through the door.

'I don't care that you've got footage of them stealing the uniforms. You can prosecute them for that but I will not prosecute Charlene for the theft of the paintings. You haven't even asked her properly about it and you don't have the paintings?'

'We have asked her and she denies that they stole the uniforms and the paintings.'

'Well I'd like to talk to her.'

'You can't talk to her unless you are a police officer, her family or her lawyer.'

Christophe shook his head exasperated. 'OK then, I'm her lawyer.'

'You can't be her lawyer because of a conflict of interests.'

'Well then Bernard Chauvenon can be her lawyer.'

'If you insist, but then he can't be your lawyer as well as Charlene's lawyer'

'Fine.'

Christophe nodded to Bernard. 'You OK about this?'

Bernard shook his head in despair.' I am Christophe but I really can't see where you are going on this one.'

'If you'd like to come this way,' said Guillemain ushering Bernard through the Gendarmerie to the cells.

Christophe turned to Julia and Rochelle.

'Did you get it? Did you get the house?'

Julia went over to Christophe and kissed him. 'Hello to you too Christophe.'

'Oh sorry. Just a bit frustrated with how things are going.' He gave her a peck on the cheek. 'The whole thing is ridiculous.' He turned to Rochelle. 'Sorry Rochelle, hello, how are you holding up?' Rochelle smiled hesitantly. 'OK, but I'm a bit worried about you Christophe.'

Christophe sat down with his head in his hands for a moment. 'I'm just over tired that's all, Rochelle, and trying to do what I feel is right.'

'Christophe you've always tried to do what is right and you always have but sometimes you have to think of yourself and those closest to you.

Christophe stared at the floor and said very quietly, 'I am thinking of those closest to me Rochelle, you know I am.'

***

Bernard returned. He shook his head when Christophe opened his mouth to say something.

'Let's all go back to the lodgings and grab some lunch.'

He drove the car out of the village and pulled over down a country lane.

'We won't be overheard here. You know how small this village is and how quickly the gossip travels. We all need to be very careful. I'm not sure what is going on but Charlene said that she and Petit-Jean were nowhere near the Chapman gallery and I believe her. She said they did go to London to try and see you, Christophe, because Petit-Jean desperately wanted to talk to you. At the last minute he buckled out because he thought you wouldn't speak to him. They were never anywhere near the Chapman gallery. That's when Guillemain came back in and she immediately clammed up and wouldn't say any more. I asked Guillemain if I could see the CCTV footage of them stealing the uniforms just to get rid of him. He was only out for two mins but that was long enough for Charlene to tell me that they weren't doing drugs because she is pregnant and she doesn't think Petit-Jean had an accident. I think there is more that she wants to tell me but she obviously doesn't trust Guillemain. She asked me to go and see her again as soon as possible. If anything I'd say she's scared.'

'Can't we do anything to get her out. Even if it is only on bail?'

'Not yet. Guillemain's excuse is that he wants to keep her until Denton arrives as the paintings were stolen in London. So were the uniforms so it's officially Denton's case.'

'But there is no case. I've dropped the charges. So, what do we do now?' Asked Christophe. 'Have you got the CCTV footage?

'Yes, I have a copy on a pen drive. He pulled his laptop out of his bag and loaded it.'

Two people in hoodies entered the back door of the gallery building, then a small portion of the face of the man was caught on camera as he turned and quickly grabbed two uniforms and the papers on a desk nearby. Then they left.

They watched it over and over again.

'It's ridiculous,' said Christophe. What the hell is

Guillemain thinking? They can't hold Charlene on that. At best, it might be Petit-Jean but it's not convincing and you don't even see the other person.' No detective in their right mind would hold someone based on that.'

'I agree,' said Bernard. 'It's really weird and highly unprofessional. Whatever you say about Guillemain, Christophe, he is usually very professional.'

'How long can they hold her without any new evidence or bringing any charges?' asked Christophe

'Twenty four hours maximum.'

'Well she's been there for at least forty eight now. Let's go and get her released.' said Christophe. He got out of the car and found himself face to face with Inspector Guillemain.

'I have some good news for you de Flaubert. They've found your Chapman painting.'

Guillemain was very pleased with himself.

'Great,' said Christophe. 'So, you can release Charlene now.'

'Don't you want to know where we found it?'

'Of course, I do. Where did you find it?' Christophe asked exasperated.

In Charlene Madec's old caravan over at the commune.

Twelve

IT WAS PAST MIDNIGHT and Christophe was still pacing up and down their room.

'Christophe come to bed please?' said Julia. She looked up at him beseechingly. 'You can't do any more tonight.'

He sat down on the bed. 'I just can't get my head around it. I don't believe Charlene took it, nor Petit-Jean. Even if they did, it's my own fault. I should have made up the quarrel. I should have spoken to him years ago. He came to see me to talk to me and I wasn't there for him. I haven't been there for him and now he's dead and Charlene has been arrested.'

Christophe it is not your fault.

'Isn't it, Julia? Isn't it?'

'No. It is not!'

'It is!' He started pacing up and down again, like a trapped animal. 'Just like that business with my parents, with my sister Simone.'

'Christophe if it's anybody's fault it's mine because

I'm the one who let the fake gallery people take them in the first place.

He shook his head. 'No, Julia. How were you to know? And I was really horrible to you about that too.'

'You were no worse than I was to you. I told you that you had a huge ego.'

'That's the whole point. You're right. If I didn't have such a big ego maybe I would have been understanding and maybe I would have swallowed my pride. Maybe I would have been kinder to my friend.'

'Lots of people have arguments. And sometimes it takes time to get over them.'

'I left it too late. All I ever do is let people down. All the people that I care about in my life end up hurt. Maybe you should just get out now while the going's good, before the same happens to you.'

'Christophe. You can't mean that.'

She realised he was so emotionally exhausted he'd become completely irrational.

'I do. Julia. My parents, Simone, Petit-Jean. You're bound to be next.'

'Nice try but you don't get rid of me that easily.'

'I'm not trying to get rid of you! I am trying to save you.'

'I don't need saving.'

'Not yet, but it's bound to happen eventually, that's what happens when I love someone. If I was you, I'd head for Simon Chapman. I'm sure he's dying to look after you.'

'Christophe! You're being ridiculous. You must be absolutely exhausted to be behaving so irrationally.'

'Am I Julia? Am I being ridiculous? You seem to cosy up to each other an awful lot.'

'I cannot believe that you have just said that.' Julia's

face went bright red, sending Christophe completely the wrong signal.'

'You're looking very embarrassed and guilty Julia. Is there something you need to tell me?'

That was the final straw.

'Me? What about you and Sophie Petrarch? You lied about her being on the plane with you. Don't you think that's something you should have told me? Why did you lie about that?'

'I didn't lie. I was just economic with the truth. I know how jealous you get and I was just trying to avoid it.'

'You sure about that Christophe? Are you sure it's not guilt?'

'Of course, I'm sure. I was thinking of you.'

'Yeah right! And then there's the lie that you told at the castle. 'Julia can stay, we don't have any secrets' Well from where I'm sitting you seem to have more secrets than the French resistance.'

'Like what?'

'Like the reason you and Petit-Jean weren't speaking to each other and…'

'I told you. I made a promise. It is not my secret to tell!'

They glared at each other. Then Julia couldn't help herself. She knew before she even opened her mouth that it was going to end badly but she couldn't stop herself.

'And what?' asked Christophe, daring her to continue.

'The reason that Inspector Guillemain thinks you hit women' Her words hung in the air, frozen.

Christophe picked up his dressing gown and went over to the door. 'I'll go and find another room to sleep in. I can see that I am only going to keep you awake.'

***

Julia couldn't get to sleep. She tossed and turned in the bed going over the argument in her mind time and time again. In the end she gave in and took a quarter of a sleeping tablet. She desperately needed to sleep. If she didn't get some sleep, she would never get through the next day. The tablet finally calmed her and her body surrendered to the wave of exhaustion.

Later, she vaguely sensed a weight on the bed and a movement beside her, but she was too deeply into her dream, to wake up. She was running hard, running away down a leafy lane and she had the paintings in her arms. Christophe was tearing after her down the road. He was shouting at her to give him the paintings but she wouldn't, she couldn't. She really wanted to give them to him but no matter how hard she tried she couldn't stop running in the opposite direction. She tried to turn and run back to him, but as soon as she faced him her body turned around the other way and kept running even faster in the opposite direction.

'Aargh! Bloody hell,' she shouted, not realising she was shouting out loud in her sleep. She vaguely felt another movement next to her in the bed but still she didn't wake. The dream carried on even faster, running, furiously away from Christophe and then she saw someone running towards her. It was Simon Chapman. He reached her, picked her up off her feet. He was laughing and spinning her around carrying her in his arms.

'Good decision Julia,' he said 'Let me carry you over the threshold.'

This time she shouted so loudly she did wake herself up.

'No! PUT ME DOWN! You just put me down, right now!'

'Julia?' asked Christophe. He was snuggled up to her like spoons. He moved away, worried.

'Christophe?' she asked sleepily.

'Yes. Do you want me to go?'

Suddenly fully awake, she blinked in surprise.

'No, why?'

'Because you just told me to put you down.'

'Oh no. I was just having a weird dream.'

'Oh. So, we're good then?'

'Yes. I think so. Well I am if you are.'

'I am so sorry. Julia. I just don't know what got into me.'

Julia turned around and hugged him as tightly as she could.

'I'm sorry too. I should never have said that about what Guillemain said. I should have trusted you.'

'No, you were right I was being hopelessly irrational.' he smiled apologetically.

'It's OK, Christophe. This has been emotionally draining for everyone but especially for you.'

He drew back and looked seriously at her. 'I really want to tell you everything but I can't tell you some things because as I said, they are not my secrets to tell. Please, I'm asking you to trust me on this.'

'I do trust you.'

'But I will tell you this...'

She put her finger to his lips, to stop him. 'No, you don't have to. I promise I will never ask you to. We have both led destructive lives that have made us mistrustful, it brought us together, but if we do not trust each other, we are ruined. You do not have to tell me.'

He smiled. 'You are right about the trust, but wrong about me telling you this. I do have to tell you.' He took a deep breath.

'When we were all partying and living it up here in our late teens, the parties could get pretty crazy sometimes. Petit-Jean would get the dope out and everybody would party out in the fields. At the time, Sophie and I had a thing going but she was also going out with Petit-Jean.'

'The free love and peace.'

'Yes. Sometimes it felt as if everybody was going out with everybody else. One night, things got out of hand and Petit-Jean had mixed too much drink with his dope. On top of it, some of the diehards had been out looking for magic mushrooms. I'm guessing they may have got one or two bad ones mixed in. Or maybe the whole mix of things was too much. I don't know, but it all went horribly wrong. I'd already had a lot to drink and had bedded down for the night as had most of the others except for Sophie, Petit-Jean and a couple of others. We heard shouting and screaming, so got up to go and see what was wrong. I'd sobered up by then. Petit-Jean and Sophie were hallucinating badly. She was screaming because he was attacking her. Petit-Jean thought she was some kind of sea serpent. He was using a tent pole as a weapon and trying to hit her. It was awful. I grabbed the pole from Petit-Jean and pulled Sophie out of there. Somebody panicked and the police got involved. She said Petit-Jean attacked her and she wanted to press charges. She was angry with him because he was always sleeping with so many different people. She was in a terrible state, a mixture of jealousy, coming down from tripping and fear because she couldn't really remember what happened.'

'Anyway, I could see that she was out for revenge and wasn't going to let it go so I told her and the police that it wasn't Petit-Jean that attacked her, that it was me.' I thought by the next day she would have calmed down. As it was, she didn't remember anything.'

'But why Christophe?' asked Julia gobsmacked. 'Why would you do that?'

'Because at the time she was closer as a friend to me than she was to Petit-Jean and I thought if she thought it was me, she'd accept that it was a mistake.'

'And she'd drop the charges.' said Julia

'Yes.' He shrugged 'and she did. And I never told anyone else until now.'

'Not even Bernard and Rochelle?'

'No.'

'But why didn't you tell anyone?'

'Because Petit-Jean was already tainted with the Baudoin stigma. He'd already been in trouble God only knows how many times and I knew it was an accident so …'

'Did Petit-Jean remember that it was him?'

'Yes.'

'Oh Christophe'

'Julia, I love you more than anything else in the world. I will never ever hurt you.'

'I know you won't. I should never have doubted you.'

'As for the comments about Simon Chapman. I've lived a life where nobody could be trusted in relationships. I saw my mother being torn between two men, her infidelity taking her backwards and forwards causing terrible emotional torment to the family. In the end she left my father and he died of a broken heart. I've never allowed myself to love anyone until I met you. You are the only woman I have ever trusted. It really scares me. I've never seen you look interested in any other man and seeing the way you smile at Simon Chapman worries me.'

'But there's nothing in that, Christophe. He's just a terrible flirt.'

'He's just a terrible flirt? I don't think people can be a terrible flirt unless they get a response, do you?'

'I don't know. Perhaps you should ask Sophie Petrarch that one,' replied Julia icily

There was silence for a moment.

'Ah. Yes, fair point,' said Christophe.

'Look, let's not go down that road again,' said Julia. 'I will do my very best not to reciprocate Simon Chapman's flirting if you do the same with Sophie Petrarch. You know we really are two of a kind. You're right I would have gone crazy about Sophie being on the plane with you. But, on a 'check me into the asylum' scale it would have been a lot lower if you'd told me rather than me finding out from Simon Chapman.'

'I'll bear that in mind next time, if I ever have to confess to being alone with another beautiful woman.'

'Would probably be better, if you just never get into a situation where you are alone with a beautiful woman.'

He laughed in disbelief. 'You mean live the rest of my life being chaperoned like some Victorian Miss?'

'Yes.' said Julia. An image of him dressed up in a corset and bustle shot into her head and she laughed even more.

'Seriously?' he laughed back. 'Well then the same goes for you too. In fact, I'll get Hilda over right now so that you are never left alone with Simon Chapman.'

'I'm safe there. There's no way in a month of Sundays she'd come. She'd be terrified we'd make her eat snails.'

'True.'

'So, we will just have to settle for a total trust pact and slay the green-eyed monsters as soon as they hatch. We could have a little code word to let each other know that they are hatching.'

'Excellent idea, how about green eggs.' He pulled her to him.

'Green eggs, it is. What a relief Christophe. Last night was awful. I never ever want to go through that again.'

'Me neither and I promise we never will.'

'Still at least I now know why you fell out with Petit-Jean.'

'Well no, actually. That's something else entirely. And I really can't tell you that.'

'Oh.'

***

Inspector Denton arrived at the Gendarmerie the next day. Bernard, Christophe, Julia and Rochelle headed off there in force. They were all fairly confident that they would be able to get Charlene released and give her the keys to the house.

Christophe was in an extremely good mood. Rochelle hooked her arm through his.

'It is a beautiful thing you are doing. Christophe. I am sure Petit-Jean is watching from up there and is thanking you.

'We're not quite there yet, Rochelle. Don't uncross your fingers yet, any of you. He put his arm around Julia. 'It is only right and fitting that Charlene lives in the Baudoin house with Petit-Jean's child.'

Inspector Denton was waiting for them and he shook Christophe's hand and smiled politely.

'How nice to see you again Mr de Flaubert, and you Miss Connors. So, things have all turned out right in the end. You have your Chapman masterpiece back in perfect condition.'

'Yes. Inspector Denton. And I thank you for that.'

'Well, you're thanking the wrong person. It is all down to Inspector Guillemain's wonderful work.'

'Oh really?' replied Christophe in total disbelief

Julia looked across at Rochelle and they both winced.

'And sadly, we do not have the Baudoin,' said Christophe.

'Yes, very unfortunate. I remember you saying that it held great sentimental value for you.'

'And odd. Don't you think it is slightly odd that the Chapman should turn up but not the Baudoin, Inspector Guillemain?'

'No. Not really,' Guillemain interrupted, stonily. 'As you said yourself the Baudoin was not really worth anything, a few hundred at most. They probably gave it to a junk shop or binned it so that they could concentrate on the big bucks.'

'You really think that, Guillemain? You think Petit-Jean would have thrown away one of the few pictures in existence that his Grandfather painted?'

'People will do a lot for money or revenge, de Flaubert.'

'Revenge?' asked Christophe. 'Revenge for what exactly?'

Inspector Denton looked surprised and a little exasperated.

'Revenge Inspector Guillemain? Is there something you haven't told me?'

'I don't know. Perhaps de Flaubert can enlighten us.'

Christophe shrugged his shoulders. 'I have no idea what he is talking about.'

'Oh, come on de Flaubert. It's a well-known fact that you and Petit-Jean hadn't spoken in years!'

'Would you like to tell us why that is Mr de Flaubert?' asked Inspector Denton. 'It would certainly help us put this case to bed.'

'No. I'm sorry Inspector Denton, I can't do that.'

'Well then. Let's hope that now that Miss Madec is being charged with the theft of the paintings, she will tell you where the other painting is, it would certainly help her case.'

'There is no case Inspector Denton.'

'Oh?' he asked, surprised.

'I don't want to press charges.'

'I beg your pardon?'

Everyone shuffled uncomfortably. Bernard, although not a religious man, looked to the heavens for help.

'Hum. And why exactly is that?' asked Inspector Denton.

'Because I don't believe that they took the paintings.'

'Ah. I was afraid you were going to say that. Most unfortunate.'

Inspector Guillemain shook his head in disgust. 'You can't do that de Flaubert. That's a ridiculous suggestion. We are on the verge of a solid conviction and you don't want to press charges. You can't do that.'

'I can,' said Christophe.

Bernard started to say something. But Inspector Denton interrupted.

'Perhaps we could put this conversation on hold for a moment while we look at some other information that I have. Do you have a screen available please Inspector Guillemain, there's something I'd like to show you. Would you mind waiting here, Mr de Flaubert, Miss Connors. In fact, all of you if you wish.'

***

Bernard and Rochelle waited with them.

'They can let Charlene go now Bernard, can't they?' asked Christophe.

'I don't know. You're playing with fire here. The Chapman is a registered masterpiece and as such the rules are different. It is not up to you as the owner to decide. The painting has cultural heritage value and that changes everything. Even if you don't want to press charges, they have enough proof to keep Charlene and investigate her for possible other art thefts. They'll probably try and claim that this may be one of many thefts and that they the need to investigate further. Every unsolved art theft case on the books, I would imagine. They'd probably get the right to at least hold her for a longer period of time. Also, the state can decide to prosecute and it will be out of your hands.'

'Have you managed to talk to her again yet?'

'No, I haven't but as soon as they come back, I'll go and see her and try and find out what else she wants to tell me.'

'OK'

Bernard was worried. 'Are you absolutely sure about this Christophe? Have you even thought about the possibility that Charlene and Petit-Jean did steal them? Perhaps you are letting your own feelings of guilt cloud your judgement.'

Christophe looked across at Julia and smiled hesitantly.

'I know that but even if they did, I don't want her to go to prison. Sorry Bernard. On this one I know it's irrational, even mad but I just have to go with my gut reaction.'

'OK. If that's what you want,' Bernard replied, sighing. 'As your friend I accept that this is totally out of character for you and that you are not quite yourself, but as a lawyer my advice …' He looked at Christophe's face and shook his head in despair, '…will clearly fall on stony ground. You win. I'll talk to her again.'

Inspector Denton and Guillemain returned. Guillemain looked extremely pleased with himself as he advanced towards Christophe. He took out a pair of handcuffs and gestured that Christophe should put his hands behind his back.

'Christophe de Flaubert I am arresting you on ...'

'Are the handcuffs really necessary?' interrupted Denton, irritated by Guillemain's behaviour. 'Mr de Flaubert is in a Gendarmerie full of police officers and highly unlikely to run away.'

Guillemain put down his handcuffs and grabbed Christophe's arm instead. 'I am taking you into custody on suspicion of arranging the theft of the William Chapman *Enfants au rivière en hiver* painting. And for fraudulently claiming an insurance payout for said painting.'

'What?!!!' Exclaimed Julia and Rochelle in stereo.

'You have the right to remain silent. Anything you say can be used against you in court. You have the right to talk to a lawyer for advice before we ask you any questions. You have the right to have a lawyer with you during questioning. If you cannot afford a lawyer, one will be appointed for you before any questioning if you wish. If you decide to answer questions now without a lawyer present, you have the right to stop answering at any time.'

Bernard immediately turned to Guillemain. 'I would like to know what evidence you are arresting my client?'

'Which client is that, Mr Chauvenon?'

Bernard looked at Christophe, who shook his head.

'And my advice to you M. Chauvenon,' continued Guillemain, 'is to decide who your client is. Mademoiselle Madec or Monsieur de Flaubert? It is inadvisable and you cannot possibly do justice to representing two people who are involved in the same crime.'

'I am very well aware of that, Guillemain, and I am also very well aware that it is not against the law.'

'Charlene.' said Christophe firmly. 'Represent Charlene. 'I'll represent myself.'

'But Christophe!' said Rochelle.

Christophe shook his head and then turned and smiled at Julia. 'Charlene. Bernard must represent Charlene. She needs him more.'

Julia bit her lip, attempting to hide the wave of emotion she felt. He was always trying to do what's right for everybody else.

Christophe turned to Guillemain. 'I imagine I'm entitled to kiss my wife before you lock me up for good Guillemain.'

'You would be, if she was your wife.' Guillemain replied tersely.

Inspector Denton looked at Guillemain with exasperation.

'Of course, you may kiss Miss Connors.'

Christophe crossed over to Julia smiling affectionately.

'Make sure you visit me my darling. Bring some decent food.'

Inspector Denton smiled wryly.

Christophe bent his head and kissed Julia passionately on the lips. Then he nuzzled into her neck and hair, sighed in fake despair and said very loudly' 'I hear Inspector Guillemain's cooking is dreadful.' While people were busy laughing, he whispered quietly in her ear. 'Move into the Baudoin house immediately.'

Thirteen

'ROCHELLE IF YOU KNOW anything, anything at all about what's going on for God's sake tell me! I'm terrified.'

'Julia, I don't know anything. We'll know more when Bernard gets back from seeing Charlene.'

Julia put her bags down in the middle of the huge hall where Petit-Jean's body had been laid out earlier in the week. It felt cold, hollow and would have been completely empty if it wasn't for a small wooden stool placed near the inglenook fireplace.

'Why do you think Christophe wanted me to move in here?' she asked.

'I don't know *cherie*. Maybe he thinks that it is better for you.'

'Better for me? You're kidding right! Being here in this freezing mausoleum is better than being in our wonderful cosy room in the Castle Lodgings? Even if he thought I'd had an affair with Simon Chapman, he wouldn't punish me by sending me here.'

'Listen. I don't know!' Rochelle threw her arms up in the air and started stomping up and down the room. '*Je ne sais pas!'* Maybe he thinks they will freeze his money. Maybe he thinks they can't take the house if you're in it. Anyway, here you are nearer to him.'

Julia stared in disbelief. 'I'm the same distance as I would be in the Castle Lodgings. As for freezing his assets they'd have to freeze them in four continents and that would be a lot of paperwork and time based on a tiny suspicion. What did Bernard say?'

'Look Bernard couldn't tell me anything. He wants to try and talk to Charlene as quickly as possible. He said she thinks Guillemain listens to what she tells him.' She shrugged. 'I think it is more complicated that we realise Julia.'

'It is definitely more complicated than I realise. You know why?'

'No Why?' asked Rochelle looking slightly scared of the forceful Julia that had suddenly appeared from nowhere.

'Because I know you are not telling me something.'

Rochelle hesitated. 'I can't Julia.'

'Really?'

She shook her head and sat down on the stool. I can't. I promised.

'Great and does Bernard know?'

'No. He doesn't, so please don't ask him. He knows nothing.'

She really does look scared, thought Julia. Well at least I'm not the only one in the dark about this one.

'OK, I'll let it go for now, Rochelle but I'm not happy.

'You just have to accept it.' said Rochelle.

'I might be letting it go. But don't think I'll forget. '

Rochelle looked even more scared.

'I wonder what Guillemain's got on him.' said Julia.

'Christophe will call as soon as he can. I am sure of it,' said Rochelle 'And if not, then Bernard will find out somehow. Come on, I will show you around. I know this house from our student days. Even though they have started to change it a little, the layout is still the same. There is a very beautiful room at the top of the house where we can see the whole village and the castle. You can even see as far as the old *lavoire* where they washed the clothes in the river. It was the room that Baudoin used for his painting studio. Petit-Jean told me once that his grandfather went onto the roof to paint.'

'You're kidding? He must have been very brave.'

'I think perhaps he had a big motivation. Petit-Jean said it was the only way to get away from Yvette because she would annoy him.'

'But she was only very young, wasn't she?'

'Yes, but I think perhaps she has always been quite *terrifiante*. It's a miracle Baudoin did not fall down, I think. These mediaeval *pan de bois* houses have very steep roofs.'

They made their way up the stairs to the minstrel gallery and then up an old wooden staircase right to the top. The bedroom door was old oak, black with age just like the beams in the house and ceiling.

'You know,' said Rochelle, 'these beams and doors are as old as the fifteenth century. This is even before you burnt our Joan of Arc.'

'I didn't burn her, the English did and anyway she was half mine too Rochelle.'

'Ah *oui*, sometimes I forget that you are also French.'

They pushed open the door.

'This feels so wrong,' said Julia. 'It is Charlene's home.' Then she gasped.

The room was huge and ran the length the top floor of the beamed house. Beautiful colourful saris and other fabrics covered over the peeling paint of old wattle and daub walls. Above the bed three romantic erotic pictures of the Kama Sutra caught your eye. The smell of damp that had pervaded the rest of the house had gone and a sweet exotic smell had taken its place.

'Sandalwood and jasmine,' said Julia

Rochelle looked at her surprised. 'How do you know this?'

'Aromatherapy massage. Christophe and I have got to keep the demons at bay somehow.'

The wooden floors had been covered in rugs but they still had the old paint stains on the floor from Odilon Baudoin's painting days. At both ends of the room the original dormer windows jutted out of the roof. Light could pass right through from one end to the other.

'The windows are *magnifique* aren't they,' said Rochelle. 'We call them the eyes of the house.'

'Why because you can spy on the neighbours?'

Rochelle laughed. 'Possibly. But I believe it is because they allow the light into the house. The same way that your eyes allow light into your world. Without them all is black. This room is wonderful, there is so much light in here, even when it's a grey depressing day in Brittany.' She wiped the condensation off the window with her sleeve. 'You can see why he made it his studio and as for the views.' She opened one of the windows and leant out to look around. Julia joined her; you could easily fit the two of them side by side. Julia turned her head and looked up at the roof.

'He climbed out there? Brilliant!'

'But look how steep the roof is, ' said Rochelle.'

'Yes, but look at the views, it must have been so worth

it! I'm going out to have a better look.'

'Julia, for God's sake be careful.'

'Come on Rochelle, come with me. Don't you want to see what he could see?'

Rochelle hesitated.

'I do, but I am only going because I am worried for you to go alone.'

'Look. There are metal pegs that have been cemented into the sides of the Dormer casing, hold on to those,' said Julia. 'Odilon Baudoin must have put them in so that he could climb up.'

Julia made her way slowly up the side of the window to the roof. It was easier than she expected because you could grab the upper stakes and put your feet on the bottom ones and work your way up gradually. It was fine, so long as you didn't look down. She turned to check on Rochelle but she'd disappeared.

'Rochelle?' she called out.

Rochelle's head appeared over the other side of the peak of the roof.

'This is amazing. Julia, look what I've found. Come and see.'

In the dip between the Baudoin house and the next house was a small flat area where you could sit and gaze out at the scenery. Rochelle was sitting on top of a trap door that had been inserted into the roof at the bottom of the dip.

'Look this is where he sat to paint, look at all the paint stains on the roof tiles. And you see, he was using the roof slates as a palette.

'Just look at the view,' said Julia. 'Bet it's a great place to sunbathe or drink a sundowner too.' She pointed to the burnt-out incense sticks on one of the tiles.'

'Yes, or smoke a joint or two,' said Rochelle gesturing to a small jar that had stubs in it.'

'Charlene and Petit-Jean must have been coming up here.'

'Yes.' Said Rochelle, suddenly feeling sad. 'Let's go in. You are right, Julia. It is Charlene's home. It does not feel correct to look around their house in this way.'

They climbed down carefully. 'I've changed my mind on the sundowner idea,' said Julia. 'Wouldn't want to be even a tiny bit tiddly going up there. They must be crazy to go up there and smoke joints!'

Back in the bedroom, as they were about to leave Rochelle caught sight of a small old carved wooden crib with clean folded baby linen in it.

She put her hand over her mouth.

'Oh Julia. We have to do something. Charlene is having a baby. We have to do something. She has lost the great love of her life, she is carrying his child and now she will go to prison. She will be a mother, and she's facing it alone. It is so wrong.' And she burst into tears.

Julia hugged Rochelle. 'We will. Christophe will, Bernard will Rochelle. We will all help her.'

'Hello!' shouted a male voice from the corridor outside. Simon Chapman poked his head around the doorway. 'Sorry to interrupt, do you mind if I come in?' he asked. 'The door was open downstairs and I'd heard that you were moving into the house.' He smiled his slightly less lazy than usual, but equally charming smile.

'Hi Simon,' said Julia. She continued to hug Rochelle shielding her from him, to give her time to compose herself.

'In truth, I came to help. If there's anything I can do Julia, please let me know. Anything, anything at all. This business of Christophe being arrested is just ridiculous. I think my cousin Guillemain may well have lost the plot. Which is really quite serious as he's a detective.'

Rochelle had brought her emotions back under control so Julia let go of her.

'Thanks Simon, I'm not sure what we can do at the moment.'

'I also came to see if you would like to come for dinner, and to ask a favour of you, to be truthful.'

Julia looked surprised, and a little nervous. This could definitely be a green eggs moment. Christophe's in prison, and I just pop out for a candlelit dinner with Simon Chapman. I don't think so!

'A favour?'

'Yes.' He hesitated as if not sure of his ground. 'I know Madame Yvette often seems very harsh but underneath it she is an elderly woman who has suffered so much loss in her life. Tragic loss. You know she was as much my grandmother as my own grandmother and when my mother died young, she took over that role too. I think it may help her to come back and make her peace with her past. If she could see what Petit-Jean and Charlene were doing with the house, how they were changing their life. Would you allow me to bring her to visit?'

'Of course, Simon. If you think it will help her.'

'Would tomorrow be convenient?'

'Yes, no problem.'

'And dinner?'

'I don't think so, Simon. I want to visit Christophe and take him something to eat.'

'Of course,' he said, smiling warmly enough but with a definite glint in his eye. 'Why don't you give me a call in the morning,' he said, writing his number down for her.

'Maybe I can get you to change your mind.

Julia passed him her phone. 'Probably easiest if you just put your number in my phone. I have a number problem. A sort of maths dyslexia.'

'You have dyscalculia?' asked Simon.

'Yes.' said Julia surprised 'I've never ever met anyone who knows what that is. How incredible.'

'That explains the mix up with buying the house I imagine.'

'Well only partly. The Breton had a lot to do with that too.'

Simon put his number into her phone. 'Yes, that was rather bad of them but it was done for a good cause. There you go. I've put myself in favourites so you can find me quickly.' He gave her a wink and turned to go.

'Lovely to see you Rochelle.'

'You too Simon.' Replied Rochelle without looking him in the eye. They both watched him as he sauntered down the stairs. He smiled up at Julia before leaving the main hall.

'You want to watch him,' said Rochelle

'What? Why?'

'Julia you can't hide it. There is a definite frisson in the air when he is near you.'

'Don't be silly Rochelle.'

'And as a friend, I have to tell you,' continued Rochelle, 'that frisson is not one sided!'

'Rochelle you're being ridiculous.'

'Am I?' She put her arm around Julia. 'Honestly, do you believe he cares even a little about Yvette?'

'Well he probably does if she's been there like a grandmother and then mother for the whole of his life.'

'Well what if you look at it like this. Do you think

Yvette is the type of woman that would want to revisit her past here? She has had this possibility open for more than seventy-five years?'

'Probably not.'

'No. Do you remember how she couldn't wait to rid herself of this house and all memories of the Baudoin family - her husband, son and her grandson? What did she say at the funeral? And more than this, the argument in the castle when she refused the idea of giving the house to Charlene?'

'You're right Rochelle, you are so right, it was just an excuse.'

'Exactly, an excuse to see you and did you see his face when he saw I was here?'

'No, I didn't'

'Well I did!'

'Come on Rochelle, let's go down. This is all very uncomfortable for so many reasons.' She looked back at Charlene's and Petit-Jean's bedroom. 'I'll sleep in one of the other rooms.'

She sighed. The last thing she needed was Simon Chapman prowling around.

'Why oh, why did Christophe want me to move in? I wish I could stay back at the Castle Lodgings with you and Bernard.'

Rochelle nodded. 'Perhaps we could move in here with you? Then we will be *sur place* to keep our eyes on you. But, there is only half a bathroom and it does not function so well'

'Yes, and a lot of the rooms seem to have rubble in. Anyway, I imagine Bernard needs to work.'

'He does and he is terrible about everything being just so with his desk and papers. And if the internet is slow he completely blows. The problem is Julia, can I trust you to behave?'

'After our conversation the other day about lovers, that really is…'

'La poêle qui se moque du chaudron,' said Rochelle at the exact moment that Julia said, 'The pot calling the kettle black.' They both laughed.

Julia smiled. 'Exactly.' She put her arm around her friend. 'You don't have to worry about me Rochelle. I would never jeopardise my relationship with Christophe, not for all the tea in China, not for all the Chapman charm in Christendom, not even for revenge should Christophe have slept with Sophie Petrarch.'

Rochelle raised her eyebrows at the mention of Sophie Petrarch, then kissed Julia's cheek.

'In affairs of the heart and the *inguen* Julia, one can never say never.'

***

After Rochelle had gone, Julia tried to call Christophe again. He didn't answer, his phone was either taken from him or switched off because he was being questioned. She tried three more times in succession then glared at the mobile and threw it on the table. Thumping her fist on the table, in frustration she shouted out loud. 'I just want to talk to him! Why can't I talk to him? Why won't you let me talk to him? You nasty piece of work Guillemain!'

She slumped down in a heap in the middle of the floor because there were no chairs, in complete despair. If only she'd been more careful. If only she hadn't signed those papers and let them take the paintings, none of this would have happened. God I could kill myself for this. She felt the tears of frustration and anger start to well up. She allowed herself a few tears and then got up and dusted herself off. Julia Connors you've been through worse and so has Christophe. You will get through this! He will probably be out by tomorrow and anyway there is nothing you can do about it now.

Then she had a thought. But she could do something for Charlene. She was sure Christophe and Bernard were going to come up trumps and when they did she would need her home. And what's more, she was going to come home to the most wonderful surprise.

She hesitated for a second. Honestly, there goes that conscience bird again. She pulled her coat around her and headed up the stairs to have a better look around.

'Listen, conscience bird,' she said out loud. 'You can keep quiet for a while, I've got this.'

She wondered how long it would take to complete the bathroom. The tiles were there and so was the bath and shower, although it didn't look as if they were plumbed in. At least the loo worked.

She decided to take the biggest bedroom on the second floor as it was the nearest to the bathroom, and anyway most of the other rooms were either full of rubble from the building work they'd been doing or they were used as storage. One was full of old tiles that they must have been planning to recycle. If the house was that old it was almost certainly listed and had huge restrictions on what they could use to renovate it. She'd need to find someone to help who knew about the rules. Maybe Simon Chapman. They must know all about that from having done the castle. It must need a lot of maintenance, an old building like that. They probably even had permanent staff doing it.

Hum. Now why would I go out of my way to have

more contact with him? What was it that Rochelle said about having your cake and eating it? She thinks he is a little caramel cupcake that could easily balloon into a full-blown gateau Saint Honoré. Or in Julia's view no honoré. I'll keep it safe, call him and get some numbers of people to ring.

He answered immediately.

'Julia, I was just going to call you. Would tomorrow morning be alright to come over with Yvette?'

'Yes of course. I wasn't calling about that though. I'm trying to sort out the bathroom in the house and I wondered if you could put me in touch with some plumbers and workmen. I don't know anyone around here and it's always best to get someone who has been recommended.'

'Don't worry I'll sort something out for you. No problem at all.'

'Please, just send me the contact details. That will be fine.'

He laughed. 'Julia, It's nearly Christmas. If you are lucky, they will give you an appointment in three months' time and if they give you an appointment immediately it is because they are not very busy and that means...'

'They are not very good,' Julia finished the sentence.

'Exactly. I'll be over the first thing tomorrow, and we'll get it sorted.'

'Thank you, Simon. That is so kind of you.'

'Not kind at all. Nothing would give me more pleasure than helping out a beautiful damsel in distress. I shall see you tomorrow.'

Julia put the phone down. Damsel in distress? Honestly, the man had no idea what real distress was. Still, with a load of workmen in the place and Madame Yvette too, that's enough chaperones to satisfy Christophe. She thought about what Rochelle had said a few days ago at the funeral, when Julia had been covered in green dragon scales over Sophie Petrarch. Just because you have chemistry with one person doesn't mean you won't get attracted to other people. One thing was for sure if he kept coming up with Cinderella and damsel in distress comments like that, no chaperone would ever be needed.

On the ground floor, just off the main hall she found a small room that was kitted out as a temporary kitchen. There were a couple of camping gas rings and a kettle, and an old ceramic sink. She made herself a cup of tea and then started a list of things she needed to buy.

Tomorrow she'd do a shop and then go and see if they would let her see Christophe. The sun had gone down and it was starting to get cold. There was a fireplace but no wood apart from bits that had been removed during the renovations and were stacked in the corner. She hesitated. Could she burn them? Better not. Knowing her luck they'd be registered antiques dating back to Joan of Arc. Then she'd be in big trouble. She tried ringing Christophe again, but it was unobtainable. Either it had no battery, they'd taken it away from him or he was still being interrogated by that dictator Guillemain.

It was infuriating.

Two minutes later, the phone rang. She grabbed it like a child grabbing its Christmas stocking.

'Christophe! At last! I've been trying to call.'

'It's OK. Everything will be alright. They've had me in interrogation for the allocated eight hours but legally they have to give me a break. Guillemain didn't want to give me my phone but luckily Inspector Denton has a sensible brain in his head.'

'That's pretty mean of him. Are you OK?'

'I'm fine sweetheart. How are you doing?'

'OK, but I've been so worried.'

'Don't be, my darling. Well unless you think I'm guilty - then I think I'd be extremely worried too, if you thought that.'

'Christophe, don't joke like that.'

'Sorry. It's just such a farce. Have you seen Bernard since he came back to see Charlene?'

'No, I haven't. Christophe, why did you want me to move in here?'

'Can't talk right now.'

'Is someone listening?'

'Yep. Anyway, they don't seem to have very much on me,' he said in a very loud voice so everyone on the other end could hear. 'Just some Street CCTV in Eton Square of two people going towards our flat that they say facial recognition identifies as Petit-Jean and Charlene. They claim it is evidence that I was meeting them to discuss the fake theft.'

'That's it? That's what they are basing this on?'

'Yes, which is nothing. Look, I'll be out tomorrow. They can't hold me for longer than twenty-four hours based on a bit of CCTV of a couple of hoodies.'

'Hoodies?' asked Julia. 'Christophe, did you say hoodies?'

'Christophe?'

But he'd gone.

Hoodies? She'd seen them! When she ran into the traffic light post, well at least she'd seen Petit-Jean. That's why he looked familiar.

Fourteen

BERNARD ARRIVED EARLY THE next morning with Charlene. He gave Julia a quick reassuring kiss on the cheek and went straight into lawyer mode.

'The judge agreed to set bail and release Charlene.'

Julia sighed with relief.

'But,' Bernard continued. 'Her release is pending a further investigation. Guillemain refused to drop the case. He's using the irrational branch of his detective skills to investigate a supposed organised crime ring dealing in a series of major art thefts, insurance scams and stolen antiques.'

'And Christophe?' asked Julia. 'What about Christophe?'

'He'll probably be out tomorrow morning once they've tied up the loose ends. I don't think they've even got enough to charge him with anything so he won't need bail. I obviously couldn't do anything about it because he is representing himself. Don't worry Julia, I am sure he will be out tomorrow.'

Charlene hugged Julia.

'Julia, you know that Petit-Jean and I had nothing to

do with this don't you? Somebody put the painting in my caravan, we did not steal it.'

'I believe you Charlene, and so does Christophe, but …' She hesitated. Should she mention the Eton Square thing?

'Thank you both of you for everything you are doing, and of course, you too Bernard. Petit-Jean will know I am sure.' She caressed her slightly swollen stomach as she spoke. 'And so will his son.'

'Or daughter?' suggested Julia.

Charlene smiled. 'I can feel his spirit, it is a son.'

'Really? You're that sure?'

Charlene smiled at Julia. 'Yes, and you know it is too, don't you?'

Julia had to admit it, even though she had mentioned a daughter, she had seen a boy in her mind.

'Why do you hide your psychic gifts, Julia?'

'That would be because I don't have any,' Julia gave an embarrassed laugh.

'You are the most terrible liar,' said Charlene, shaking her head.

Julia grimaced. That was twice in as many days that she had been called a terrible liar. Hey Maybe not being able to lie well was the real gift.

'I only stopped by to say thank you and to collect some things,' said Charlene. 'This is your home now. I will go back to my friends at the commune.'

'No Charlene,' said Julia. 'It is your home, Christophe bought it for you and Petit-Jean's son.'

Charlene shook her head sadly.

'Perhaps, but I don't know, I feel such sadness. Sadness for what might have been here and what should have been. At the commune, I remember the happy times.'

'I can move out,' said Julia. 'I don't mind if you want to be alone here.'

Charlene held her hand. 'No, not at all, that is not the problem at all. I'll see how I feel in a couple of days. I just feel I want to be over at the commune where I feel safe. I no longer feel safe here. I need to see the others and check on a few things. I will come tomorrow and see you and Christophe. There is so much that I want to say to you.'

'Does that include your explanation for being in London near our house and following me?'

'Charlene's eyes lit up. I knew you had seen us! Yes. We did follow you to the house, and I can explain that, but tonight I am so tired. Tonight, baby Baudoin is telling me that I need to rest.'

'Of course.'

'And it will be better if Christophe is here because there are some things I cannot talk about without him here, it would be unfair.'

'I understand. Also, it will save you having to say everything twice.'

Charlene nodded and sighed sadly. 'It is very important that he understands. And we must all be very careful, there are very bad, bitter feelings behind this. I am sure Petit-Jean will tell me more tonight.'

'Petit-Jean?' asked Julia

'Yes. Of course. Some of us have the gift of understanding the spirit world Julia. And we are not afraid to use it.'

Bernard looked more than a little worried. If he had to put Charlene channelling Petit-Jean on the stand, he was on a hiding to nothing. He opened his mouth to say something, but then Julia winked at him, so he changed his mind.

'The most important thing is that you and your baby rest,' said Julia. 'Get some rest and you can tell us tomorrow.'

'Yes, and you and I can get to know each other better. I'd like to get to know you.' She took Julia's hand and placed it on her stomach. '*We'd* like to get to know you better.'

Julia felt a tiny pop beneath her hand.

Charlene laughed. 'Baby Baudoin likes you, I think.' she smiled her ethereal glowing smile and left with a very nervous Bernard. Bernard had defended a few of the World's most psychologically unstable criminals but this new age spirituality scared him far more. Even worse, it was catching, because his best friend was also going off with the fairies.

***

Julia was about to call Christophe when the door opened and a group of guys in work gear came in, followed by Simon Chapman. They put their tool kits and other equipment. down on the floor in the middle of the room and then went out again to get some more things.

'They're going to start with plumbing in the bath and shower that are already there, then get on with the tiling,' said Simon, smiling.

'That's wonderful. I am sure Charlene will be so grateful, Simon.'

'Is she not here with you?' he asked. 'I heard she'd been released on bail.'

'She wanted to see her friends and stay over at the commune tonight. She'll come over tomorrow, when Christophe is out. Bernard said he'd be released by tomorrow.'

'I'm so sorry about all this Julia. I really don't know what's got into my cousin Guillemain.'

'You don't think that they did it then?'

'Well I'm sure Christophe isn't involved.' He rubbed his chin, thoughtfully. 'Charlene and Petit-Jean however, did take the gallery uniforms and papers. And they were caught on camera outside your house in London too.'

Julia sighed. 'I know, Simon. And Charlene told me that they were following me. I saw them earlier in the day when I was out jogging. Well I saw Petit-Jean anyway.'

Simon looked surprised. 'Are you sure?'

'Yes, I have a really good head for faces. I think it's my karmic compensation for being so useless with numbers.'

'Why would they follow you though?'

'I don't know. Charlene is going to explain everything tomorrow. She did say Petit-Jean wanted to talk to Christophe. I would love to know what he wanted to talk to Christophe about.'

'Me too,' Simon agreed. 'I think half the village would love to know what that fallout was about. Are you saying Christophe hasn't even told you?'

'No. He hasn't.'

Julia felt very uncomfortable, seeing the surprise in his eyes.

'Well I believe Charlene,' said Julia. 'Call it instinct whatever you want. Or at least she didn't take them. Or maybe she didn't know that Petit-Jean took the paintings.'

'I guess that's possible. You know Petit-Jean really was a loose cannon, Julia. He may have improved since being with Charlene but it doesn't mean he had completely given up his old habits.'

'But why would he take the paintings?'

'I don't know. Almost certainly it's got something to

do with his grandfather though. For as long as I can remember he has been obsessed about it. The shame over his grandfather being a traitor. It's understandable I suppose. It was tough growing up in a place where everybody knew and ostracised you. My grandfather and even my father tried to shield him from it, but it didn't seem to do any good. Maybe he just wanted his grandfather's paintings and maybe at the same time he could get back at Christophe for whatever it is they argued about. Far be it from me to gossip, but you do know that Christophe has a rather shady past?'

Julia felt her hackles rise and broke into a beaming smile.

Simon Chapman was confused. Why would she be pleased about Christophe's shady past?

Julia smiled even more at the confusion on his face. It was brilliant. He had cast aspersions on Christophe. Rather than worry and ask Simon more, her instinctive reaction had been to protect the man she loves.

'You're smiling Julia,' he said, breaking into her thoughts.

'Am I? Oh. I was thinking about something else. So, you agree with Inspector Guillemain then?'

'No. But I just can't see any other explanation. Hey, let's not think about the bad things.' He put his hand on her shoulder. 'The important thing is to get Christophe out and prepare the house for Charlene, if that's what you want. Or for you? For whoever ends up as mistress of this…' he ran his hand along the wall and a large lump of plaster hit the floor '… lovely crumbling antiquity.'

Julia laughed. 'Yes. I'm not sure I would have chosen it but you know it is growing on me.'

'Now that I am very pleased to hear.'

***

The door opened and General Chapman marched in without knocking. The sound of his highly polished shoes made loud drum beats that echoed around the spartan room, like somebody had let off firecrackers.

Julia's eyes narrowed. What an arrogant man he is. She didn't usually take an instant dislike to people but something about his rigid unbending military persona really annoyed her. Who the hell does he think he is? Walking into someone else's house without knocking?

'So, Miss Connors. De Flaubert took the house anyway.'

'General Chapman. He did not take it.' Julia retorted. 'He bought it!'

'Father …I really don't think…' Simon started to speak.

'I'll deal with this, Simon.'

Simon Chapman threw Julia an apologetic look.

Seems as if General Chapman is a bit of a bully, thought Julia, feeling quite angry on Simon's behalf.

'I have been told that Simon is loaning our maintenance staff to you. What exactly are they doing?'

Simon threw Julia an exasperated look from behind his father's back. He then jumped to attention when his father turned around.

'Not much Father, just sorting out the bathroom and a few other things.'

'And who is going to pay for this, Simon?'

'Don't worry about that father, it's all settled.'

'It had better not be coming out of the Château maintenance budget Simon.' said Charles Chapman marching across the room towards the stairs.

Simon Chapman threw Julia a conspiratorial look,

nodding his head to indicate that in fact it was.

'No of course not father,' he said. 'Come upstairs and we'll show you. That's OK isn't it, Julia?'

'Yes, of course,' said Julia. 'Would you like some tea? I'll put the kettle on.'

She dived into the kitchen. She didn't trust herself not to go up there and push General Chapman off the top of the minstrel gallery.

Simon led his father upstairs where two of the workmen had already started on the bath. She could hear Charles Chapman barking out orders that they needed to move the bath further over and that they didn't have enough tiles to do the whole bathroom.

Interesting, thought Julia. General Bully-bluster doesn't want Christophe to have the house, he doesn't want Simon to let us use his workmen and he doesn't want the château to pay for it, but he does want to tell everyone how it should be done.

General Chapman and Simon came back downstairs just as the kettle boiled and there was a knock on the door.

'That's probably Madame Yvette,' said Simon. 'Shall I open the door?' Julia put her head around the kitchen to nod in agreement but Charles Chapman was already there and had opened it.

'Do come in,' he said, inviting her into the house. Julia shook her head in despair. That's twice now, he's stepped on my toes. If he does it again, I swear to God. I'm going to get some building rubble and drop it on his feet from a very great height. That'll take that shine off his shoes and cripple him at the same time.

'Miss Connors, how are you?' asked Yvette, holding the tips of her fingers out like royalty not wanting to touch the great unwashed. Julia felt as if she was expected to bob in a curtsy.

'Very well thank you. How are you?' Julia replied. She took Yvette's hand in hers and gave it a good extra firm business-like handshake. Two could play at status games.

Yvette nodded politely but without warmth and then rubbed her right hand as if in pain. Julia immediately felt guilty. Maybe she suffers from arthritis, honestly, what was I thinking?

Yvette got straight to the point.

'Why did you want me to come here Simon?'

'I thought, *Mémé.*' he said, calling her affectionately by a pet name used for the elderly.

She smiled, again without warmth. 'You know I do not respond to that name. It is for old women in aprons, which I am not.'

She certainly wasn't, thought Julia. She was an extremely glamorous older woman who still stunned people when she entered a room. She must be really old, but she doesn't look it.

'I wanted you to have a last look at the house and see if there is anything here that you would like to keep as a memory.' said Simon.

'And why would I want to do that Simon?'

'Because, one day, Yvette, when you are nearing your death bed, you may have many regrets.'

There was silence.

'There cannot possibly be anything that I would want here.' She seemed hesitant and they all held their breath.

'No!' She broke the silence angrily. 'Regrets are for the weak and feeble.'

Charles Chapman turned and looked at Simon, shaking his head.

'I told you. You are a sentimental idiot. I rue the day I ever let you refuse the army and go into the art business.

Stupid it was a stupid thing to do. It's turned you into a complete wimp.'

'Thank you, father for that vote of confidence.'

'Make sure Miss Connors pays the bill!' he said, leading Yvette out.

'Of course, father.' Replied Simon, shutting the door behind them.

Ouch thought Julia. I'd much rather have no father than have one like Charles Chapman.

'That went well then,' said Simon. They both started laughing.

'He's not that bad, honestly,' said Simon.

Julia laughed even more. 'Simon there was absolutely no ring of truth whatsoever in your voice.'

They both got the giggles and ended up sitting on the floor laughing, because there were no chairs.

'The army is supposed to be the making of people,' said Simon when they managed to stop laughing. 'But I think he must be the exception to the rule. In his case I think it ruined him completely.'

When Christophe walked in, closely followed by Inspector Denton, they found Julia and Simon still falling about laughing.

Julia froze slightly when she saw Christophe. For God's sake, she said to herself, you are laughing, nothing more, there's nothing to feel guilty about.

Unfortunately, Simon then made things worse. He smiled a very satisfied smile, held out his hand and helped Julia up off the floor.

'Julia was just trying to decide if anyone on this earth could stomach my father as a father in law.'

Christophe went over and kissed Julia possessively on the lips, clearly marking his territory. Green eggs, he whispered in her ear.

'Well luckily that's not something she will need to worry about, is it darling?' he said.

'Christophe you're early. Bernard thought you wouldn't be out until tomorrow.'

'Early? I'd say I'm just in time,' said Christophe looking daggers at Simon.'

Nobody had taken any notice of Inspector Denton, so he coughed politely. With what Julia was beginning to realise was a real talent of his, he diffused the tension immediately.

'Lovely to see you again Miss Connors, Mr Chapman. We have good news. The charges have been dropped. As I was on my way to the airport, I thought I'd drop Mr de Flaubert back on the way and take a look at this lovely old building. I'm quite a fan of architecture and this really is something.'

'You should stop off at the château before you leave, Inspector Denton,' said Simon. 'If you love architecture. It's a perfect renovation.'

'Sadly, I won't have the time, but I thank you for the offer. Also, I confess, I rather like to see buildings in their original bare bones form. I think it must be the detective in me that wants to see the evidence of the hundreds of years gone by.'

'Well this is certainly bare bones at the moment,' said Julia.

'I'd better be going,' said Simon. 'Give me a call when the men have finished doing the bathroom, Julia.'

Christophe raised his eyebrows.

'Simon kindly got his workmen to do the plumbing in the bath and shower,' she said defensively.

She walked with him to the door. 'I will Simon, and thank you so much for your help.' She closed the door behind him.

'Is there any coffee Julia?' asked Christophe, slightly terse. 'Would you like a coffee Inspector Denton?'

'No thank you Mr de Flaubert. Now that we are alone. I think it is better that we get straight down to business.

Fifteen

'MISS CONNORS I WOULD just like to confirm a few things with you. I do not believe for a second that the theft of the paintings was an insurance scam. Mr de Flaubert's finances are more than satisfactory. In fact, not even a trace of tax avoidance let alone anything illegal.'

'So why was Inspector Guillemain so quick to arrest Christophe?'

'Yes, he was worryingly quick off the mark,' Inspector Denton agreed.

'And all over a small piece of CCTV footage,' said Christophe

'Taken when you were not even in the country,' said Inspector Denton. 'Which brings me to you, Miss Connors. 'Did you have any contact with Petit-Jean and Charlene in London?'

Julia hesitated.

Christophe looked surprised. 'Julia?'

She really didn't want to get them into trouble, especially because Charlene hadn't even spoken to Christophe yet, but she couldn't lie.

'Not directly, no.'

'In what way?' asked inspector Denton.

'I saw them when I was out jogging in Kensington Park. Well I can't say for sure about Charlene because she never actually turned and faced me. Also because of the hoodie she was wearing I didn't see her hair. But Petit-Jean looked at me. Just before I ran into the traffic light post.'

'And you know for certain that it was them?' asked inspector Denton, not disbelieving but slightly surprised.

'Yes, they were also behind me when I stopped to get my breath outside a shop.'

'Behind you?'

'Yes, I saw their reflection in the window and then when I turned around, they'd gone.'

'And you recognised them even just from a reflection?'

'Julia has an excellent visual memory,' said Christophe. 'Julia why didn't you tell me, you'd seen them?'

'I was trying to tell you yesterday on the phone, when you mentioned the hoodies in the CCTV. That's why I recognised Petit-Jean in the coffin but before I could tell you the phone was cut off.'

Christophe shook his head and turned to Inspector Denton. 'Inspector Guillemain, had his stopwatch on the allocated three minutes for a phone call and cut me off.'

'He's very diligent, isn't he?' said Inspector Denton. 'Am I right in saying that you haven't seen the CCTV footage, Miss Connors?'

'No, I haven't seen it,' Julia confirmed.

'Has Mr de Flaubert or Mr Chauvenon given you any more information about the CCTV footage Miss Connors?'

'Apart from Christophe saying about the hoodies, no.'

'Do you think you could describe the two people you saw, Miss Connors?'

'Yes. I'll try.'

He held out his phone. And would you mind if I record it?'

'No, not at all, although I'm not sure how much help I can be.'

'Don't worry. When you're ready, just go ahead.'

Julia didn't know why she did it, but instinct just made her close her eyes so that she could take herself back to the moment.

'When I first see them, I'm talking to myself about Christophe being away so much and how I always start to worry and get anxious about him being unfaithful.'

Christophe smiled wryly at Inspector Denton.

'I'm remonstrating with myself not to be so stupid. I'm shouting 'stop it, stop it' and I sense someone is behind me. I think that they might think that I am shouting at them, so I turn to apologise and Petit-Jean looks straight at me.'

'Thank you, Miss Connors, but what I really wanted was a description of …'

'Please, don't interrupt me. I don't know why but I think I have to do this to get to the moment where I can see the image in my head and sort of freeze it.' Said Julia. She stared at Inspector Denton, without really seeing him.

'Oh. My apologies, do carry on.'

She closed her eyes again.

'One is tall and slim, very straight posture, no slouching at all. Could be male or female, no obvious curve of hips but can only see the back view. The hood on the grey tracksuit is up. No hair is showing out of the hood, so I can't say what colour it is. There's a small cream label sewn on the back of the sweatshirt, with black writing on it. Can make out letter shapes but I cannot read it. The jeans are dark indigo, baggy and slightly short, showing tanned bottom of the legs at the bottom. They are new and I think they are Levis. She's not wearing socks, old black and white Adidas trainers. The ankles are female, slim, no hair.'

Inspector Denton and Christophe stare at Julia in amazement. Julia carried on without opening her eyes.

'Petit-Jean's hood is also up but his hair at the front is oily and sticking to his face, where it parts on the right-hand side, it's unwashed. He has a red mark on his face on the left side, looks like a rash. The sweatshirt is also grey but the toggles are on black string, hanging down. The right plastic toggle is missing and it's just tied in a knot. The sweatshirt is open at the front and he is wearing a dark blue and white striped t-shirt. It has a hole in the bottom at the front. There are two black straps of a rucksack going over his shoulders. The jeans are pale blue, ripped at the knee, the right knee tear is shorter than the left and the jeans are too long; they hang over the trainers and are frayed at the bottom. The trainers are black and fairly new. He looks scared when I speak to him. She, yes, it is a female hand that grabs him and pulls him away. It is Charlene's hand. I turn around to jog across the road and hit my head on the traffic light post.'

Julia opened her eyes.

'That's all, I'm afraid'

'I don't think that is anything to be afraid of, at all Miss Connors. In fact, it's really quite impressive. You have just described the exact clothing of the people on the CCTV in Eaton Square. Have you always been able to do that? Recall a memory so accurately?'

'I've always had a good visual memory but I've never done that before. I'm quite surprised.' She smiled at Christophe.

He gave her a big hug. 'Now I know I am in deep trouble because you will remember every little thing, glance, touch, everything that I do and it will be replayed with incredible accuracy and held as evidence against me, and I will have no defence!'

'Well you'd just better behave then forever more Monsieur de Flaubert.'

'Inspector Denton smiled. 'You have my sympathy Mr de Flaubert. Miss Connors could well have a photographic memory and may even be a super recogniser.'

'What's a super recogniser?' asked Christophe

'They are people that have almost superpowers at recognising people. The scientists don't know why but super recogniser brains pick up more information than other people's, for recognising faces. They are highly prized by the police force especially when looking for specific known suspects in crowds.'

'But I thought facial recognition software was doing all that now.'

'It does some of the work but it's by no means fool proof. The latest statistics showed an extremely high percentage of false positives.'

'It makes Guillemain's case using CCTV extremely doubtful,' said Christophe.

'Until I just confirmed that it was Charlene and Petit-Jean, in Eton Square,' said Julia, shaking her head.

'Miss Connors. I am rather out of order here, but I'm getting to the end of my career. I've worked on thousands of cases and you develop an instinct for these things. It's something they try to drive out of us very early on in our careers so that we concentrate on evidence, but it hasn't always worked for me. I do not think for one minute that

Charlene Madec and Petit-Jean Baudoin stole the paintings, despite the fact that the Chapman was found in her caravan. They are just not the type. Where would they find the money to hire two people to dress as security guards, steal the paintings and then get them out of the country and over to Brittany? It simply does not make sense.'

'I am quite relieved to hear that Inspector Denton.' said Christophe

'I shouldn't be too relieved just yet because I don't have any other explanation but I shall try and find one when I get back to London. You have my details. If anything at all comes to mind that might help explain the case, anything at all, call me, please.'

***

The workmen left. Julia and Christophe were finally alone.

Christophe sat on the bed that Julia had made up in the bedroom on the second floor. He bounced up and down on it to see how it felt.

'Feels very soggy and dips very badly in the middle. It will be impossible for us to get away from each other now because we will keep rolling back into the middle.'

'I don't want to get away from you.'

'Are you sure about that? You were having a very good time with Simon when I came back.'

'If you're jealous about us laughing you shouldn't be. Things could have been very different. You could have come back to find that I'd pushed General Chapman off the minstrel gallery.'

Christophe lay down on the bed, gently pulled her on top of him and stroked her back.

'Sorry. I'm not doing very well on the green-eyed monster slaying, am I? Fallen at the first hurdle.'

'I forgive you.' She kissed him and then rubbed his cheeks. 'Nice stubble.'

'Yes. Am dying for a shower.' He sat up and then fell back again into the huge dip in the middle of the bed.

'Lord, I'm tired.'

'Christophe, why did you want me to move in so quickly?'

'I don't know. I just felt it was important. I had this feeling that they might freeze my assets and General Chapman might make some excuse to take the house back because the funding stopped. He was so angry that we'd got it for Charlene. I thought if you were already here, it would be harder for him to do it.'

'Do you think it was him that bid against us in the auction?'

'I don't know, but something very strange is going on. I can't get my head around it at the moment. I just want a decent bath and to spend a quiet evening with you, my darling. We'll see what tomorrow brings.'

'You can't have a bath, Christophe, the grout isn't dry.'

'Great.'

'And you know what?'

He shook his head, smiling to himself. That was usually the way she started a very imaginative treatise aimed at getting him to do something.

'As you have already pointed out, the bed is terrible. And it's really cold here at night too, there's no central heating and no wood for the fire. And there's no food either. And there's this awful insomniac cockerel that wakes you up every hour. And the pigeons here are huge gossips, they have really loud coos and they all meet on the windowsill outside the bedroom window early in the morning and …'

'And you want to go back to the Castle Lodgings.' Christophe finished the sentence for her.

'Yes. And for a far more important reason.'

'Which is?'

'The bath there is big enough for two.'

***

Christophe leant over the bath to pick up the bottle and topped up their wine glasses. The steam rising from the bath was like a sauna. It misted the glasses and the mirror opposite, leaving them cocooned in a cloud of steam.

'You're not going to put womb music on are you Julia? Don't think I could handle that.'

'No, I'm not.' Julia laughed. 'I'm not that extreme, well not yet.'

'Still, it was a good call coming back here,' said Christophe.

Julia gently pushed him forward in front of her so that she could massage his back and neck with the scented gel.

'That feels good.'

She took another sip of wine and Christophe leant his head back against her chest.

'I could easily sleep here all night I think,' he gave a deep sigh.

'Except that the water will go cold,' said Julia.

'Not if you stay awake all night and keep topping it up.'

'Thanks Christophe. And what if I fall asleep?'

'Then we'll both drown.'

'No. I'd wake up and I'd save you.'

'You already have saved me.'

'Have I?'

He turned around to face her, sloshing half of the water out of the bath. He moved her nearer to him and looked deep into her eyes.

'You've saved me from myself. I've been living this life always trying to absolve myself from the guilt I feel. Always trying to make amends for what happened in the past, and protect people that I think I've let down. Driven by guilt. You've changed all that. Oh, I still want to do what's right, to make amends, but not at the expense of us. Never at the expense of us.'

Julia leant forward and kissed him, her pupils growing even larger in the dim candlelight.

'Then I know we'll be alright, always.'

'Always. I promise.' He clinked his glass on hers. 'Let's drink to that.'

'Do you mind watching where you're putting your foot please,' she said.

He pulled her even closer to him.

'That's not my foot.'

***

There was an urgent banging on their door with voices arguing outside.

'*S'il vous plait, s'il vous plait!* Monsieur de Flaubert.' A deep male voice was full of panic. 'It's Charlene. She needs to talk to you urgently!'

'I told you to wait. You cannot come up here and disturb our guests!' said another agitated voice.

The fist banged on the door again.

'It's me, Stefan from the commune. It's an emergency! She told me to come and get you. Let go of me,' he said to the other person. 'You don't understand.'

Christophe jumped out of the bath and pulled a bathrobe on. He threw the other to Julia and then opened the door.

The tall leader of the commune was standing there. He was very distraught and out of breath from running.

'Shall I call the police, Sir?' asked the night manager.

'No, it's OK,' said Christophe. 'I'll deal with it.' He gestured for Stefan to come in. 'What's the matter?'

'It's Charlene, she said to come and get you. She said it's urgent. She's not well. I think it's the baby.'

'Then for goodness sake, you need a doctor, not me.'

'I tried. She said no, she said she has to speak to you. She said it was more important to get you first.' He was worried and doubting that he'd made the right decision.

'OK,' I'll come but you need to go and get a doctor.' Christophe grabbed his jeans and went into the bathroom to get dressed.

'I'll come with you,' said Julia.

'No,' Christophe shouted from the bathroom. 'Call the doctor and make sure he comes here to pick you up. Bring him to Charlene's caravan at the commune. Stefan will give him the directions.' He emerged from the bathroom and grabbed a jacket. 'I'll go straight there on foot more quickly. I can run through the back field path.' He ran out of the door.

Julia dialled the number for the doctor on call and he said he'd leave immediately. Stefan paced up and down the room, muttering. He turned tearfully to Julia.

'She wouldn't let me go get the doctor first, she insisted I come here. She is not good. I am so worried. I shouldn't have listened, I should have gone to the doctor.'

'Is someone with her?' asked Julia

'No, they are all up at the Peaks. It's the Festival of

Light. They always go there. I stayed to be with her. I sensed something was wrong,' he said. 'I should go, I should run back as fast as I can.

'No if you do that, I won't be able to explain to the doctor how to get there. Christophe will be there by now. Go downstairs and wait outside the front entrance so the doctor will see you. I'll get dressed.'

When Julia got downstairs the doctor still hadn't arrived and Stefan was in a bad way.

'I should have gone for the doctor. I should have followed my instincts. He won't come in time, I know he won't.'

'He will come, I am sure of it.'

He looked at Julia, his eyes emotional, and suddenly stopped pacing about.

'It's too late,' he said.

'You don't know that, Stefan,' said Julia. The look in his eyes was worrying. Then they glazed over.

Very calmly, he took her hand in his and held it for a moment.

'It is too late, Julia. Some people just know things. Charlene was right, you know things but you do not want to listen in here.' He touched her solar plexus, and Julia felt sick with fear. Deep down she had been feeling that for some reason Charlene was not going to make it but she couldn't bear to think about it.

The car pulled up and Stefan jumped in the front.'

'The doctor was an elderly man with a kind face.'

'Don't worry,' he said. 'We'll try and get her sorted out.'

They headed out of the village on the old *lavoire* road and then Stefan directed them to go off on the tracks that ran through fields towards a copse. They could see the light of a fire in the distance at the end of the field.

'Head towards the light of that fire,' said Stefan.

The caravan was in the field under a tree, a long way from the other group of teepees of the commune, which was in darkness. A faint flicker of candlelight was coming from the inside of the caravan. The elderly doctor pulled the handbrake on, grabbed his bag and got out of the car quickly, but without panic. He was extremely experienced and Julia felt comforted merely by his presence. He handed her a torch.

'Now, let's go and see what the trouble is,' he said and Julia followed him into the caravan.

Christophe was sitting on the bunk cradling Charlene's head in his hands. Her eyes were open, staring blankly, lifeless. Christophe had tears in his eyes as he looked up and said,' she's dead, I think she's dead. I can't bring her round.'

The doctor took hold of Charlene's arm, feeling for a pulse and looked into her eyes with a small light he took from his bag.

'No. There's a pulse,' said the doctor. 'There's no time for an ambulance. Quicker if we take her. Move her into the car, gently' he said. 'One of you will have to drive. I will do what I can on the way.'

'It's probably best if you drive, Stefan, you know the area better.' said Julia turning around.

He wasn't there.

'What the hell? Where's he gone?'

The panic in Julia's voice mobilised Christophe into action.

'Let's move it,' he said, jumping up. 'There's still a chance she might make it, if we hurry. 'I'll drive. You help the doctor in the back.'

On the way to the hospital the doctor asked them a lot of questions while he continually checked Charlene's pulse and tried to bring her round. Did she do drugs? Had she been drinking? Was she on any medication? They couldn't answer any of them. The only thing they could say was that she was pregnant.

They reached the Hospital, and the Emergency Department staff rushed her through.

'Will she make it?' Christophe asked the doctor.

'I don't know,' he said. 'Until they find out what she has taken or what is wrong, I cannot give you an honest answer.'

'You think she has taken something?' asked Christophe.

'It looks very much like an overdose but honestly I cannot say. I'm very sorry.'

Julia and Christophe filled in the paperwork in admissions as best they could but apart from Charlene's name, they couldn't do anything else, not even provide a next of kin or contact number. In the end they left Christophe's number and headed back to the Castle Lodgings.

'Where the hell did Stefan go?' asked Christophe.

'I don't know,' said Julia. 'Maybe he went to get the others from the commune. He said they'd gone up to the Peaks for the solstice.'

'That's madness. Couldn't he see the state Charlene was in? And why didn't he come to the hospital? He might be the only one who knows where to find her family.'

As they walked into the reception of the Castle Lodgings, Bernard and Rochelle arrived back from Rennes. A good family dinner with Francoise had made Rochelle pleasantly merry and totally desensitised to picking up any clues on anyone's state of mind.

'Hey! You're out. How did you manage to do that Christophe without the help of my amazing, clever and talented criminal defence lawyer, husband? Rochelle asked. She gave him a big kiss. 'And this one's from Francoise.' She gave him another. 'We've just had the most wonderful dinner with her in Rennes. She is so clever, that girl. I just don't know where she gets it from? Do you know your god-daughter has just been given confirmation that she has won the sponsorship for a final year in Polynesia. So in two years' time she will be living on some remote Polynesian atoll. She was up against a thousand other shortlisted candidates from all over France and ...'

'Shh, Rochelle. Just for a minute,' said Bernard gently squeezing her hand. 'Christophe what's the matter?' he asked, immediately seeing that something was wrong.

'It's Charlene, she ...'

Christophe's phone rang and he immediately answered it. He listened carefully and then said. 'No, I don't, I'm sorry.'

'That was the hospital. They wanted to know how to contact Charlene's next of kin. She didn't make it.'

Sixteen

IT WAS A FEW days before the autopsy report indicated a death by probable suicide. Charlene had taken a large dose of tranquilisers and that had triggered a pre-eclampsia because she was pregnant.

Christophe was the most distraught that Julia had ever seen him. He wouldn't eat, and wouldn't talk about it - not to her nor Rochelle and Bernard. He lay in bed as if in a trance, either sleeping too much or not at all. They'd suggested just about everything they could think of to get him out of the depression he seemed to be falling into. Cooking a sumptuous dinner, taking him out for dinner, staying in for dinner. Julia had even offered to organised for them to go back to London, or down to Provence to the old family home but nothing worked. Exercise, long walks - not even her usually highly successful seduction techniques worked.

She was so worried, she got up early before Christophe stirred. She drove over to see a doctor in the next village. She was relieved to find that it was the same one who had come out to Charlene.

Going to see a doctor secretly on someone else's behalf did not seem very ethical, but she had to do something. She sat down in the chair that he offered. He gave her a reassuring smile and she just blurted it out.

'I'm really worried about my husband. Well he's not my husband but he is my sort of husband and he is …' she hesitated, not sure of what his real state of mind was.

'In a state of shock?' said the doctor

'Well yes but I think it's worse than that. I think he is falling into a deep depression.'

'Ah. Yes, I could see that he was very shocked when we found your friend. You know, deep depression is normal after bereavement, as is anger, guilt, denial and so many other emotions.'

'The thing is, we had only just met her. We didn't know her very well. She was a friend because we both liked her instantly. But this seems to have hit him so much harder than his friend Petit-Jean's death.'

'So, he had already suffered a bereavement recently. Was he a very good friend of Petit-Jean?'

'Yes, that's why we came over here. And he felt bad because he hadn't spoken to his friend for many years, they'd argued and he never managed to make it up with him.'

'Perhaps he is displacing his feelings on the loss of Petit-Jean to Petit-Jean's partner'

'Maybe. And he has been behaving quite irrationally too. Well irrationally for him.'

'In what way?'

'Well trying to follow his gut feeling and buying the house for Charlene and telling me to move in there but he didn't know why.'

'It sounds as if he is trying to make amends for his

guilt feelings by looking after his friend's partner. And of course, her being pregnant with his friend's child would make him feel even more …'

'Guilty…' said Julia

'Yes. Guilty that he has been unable to look after her but also desperate that he could not make amends.'

'Of course. That's what it is,' said Julia.

'The best thing to do is to give it time. Try and keep him occupied. If you could get him to come and see me and talk, I could prescribe some anti-depressants. However, I'll be honest, I believe talking is a much better healer than medication, if he can handle it. Don't forget it is early days, it's only been a few days since your friend died. Time of course is the other great natural healer.'

'Yes, I suppose so, and Charlene's suicide coming so soon after the death of Petit-Jean.'

'I was so very sorry that your friend didn't make it,' he said. 'That is one of the hardest things in my job, seeing the passing of someone so young who had everything to live for.'

'Yes, it was a terrible shock and Christophe took it very badly. I think he blames himself and it brought back terrible memories of when his sister died.'

'Did his sister die from suicide too?'

'No, from a drug overdose.'

'Well if he has already lost someone close to him, through drugs, it would indeed make his loss even harder.'

'Charlene's wasn't drugs though was it?'

'Tranquilisers and drugs, mixed together, I think.

'So sad.'

'Yes. And very unusual.'

'Oh?'

'It is extremely rare indeed that a pregnant woman takes her own life, but if she had recently suffered the loss of the father of her child, and if she had a history of drug use, which I believe she had, then that could explain it.' He shook his head sadly. 'And even worse, she must have regretted it because she sent your tall friend to get me. We were just too late.'

'He wasn't our friend, he was one of the commune people. To be honest we didn't know any of them very well, but Christophe knew Charlene's partner very well, he was a childhood friend. The tall man, Stefan, wanted to get you first but Charlene insisted that he get Christophe first, but none of us know why.'

'That would probably make it even worse for your husband. My advice to you is to get him to come and see me if you can. Men are always very loath to talk about these things but we must always try and help them to speak about them. And if you see any extreme changes in his behaviour, call me.'

He handed Julia a piece of paper. 'Here is a list of things to watch out for. If you see any of these changes in him, call me immediately. Try to get him involved in some kind of project. Especially if it involves a lot of thinking that will take his mind off things. If he has a goal to work at, it really can help. And be patient. We spend many years deepening our love for people and we cannot just set that aside in a couple of days, as if we've lost a broken toy.'

***

Julia drove back to Pont Carnac on the back roads, through the windy lanes. She watched the big dark heavy clouds approaching from the east. The temperature was dropping dramatically and it looked like it might snow.

She was dreading Christophe saying that they should move back into the Baudoin house. If she'd thought it was cold before it was going to be a lot colder now. Chances were it would make depression even more likely – but this time, for both of them.

What a disaster that had been, first buying the wrong house then paying a fortune for the right one and now having nobody to give it to. They'd saddled themselves with a huge listed building project for something that they didn't even want. Boy was it a mammoth project. A project. Of course, a project for Christophe! But how to convince him, that was the problem. They could finish the house in memory of Petit-Jean and Charlene. Then sell it or rent it out. Or even better! They could give it to Françoise then she wouldn't have to rent in Rennes.

Julia hadn't realised that she had been driving extra slowly while she'd been thinking. Now that she had a goal, she put her foot down a bit, to the relief of the long tailback of cars behind her that had been flashing their lights at her and tooting in frustration. Yes. She'd speak to Rochelle and Françoise and get them in on it. Yes, it all fitted perfectly. They would tell a little white lie to Christophe, that Françoise had nowhere to live and needed the house. That may work. He would do anything for Françoise. At the next roundabout, she went right around and headed off back towards Rennes.

***

It was nearly lunch time when she'd finally got everything organised and arrived back at their rooms in the Castle Lodgings. Christophe was still in bed and the shutters were closed, but she knew he wasn't asleep.

She kissed him on the forehead. 'High sleepy. Do you

mind if I open the shutters, I need some natural light to see these building plans.'

'OK,' he murmered. He put his head under the pillow to block out the light.

She swept everything off the table and laid the plans out.

'Do you want anything to eat?' she asked

'No,' he mumbled.

'Rochelle and Françoise will be here soon. They are going to come and look over the plans because poor Françoise has got to move out of her lodgings and she has nowhere to live so we thought it would be a good idea for her to move into the Baudoin house. What do you think?' More mumbling came from beneath the pillow. Julia thought it resembled something like, 'if you want'.

There was a knock at the door and Rochelle and Françoise came in with a box full of piping hot *Galette Bretonne* and a couple of bottles of the local organic cider.

'Are you going to eat with us, Christophe?' Julia asked.

'No,' he mumbled again. 'Just leave me alone for God's sake!'

Rochelle and Françoise shook their heads at Julia. The worry was clear on their faces.

They took the plans off the table and laid out plates and glasses. Rochelle accidentally dropped the cutlery on the floor and it rang out like the church bells, but it didn't seem to register at all with Christophe.

Françoise shook her head, in despair. She went over and sat on the bed next to Christophe who was so tightly wound up in the duvet he looked like an Egyptian mummy.

'I am so sorry about Charlene, *Tonton* and about Petit John's baby. It is so sad.'

Christophe pulled the pillow off his head and turned to look at her.

Françoise was shocked by the redness of the eyes probably due to lack of light and too much time in bed and possibly crying too.

'I wish I had known them better. I only met Petit-Jean once, many years ago,' she said.

Christophe raised his head and looked confused. 'You only ever met him once?'

'Yes. We came for a holiday with Mama and they were talking about old times. It all sounded great fun.'

'It was,' said Christophe, sadly. 'It really was.'

'Will you tell me more about those days, *Tonton*? So that I feel I know them better. I want to do what's right for the house, like they would have wanted.'

Christophe took her hand in his. 'Of course, I will.'

Françoise gave him a hug and Christophe didn't pull away.

Rochelle and Julia exchanged glances. They were both thinking the same, this might just work.

'She couldn't have been that much older than you,' said Christophe.

Françoise smiled. 'I know, and she had so much to live for.'

'That's what the doctor said too,' said Julia. 'He said it is so sad because she had so much to live for. He also said that it is very unusual for a pregnant woman to commit suicide.'

'What did you say?' asked Christophe. 'You've been to see the doctor?'

'Yes...I was...' Julia hesitated. She didn't want to tell him she'd been to see the doctor about him. Certainly not in front of Rochelle and Françoise. It would be embarrassing for him and make things worse.

'I needed some more sleeping tablets so I went to see

the doctor and it was the same one who came out to Charlene.'

'No, not that. The thing he said about pregnant women.'

'He said it was extremely rare for a pregnant woman to commit suicide.'

Christophe sat bolt upright. 'Pass me my bathrobe, will you Françoise *cherie?*'

Françoise went into the bathroom and then handed it to him. Christophe put it on, jumped out of bed and went over to Julia. He hugged her from behind.

'Wow those Galettes smell fantastic,' he said. 'I am starving.' He pulled the corner off one and put it into his mouth. 'Galettes Bretonnes *a la forestiere,* my favourite.' He gave her a big kiss. 'Sorry I've been such a bear with a sore head. I will make it up to you this evening. I'd like two galettes please.'

He looked down at the plans on the sofa. 'Great idea to do the house. Françoise you choose what you want, you don't have to stick to Petit-Jean and Charlene's house plans because it is going to be yours. Make it the way you want and don't worry about the cost.'

He wandered over to the wardrobe and opened it. 'Julia you are a star, you got our stuff laundered. I'm going to take a shower and then I need to sort out a few things. First on the list is calling Inspector Denton.'

***

Christophe didn't bother to pack any clothes. He picked up a small case to put some paperwork in.

'I'll leave the car with you Julia. You'll need it here more than I will in London.'

'OK,' she replied, happy, but flabbergasted at the change in him.

'Françoise is dropping me at the airport in Rennes on her way back to University. I'll get the first flight I can back to London.'

'OK. But are you going to tell me what's going on?'

'I'm not sure and you will be the first to know when I am sure. But I do know this. There is no way Charlene committed suicide and I don't believe Petit-Jean had an accident either. And I am certain they didn't steal the paintings.'

'And you know this, how?'

'Gut instinct Julia.'

'No Christophe you can't use that as a justification. That can only be used when you don't have any clear logical facts to go on.'

'Ah. So, you admit that's what you do!'

'Well sort of. Anyway, why do you need to go back to London?'

'Because I know that Denton is the only person that I can count on to help us in this. Guillemain is too close to everyone in this village and if I try and talk to him, our natural dislike of each other is guaranteed to shut down any investigation before we even set foot in the gendarmerie.'

'So, call Denton. You don't have to go there.'

'I do. There is something else I want to check.'

'So, why don't I come to London with you? Christophe we haven't even spoken properly about this since Charlene died. You've been so upset and instead of talking and supporting each other, I feel like we've been more distant than ever and we haven't even …'

'…made love.'

'Yes.'

'Well we could, now, a quickie …' He realised immediately the suggestion was a big mistake.

'I do NOT want a quickie! I want to go to London with you. I want to sleep in our own bed, make love. I want everything to go back to normal. Us as we usually are. When we don't get up, except to get a huge plate of buttered toast and a glass of wine, then go back to bed again.'

'Julia, I'll be back in a day or so. As soon as I've got a plan sorted out with Inspector Denton, I'll be straight back.'

'Even more reason why I can go with you, because it is not for very long.

'Somebody has to help Francoise sort out the house. It needs builders, plasterers and decorators organising. You can get Simon Chapman to help with that.'

She stared at him, stunned.

'You are asking me to ask Simon Chapman for help?'

'Err Yes.'

'Really? You want me to spend time with Simon Chapman?'

'No. No I don't. I'd like you to speak to him on the phone and not see him in person.'

'That had better be tongue in cheek, Christophe.'

Christophe grabbed his mobile and kissed her. Then he saw the upset in her turquoise eyes and stopped in his tracks.

He sat down and pulled her onto his knee.

'I know it sounds crazy and it won't bring Charlene and Petit-Jean back, but I owe it to them to clear their names and find out who did this.'

Julia shook her head in disbelief.

'But it's illogical and there is not a shred of proof.'

He turned her to face him and looked straight at her.

'You've got to be kidding me. You are telling me there

is no proof. Where did this role reversal come from?'

'I don't know. Really I don't.' She was thoroughly confused. 'Maybe it's the way the Universe works. Maybe the spiritual balance has to be constantly reset and balanced. If you go touchy-feely, I have to go logically-proofy to compensate.'

'I love it when you come up with a take on things right from left field. OK, in order for you to reset your gut reactions and instincts, here is my rational reasoned logical take on things. First, not stealing the paintings. As Denton said, how would they pay two people to steal and transport the paintings and get them here in such a short space of time. We know Petit-Jean wanted to talk to me about something and there is no logic to them binning the Baudoin. If they were really in it for the money, which I very much doubt, because their lifestyle was not based on money, it was based on freedom, renouncing the modern materialistic world then they would have sold the Baudoin too. So, there is no motive.'

'Agreed,' said Julia.

Second. Petit-Jean's death. He hadn't touched any heavy drugs for years. As much as he could be crazy on his motorbike, he was an incredibly good rider. He even did motor cross and could cope with ridiculously difficult terrains in all weathers. A motor bike accident on a small country lane in a place that he knows like the back of his hand with no one else involved, it just doesn't stack up.'

'OK. I accept that.'

'Third, Charlene's death.'

Julia flinched and Christophe squeezed her hand reassuringly.

'Charlene's alleged suicide. Petit-Jean and Charlene were making a great life for themselves. They were doing up the house, starting a family. According to Stefan, Petit-Jean was really excited about it all.'

'Yes, but maybe Charlene was in a deep depression after Petit-Jean's death. I mean, she was having to deal with that, and so many other things. Losing the love of her life, the father of her baby, facing that alone. Being made homeless by Yvette and being arrested for something she didn't do. That's enough to make anyone suicidal.'

'Julia, what does your gut tell you?' He took her hand and placed it gently on her solar plexus. It reminded her of the way that Charlene had taken her hand and placed it on her swollen belly and she'd felt the little pop of the kick of the baby Charlene was carrying.

She felt a sudden wave of tears rising. No. Charlene would not have done that. She would never have harmed her baby. She hugged him tightly.

'My God you're right Christophe, I know you are. But be careful.'

'You too.' I'm leaving you the laptop. We can video call. Best if you stay here at the lodgings as you've got Wi-Fi.'

'Thank God for that. The Baudoin house is freezing.'

'I mean it, Julia be careful. If they didn't steal the paintings, somebody is doing a lot to make us think that they did, and that possibly includes resorting to murder. Don't discuss it with anyone apart from Bernard and Rochelle. See if you can find Stefan from the commune. Find out a bit more about what Charlene said to him that night. He might know what she wanted to tell us. Ask him if he knows anything about why Petit-Jean wanted to talk to me.'

Julia looked slightly scared.

'Don't worry. I know Denton will help us. I trust him.'

***

After he'd gone, Rochelle and Julia donned their biggest sweaters and headed over to the Baudoin House.

'We need to get some wood for the fire,' said Julia. 'It would make things a lot nicer for us and for the workmen too.'

'This didn't work out quite as we planned, did it,' said Rochelle.

'No. It was supposed to be the wind that filled Christophe's sails and pulled him out of the doldrums.'

'Well it did that,' said Rochelle.

'Yes, but I think it's thrown him straight into a raging maelstrom.'

'And my family has abandoned the ship. Françoise believes her mission is complete. Bernard is playing his 'too much work' card and has run back to Nice. Maybe we can just quickly ask Simon Chapman to tell the workmen what to do and then run away ourselves shopping or something'

'Well maybe you can but I have to do a bit of detective work. Christophe wants me to try and find Stefan and talk to him. And anyway, you can't go and leave me.'

'Why not?'

As you said yourself, I need a chaperone, if I'm going to be seeing Simon Chapman.'

'But I have so many things to do, Julia.'

'Really? Like what?'

'Well I've got my painting.' Rochelle's eyes narrowed.

Julia threw her a look of disbelief. Rochelle looked away and something dawned on Julia.. She felt it in her solar plexus. Her gut reaction came back even stronger than it had been before. 'I bet your bottom dollar you haven't painted anything for years.'

Rochelle squirmed. 'Julia, that is a terrible thing to say to me!'

'Is it?'

'Yes. Why would you say that?'

'Because that's the reason that you have affairs! Not because you are unhappy in your marriage or because you are French and that's what French people do, or because marriages get eczema every seven years. It is because you are not happy with yourself.'

'Julia when did you suddenly change from high fashion princess to doctor of psychology. Are you having a midlife crisis?'

'No, I'm not having a mid-life crisis. I am too young for a mid-life crisis. But I will admit that I've just got this sort of instinct conscious thing going on. Ever since Christophe went away on business the last time. I've been feeling guilty about all the money and privilege and I want to do something more with my life. Anyway, don't change the subject. You haven't painted anything have you?'

Rochelle shrugged unhappily and pouted. 'But of course, I have.'

'Yeah and that's got as much ring of truth about it as a clock striking thirteen!' She threw Rochelle a look that would have made the Angel Gabriel squirm.

'I have then! I have painted recently.' Insisted Rochelle, a note of panic in her voice.

'Yeah the kitchen ceiling probably.'

'No. Bernard's Porsche. I painted it in love and peace flowers after the last time that I ... Well that we had an argument and I thought it would make him happy but it didn't. He said those days are gone and it is time I grew up.'

'I am right then?' Julia asked with surprise. 'My instincts are so hot lately.'

'Well don't expect miracles,' said Rochelle in a huff. She didn't like this new side to Julia at all. 'Listen, I don't even know which brush to pick up. And as for colour whatever I do comes out looking like mud.'

'Well here you can find your inspiration. Imagine. You can go up on the roof and paint like Baudoin and Chapman did. You could even paint a copy of the Baudoin that Christophe lost and it would be a wonderful present for him.'

'But I can't remember what it looks like.'

'Stop making excuses.'

'I'm not making excuses. I only saw it once, the day Françoise brought it home.'

'I'll get Christophe to send a photo of it over. Come on. Let's go up on the roof and see if we can get through that little trap door that we saw, where Baudoin painted. Maybe he left his paints there and you could even use his own paints and brushes, imagine that.'

They went into Charlene's bedroom and stopped for a moment, staring at the wooden crib.

'I will never understand it' said Rochelle. 'I will never understand why …' Rochelle shook her head, suddenly overcome with emotion.

Maybe I am being a bit hard on her, thought Julia and she rushed over to hug her. 'I know. I agree with Christophe though. I just don't think she would have deliberately killed herself. She was so happy about the baby.'

'She was' said Rochelle, her voice almost a whisper.

'I suppose we ought to pack her things up so that they workmen can get started. But it just doesn't feel right, none of it does. And what will we do with it all? We don't know who her family are, we know nothing.'

Rochelle continued staring down into the crib.

'We could take it to her friends at the commune.' Julia continued. Maybe keeping busy would help. 'They can decide. I have to go there anyway to try and see Stefan. It's one of the jobs Christophe left me to do.'

Rochelle did not reply. Still she did not move.

Julia realised that Rochelle was beginning to fall into the deep pit that Christophe had just emerged from. She watched her friend for a moment, not knowing quite what to do. She had to do something.

'Come on.' She took her friend's hand and manoeuvred her towards the window. 'Let's go and see if we can get that trapdoor open. Even if you don't want to paint, don't you want to go and see what's up there, Madame Chauvenon?'

Rochelle gave a hesitant smile and nodded. Julia climbed out of the window first. She carefully pulled herself up from the dormer window top, using the metal pegs. Just as they reached the top, the white winter sun appeared from behind a cloud, lighting up the countryside and reflecting on the heavy frost that covered the land.

'Look at the light,' exclaimed Rochelle, cheering up immediately.

'Exactly the same time of year as the Chapman painting.' said Julia. 'So beautiful.'

They slid gently down the other side of the roof onto the trap door. It had a chain attached to a hook that was soldered into the very solid metal frame. Julia tried to pull it up by the chain but it was stuck solid. She yanked it harder.

'Julia be careful!' said Rochelle. 'If it suddenly opens, you'll go shooting off the roof. Here, let me have a look.'

Rochelle looked around the sides and found the other end of the metal chain had been passed through two loops and it had been padlocked.

'Zut!' said Rochelle, disappointed. She sat back down dejectedly.

'Why would anyone padlock it?' asked Julia. 'I mean it's not as if anyone is going to nip up here to steal anything is it?'

'Maybe it is not safe?' suggested Rochelle.

'Yes, but the only people clambering around up here would be Petit-Jean and Charlene.'

'Or Yvette?' suggested Rochelle.

'Yvette?' Julia started laughing. 'You think elegant Madame Yvette who hates the Baudoin family would come clambering around up here in her latest designer shoes?'

'Well she might have done, years ago.'

'But the padlock is new and Yvette, she's what? I don't know, hundreds of years old. I know she looks good for her age but do you really think she would come up here?'

'Age is just a number, Julia. You of all people must know this because you hate numbers. I have seen a yoga teacher that is a hundred years old on the internet. She'd easily climb up here.'

'I have a better explanation,' said Julia. 'Maybe it's where Petit-Jean and Charlene kept their stash of dope and other stuff.'

'Dope maybe,' said Rochelle. 'They hadn't been doing hard drugs for years.'

'Hello. Anyone there?' shouted Simon Chapman from below.

He poked his head through the dormer window to look out and then immediately disappeared back inside the bedroom.

'Simon we're on the roof, come on up.' Shouted Julia 'No! I can't!'

'It's easy,' Julia shouted back. There are special pegs you can use to get up.'

'No. Still can't

'Why?'

'Vertigo. Very bad vertigo!'

Julia and Rochelle climbed back down into the room.

Simon was sitting on the bed, his head in his hands, looking extremely pale and he was trembling.

'Yes, sorry about that. It's a family thing. Both grandfather and my father suffered.'

'You don't look good Simon,' said Rochelle.

'I'll be OK in a minute.'

Julia couldn't imagine General Bully-buster Chapman having a phobia about anything.

'So how did the General cope with all that parachuting into war zones?' she asked.

'My father being my father battled it and in his own words he *showed a bit of backbone.*'

'I hate that expression,' said Julia.

'Me too. General Charles Chapman believes a decent Sergeant Major and the proper training could cure a soldier of everything except the pox.'

Julia laughed. 'He's quite a character, your father isn't he?'

'That's one way of putting it. And a pretty awful one most of the time. I'm used to it now so I've given up apologising for him.'

'Well you don't have to apologise to me. Anyway, you are getting a bit of colour back now, poor you.'

'I'm very embarrassed.'

'Don't be. Goodness if you only knew about some of my phobias. I once…'

Rochelle had been watching the exchange with

interest. It was as if she wasn't even in the room. She was feeling a sense of panic, now though. *Mon dieu*, what is Julia going to say?

Seeing the look on Rochelle's face, Julia immediately stopped herself. Whatever was I thinking? I was about to tell him about being frigid after being raped as a teenager. Why in heaven's name would I tell him that?

'You once, what?' asked Simon, his gentle voice belying the intensity of his interest.

'Oh nothing. It's mainly to do with my dyscalculia.'

Rochelle let out a huge sigh of relief.

Good recovery, Julia congratulated herself.

'You know, I panic at the sight of numbers and any kind of calculation. No amount of military training could overcome that I'm sure.'

'Yes, well father's military training didn't solve my problem either. He used to make me stand up on the top of the castle ramparts. I had to stand there looking over the edge for three minutes at a time and if I looked away, he would add another minute. I never managed more than two minutes before I passed out.'

'Simon that's awful!'

'That's my father for you.'

'You've gone very pale again, Simon.'

'Probably not a good idea to relive the standing on the ramparts memories. I'll be fine in a minute.'

'You don't look fine,' said Julia. 'Shall I make you some tea?'

Simon laughed. 'You English and your tea.'

Julia laughed too.

'It works though, it really does.'

'Let's all go down and make the tea together,' said Rochelle, reminding them that she was there. Yes, she definitely had to stay as a chaperone. Julia and Simon's frisson was increasing exponentially. If it got any worse it would reach thunderbolt level that would be a tragedy.

The tea didn't only cure Simon, it cured Rochelle too. She was well out of the doldrums and she had a new mission. Get rid of Simon.

'*Allez, allez,*' she said, chivvying him off back to the château. She'd extracted all the important numbers they would need to get the work done. She had a schedule of the order that the work needed to be done in. She would organise everything and he wouldn't have any excuse to come and chat to Julia. She was well aware that she had made an enemy from the look on his face when he finally left.

'Ok. Let's start at the top of the list and go and buy the things we need.' said Julia.

'Yes, and we'd better make a budget,' said Rochelle.

'No. Not going to happen - numbers.'

'Ah *oui,* I forgot.'

'Anyway, Christophe said to just get on with it. First thing is to pack up Charlene's things and clear their bedroom. That will be your studio for painting, which means you can start straight away.'

Rochelle looked slightly terrified. 'No pressure then,' she mumbled.

Julia carried on with her own express train of thought.

'I vote we get the rubble cleared from the bedrooms, clean up the walls, get the chimney swept and repaint the whole place. Then buy new beds, well new mattresses at least for the bedrooms on the second floor. We need to get a wood delivery as soon as possible. We'll need to buy sofas. We'll leave the kitchen until last.'

Rochelle suddenly felt physically sick. She'd been fine

when she had been concentrating on getting rid of Simon but now she was back in terrified artist and weepy mother mode. She couldn't possibly look at that crib again.

'Rochelle are you listening?'

'Yes, I am. But Julia I can't do it.'

'Why?'

'I don't know. I just can't.'

'Which part can't you do?'

'All of it. Clearing out Charlene's things for a start. I've had four babies, I just can't understand how any woman can do what she did.'

'But she probably didn't Rochelle.'

'Even so, that poor little baby. I only want to be back with my babies, love them, hug them, protect them and never let them go.'

Julia gave her a big hug. 'Sorry, maybe I am being too bossy. Do you want to go back to Nice?'

'No. They're not there, they're all off on the school ski trips anyway.'

'How about if we start with the studio?'

'You're right about that too. It's physical. I get sick when I think about painting. I can't do it. I know I can't. I haven't painted for years. I've got painter's block, the worst kind. It is chronic and terminal.'

'How about I promise you that I won't bully you into going into the studio?'

Rochelle didn't look convinced.

'Well what if I get Francoise to come and help us do the packing up bit?'

Rochelle really shook her head at that one. 'No. Too emotional.'

'What if I do the packing up while you go and organise the wood and get the skip people to take away the rubble? Then you can go to Rennes and decide with Francoise what furniture she wants. By the time you come back, Charlene's room will be an empty studio that only needs artist's materials and an artist.'

Rochelle still looked wary.

'Or...' Julia paused, racking her brains. 'I know. It will be just a blank room with paint stains on the floor and if anybody should just happen to stumble in there with an easel and paints, or wants to paint flowers on the wall, then they can.'

'OK.' Said Rochelle finally convinced and beginning to show some enthusiasm. 'And we can try and remove the padlock and see what is under the roof.'

'Great idea.'

'It's quite late now though,' said Rochelle. 'I won't be able to organise that until tomorrow so I'll probably stay in Rennes with Francoise and come back the day after. How's that?'

'I guess you're right. It is getting dark already.

'Superb!' said Rochelle, jumping up and heading for the door so fast you'd think she was in training for the 'eat and do a runner' Olympics. 'See you'

'See you.'

Great, thought Julia. Why am I always the last woman standing?

Seventeen

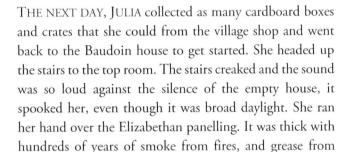

THE NEXT DAY, JULIA collected as many cardboard boxes and crates that she could from the village shop and went back to the Baudoin house to get started. She headed up the stairs to the top room. The stairs creaked and the sound was so loud against the silence of the empty house, it spooked her, even though it was broad daylight. She ran her hand over the Elizabethan panelling. It was thick with hundreds of years of smoke from fires, and grease from cooking that would easily drift upstairs from the open hall below. If only the walls could talk.

She jumped out of her skin when her mobile rang. It was Christophe

'Crikey Christophe, you made me jump out of my skin,'

'Sorry darling. I'm just ringing to check that you're not alone with Simon Chapman.'

'Very funny. And if I say I am, will you come back quicker?'

'Yes.'

'Well then I am. He is just helping me get out of my

work clothes because I spilled all this paint down my cleavage and it made my boobs stick together.'

'I'm on the next plane.'

'Seriously, when are you coming back?'

'Tomorrow, most probably. Denton has got hold of the autopsy reports on both Petit-Jean and Charlene and shown them to a coroner here. The coroner has done a report, questioning the suicide theory, for Charlene at least. He couldn't comment on Petit-Jean. He sent it to Guillemain and after a lot of discussion they finally agreed to open an inquiry into Charlene's death, but not into Petit-Jean's.'

'Well that's something then.'

'Yes, but it won't mean much. I am certain that Guillemain will go a long way out of his way not to find anything. Did you manage to see Stefan yet?'

'No, I'm packing up Charlene's things then heading off to give them to the commune. I thought I'd try and see him then and it wouldn't look so suspicious, me talking to him.'

'Good idea, but don't stay up at the commune, it's a full moon and they are prone to dance naked in the moonlight, even in the depths of winter.'

'Super. I'll take Simon Chapman with me to keep me warm.'

'Warning! Warning!' said Christophe, making the sound of an air raid siren. This is a public green monster alert!'

'Well hurry up back then!'

***

Julia had only just started on the room when there was a loud knock at the door, making her jump out her skin again. One thing she knew for sure, it wasn't going to be

General Chapman because he would have just walked in.

She hopped down the stairs, grateful for an excuse not to have to start going through Charlene and Petit-Jean's things just yet. Maybe she wouldn't go through them. She'd just box them all up without looking.

She opened the door to find a couple of people looking very apprehensive. They were probably from the commune by the look of their boho clothes.

The girl seemed less twitchy than the man. He was looking up and down the street, like he was a lookout for an illegal street trader.

'Stefan said we had to come and give you this,' said the girl pushing a small envelope into Julia's hand.

'Oh, thank you. Come on in,' said Julia. 'Your timing is perfect. I wanted to talk to Stefan. Do you know where he is?'

'Yes, said the girl at the same time as the man said no.

'Please come in.' Julia opened the door wider and stood back to let them through. 'I have things to give him, Charlene's things.'

The girl stepped forward to go in but the man pulled her back.

'No, we don't know where he is.' he said. 'And if we did, we wouldn't be able to tell you. He is very upset. He wants to be on his own and he's gone off on a retreat.'

The girl hesitated as if she wanted to say something more but he grabbed her hand and they both ran off down the street at a speed rarely seen in hippy communities.

Julia closed the door and opened the envelope. Inside was a small key. There was no note nor explanation.

She bet it was for the trap door padlock! She charged over to the stairs in excitement. She'd go on the roof and take a look. Any excuse not to go through Charlene and Petit-Jean's things.

As she got to the stairs she missed her footing on the uneven floorboards and fell flat on her face. She stayed sitting on the floor for a moment while she got over the shock. She'd had years of experience of falling down and knew it was better to wait and assess any damage rather than getting up suddenly. Her knee was bruised but other than that she was OK. Probably not a good idea going up on the roof alone. She looked out of the window at the snow that had started to fall. It would be slippery up there. She would be sensible and wait for Rochelle.

She made her way back up the stairs, very carefully and walked into the bedroom, steeling herself. You must not get emotional about this. You hardly knew her.

She opened a drawer and started to pull out some photos, herbal creams and various other personal items. There were packets of incense sticks, a miniature statue of a Buddha, some South American worry dolls. Julia put them all straight into the first box. She decided it was best not to look at the photos.

Is this it? She thought to herself. Is this what happens to us all? We end up with a few photos, some clothes and a couple of old toys thrown into a box that nobody wants.

She turned around to start on another cupboard and caught sight of the crib. The tears started to fill her eyes. That tiny kick of life. She brushed the tear away and gave herself a good talking to. Just get on with it. People die all the time, yes even babies. They shouldn't but they do. It is probably just hormones making you feel like this. It's body clock, lack of sleep and hormones.

After an exhausting couple of hours, she'd finished. She lugged the boxes down the stairs one by one and stacked them in a free corner of the ground floor hall.

Rochelle had messaged to say that the wood would be delivered tomorrow and the skip people would collect the rubble the day after, and she promised to be back early the next morning to help.

Good of her, but she was probably feeling guilty. She knew damn well she'd left Julia to do the toughest bit on her own. She headed off to the Castle Lodgings. All she wanted to do was sleep and make the sadness disappear.

***

She woke up with cold feet, moved them around in the bed trying to find a piece of Christophe to warm them on, then remembered he was in London. When she leant over to try and work out what time it was, every bone in her body seemed to object to even the tiniest movement. That's what comes from falling and then carrying a load of heavy boxes around on your own.

'OK Google, what time is it?' she asked

'It is ten o'clock in the morning,' replied the Google lady far too happily.

Hell, Christophe had said he landed at ten something and she still had to drive to the airport.

Rochelle walked in just as Julia was leaving.

'Oh heck. Why didn't I think of that Rochelle!'

'What?'

'You could have brought Christophe back with you. I'm going to the airport.'

'Oh no. I've just come from Rennes.'

'That's what I mean.' Julia handed her the keys to the house. 'You'll have to go and wait for the wood delivery.'

'Is it…?' Rochelle hesitated

'Safe?'

Rochelle nodded.

'Don't worry. It's now a full-blown safe zone. It's emotionally sterile. Not a cute thing left anywhere. Everything is boxed up without a single thing poking out that might set you off. It just needs taking up to the commune, if you can find someone to give it to. Stefan seems to have disappeared on some kind of retreat.'

'OK. I'll do that,' she smiled apologetically. 'I'll try and find someone from the commune before I load it all into the car.'

Julia managed to park easily. She rushed into the airport arrivals and looked for London on the monitors. It was showing green as 'landed on time'. Of course, it has, she thought. When you're early they land late, and when you are late, they land early. It is a global confirmation that sod's law is as real as Newton's law of apples falling on people's heads. She'd hated maths classes but now and then there were one or two things that clicked and the image of an apple falling on Newton's head and knocking off his curly wig, was one of them. Sod's law she'd learnt by first-hand experience. She charged to the arrival gate and stopped dead in her tracks.

Inspector Guillemain was standing in front of Christophe and he had three armed gendarmes with him as back up. What the ..?

She rushed over to Christophe and he hugged her tightly.

'Hello darling. I am very popular today, look at all these people that have come to welcome me back.'

'Christophe what's going on?'

'Monsieur de Flaubert is a suspect and wanted for questioning over the death of Charlene Madec,' said Inspector Guillemain.

Julia couldn't help herself. She could try and put it down to being overtired, tetchy and sore from her fall, but it wasn't that at all. She was furious with Guillemain. She turned on him, and thrust her face right up to his.

'What the hell is wrong with you?!!!'

Guillemain was so shocked he looked almost scared.

'You've got such a bloody chip on your shoulder,' Julia continued. 'Why the hell are you running around trying to pin every unsolved crime in the whole of France on my husband?'

Christophe was torn between feeling ecstatic that she had referred to him as her husband and wincing at the fury in her voice. Julia's eyes didn't often turn combat green these days but he could see a whole platoon in there.

'Julia …' he said.

'Don't interrupt me please Christophe. Well Guillemain what do you have to say for yourself?

Guillemain stared back at Julia, lost for words for a second.

She noticed his jugular was pulsating and she really hoped he might be having a medical emergency and would have to be loaded head first into an ambulance.

Guillemain carefully took out his notepad and pen.

'If you have a husband that you haven't told us about and if he is a possible suspect in the murder of Charlene Madec, *Mademoiselle* Connors…' he said, putting heavy emphasis on the Mademoiselle. '… I'd dearly like his name. If not …' He snapped his notepad shut for dramatic effect. 'I suggest you calm down otherwise you will find yourself arrested for assaulting a police officer in the execution of his duty.'

Julia was sure she saw one of the gendarmes raise his eyes to the heavens.

'That's a joke, Guillemain, right?' said Christophe, laughing in disbelief. Then he remembered that Guillemain had never had a sense of humour. He turned to Julia.

'Sweetheart, don't worry. Inspector Guillemain was born with EHD, you'll have to forgive him.'

'What's that?' snapped Julia, still glaring at Guillemain.

'Extreme humour deficit, my darling. It's a terribly sad condition, difficult for him to live with and very hard for him to make friends, you need to show a little sympathy for him.' He winked at her and was relieved to see the combat green of her eyes dissipating into gentle turquoise pools. 'Now, could you let Bernard know that Inspector Guillemain has arrested me *yet again* and if you want to throw Police harassment into the conversation, while you are at it, feel free.' He blew her a kiss as they led him off.

Eighteen

BERNARD HOPPED ON THE first flight from Nice to Rennes and headed straight for the Gendarmerie. He could have done without this. He had so many cases he was trying to clear up before Christmas, not to mention getting extra Christmas visiting rights for the families of people serving time in prison.

Christophe pottered around his cell, refusing to speak to anybody until Bernard got there, not because he couldn't handle it himself, but because he knew it would really rile Inspector Guillemain. He spent the six hours in the police cell reading and when he felt the need to up the irritation factor, he asked for food, a coffee, lots of bathroom breaks, and a change of cell because the one he was in was making him sneeze and he decided he was most probably allergic to the police.

After many hours of this torment, Guillemain finally cracked and went to see Christophe.

'You seem to think this all a big game de Flaubert. I can assure you it is not.'

'Guillemain. I did not start this game and I certainly did not ask to play it.'

'No but you finished it. You finished it by killing Charlene Madec!'

'Do you realise how ridiculous you sound Guillemain? I was the one that got Inspector Denton involved in looking at the autopsy report and suggested that it might not have been suicide. Why the hell would I do that if I murdered her?'

'Because you were bluffing and that failed dismally. Because, given our mutual dislike and your arrogance, you thought that I would refuse to listen to or act on anything that you said.'

'Good God Guillemain, isn't it time you took a chisel to that log on your shoulder? They all tell me you are an excellent detective, but you hide it extremely well when I'm around.'

'I'm guessing you also thought that my starting the enquiry at your instigation, would bode well for your defence. And let's face it, you've got form when it comes to hurting women, haven't you?'

'Don't answer that,' said Bernard, arriving at the cell. 'Let's head for the interview room, shall we? And we can make this all official.'

They went into the room which was stark, painted in a bland grey gloss with one large blacked out observation window at one end and a grey desk in the middle. There was a webcam up in the corner. Guillemain sat one side of the desk and Christophe and Bernard sat the other side.

'Just for the record. I will be filing police harassment charges against you if this turns out to be another case of you taking two plus two and making two hundred and two, Inspector Guillemain.' said Bernard.

'Of course. I would expect no less from a good lawyer, Mr Chauvenon.' Replied Guillemain, not in the least phased.

Bernard and Christophe looked at each other surprised.

'And the alleged crime?' asked Bernard.

'The autopsy shows that Charlene had indeed taken tranquillizers, but not enough to commit suicide. The residue in the stomach indicated that it was a very low dose of diazepam, just enough to sleep. She therefore must have been given or also injected herself with a lethal dose of intravenous tranquilisers.'

'Yes, all of which we know from Denton's second opinion on the coroner's report. A report that my client requested. How is this relevant to my client?' asked Bernard.

'All in good time. Mr Chauvenon,' said Inspector Guillemain, savouring the tang of whatever bitter morsel he had on Christophe. 'Can you tell us exactly what happened on the night of the nineteenth please de Flaubert?'

Christophe sighed to himself. Why was Guillemain being such an idiot? Well he'd been there six hours. Only another eighteen to go. Might as well enjoy himself a little at Guillemain's expense.

'Well, Julia and I were in the bath together, enjoying a glass of wine. It was rather a good chilled P*ouilly fumé* I think. One that we'd found in that little delicatessen they've opened down by the *marché* in Rennes. Have you ever been there?' he asked Guillemain.

'No.' replied Guillemain tersely.

'You should go there, really, they have some truly wonderful wines at very reasonable prices.' Christophe hesitated while he thought a little more. 'Yes, I think we also bought a burgundy and a couple of nice clarets. Julia usually prefers a chilled white when we're in the bath together but we prefer a spicy red burgundy when it's cold outside and we are cuddled up naked in front of a roaring fire…'

'And?' interrupted Guillemain impatiently.

Christophe noticed his face was turning the colour of Côte de Provence rosé. Excellent, he thought, I wonder if I can get him to turn full bodied claret.

'Christophe,' said Bernard, giving a gentle warning.

'Oh Yes. So, there we were, relaxing. She gave me an aromatherapy back massage with, let me see, I think it was jasmine oil.' He frowned slightly, over acting being deep in thought. 'Hum, or no maybe it was lavender. Yes it was probably lavender, because Julia says jasmine is an aphrodisiac, and we certainly don't need that! Yes, it was probably lavender because that helps you to relax and after all that ridiculous business of being holed up in the police station for hours, I really did need a nice romantic, relaxing bath with Julia.' He sighed dramatically. 'She is such a darling, isn't she Bernard?'

Bernard nodded but looked slightly nonplussed. What the hell was Christophe playing at?

'Beautiful too, but there is so much more to her than that. She really isn't just a pretty face. She has an interesting rather unusual way of looking at things. She always comes up with the unexpected and follows her gut reaction and do you know, she's invariably right. It's quite something to behold. For example, she really doesn't like you Guillemain.'

Bernard put his hand up to his head in despair.

'Fortunately, I don't really care about what people think of me,' said Guillemain tartly.

'As you say, that's extremely fortunate,' said Christophe, nodding.

'Get on with it de Flaubert. What happened?'

'Well, there we were chatting about how awful it must be for people who haven't found the love of their life yet. Or maybe they have but the love of their life doesn't love them back. Are you married, Inspector Guillemain?'

'I will not answer that,' said Guillemain, the irritation clear in his voice.

'I think you need to make a note Bernard, that Inspector Guillemain is refusing to answer my questions.' said Christophe, very pleased that Guillemain's complexion had moved on to a pleasant pinot noir.

'Get on with it de Flaubert!' said Guillemain.

'Yes,' sighed Christophe. 'Now, where was I? Oh yes, in the bath with my adorable darling Julia. So, we were laughing and joking and I was quite tired but you know how it is, sometimes you just see that look in their eyes and suddenly you're no longer tired at all. Well a certain part of your anatomy isn't anyway.' Christophe winked at Guillemain. 'And well then she thought I'd put my foot somewhere, but in actual fact it wasn't my foot.'

Bernard looked at Christophe with raised eyebrows. 'For goodness sake, Christophe,' he muttered, irritated. Why did Christophe always insist on riling Guillemain? It was no help whatsoever.

'Oh sorry. I was getting lost in the moment. That's what tends to happen when you have a strong, loving, CARING relationship.' Christophe said. 'But of course, you wouldn't know that, would you Guillemain?'

Ka-ching, thought Christophe. Nailed it. Full bodied claret.

'Get to the point de Flaubert!' said Guillemain.

'Why? We've got plenty of time, haven't we? Eight hours of interrogation and another eighteen to make up the full twenty-four before you have to let me go.'

Bernard was now completely exasperated. He wanted to know exactly what Guillemain had or hadn't got on Christophe and then get out of there. If he was defending someone who may have been guilty, he could understand this holding out until the full twenty-four hours were up, but he knew Christophe was innocent. He decided to take matters into his own hands.

'Perhaps, Inspector Guillemain, if you were to ask a more direct question, we may be able to proceed.'

Christophe threw Bernard a crestfallen look that reminded Bernard of school days when you managed to tackle him and bring him down in a rugby match, just before he could have scored a try. Bernard found it hard to keep a straight face.

'What made you leave the Castle Lodgings and go to see Charlene Madec?' asked Guillemain.

Bernard, having regained his professional composure, gave Christophe his serious lawyer look and nodded that Christophe was to answer.

'Well there was a loud bang on the door – we were still in the bath you understand. Stefan from the commune was arguing with the Castle Lodgings manager. He said Charlene was ill and she'd sent him to get me.'

'Why you? Why not a doctor?'

'He said that Charlene had said to get me first then a doctor. He was very upset because he wanted to get the doctor first but Charlene had insisted. I suggest you verify it with him.'

'Well we would but he has mysteriously disappeared.'

'Oh?' said Bernard. 'I presume you are actually looking for him?'

'Yes, of course we are.'

'That's a relief! Christophe exclaimed. 'I'm a bit surprised that you haven't found him already though,' said Christophe. 'I would have thought even the worst detective in the world could find a seven-foot tall man wearing a multi-coloured coat and a pointed hat, in a small village. He does rather stand out.' said Christophe.

This time Bernard glared at Christophe.

Christophe smiled, feigning innocence.

Bernard switched to serious mode. 'A young woman has tragically lost her life and her child,' he said, looking from Christophe to Guillemain and back again. 'Carrying the child of a good friend. A mutual friend to both of you. It's time to stop these ridiculous schoolboy antics.' Guillemain and Christophe looked at each other and nodded in agreement.

'What happened next?' asked Guillemain.

'I asked Julia to ring the doctor and told Stefan to stay with her until the doctor arrived so that he could show them the way. I got dressed and ran along the back field path to Charlene's caravan.'

'When you got there, was there anybody else there?'

'No, they'd all gone up to the Peaks for the winter solstice.'

'And nobody saw you?'

'Not that I know of.'

'And you didn't see anyone else near the caravan?'

'No.'

'What did you do when you got there?'

'I went straight into the caravan.'

'Was the door open or shut?'

'Open and there was a camp fire burning outside.'

'And when you got inside?'

'Charlene was lying on the bunk. Her eyes were closed

and I looked for a pulse and couldn't find one. She felt cold. I thought she was dead. I pulled a blanket around her and then Julia and the doctor arrived with Stefan.

'Then what happened?'

'The doctor said there was a pulse and that we had to get her to the hospital quickly. He said one of us should drive and he would do what he could for Charlene in the back. We were deciding who was going to drive, that's when we realised Stefan had disappeared.'

'I see. He just disappeared? Without saying anything?'

'Yes.'

'Which way did he go?'

'I don't know, none of us do.'

'And the doctor and Miss Connors can verify that.'

'Yes'

'How long would you say you were alone with Charlene?'

'I don't know… not long I suppose, minutes rather than hours. I don't know, a maximum of fifteen minutes.'

'But long enough to administer a lethal injection?'

Christophe glared at Guillemain.

'What? Are you out of your mind? I only went there because Stefan asked me to.'

'And he has disappeared.'

'Find him then,' said Christophe. 'Do your bloody job.'

'I am de Flaubert. I am doing my job. We went back to Charlene Madec's caravan with the forensics team,' said Guillemain.

'Good' said Christophe.

'Did you touch anything in the caravan de Flaubert?'

'Well apart from the blanket from the bed. I can't really remember. I was very upset.'

'I see,' nodded Guillemain. 'You touched nothing else, no hairbrush, no pots, no bottles, no clothes, towels ...'

'Not that I remember,' said Christophe.

'I see. Can you explain why your fingerprints are on the small bottle that contained the intravenous tranquiliser concentrate?'

'What?!!'

'Yes. Your prints are on the small bottle that the liquid tranquiliser was in.'

'That's impossible!'

'Maybe you touched it when you were there, but don't remember doing it?' suggested Bernard, his voice immensely calm considering the bombshell that Guillemain had just dropped.

'I suppose so, but no, I don't remember touching anything.'

'That bottle had been used previously for shampoo and contained a slight trace of that shampoo. What shampoo do you use de Flaubert?'

'I don't know. Nothing specific when I'm travelling. I use the ones that they put in the hotel or give us on the plane.'

'I see. Do you travel on British Airways?'

'Sometimes I do, yes.'

'Recently?'

'Yes. After I took the private jet to New York last week, I flew back on British Airways.'

'Well that bottle was a British Airways shampoo bottle.'

'This is ridiculous,' said Christophe. 'You cannot be serious.' said Christophe, shocked. 'You cannot seriously think that I did this?'

'I am very serious de Flaubert. You had motive,

opportunity, and your prints are on the nearest thing we have to a murder weapon.'

'Motive? What motive?'

'You wanted to sell the supposedly stolen Chapman to a private art collector. We have records of you contacting people who deal in stolen artwork. You contacted them from London the day after the paintings had been stolen. From outside the restaurant...' Guillemain paused to check his notes, 'Clarke's Restaurant.'

'What? I was putting feelers out to see if we could find who had organised the theft.'

'We have only your word for that. I think you organised the theft to get both the insurance money and the money from selling it to a private collector. I also think you refused to give Charlene her share once we found the painting and that you killed her to make it look like suicide. There's your motive and your weapon is obvious.

'Anybody could have put that shampoo bottle there, Guillemain,' said Bernard.

'That shampoo bottle also contained a couple of hairs that gave us a small amount of DNA. Would you be willing to submit to a DNA test?' Guillemain asked Christophe.

Bernard looked at Guillemain. He gave him a professional smile, drawing Guillemain's attention whilst he weighed up both him and the situation. It was obviously a set up, but how and why? He took in Guillemain fiddling with his pen. Even though he was sure of his ground on the bottle, something else was making Guillemain a little nervous.

'No!' said Bernard, quickly. 'My client will not submit a DNA test at this point in time.'

Christophe looked at Bernard, thoroughly confused.

'Why?' asked Christophe.

'Just no,' said Bernard. 'I'll explain later.'

Guillemain looked furious.

'Christophe de Flaubert I am keeping you in custody as the prime suspect in the murder of Charlene Madec. We will be requesting a court order for a DNA sample, and you will be remanded in custody until a court decides on whether to proceed with a prosecution.'

Nineteen

~~~

JULIA WANDERED LISTLESSLY AROUND the Baudoin house. She hated Guillemain. She hated being alone in this place. Maybe Yvette was right about the Baudoin family and maybe it was this house too. She shivered slightly. Maybe it was cursed with misfortune just like them. But she'd never felt that. When she'd first come here and gone into Charlene and Petit-Jean's room, that's not what she'd felt at all. She'd felt sadness that such happiness had been cut so short by Petit-Jean's death.

She hated waiting to find out what was going on. Bernard had been there for ages which was not a good sign at all. He'd called Rochelle quickly to ask her to get some things for him to set up an office at the Castle Lodgings, but hadn't said anything else. Not a good sign at all if he needed to set up an office. Maybe she should have gone to Rennes to help Rochelle get the things Bernard said he needed but she just couldn't face it. She knew Rochelle would chatter away, trying to convince her that everything was alright but deep in her solar plexus Julia knew it wasn't. She looked at the house that was crumbling around her.

She'd got to do something to keep herself busy otherwise she'd go crazy. Her eye caught the envelope with the key in it.

Yes. That must be important, and even more so now, otherwise why would Stefan have sent it to them?

She pushed the key into her pocket and walked upstairs. She heaved open the heavy window in Charlene's room. It had been sleeting and the guttering was still damp. She didn't care if it was dangerous, she wanted to see what was in that room, she wanted to take her mind off everything.

She climbed up holding on carefully to the slippery pegs. It was even windier once she got on the top. The gale seemed to be being corralled by the narrow streets and gusting violently. Maybe this was not a good idea. What the hell, she was up there now.

She lay down as flat as she could to stop herself being blown about by the wind. She gazed out across the village to the hills and river beyond. The trees bent over horizontally with each gust. The sky was a depressing dark grey, the kind of grey that seems to make all living things disappear against the sky and the earth.

The sleet was turning to heavy rain. She carefully rolled down into the dip where the trap door was and propped herself up on her left arm and elbow so that she could get the key out of her pocket. Moving forward, carefully on her forearms, she put the key into the padlock and tried to turn it, but nothing. She took the key out and tried to see if it would go in the other way, but again, nothing. She put it into the padlock the other way again and wiggled it furiously. Again nothing.

'Bloody hell,' she couldn't believe it. It had to be for that, surely? She tried again, but nothing. She lay in the dip in the rain, staring up at the dark grey sky. The clouds seemed to be moving at a furious pace. She felt miserable, frustrated and angry. She sat up determinedly. I will get that padlock off if it's the last thing I do. She thought she'd seen a saw in with some of the work materials downstairs. Maybe she could cut through the padlock chain with that. She put the key back in her pocket and carefully crawled up the side of the dip, so that she could ease herself over and get her feet on the pegs. The sleet and rain had made the pegs even more slippery. She got down as far as she could and then very carefully sat on the edge of the window with her feet pointing into the room whilst she held on to the top of the window overhang. Suddenly a huge gust of wind caught her and she felt herself being thrown sideways, she lost her grip on the top of the window and fell backwards.

As her head hit the wall below the window, she felt as if she was in slow motion. So, this is how it ends. Julia Connors rags to riches, one time socialite dies falling off a mediaeval roof top in Brittany and is cremated in a very unbecoming shroud.'

She felt strong hands on her feet, yanking her back through the window. The window frame grazed her back and she hit her head on the brick surround as she was dragged into safety. She fell forwards and landed on top of Simon Chapman on the floor.

'Christ Julia!' said Simon, as they lay there in a state of shock. 'Are you alright?' he asked as she rolled over to the side and put her hand to her head. It was bleeding slightly. He stood up and helped her to her feet.

'Julia. What in heaven's name were you thinking?'

'I don't know. I just wanted to help Christophe.'

'By throwing yourself off the roof?'

'No... I ... I've got this key and I thought it might open the padlock on the roof trap door.'

Simon grabbed a towel that was on the bed.

'Look at you, you're soaked to the skin, and your head is bleeding.' He handed her the towel.

'Have you heard?' she asked. 'I expect the whole village knows he's being accused.'

'Yes. I'm afraid they do.'

'You know he's innocent don't you, Simon?'

'Of course, I do. I'm sure it has all been a huge mistake. I thoroughly regret even involving Guillemain in London now. It's such a mess.'

'I haven't even been able to see him since they arrested him.'

'Well I think I can help there,' he said. 'Grab your coat and let's go.'

She gave him a big hug and kissed him on the cheek.

'Thank you so much Simon.'

'For what? Taking you to see Christophe or saving your life?'

***

It was impossible to park in front of the Gendarmerie because a huge crowd had gathered. Simon parked on the pavement a couple of streets away and they went on foot. It was now snowing again and had started to settle. The village was turning white.

Barricades had been put up around the entrance of the Gendarmerie with two local police there to control the crowd. It was made up of a few local people and a huge pack of paparazzi.

'Why are there so many people here?' asked Julia. 'This is ridiculous.'

'I don't know, said Simon. 'Maybe something else has happened?'

'We're here to see Christophe, said Simon to one of the local policemen. What the hell is going on?'

Before he could reply the doors opened and Sophie Petrarch stepped out. The barrage of TV reporters lurched forwards. The TF1 reporter got there first and pushed his microphone under Sophie's nose.

'Sophie, can you tell us what is happening?'

'As you know, I have a great fondness for Pont Carnac. I spent much of my youth here and have many friends here. Unfortunately, one of those friends has been accused of a serious crime and I am here to support him in any way I can.'

'Do you think he did it, Sophie?' asked one reporter

'No, I don't. I know him well and I will be giving a character reference for him in court. I'm sorry I can't say any more than that.'

As Sophie turned to leave, Simon led Julia over to her.

'Simon,' she said, giving him an air kiss so that it didn't spoil her makeup. 'This is awful isn't it?' 'Hello, Julia, isn't it?' she said smiling.

Julia nodded, taking in the beautiful face that was perfectly framed by the fake fur hood of her coat. You had to admire her, she never got it wrong. Always gave the right image for every occasion.

'It is so good of you to come and be so supportive of him,' said Simon, kissing her hands over enthusiastically. 'You really are wonderful.' Again, lots of flashbulbs went off as the press zoomed in on the trio.'

'He's holding up, I think,' said Sophie, playing to the gallery. 'I took him a hamper of goodies, I hear he's not been eating very well.' she smiled slyly in Julia's direction.

'So, I'm doing my best to feed and cheer him up.'

'I was just taking Julia in to see him. She hasn't seen him since he was arrested.'

'Oh,' said Sophie. 'That's so sad, Julia. I think his break is over and they've just taken him back in for questioning.' She took Julia's hand in hers and gave her a fake look of concern. She then moved Julia's hair slightly to look at the cut and bruise that was developing. 'Oh dear, what have you done?'

'She was trying to throw herself off the roof of the Baudoin house,' said Simon.

'Goodness.' She patted Julia's hand again. 'I know it's awful being in love with Christophe, especially when it all starts to fizzle out. He's not worth getting suicidal over, though, really he isn't, Julia. No man is.'

'She's right you know,' said Simon, smirking slightly. Then he took pity on Julia. 'Look she wasn't committing suicide Sophie, she was on the roof looking for something.'

'You can believe that if you want Simon, but you know how women get over Christophe. It wouldn't be the first time.'

'Seriously!' said Julia. 'I was up on the roof with a key trying to…'

'She was just messing about, Sophie, honestly. 'Simon interrupted quickly. 'She's a bit of a wild child underneath.'

Sophie sighed dramatically. Then lowered her voice. 'Well I don't think you should go and see Christophe looking like that. We don't want Guillemain thinking Christophe has been beating you. It wouldn't do his cause any good at all.'

And you would know all about that, thought Julia. She turned on her heel and stormed off. She was right, though. That was what was so annoying. Sophie Petrarch was right.

Twenty

INSPECTOR DENTON, BUSTLED INTO the room at the Castle Lodgings. He was very out of breath.

'It's nice to see you again Miss Connors, but sadly in such circumstances. Just to bring you all up to date.' He sat down and placed his briefcase on the table. 'I am no longer the lead detective in this case as it is now a murder investigation.

'Oh, no!' said Julia, unable to hide her disappointment.

'It is now under Inspector Guillemain's charge.'

Julia put her head in her hands. Her hopes had been pinned on Denton being able to sort it out.

'However. Mr Chauvenon contacted me and asked if I could come over and share some of my knowledge with you and help you build your case.'

'Oh. I am so glad Inspector Denton.'

'You are very welcome, Miss Connors. Even though I am not the lead investigator on the case I do have the authority to be involved in anything that may relate to the paintings. I have only been able to achieve that by making the Baudoin still registered as a stolen painting and by keeping the Chapman under the control of the British fraud squad as evidence. So, I'm afraid, theoretically, Mr de Flaubert is still going to have to be investigated for insurance fraud.'

'Oh,' said Julia. 'Well I suppose that is the least of our worries.

'It's Okay Julia. It's only been done to keep Inspector Denton here because it will make life easier for our investigation.'

'Basically, you will need to flash an authoritative badge to access information,' said Inspector Denton.

Julia smiled gratefully at Denton. 'Isn't that going to make things difficult for you Inspector if you are working with us?'

'Probably, given Inspector Guillemain's strict character, but it is not illegal. And what is important to me, Miss Connors, is the truth.'

'Very well said, Inspector.'

'Okay,' said Bernard. 'I have advised Christophe not to give a DNA sample at this point.'

'But won't that prejudice his case?' asked Julia. 'Isn't that like saying I'm too scared to because I'm guilty.'

'In theory, yes. But, Christophe has obviously been set up here, and if his prints match, you can bet your bottom dollar the DNA will match too. I know that Guillemain is very diligent and usually sticks to the letter of the law, but for some reason, where Christophe is concerned, he does seem to be on a bit of a mission. From the smug look on his face yesterday, I think he may have run Christophe's DNA immediately.'

'But where would he have got it?'

'He could have got it from anything in the police

station, a cup he drank from, a fork after he'd eaten, a tissue he sneezed in.'

'And running it without authorisation means it is not only inadmissible, but also could be used to show that Guillemain is guilty of professional misconduct and police harassment' said Bernard. 'If we decide to go down that route.'

'Good point,' said Denton.

'And if I'm wrong and he hasn't already run the DNA, then we have lost nothing.' Bernard added.

'If you give me the details of the nearest DNA processing lab, I'll check it out using my British police authority. Guillemain would not be stupid enough to use the police lab.'

'I am so relieved that he has you, Bernard, and you too Inspector Denton.'

'I'll need to head off to be with Christophe during the next lot of questioning, soon. It will probably be a hard push to try and get a confession. Given that it's Guillemain versus Christophe and that Christophe is doing his utmost to rile Guillemain, I suggest you don't wait up for me Rochelle.'

'Oh Bernard. This is awful, poor Christophe.'

'Don't worry. We can get this sorted,' he said. 'I've had worse cases. And they really don't have much to go on for the moment. Before I go, Inspector Denton is going to give us some advice on how we go about investigating this and tracking down anything that will help our case.'

'Now then,' said Inspector Denton. He stood up, moved over to the white boards that they'd set up and picked up a pen. 'Firstly, I'd like to say that I think this is a ridiculous accusation on the part of Inspector Guillemain. It was Mr de Flaubert who suggested that the verdict of accidental suicide was wrong and the case should be reopened. Why would he do that, if he was implicated?'

'Exactly,' said Bernard.

'I also think that you now need to change the way that you are looking at this,' said Inspector Denton. 'You've - well all of us, in fact - we have been focusing on trying to understand and prove that Petit-Jean and Charlene, 'did' in my case, and 'did not' in your case, steal the paintings. What you now have to do is look for a reason why someone would want the paintings and why they might also want Petit-Jean and Charlene dead, because that is where it all started, with the paintings.'

'Agreed,' said Bernard. 'And we should also think about why someone might want to pin it all on Christophe.'

'My money's on Guillemain for that!' said Julia, folding her arms crossly.

'I'm sorry I cannot comment on that except to say that whatever your dislike of him, he has an impeccable track record.' Said Inspector Denton. 'But I agree he is making it personal.'

Bernard had stood up and was pacing the floor. His eyes flitted to and fro as his legal mind organised his thoughts. He stopped pacing, sat down and leant his arms on the table.

'Or,' he said. 'What if the target has always been Christophe? And the paintings, Charlene and Petit-Jean were just a means to an end.'

'They were just a means to an end, or collateral damage?' asked Denton.

'Yes,' said Bernard.

'Well if that is the case, I would suggest that whoever it is would have to have a serious grudge against Mr de Flaubert. They would also have to know him very well and have a lot of financial clout to pull this off. So, who would want to get at Mr de Flaubert?' Asked Inspector Denton. 'Does he have any enemies?'

'Well there's his half-brother Jaime Girault,' said Bernard.

'And Girault's sister, Cassandra,' added Rochelle.

'Christophe and Julia were both responsible for them getting accused in the Moreno drug cartel case,' said Bernard. 'She disappeared, but he was caught. Christophe smuggled him back from South America and he was taken into custody but then he escaped. No one has seen either of them since.'

'There's the rest of the Moreno family too,' Rochelle added. 'They weren't happy at all.'

'Good Lord!,' said Inspector Denton wide eyed. 'Usually when I ask that question people have great difficulty in thinking of anybody at all, let alone major drug cartels. I wonder why I wasn't told of this. Inspecteur Guillemain didn't say anything.'

'He won't know about it,' said Bernard. 'It was an undercover operation run by the police down in Provence. Jacques Morell was in charge, I'll give him a call, and see if there has been any developments on that front.'

'Are you sure he'd tell you, if it's undercover?' asked Inspector Denton.

'I hope so,' Bernard was thoughtful. 'He's a friend of Christophe's.'

'He is the person Christophe called to ask about people that he could approach when the paintings were stolen.' Julia added.

'Ah. Yes. Giving more information that led to Inspector Gillemain's art theft theory. ' said Denton. He turned to the first board and wrote a title, 'List of Suspects.'

'I'll be honest, framing Christophe is not really drug cartel style. They would just send someone to execute him after torturing him first.'

Julia gasped, putting her hand over her mouth. Denton turned around quickly.

'Oh. My apologies, Miss Connors. Don't worry I'm sure if that was going to happen, they would already have done it.'

'That doesn't make me feel any better, Inspector.' said Julia, shaking her head in despair.

'Nor me,' said Rochelle.

'It may not be drug cartel style, but it could be Girault's style,' said Bernard. He had never been given the full details of what had happened to Julia. 'He's a bit of a coward underneath. He wouldn't go for the brutality and torture, too squeamish, isn't he Julia?' asked Bernard.

Julia's mind drifted back to the time that Jaime Girault had caught her spying for Jacques and Christophe. A beam of sunshine flickered through the window. It should have made her feel better rather than anxious, but it didn't because it hit the mirror and started flickering. She watched it, mesmerised, as if she was being hypnotised. It reminded her of something. The glint of the silver foil when someone holds a flame underneath it. She started trembling. When someone is burning crack. She was no longer in the room. She was back at Chateau Lacoste. She could see Girault's henchman Hernandez. She could smell the smoke rising from the burning crack, she could feel the weight of Hernandez on top of her. She saw the ecstasy on Jaime Girault's face as he watched Hernandez ripping her clothes and she heard her own screams.'

In the distance someone called her name, but it was so far away.

'No, no,' she was shouting and pulling at her clothes to cover herself.

Inspector Denton, jumped up and grabbed a bottle of aftershave and sprayed a little in front of Julia's nose.

Julia glanced around in shock then realised where she was.

'Are you alright?' asked Denton.

'What the hell just happened?' asked Rochelle.

'Miss Connors is what we call a Super Recogniser, it's like having a photographic memory. Some people have it for faces but Miss Connors also has it for events, she runs it like a film, seeing and feeling every detail.'

'Oh Julia!' said Rochelle, reaching out a hand to reassure her. 'That must have been terrifying.'

'And the aftershave?' asked Bernard.

'Smells are a much bigger trigger of memories than most people realise, so a sudden change of smell to one associated with a good memory can help break the trance.'

'Christophe's aftershave,' said Julia, smiling. 'I usually carry it in my pocket when he is away. 'Sorry everyone, that just came out of nowhere. I thought I had all that under control now.'

'Well I think you have your answer to your question Mr Chauvenon. The cartel style is indeed Jaime Girault's style.'

'Does anybody want a cup of tea?' asked Julia. She felt very shaky. 'I think I need a cup of tea.'

Rochelle smiled to herself. She loved that Englishness about Julia, tea to her was like chocolate against dementors.

'I'll make it Julia.' She stood up and put the kettle on. I'll get you some chocolate too?'

'Do you feel ready to go on?' Inspector Denton asked Julia.

Julia nodded. 'Yes of course. It's important we get on with it and I wouldn't completely rule out Jaime Girault and Cassandra, the hatred runs very deep indeed. They like to take their revenge and serve it cold. She is prepared to put a lot of time into getting that revenge.'

'Anything else a bit closer to home? asked Denton, hopefully He had no desire to get embroiled in a drug cartel case so late in his career. 'What about this feud with Petit-Jean that remains unexplained. Miss Connors?'

Julia hesitated. 'I can't say on that one. Well I can say one thing but I don't think it's related. Christophe said it wasn't.'

'I think it is extremely important Miss Connors,' he turned to Bernard and Rochelle in turn. 'Mr and Mrs Chauvenon, that everyone mentions absolutely anything they know about Petit-Jean and Christophe's past. However small a detail it might be.'

Julia took a deep breath. 'Well this is what Christophe said.'

Rochelle looked wide eyed and shook her head at Julia.

'Rochelle! Christophe may be charged with murder. This is no time for secrets!'

'What's the point if it is not relevant?' insisted Rochelle.

'We don't know if it is relevant or not until it's out in the open.

'Please continue Miss Connors.' Denton said encouragingly.

'When they were young they would hang out in Pont Carnac. One night they all got high but Petit-Jean and his girlfriend Sophie took more than just dope.'

Rochelle looked upset.

'Sophie had been having flings with Christophe and Petit-Jean. Sophie and Petit-Jean went off and collected magic mushrooms, and were eating them on the way back. Some weren't the right ones, and maybe they were more poisonous. Things went wrong and they started hallucinating. Petit-Jean saw Sophie as a snake or something that was attacking him and he started fighting her, hitting her. Christophe and the others didn't do mushrooms and were clear headed enough to pull Petit-Jean off and get him away, but the police had been called. Petit-Jean had already been in a lot of trouble. Sophie accused him but she couldn't remember properly and Christophe took the blame saying it was him. He thought because Sophie was more interested in him at the time, she would drop the charges and she did.'

Bernard and Rochelle both looked shocked.

'He never told me!' said Bernard. 'All these years we thought it was Christophe who lost it. We weren't there that day but we all heard about it.'

'We should have known better, Bernard. We should have known it was Petit-Jean and not Christophe.' said Rochelle.

'Ah, said Inspector Denton. I am assuming that that is the reason behind Inspector Guillemain's accusation of Mr de Flaubert having been violent with women in the past.'

'Has he accused him of that?' asked Bernard. 'That is harassment because nothing was ever proven and the charges were dropped.'

'I agree,' said Inspector Denton. 'It's something to keep in mind in Mr de Flaubert's defence. Now, the girlfriend. Do you think the girlfriend could have found out? Was she a violent person herself, maybe she wants revenge? Just a thought.'

'I doubt it,' said Rochelle. 'It's not just any Sophie, it's Sophie Petrarch, the actress and she's had more than enough drama in her life both on and off screen.'

'She's also very keen on keeping her private life very private indeed,' said Bernard. 'She certainly wouldn't want to rake up the past.'

'Well that could be a motive.' said Denton, adding her name to the list. What if they were raking up the past, Petit-Jean and Charlene?' asked inspector Denton. What if as part of their new life together they wanted to make amends for the past. I am certain she would not want all of that coming out in the press. Perhaps that's what Petit-Jean wanted to talk to Mr de Flaubert about?'

'Possibly,' said Bernard. 'Although I don't believe for a minute she would resort to murder. I don't think she can even be placed in the area. 'She came for Petit-Jean's funeral but then she went back to London, didn't she, Rochelle?'

'She didn't,' said Julia quietly. 'She was there at the Gendarmerie yesterday when I went to see Christophe. She was offering to post the bail money and save him. I'm sure it will be all over the press by now.'

'That is extremely unfortunate,' said Inspector Denton. 'It means our investigations will be seriously hampered by interest from the press.'

Twenty-One

'WE ARE GOING TO have to find somewhere else to use as our operational base,' said Bernard. He was sweating as he arrived back at the Castle Lodgings office. 'Somewhere with gates that close so the press cannot get in. And not in a hotel, where they are waiting in the corridor like a pack of velociraptors, the moment you step through the door.'

'These lodgings are not ideal but for the moment I think they will have to do,' said Inspector Denton. 'If we try and move now, it will be even worse and at least here there is a reception that's manned twenty four hours a day.'

'I suppose so.' But if we are keeping this as our base, it has to have foolproof security. Everything here is for our eyes and ears only.' He gave Rochelle a meaningful look. 'Nobody comes in or out apart from us. It must be kept locked.' He walked over andrew the black out curtains. 'Keep these closed at all times. We don't want anyone poking a telescopic lens at the window. Someone will have to be here when the cleaners do the rooms.'

'I'll get all the spare keys that they have for this room from reception.' said Denton. He walked over to the desk and picked up a couple of marker pens. 'Madame Chauvenon has kindly sorted out the pin boards, whiteboard markers and everything else so that we can get all the case material visual.'

'We'll need a printer too,' added Bernard. I've asked them to install a secure direct line into the room too."

'Good idea,' agreed Denton. 'I'll talk to the management and suggest we pay for our own security guard. Their own people are receptionists rather than security.'

'Yes, let's do that.' said Bernard, 'I'd feel a lot happier. Let's make it twenty-four hour. I'll call the nearest authorised security company.'

Inspector Denton stood up. 'Let's get started. This is our operations room and we're setting up in the same way that the police go about an investigation. We are going to split the workload into two teams. I will work with Mr Chauvenon as one team as we can use both my police authorisation and his legal mind to bypass some of the privacy rules. Miss Connors and Mrs Chauvenon, you'll be concentrating on coordination and reacting to any leads that come up. It is very important that you stick together as much as possible. Never forget that we may be dealing with a murderer. If he or she has killed Charlene Madec he has almost certainly killed Petit-Jean Baudoin too.'

Julia did a sharp intake of breath.

'However, we must all keep an open mind and let us not forget that it is still possible that Charlene did in fact commit suicide.'

'*Non*, I do not believe she would do that to her baby!' said Rochelle.

'An open mind, Rochelle!' Bernard repeated.

Julia was surprised at the frustration in Bernard's voice. She'd never heard him snap at Rochelle before.

'We will create a series of boards that relate to different aspects of the case and look at any connections between the information and suspects.' Denton continued. 'Board one is what we know about the theft of the paintings. I'll transfer everything I've got to the computers here and we'll need pictures of the paintings, and a timeline of events.'

'Board two will be background information about the people involved,' said Bernard. 'This includes family relationships, friendships, arguments, business dealings, finances, anything that could provide a motive. Rochelle, you are the best person for this. You've known the people involved and this area the longest. I'll chip in too. We'll also need to speak to Simon Chapman, and Sophie Petrarch. Julia you'll have to add in everything you know about Jaime Girault, and Cassandra.'

'Board three will be Petit-Jean, Charlene and the commune.' said Denton.

'I'll do that,' said Julia. 'I've packed up their things. I did it without really looking, but thankfully I didn't throw anything away.'

'Good job I didn't manage to take it up to the commune,' said Rochelle.'

'Go through every detail, no matter how small,' said Inspector Denton. 'Turn the house upside down. People always make mistakes and the truth will out in some form or another. We need to know what they wanted to speak to Christophe about. We need to try and trace their steps. When they were in London, where did they go? Where did they stay? Did they take any deliveries? They must have paid for things. You'll need to find credit card bills – if they used them, access to bank accounts. Phone records. That will all be in their paperwork. If you need me to, I can access bank information directly via my fraud investigation.'

'Board four, Charlene's murder. I'll coordinate this one,' said Inspector Denton. 'Miss Connors, I will need everything you remember about that night, we'll sit down and go through it thoroughly. We have two priorities. First is to find Stefan. He is key to this as well as being the only other main suspect. He is the only person that we know for sure was with her on the night she died. We only have his word for it that he said Charlene had told him to get Christophe before going to the doctor.'

'But I can confirm that Stefan said that to Christophe.'

'Yes, but it won't be enough for Guillemain, Julia. We need to get hold of him as soon as possible.' said Bernard. 'Stefan knows more about what Charlene and Petit-Jean were doing than anyone.'

'We also need to find out more about the tranquilisers,' said Denton. 'Where did the tranquilisers come from? I'll get hold of the forensic analysis to see if they can identify the brand of tranquiliser. They won't have been able to do it from the blood analysis but they might have been able to do it from any residue left in the bottle. If the tranquiliser was in liquid form not many people have access to that and there will be a record of purchase and prescription somewhere. If the tablets were crushed and dissolved before injecting them, it won't be so easy to follow the source. Charlene could have purchased tablets herself.'

'And the other priority?' asked Julia

'The bottle,' said Bernard and Denton in unison.

'You are going to have to take your mind back to the day the paintings were stolen and write a list of everyone who could have got their hands on a shampoo bottle that had Christophe's prints on it.'

'And hairs in it.' said Julia

Bernard shook his head. 'That's not so important. Hairs could have been picked up easily and put in later, but the prints couldn't.'

'The final board,' said Denton, 'will be the suspects.' He paused

'And that I am afraid includes all three of you.'

'What?!!!' cried Julia and Rochelle in synchrony.

Bernard smiled at their outrage.

'The truth,' said Bernard.

'Yes,' said Denton. 'The truth is all I'm looking for.'

'Quite right,' said Bernard.

'The premise of any investigation is that a suspect needs to have means, motive and opportunity.'

Julia stood up looking very angry. 'This is all so wrong! It is bloody Inspector Guillemain's job to investigate that Christophe has been framed' she said. 'I am grateful that you are doing this Inspector Denton, but you need to go and have a word with Guillemain, you too Bernard. This is just madness. And there may be a killer out there!!'

There was silence for a moment.

'And what if Guillemain is involved?' said Bernard, quietly.

'I knew it!' said Julia. 'I bet he bloody well is! Can't you just call another police officer and get him arrested?'

There was a gentle cough from Inspector Denton.

'Oh!' said Julia. 'Of course, you are another officer.'

'However,' said Denton. 'For the record I want it known that I do not think that Inspector Guillemain is involved. But, I agree his actions are unprofessional and difficult to explain. That is why we need to work on this separately from his inquiry.'

'I also agree with you that Guillemain should be investigating this, Julia,' said Beranrd nodding. 'But what we are trying to do is push him in that direction. We're providing him with other evidence. And if he continues to refuse to see sense, then, yes, I am prepared to look at the possibility that he is involved.'

'He is doing his job by looking for Stefan,' Denton added.

'Quite.' Bernard agreed. 'But Stefan's prints are not on the bottle and for the moment that bottle is as near as dammit a murder weapon.'

'I suggest we compile all the information and treat the three of you as suspects, just to show you how this works,' said Denton. 'Call it an intensive training exercise. Do you agree?' They all nodded.

'Let's start with you Madame Chauvenon.' Denton. Suggested. Rochelle looked uncomfortable.

'Did Madame Chauvenon have the means? That includes the money to organise the theft of the paintings, access the tranquillizers and access to the murder weapon, i.e. the shampoo bottle.'

'Yes, to the shampoo bottle, yes to the tranquilisers and no to the finance,' said Bernard. Rochelle looked affronted. 'Well not really to the finance, but she couldn't have accessed that amount without me knowing.'

'Did she have a motive?'

'No,' said Rochelle

'Did she have the opportunity? According to the autopsy report Charlene was given the injection sometime between before Stefan left to go to get Christophe at the lodgings and his return there with Julia and the doctor.'

'No,' they all replied. 'Because we were in Rennes having dinner with our daughter,' said Bernard.

'The same is therefore true for you Mr Chauvenon, no motive, no opportunity.'

'Yes, but also it's a yes to financial means.'

'Right. Miss Connors. Do you have the means?'

'I have the use of Christophe's bank cards and credit cards. I had access to the shampoo bottle. I keep sleeping tablets in my wash bag, and I was the one who let the paintings get taken away.'

'And motive?'

'No. What would the motive be?' said Julia.

'Motive is always the hardest thing to find,' said Bernard. 'But it's usually the thing that clinches it.'

'I do NOT have a motive Bernard!'

'I know you don't but remember why we are doing this, Julia.'

'Opportunity?' asked Denton.

'Were you alone at any point between Stefan arriving at the Castle Lodgings and arriving with the doctor at Charlene's caravan?'

'Only for the few minutes that I went into the bathroom to get dressed.'

'Which is not long enough for you to get up to the caravan and back down again to the Castle Lodgings.'

'No.'

'So, the only way you could be guilty is if you and Christophe were working together.'

'In which case she wouldn't have framed him,' said Bernard.

'Agreed,' said Denton. 'So you are all crossed off the suspects list with the exception of Miss Connors.'

'What?' 'Why am I still on the list?'

'You could have a motive if you and Mr de Flaubert had fallen out,' said Denton. 'Perhaps you organised the theft of the paintings and the sale to collect insurance. Then you disagreed over Charlene and you were looking to get out of it and you were looking for revenge and to secure money for yourself. Framing him would be killing two birds with one stone, so to speak.'

'But?' Julia looked close to tears, 'I would never do anything like that.'

'I know Miss Connors but what we are trying to do is understand the way an investigation works and trying to find possible motives. I needed to use you as an example. And believe me, if Inspector Guillemain can't get his case to hold together, and he won't let it drop, you can bet your bottom dollar that you will be top of his list of accomplices!'

'I don't think I have ever hated anyone on sight as much as I did Guillemain,' said Julia shaking her head.

'I did rather get that impression in London,' said Inspector Denton, gently. 'But you must not let it cloud your judgement. Right. Let's set up a list of credible suspects. People who had access to the shampoo bottle, right from the beginning.'

'Air hostess on BA flight,' said Bernard

'Anyone on a flight that Christophe was on,' said Rochelle.

'Sophie Petrarch!' said Julia and Rochelle together.

'Anyone who cleaned or came into our rooms here at the lodgings.' Added Julia.

'It would help if you could remember Miss Connors if you brought a British Airways travel shampoo bottle here with you.'

'I can't say for certain. You'll have to ask Christophe. He always does his own packing.'

'I'll check with him,' said Bernard.

'Wait a moment,' said Denton. 'You've jumped from the flight to the Castle Lodgings. What about the time in between? At home in London?'

'Well there is Hilda the cleaner. Although frankly if she was going to frame anyone, it's much more likely to be me for the state of the house.'

'Did anyone else visit the house?'

'Well, You Inspector Denton and Inspector Guillemain.' Julia started to get excited. 'And Inspector Guillemain went off around the house on his own while we were talking. He could easily have gone into the bathroom!' said Julia. To her mind it was an open and shut case and Guillemain was guilty.

'He could indeed,' said Inspector Denton.

'Did anyone else visit? Did anyone else ask to use the bathroom? Did the fake security men perhaps?'

'No. Not that I can think of. After you'd left, Christophe and I had little argument and I went out. When I got back he was chatting to Simon Chapman. He was the only other person. I've no idea if he used the bathroom.'

'So, we'll put a question mark on that one. Then you came here to Brittany?'

'Yes. We came straight to the lodgings.'

'So, we need to check if anyone came into the room apart from the cleaners. Is it possible that the bottle was empty and put in the bin for the cleaner to throw?' asked Denton. 'Then somebody could have picked it up from there?'

'I'm not sure, that's one you'll have to ask Christophe again,' said Julia. 'But I can say for sure that I threw a couple of empty shampoo bottles in the bin at home. I tend to hoard them and then do a blitz.'

'Don't forget you moved into the Baudoin House, Julia.' said Rochelle. 'Did you unpack all the wash things there?'

'Yes. Of course, I'd forgotten about that. And there

were lots of people that went there, because we started work on the bathroom. There were three men from the château maintenance team, Simon Chapman, General Chapman, us and even Yvette.'

'Our list is getting longer by the minute,' said Rochelle, dejectedly. 'We'll never find who did this.'

'I know it probably feels a little depressing,' said Inspector Denton, 'but there is a method to the madness.'

Bernard squeezed Rochelle's hand. 'Don't worry. The more people that could have taken the bottle, the better, because if it ever gets to court it casts reasonable doubt on the murder weapon. Guillemain would be mad to take this to court.'

'Then you moved back in here to the same room at the Castle Lodgings?' asked Denton.

'Yes. We came straight back to have a bath. That's what we were doing when Stefan came.'

'Was the bottle here then?' asked Denton.

'I don't know,' said Julia. 'Christophe brought his wash bag but we didn't open it, we used complimentary bath gel.'

'And you have no recollection of when you last saw the bottle Miss Connors? Think carefully, use that excellent visual memory you have.'

Julia shook her head. 'I really don't recall seeing it here. It was definitely in the bathroom in London because we'd run out of shampoo. I think Christophe took it out and it was on the side. After that I can't say.'

Julia sat down with her head in her hands.

'This is awful. I know that you think Guillemain is not involved, Inspector Denton. But supposing he is? Just supposing he is! He was in London when the paintings got taken. He works for the fraud squad and could easily move the paintings over to Brittany without any questions being asked. He had access to the shampoo bottle. He could easily have gone to the commune. Why hasn't he found Stefan? And I bet if you check, he was here when Petit-Jean died in the motor cycle accident. Why wasn't that investigated? Christophe said Petit-Jean was a brilliant motor cross rider. How the hell did he have an accident on a country road with nobody else involved?'

'Julia, that's all true but I just can't believe he would do it. He is one of the most respected fraud detectives in the World. Why would he risk all that?' said Bernard.

'And' said Julia, 'He has motive.'

'Oh. What's his motive?' asked Inspector Denton, surprised.

'Revenge, hate. He dislikes Christophe intensely and has never forgiven him for embarrassing him when Christophe exposed his Van Gogh as a fake. That probably lost him a lot of money too.'

'OK.' said Inspector Denton, nodding thoughtfully. 'All the more important, for us to keep this quiet until we have built a concrete case. 'I think that is a very plausible scenario Miss Connors but I do not think it is Guillemain. He may well be taking out his revenge on Mr de Flaubert. He is certainly enjoying the discomfort he is going through but I think that is just him being opportunistic.'

'And,' said Julia, standing up. 'What if he is working with Girault?'

'What makes you think that?' asked Bernard.

'Because the fake Van Gogh he found was in Lacoste! So he must know the Giraults'.

And if it IS him, and he realises we are near to proving it, then Christophe is in danger and he is in Guillemain's custody. Bernard, you have to get him out.'

'Christophe is not in danger, Miss Connors. If Guillemain did this he needs Mr de Flaubert alive to be convicted of the crime and he certainly won't risk killing him in custody.'

'Are you sure inspector? What if he just lets Girault in and they make it look like suicide? It happens all the time doesn't it?'

'There would have to be a clear case of Mr de Flaubert's mental state pointing to a risk of suicide for that to hold and he strikes me as a man who is very happy.'

'But can't we get Christophe out? On bail or something?'

'We can't. France doesn't have a bail system.'

'But you got Charlene out,' said Julia.

'That was because British rules applied because the crime was committed in the UK and Inspector Denton was in charge.' said Bernard.

'Well at least let me go and see him,' said Julia, pleading.

Bernard, who was not one for being tactile, stood up and gave Julia a hug.

'French law is strict and the only people who can visit Christophe while he is in custody are either direct family or lawyers.'

'And Sophie Petrarch?' asked Julia.

'Exceptional circumstances I know. But Julia, trust me. I do not want to rile Guillemain any more than he already is. Please, let me handle it.'

'Let us get started then,' said Inspector Denton, standing up. 'I'll head off to the DNA Lab.'

'I'll go and stock up on the rest of the provisions,' said Rochelle.

'I'll get off to see Christophe,' said Bernard. 'So you'd

better hold the fort for now, Julia.'

Bernard closed the door behind him and she was left alone with her thoughts. Hold the fort? That was a good one. What the hell with? A cheese sandwich and a hairdryer? Not much use against a murder and a pack of paparazzi.

Twenty-Two

JULIA STARED AT THE boards for a good ten minutes before she could even get near to calming down. It was all so wrong. She stood up, took a tissue and frantically rubbed her name off the suspects list. Then she grabbed a red marker pen and wrote Guillemain on it in big bright red capital letters. She added a few exclamation marks and underlined it three times, and stood back to look at her handy work. No something was missing. She drew a skull and crossbones next to the exclamation marks. Much better. He was a horrible arrogant little man. And petty. He let Sophie Petrarch see Christophe because she's famous and the darling of the village, but she, his loving partner, couldn't see him.

She sat down again and looked for the pen drive of art crooks and fraudsters that Denton had left for her to look through. She muttered to herself as she searched. I don't want to look at art crooks, I want to look at Christophe. I want us to be laughing and making love and just 'being'. She picked up the aftershave to sniff it and heard something fall on the floorboards. When she bent down to look, the pen drive had fallen and so had a key. The key that Stefan sent. What an idiot, she'd forgotten to tell them about the key.

So here are my choices. She held the pen drive in one hand and the key in the other. Villains or key, villains or key? Tough call. No. She stood up determinedly. No, neither. It just wasn't fair. She was not having it. Nope. No. If bloody Sophie could see Christophe then so could she. Bernard was wrong. I will not sit quietly and pander to Guillemain. I will go and get this sorted out now. Guillemain simply can't be allowed to get away with it. She grabbed her coat and headed out of the door in a fury. Her pace accelerated along with her thoughts of exactly what she would say to Guillemain when she got hold of him.

It was still snowing and was getting deeper by the minute. In any other circumstances she would have taken great pleasure in kicking the snow as she walked. She would even have stopped and looked in the quaint village shops that twinkled with Christmas lights. But not today. Today, even the snowflakes caressing her face annoyed her. They didn't stand a chance of settling even for a second because of the thermal energy her anger was pumping out, it was positively volcanic.

Her walk was so brisk she was creating a snow wake as she went. She muttered to herself angrily, thinking about all the things she was going to say to Guillemain. Seasonal greetings were not on the list that was for sure. She didn't hear her name being called from behind her, her thoughts were shouting so loudly in her head.

She felt a hand on her arm.

'Woah, slow down Father Christmas isn't due for a few more days yet!'

She stopped and turned to see Simon Chapman

panting heavily. He'd been chasing her down the street.

'A penny for your thoughts, Julia? Although, the speed with which you crossed the village makes me think they might be much more expensive than that.'

He had a thick coat on, and a scarf covering most of his face. The only thing she could see were the black eyes.

'Oh. Sorry Simon. I can't chat, I have to go to the Gendarmerie. I have to see Christophe and get him out. It is all wrong what Guillemain is doing.'

She turned to go but he kept hold of her arm.

'Won't Bernard Chauvenon be sorting that?'

'Yes, but he doesn't want to rile Guillemain so he won't accuse him of being unfair about letting Sophie Petrarch see him and not me.'

'Ah, yes.' He turned her around to face the opposite direction without her even noticing. 'I can see why you're angry.' He took her hand in his. 'Look your hands are freezing, you didn't even put gloves on, let alone a scarf and hat.' They started walking back down the road. 'Let's go and get a hot chocolate. It will warm you up. Then if you still feel the same, I will come with you and see if I can help sort it out.' He guided her towards the Cafe Breton.

'No Simon. I don't have time.'

'Julia, you are in no state to do this. You won't even have to say anything for Guillemain to tell you to leave because your anger is obvious to all and sundry. I could see the steam coming out of your ears from all the way up at the château and your anger will make you irrational when putting your case. You need to let someone else handle it.'

'Simon...I ...' He took her coat and she sat down in the chair he pulled out for her. She gazed at the table cloth in a daze while he hung up their coats and ordered two hot chocolates with brandy.

She hadn't even realised that she was cold. The steaming chocolate arrived and she grasped it, warming her hands gratefully. She let the wonderful smell of warm chocolate and brandy waft around her nostrils and felt better immediately.

'I suppose you are right, Simon.'

'I know the Sophie thing is hard to take, but she is probably doing Christophe a favour.'

'How come?'

'Well, imagine if it did get to court.' She looked scared he took her hand in his and squeezed it reassuringly. 'I don't for a minute think it will. But if it did, and there is a trial by jury, Sophie has made the press and public aware of it. They would have to hunt high and low to find people who did not know anything about it, to serve as jury members. And in the court of public opinion she has already declared him innocent.'

'Hang on. How will it get to court? All they've got is a shampoo bottle that has his prints on it. Anybody could have put that there.'

'True but …

'Including Sophie Petrarch!' said Julia interrupting him.

Simon shook his head. 'Julia you can't be serious? You don't honestly think she would do something like that? And if she did, why would she then go and see him?'

'Well I don't know but whoever did kill Charlene is trying to frame Christophe.' Julia said louder than she meant to. A few people glanced over in their direction.

'If she was killed,' said Simon, lowering his voice.

'You don't think she was?' Julia whispered and the people in the cafe looked away and ignored them.

'I don't know. But I am certain that cousin

Guillemain had no option but to open a murder enquiry after Christophe got a second opinion on the autopsy. Look, I'm not a police officer nor a coroner, but I did know Petit-Jean and Charlene well. She had a drug problem. They both had for quite a long time.'

'I know, but she was pregnant. They weren't doing drugs and pregnant women just don't commit suicide.'

'Maybe she had depression. Maybe she just grabbed that bottle herself from somewhere and used it to get hold of more tranquilisers.'

'She was at the Baudoin house and she did have access to my sleeping tablets.'

'There you are then. That's another reason why they won't be able to say for certain that it was Christophe. Julia, I think you need to go back to the lodgings and wait for Christophe. Guillemain will release him I'm sure. After all it is Christmas.'

'I suppose you are right, Simon.'

'Come on, I'll walk back to the lodgings with you.' He stood up and went to get the coats.

'You don't have to come back with me Simon. I'm fine really.' said Julia when he came back.

'Sorry.' he shook his head like a parent saying no to a naughty child. 'I'm not taking any chance of you rushing off to the gendarmerie to assassinate cousin Guillemain.'

It had stopped snowing but the wind was icy on her face. She pushed her hands into the small coat pockets to warm them and Simon shook his head in despair. He held out his arm to her and handed her his gloves.

'Here, put these on. I would never forgive myself if those beautiful hands got chilblains.'

Julia sighed heavily and for the first time took in the quaint atmosphere of the village. It was quite something.

Especially now that it was decorated with real snow.

'I love this. It is so pretty and kind of timeless, we could be in almost any century.'

'The special Christmas decorations were my grandfather's idea,' said Simon and they strolled down the main street. 'It started with the Summer 'village fleurie' movement. Every house was given window boxes and hanging baskets and Pont Carnac won so many times that they aren't allowed to enter any more. So, they decided to do something at Christmas. They created a plan of lights and trees and the life size sculptures for the crèche in the village square, to attract visitors. Now people drive from miles around to visit the village, it's quite famous as being the quaintest Christmas village in France.'

'It's like a film set from a Charles Dickens novel.'

'A Christmas Carol,' said Simon, laughing. 'Or in my case Great Expectations.'

'Oh?'

'Yes. I do have great expectations for us, Julia.'

She ignored the innuendo. Flirtation was the last thing on her mind and it irritated her. She was in a very bad mood, so Sophie Petrarch got it in the neck.

'Great Expectations. A brilliant film. I'd like to see Sophie Petrarch rotting on a sofa, covered in cobwebs.' said Julia, looking Simon in the eye without a trace of humour.

***

A police car was parked outside the Castle Lodgings. Julia ran ahead of Simon not caring that the steps were slippery. She charged up to the reception area.

There was no one there. She rushed up to their rooms. She could hear voices inside. One of them was Christophe.

She opened the door ready to launch herself into his

arms but stopped dead in her tracks.

The room had been completely ransacked.

'Ah there you are,' said Denton. 'We got back here and found this.' He gestured to the papers all over the floor, the open drawers and computer discs all over the desk.

'Julia I thought we agreed that someone would be here at all times?' Bernard said in his chief prosecutor voice. You were supposed to stay here.'

'I, was .. err' She felt so bad. She'd let them down.

Bernard's voice switched back from chief prosecutor to concerned friend. 'We were worried about you. We didn't know if you'd just gone off or the person who did this had taken you.'

***

Simon appeared in the doorway. 'Do I have permission to enter or is this a crime scene?' He sauntered in without waiting for an answer.

'Where were you, Julia? Christophe asked.

'I was going to see you. I wanted to tell Guillemain exactly what I think of him and force him to let me see you, then I bumped into Simon.'

'She was wandering around lost in a daze with hardly any clothes on ... I mean no hat, gloves or scarf and she was frozen to the bone so I took her for a hot chocolate to warm her up,' said Simon. 'And to calm her down a little.'

'Really?' said Christophe, 'How fortuitous.'

'Yes.' said Julia. 'And he stopped me from doing something very stupid.

'How good of him.'

'And,' said Julia, going over to kiss Christophe. He moved away. She hesitated and continued. 'Simon came up with a very good point about Charlene, that means Guillemain has to let you go.'

'And that is?'

'That, it is quite possible that Charlene did commit suicide. She could easily have taken the shampoo bottle from the Baudoin house and used it to put some of my sleeping tablets in it which means the case against you could not be beyond reasonable doubt.'

'Yes, interesting, Julia. And that happens to be what Bernard has been pointing out to Guillemain for the last couple of hours. What an astonishing coincidence don't you think? Or perhaps you and your cousin Guillemain had already discussed that Simon?'

'No, Christophe we hadn't. I thought it made sense. That's all. Look, I think I should go. You have some catching up to do. Good to see you out though Christophe.'

Christophe nodded curtly.

Simon took his gloves from Julia, kissed her on the cheek and left.

She turned to give Christophe a big hug but the atmosphere between them was even frostier than the ground outside.

'Can you tell us if anything is missing, Miss Connors? You were the last person in the room so only you will know. Also, that photographic memory of yours would really make it all a bit quicker.' suggested Denton, noticing the coldness between them.

'Oh, yes of course,' said Julia. She closed her eyes and pictured the room as it was when she'd left it, then opened them again and looked around.

'No nothing missing that I can see,' she said. 'But I have an idea of what they might have been looking for.'

'What?' asked Christophe.

'The key'

'The USB key that I gave you, with the art fraudster database?' Asked Denton.

'No, not that. The padlock key. Only it's not a padlock key.'

'What padlock key?

'Stefan sent two people from the commune over to give me a key.'

'What? And you didn't think to tell us?' said Christophe, exasperated.

'Well I thought Rochelle would have told Bernard.'

Bernard looked at Rochelle.

'Julia, you didn't say anything about a key.' said Rochelle, shaking her head.

'Didn't I? Oh. Well … err…

'Don't you think,since we can't even find Stefan, this is important.' said Christophe.

'Yes. I do but I already know it doesn't open the padlock to the trapdoor on the roof because I tried it.'

'What trapdoor on the roof?'

'There's a trapdoor on the roof of the Baudoin house where Baudoin used to go up and paint.'

'And you didn't think that was important either?' He shook his head as if he completely gave up on them.

'I did, I mean, we did. Rochelle and I were doing our bit investigating it. I thought Rochelle would have told Bernard.'

'Well she didn't and you didn't tell me either.'

'And how was I supposed to tell you Christophe? I wasn't allowed to call you and I wasn't allowed to see you and you didn't call me. Perhaps you were too busy chatting with Sophie Petrarch.'

There was silence in the room as Christophe and Julia glared at one another.

Inspector Denton started picking up the papers. Rochelle and Bernard bent down to help him.

Denton stood up with some in his hand and looked thoughtful for a moment.

'We should sit down together and make sure we share everything we know. Everyone needs to have all the information and be aware of what's going on.' he said.

'Or,' said Julia. 'We could accept the fact that maybe we got it wrong. Maybe Charlene did commit suicide, maybe they did steal the paintings.'

Rochelle gasped.

Julia pleaded with Christophe. 'Can't we just let it go? You're out and we can go back home to London.'

'What? You can't be serious Julia? Wow! Simon Chapman really did a number on you didn't he. Took only an hour to convince you that he is right and I am wrong. You know what this is, Julia. It's not just green eggs, it's rotten green eggs, stinking rotten green eggs.'

'This has nothing to do with green eggs. This is about us, all of us and our safety. I don't want you to go to prison. I don't want anyone else to die. I don't want whoever is framing you to keep doing it.'

'And you think ignoring it will make it go away?'

'If I might suggest something,' said Inspector Denton. 'What if we close our case. I'm sure I can convince Guillemain to close it officially. The perpetrator would be put off his or her guard. It's Christmas. I shall go back to London and spend time with my family. I suggest that you all do the same. Then we can pick up the case in the New Year.'

Bernard went over to Rochelle and put his arm around

her. 'I think it is a good idea. We should get back to the children.' he turned to Christophe. 'I shall continue doing some background searching on this, but Christmas is family time.'

'Fair enough,' said Christophe, nodding. 'But I will stay here. And I *will* find a way to clear Petit-Jean and Charlene's names. I owe it to them.' He bent down and picked up the remaining papers that had been on the floor and started looking through them, ignoring everyone else.

Julia sighed. 'Christophe. You can't save everyone.'

'I know that but I have to do this, you know I do.'

'Then I suggest you go about it very carefully,' said Inspector Denton, because if you are right, there is a murderer on the loose and one thing is certain, that person does not have your best interests at heart.'

Twenty-Three

JULIA SAT ON THE floor at the Baudoin House, dragging the boxes that she'd filled with Charlene and Petit-Jean's things, nearer to the fire. Christophe looked around the room and took a box too. He then went out to the back yard. There had been no big thaw yet in their relationship. They'd both gone into hibernation for the winter, but she was ever hopeful.

Christophe came back in with some more logs. 'These should help keep us warm while we do this,' he said, putting two on the fire.

'We'll need to get central heating put in here before Francoise can move in,' said Julia. It's freezing here. The heat from the fire hasn't even thawed the walls yet. He nodded but did not look at her.

'We'll put anything important in this box.' He pulled one of the empty boxes nearer to him. He took out an empty file from another box. 'Any financial paperwork will go in this. He moved a bigger box to the side. 'Anything to go straight to the commune can go in that one.'

'Don't you think we should start on the roof?' Julia

suggested. 'You know, take a look at the trap door. It must be important if it's padlocked.'

'Go up on the roof in snow and ice?' he asked with disbelief. 'With your long history of disasters?'

She decided to let that go. She pulled a box over angrily and started going through it. She slammed things on the floor heavily as she went through them. He ignored her. She pulled out an old doll and stopped for a moment. She looked at the sad blue crystal eyes and the matted hair. It reminded her of her own china doll. It was the only thing that she had of her mother's. As a surprise, Christophe had it repaired after it got smashed by one of Girault's gang enforcers who had burgled her flat. She sighed, sadly. He had every right to be angry. She was left in charge of the office and she'd gone off in a strop following her own agenda rather than doing what was best.

There must be some way to make it up to him. She stood up and put another log on the fire. The flames were really pulling up through the chimney and she was beginning to feel the warmth. She looked over at Christophe. Still he ignored her.

She sat down again. Maybe, if they made progress getting the trap door open, he might forgive her.

'I could go up on the roof if you tied a rope onto me. Then if I fall you can save me.' She said thinking out loud.

Christophe's response was to raise an eyebrow slightly. 'I thought you said I can't save everybody.'

'Christophe! You know what I mean.'

He looked a bit sheepish. 'Look, I just need a little more time. I've never suffered from jealousy before. It's always been everyone else who got hurt and I'm not really sure how I deal with it yet.'

She moved across and put her arms around him. 'I will

go and swear on the head of the baby Jesus in the village crèche that you have nothing to be jealous about.'

He pouted, sulkily but did not move away. 'It really hurts doesn't it, jealousy? I thought it was something ridiculous, people getting angry and over-sensitive but it isn't, is it? It attacks you like an electric shock from inside and rushes all around your body.'

'Yes, then sets up a circuit loop in the unreasonable behaviour centre of your brain.'

Christophe laughed and nodded. 'It does indeed. I feel bad now about all those women who I may have put through that.'

'Don't feel too bad, otherwise my green eggs will come back.'

'You deserve them.' He said, pulling her onto his knee.

She turned to look up at him and he held her gaze. The chill had gone from his eyes.

'So are we good then?' he asked.

'Yes, we're good.' She kissed him on the lips. 'So good.'

'I think we should christen the awful lumpy mattress upstairs then, don't you?'

'No, I think we should grab the burgundy from the kitchen and take advantage of the fire.'

***

They lay cuddled up in front of the fire with big sweaters and scarves on, naked from the waist down under the duvet. Christophe stuck his foot out towards the fire.

'Now I would save you, if you went on the roof,' he said, putting his warm foot back on her leg. 'But I have decided I can't take the risk of losing you. So, we will continue here with the boxes, and then do the roof after.

I'll have to borrow a saw from somewhere to cut through the padlock chain and I'd rather do that when it's not so icy.'

He leant over and pulled two of the boxes nearer to them. 'One for you and one for me. Christmas already.'

'Denton said to keep any receipts or things related to London,' said Julia, 'credit card bills, anything to do with the paintings, anything to do with the painters.'

'When did he say that?'

'He gave us a briefing when you were being questioned. That's when we set up our operations room to prove your innocence.'

'I'm glad he's involved,' said Christophe. 'Guillemain has definitely got it in for me.'

'Well maybe he wouldn't be so bad, if you didn't deliberately rile him. Bernard said you made things extra difficult during the questioning.'

Christophe had the grace to look contrite. 'I did amuse myself at his expense.'

'I thought you'd overcome your inherent death wish,' she replied, taking a handful of photos out of her box.

'It wasn't a death wish. It was more of a wine connoisseur's colorimetry test that I was doing.'

'A what?'

'I was seeing how red I could make him go.'

Julia flicked through most of the pictures that looked like they were taken at parties up at the commune and put them to one side for boxing up again.

'And just how did you do that?' she asked, not really paying attention.

'I told him all about our sex life.'

'You what? Oh, Christophe you didn't!'

'Only a little. Not the intimate details, just about us

being in the bath and all that. He's such a prude. Sometimes I wonder if he's a Guillemain at all. The Guillemain were as prolific womanisers as the Baudoin were in their day. Either way he should have gone into the priesthood and not the police force.'

Julia was looking at an old black and white photo that had got mixed up with the party photos. 'Look Christophe, it's your Baudoin! But look at the picture that Baudoin has on his easel, it's the one that General Chapman has in his sitting room. And who is the other guy in the picture?' She handed it to Christophe.

'Looks like Andre Guillemain possibly. Must be one of the old Breton School painters. They did paint a lot together. They even had a go at each other's paintings sometimes, usually when they'd had a few drinks, according to William Chapman.'

'They look very serious in this one, don't they?' said Julia handing it to him

'Does it have a date on it?' He turned it over. '1940, just at the beginning of the occupation. That will explain it, then.'

'I'm quite shocked that Baudoin was a collaborator.'

'It's easy to say that in hindsight,' said Christophe. Who knows what we'd have done in their place.'

'We wouldn't have,' said Julia. 'We would have held strong and fast and not given in.'

'You don't know that. At the time there was no TV, only radio broadcasts. There may have been rumours but nobody knew for certain what they were doing to the Jews until later. Baudoin was probably hoping they'd get an independent Brittany out of it. Lots of Bretons thought that they should not be part of France. Also, Baudoin did fight on the good side with Chapman during the Spanish civil war.'

'You're defending him,' said Julia, disappointed.

'No. I'm putting myself in Petit-Jean's place and trying to understand what tack he was on. There must have been something in his mind.'

Julia pulled out another pile of things to look through. 'Maybe it was just wishful thinking,' said Julia. 'I can't imagine anyone would find it easy knowing their grandfather was a traitor. In one of the smaller boxes she found a small silk purse. Inside was a locket and a positive pregnancy test. The locket was engraved on the outside with the letters CG entwined. She opened it and recognised the picture of the child immediately. She felt a lump rise in her throat.

'Oh Christophe, look, she kept her positive pregnancy test. And look how cute she was when she was a child.'

Christophe took the picture and looked at it.

'We should take this to Guillemain, along with the other photos. Maybe his forensic people could find something in the picture to help them. They still haven't found her next of kin.'

'Christophe I owe you an apology. I'm so sorry. I don't know how I could possibly have believed Simon Chapman. Of course, she wouldn't have committed suicide.'

'I guess I can just about forgive you. Although my ego is very bruised.' He pulled a mock sulking face then drew her towards him smiling. 'Will we ever get over our green demons?'

'I don't know. I was all ready to kill Guillemain for letting Sophie Petrarch see you but not letting me in. Then when Bernard said I mustn't go to the gendarmerie I was even sending telepathic angry thoughts to him!'

'No risk he'd receive them. Bernard has complete control over his gut reactions and as for psychic stuff that's for lunatics and movies.' He stood up, topped up their wine glasses and handed Julia hers. 'Look, I know Simon is a lot more suave with his chat and compliments than I am. He has a real talent for it, but he's, I don't know he's always been …'

'A bit creepy,' suggested Julia.

'Yes. It's odd. I can never quite put my finger on it.'

'If it makes you feel better, his compliments and innuendos are getting on my nerves. But what he was saying was very logical.'

'Yes, it was. And Bernard was already working on it. Hang on a minute. I am getting seriously worried about you. That's twice now that you've played the logic card.'

'I know. The only excuse I can think of is that when I spoke to Simon my brain was frozen and the brandy he gave me went straight to my head.'

Julia dragged another box over, rummaged around in it and pulled out a small wooden music box. It was locked.

'Christophe. Look, maybe this is what the key is for!'

He took the box. 'Was the key that small?'

'Yes. It must be. I'll go back to the lodgings and get it. I left it in my other coat pocket.'

'OK. While you do that I will go and hunt around in the upstairs room where the building stuff is and see if I can find something to open the roof trap door. I have a gut feeling that we are onto something. Hurry back because I want us to discover this together and I miss you when you're away.'

Julia smiled. 'I'm only going for a few minutes. You're the one that goes away so often.'

'I know and I'm not going to do that any more.

There's something about this business with Petit-Jean that has made me realise that when you find the one, you never know what is going to happen. Look at Charlene and Petit-Jean, they found each other and everything was going well and then, wham, hit by a flying cricket bat from left field and it's over. You have to make the most of every second that you are together.

'I will hold you to that. It's exactly what I was thinking when I decided to leave Jean Claude and Jacquard. We have so much that we can do together.'

There's already so much that we do together very well indeed!'

Julia raised her eyebrows. 'That's nearly as bad as one of Simon Chapman's innuendoes!'

'I mean apart from sex, said Christophe. 'Although that has got to be right up there in the top one hundred.'

'Top one hundred? Only top one hundred. That really is green dragon fodder, if ever I heard it'

'Well hurry back and we can get to the number one spot,' He laughed.

***

Julia headed off at pace, skipping along in the powdery snow. She smiled to herself. He was incorrigible. That was the one thing that she was absolutely certain that they had got right. She went straight to the lodgings. She knew they were going to solve this. Now that they were working at it together, she just knew it. She picked up speed as she reached the entrance, then slipped on the icy step and would have fallen flat on her face if a strong pair of arms hadn't shot out to grab her.

'This is getting to become a habit,' said Simon Chapman.

'Oh. Gosh. Yes. I must stop falling for you like this. I mean falling over you. Em, Falling over in front of you.'

'I prefer falling for you.'

Julia grimaced. 'Simon!'

'Sorry. But you said it first, not me. And if you throw me lines like that, you can't blame me. Why the haste?'

'I need to get something from our room.'

'Do you need help?'

'No thanks Simon.'

'Are you sure? I mean what if you fall down the stairs, or walk into a Christmas tree or Father Christmas parks his sleigh on your head or something?'

'Odd as it may seem, but I don't have accidents all the time. Look, I'll just grab it and get back to the Baudoin house. Christophe is waiting for me.'

'OK well if you're going back there, I'll wait and go with you, I never did get to talk to Christophe about the Baudoin.'

'Wait here I won't be a minute.' She took the stairs two at a time and muttered to herself 'Sorry Christophe, he just sort of tagged along, couldn't stop him, you know what he's like.' No, it wouldn't do. She would have to tell Simon it wasn't convenient. Yes, she'd tell him outright.'

She said hello to the security guard on the door to their rooms and went in. She fiddled around looking in the pockets of the coat that she'd been wearing before, but it wasn't there.

She looked around on the floor, in the wardrobe and in the cupboard, but nothing. That was weird. She knew she had it in the coat and she definitely hadn't taken it out. And ever since the place had been ransacked, they had a security guard on the door. She wandered back out and asked the security guard if anybody had been into their rooms. Maybe Bernard or Rochelle had taken it. He said nobody had been there but to ask the replacement who was due there any moment, maybe he would know something.'

Julia thanked him and went downstairs.

'You look a bit disgruntled. Anything wrong?'

'No, well maybe. I've lost a key.'

'Oh?'

'Something important?'

'Maybe'

'Well hopefully it will turn up. Shall we go?'

'Yes. Err, no, actually, Simon.'

As they approached the door the replacement security guard was coming in.

'Hang on I just need to check with this guy if anyone has been in the rooms, said Julia. 'Maybe Bernard or Rochelle has the key.'

She smiled at the new security guy then stopped in her tracks as he looked up at her and smiled back. She'd seen his face before. She turned around and gave Simon a very pointed look.

'Changed my mind. Let's go.'

'Are you OK?' Simon asked, puzzled.

'Yes. I'm fine. Let's go.'

'OK.' He started to put his gloves on very slowly. Julia tugged his arm.

'Really Simon. We need to go,' her voice loaded with meaning, 'Now!'

She dragged him out of the main entrance and looked around to check the guard wasn't watching them. She diverted off into a tiny alleyway that led to the car park.

'Simon, that security guard. He's one of the people who took the paintings in London!'

'What? Are you sure?' He guided her further down the alleyway.

'Yes. I have a really good head for faces. I know it was him. That must be why I couldn't find him in the art fraud database. He must genuinely work for a security company.'

'We need to be careful,' said Simon. 'If he realises you recognised him, you could be in danger.'

'From the way he looked at me, he did recognise me!'

Simon stopped talking. He was watching over her shoulder. Someone had come into the alley way.

'Oh my god,' he said. Julia swung round to look. She felt a blow to her head and all went black.

Twenty-Four

CHRISTOPHE PACED THE FLOOR in Guillemain's office. Guillemain had offered him a seat but he'd refused it. He stopped pacing and leant forward over the desk and slammed his hand down to get his attention.

'What are you going to do? She is missing.'

'De Flaubert she has been absent for a few hours.' Guillemain did not look up from what he was doing. 'That does not constitute a missing person.'

'Well I know Julia and it does to me. She went back to get something from the lodgings and never returned. I went back to the lodgings and the security guard said she'd left just as he arrived. That's over three hours ago.'

Guillemain pushed the papers he'd been perusing to one side.

'Now look. It's Christmas. People often go missing for a few hours. For some people it's the only way they can do their secret shopping.'

'You know damn well our lodgings were broken into. You also know that someone tried to frame me for Charlene's death.'

'Honestly de Flaubert. Even though we don't particularly like each other, I always had you down for a rational kind of guy. But this? This smacks of some kind of weird conspiracy theory. One minute you think Charlene and Petit-Jean have been murdered.'

'I didn't tell you that I thought Petit-Jean had been murdered.'

'Not me no, but I know you said it to Denton and several other people. Then Denton comes to see me and tells me you've changed your mind because Charlene could have taken the tablets herself. She could have stolen them from your rooms or house or whatever. I have a lot of respect for Denton, so I close the case. Now, you come over here when your wife or partner, however you like to call her, has been gone for a few hours, just before Christmas and you're thinking she's been murdered or kidnapped or something. Forget it!' He picked up his paperwork again. 'Hey, maybe she found herself a new, more rational boyfriend!'

Christophe hesitated for a moment then calmly pulled a chair over and sat down. Guillemain ignored him.

'I'm sorry,' he said.

'What?' Guillemain, looked up in surprise.

'I'm sorry.'

'You're sorry? You're apologising to me?'

'Yes.'

'What for, exactly?' There was a pause then Guillemain answered it himself. 'For making my life as difficult as possible during my investigation? For the years that you and your friends ran rampaging through the village, making fun of me? Or for being an arrogant shit?'

'Err all of those if you want. I was thinking more of the Van Gogh thing.'

'What? What the hell are you talking about?'

'I think you've been like this towards me for so long because you are still pissed off about the Van Gogh thing. I think that's what has caused this animosity between us.'

'Good God. Don't be ridiculous de Flaubert. We don't like each other and never have. And I don't want your apologies. I want the respect I deserve for the professional that I am.'

'I can see that Guillemain. That is a very reasonable request. I will do my utmost to give you that respect.'

'You're crazy de Flaubert, do you know that? Totally off your rocker. You think trying to apologise to me will change things?'

'Yes. Hopefully.'

'Well it doesn't. Because, I'm a professional and no amount of sucking up to me will stop me from doing my job correctly!'

Christophe got the shock of his life. Guillemain started laughing. He realised that over all these years, he had never heard him laugh. And it was a wonderful laugh, a real belly rolling laugh.

'*Oh la*! she really must mean a lot to you if you are prepared to apologise and suck up to me,' he said when he finally got some breath back.

For a second Christophe saw the funny side himself too and couldn't help laughing.

'She does Guillemain. She really does.'

'Look we're short staffed and people are having to work over the Christmas holidays. I can't allow the manpower. But I promise you if she hasn't turned up by tomorrow morning, I'll get on to it. I'm sure this newly discovered reasonable side to your character can understand that, don't you think?'

Christophe hesitated.

Guillemain waited.

'Yes of course.' said Christophe quietly. He couldn't argue with that. He would have to go and look for her himself.

'If I was you,' said Guillemain, kindly. 'I'd go through the whole village top to bottom. She can't have taken a car, the snow's too deep and the village is cut off, so she can't have gone far.'

Christophe nodded. 'Yes. And thank you Michel.'

'You are very welcome, Christophe. And a final piece of advice. If you do spot her doing her Christmas shopping, best to pretend you haven't seen her. Women don't like you spoiling their surprises, you know.'

***

Christophe headed out into the snow. He pulled his long wool overcoat around him and called Bernard.

'So, what did Guillemain say?'

'That it has only been a few hours and officially she's not really missing yet and she's probably gone Christmas shopping.'

'Seems logical. I asked Rochelle and she didn't know what Julia had planned for your Christmas present.'

'But Bernard, she wasn't going shopping. She was running back to get the key that she thought would fit the box we found. We were going to go up on the roof and look at the trap door. She was excited about it, impatient even. She didn't even take her mobile with her.'

'Well maybe she got side tracked. Come on Christophe we love her dearly, but she is accident prone and a bit *tête en l'air* sometimes.'

'I know that, but not four hours head in the clouds! I'll keep looking for her on my own '

'Call us when you find her. Rochelle is asking if you've looked up at the château, maybe she went there.'

Christophe knew that should have been the first place he looked. But he hadn't wanted to. Even if she had gone there, he couldn't believe that she would be there for that long. Not with Simon Chapman. Not after everything they'd said.

***

He went through the main gates past the ten foot tree that was in the courtyard decorated ready for the chateau's Christmas party the next day. William Chapman had always fully embraced his role as Lord of the Manor. He started the tradition of the chateau Christmas party and it had been continued after his death by General Chapman and Simon, although under great duress in the General's case. William Chapman invited everyone in the village, their friends, their families and just about anyone that happened to be in the village at the time. The General wanted it scaled down but people still came, invited or not. The General may have fought the Koreans, but not even he would take on a Breton without an invitation, during the season of goodwill, so even more people turned up now than in the old painter's time.

Christophe went through the big hallway where the staff were putting up the lights and decorations. They were setting out the tables for the food and mulled wine and hanging the all important mistletoe in strategic places. He wished them a *joyeux noel* and rang the doorbell through to the private apartments.

'De Flaubert,' said the General, opening the door. He held his hand out formally.

'General Chapman,' said Christophe, shaking it.

'To what do we owe the pleasure?' he asked, making the hesitation on the word pleasure obvious that was not what he thought it was at all.

'Sorry to interrupt when you are busy getting things ready for tomorrow. I seem to have lost Julia.'

'Oh?' the General's voice boomed out. 'Lost how? Misplaced, run away or lost her to another man?' Christophe was sure every worker this side of Versaille heard, let alone those in the château de Pont Carnac.

'Is Simon here?' The irritation in his voice was badly disguised. General Chapman looked affronted. 'I thought he might have seen her,' said Christophe hopefully.'

Yvette came in with her arm full of decorations.

'Young de Flaubert how are you?' she asked, kissing him on both cheeks. 'Without your lady I see.'

'Lost her!' said the General, still shouting. 'Gone and lost her, he says.'

'Oh dear. I'm sure she'll turn up for the *reveillon* with a lovely surprise,' said Yvette. 'She seems like the kind of lady that would keep a few surprises up her sleeve.'

'Wants to see Simon. Thinks he's got her,' said the General.

'I haven't seen Simon all day,' said Yvette. 'He did mention he wanted to talk to you about the Baudoin painting though.'

'What does he want with that?' asked the General suspiciously.

'No idea,' said Yvette. 'I have not spoken about that man, his painting or anything to do with him for eighty years and I will not start now.'

'Probably got some stupid soft idea in his head about it,' said the General. 'You know what he's like about his little paintings. Should have gone into the military. Make a man out of him, not faff around with his finger paints'

'You were always far too hard on him,' said Yvette and she concentrated on unravelling the Christmas lights. 'He's done very well indeed with the Chapman legacy, give him some credit.'

'Should have been off fighting for his country. My father did even though he wanted to be a painter. Fought that fascist Franco and his thugs. And I did. Korea, Vietnam! Let us all down, he has. He's a wimp!'

What a mess they are, thought Christophe. General Chapman is still trying to control his son. Yvette has spent years defending and protecting Simon Chapman whilst loathing her own grandson. And so bitter, both of them. I promise to God when Julia and I have children no one will ever treat them like that.

'Julia?' he said. 'Have either of you seen Julia or did Simon mention going to see Julia?'

'He didn't say anything to me,' said Yvette.

General Chapman shook his head.

'Don't worry Christophe I expect everyone will be back for the Chateau party tomorrow.' said Yvette.

'Of course they will. Nobody ever misses it, more's the pity. Give too much free booze and food, we do. I expect you'll be coming to take advantage of it too, de Flaubert?' asked the General.

'Yes, if I've found Julia. We love anything that we don't have to pay for,' he added sarcastically.

'Always been good at the back chat de Flaubert. You'd have dropped and given me ten for that if you'd been in my corps.'

'Oh hush, Charles.' Yvette, interjected. 'I'm sure she hasn't gone far, Christophe. She'll turn up. Don't you worry.'

***

Julia put her hand to her forehead. It killed her, like the worst migraine ever. Through the groggy haze, she thought it must be a hangover. Wasn't it nearly Christmas? Maybe she and Christophe had drunk too much? Odd though, she hadn't had a hangover like this since before she'd known Christophe. She felt uncomfortable. She was on a bed, but it wasn't her bed. Her eyes began to focus in the dim light. There was no window in the room and it smelt damp and earthy. She held her hand to the back of her head and felt a painful lump and dried blood matted in her hair. It wasn't a hangover. And she didn't have a clue where she was.

'Christophe?' she asked. Was he there with her? She reached out in the darkness to feel if he was there, but no one.

'Julia?' asked a quiet voice.

'Who's that?' she turned her head sharply towards the sound.

She felt someone grappling for her hand.

'Julia are you OK?' This time she recognised him.

'Simon?'

'Yes. It's me'

'Where are we?' She tried to sit up but her head hurt.

He moved over to her and held a glass of water to her lips. 'Here drink this, it's water.'

She grabbed it thirstily, her mouth was so dry, she gulped it down.

'Steady there,' he said, holding onto the glass. 'Sip it first. I think you might have a concussion.'

She grabbed his hand and moved the glass nearer. She was so thirsty.

'What happened. Where am I? Where is Christophe?'

'Here, drink a little more, you've been asleep for a long time. You're probably dehydrated.' He held the glass to her mouth again. 'Don't you remember anything at all?'

'No. I'm not sure.' She looked around the room. She didn't recognise anything. There were two metal camp beds, like in army barracks. On one side of the room there was a metal door. There was no window and the only light seemed to come from a couple of dim LED stair lights that were stuck on the walls.

'We're underground. These walls seem to be solid rock.' said Simon. 'I think we've been kidnapped.'

***

Christophe wandered up the narrow street that led past the moat, back towards the lodgings. He'd looked everywhere. He stopped and turned around. No he hadn't. He hadn't looked in all the shops. He hadn't looked in the most obvious places because he really didn't believe she was shopping. What was it they said? The simplest solution is usually the right one.

Which shop would she go into? Antiques and art probably. Yes, the art shop. Maybe she went there looking for clues. He turned right off the main street down the cobbled lane that was home to several antique and bric-a-brac shops. A small crowd had gathered around someone and he could see the flashes of cameras as people took photos.

Sophie was standing in front of the entrance to the exhibition shop of the '*ecole de beaux arts*'. She was dutifully posing for selfies with her fans. She saw him and immediately rushed over and hugged him. She gave him a kiss on the cheek and put her arm through his.

'It seems I am snowed in. Lucky me, I will be spending

Christmas in the chateau at Pont Carnac,' she said to the crowd that was getting even larger. 'Are you out sneakily doing secret Christmas shopping?' she asked him, loudly so that everyone could hear. 'I can't do anything secret!'

The crowd laughed.

'The price of fame.' he replied.

'Are you out looking for a present for me?' she smiled slyly, then continued before he could answer. 'Is he?' she asked the crowd. 'Have any of you seen what he's got for me?'

Again the crowd laughed, and took photos with their cameras. They loved the free Sophie show.

'You don't have to, you know.' She said, kissing Christophe on the lips. 'You don't have to get me anything at all.' She turned to face the crowd 'This is all I want for Christmas!' she pressed her beautiful rosy cheek, framed by its fake mink fur, to his, providing a perfect photo opportunity.

'Are you two together again?' someone shouted out from the crowd.

'You'll have to wait and see,' she said. 'I might have a Christmas surprise for you. Now, please…' She put her hand up to stop any more questions. 'You've all been very sweet, coming to see us, but could we have a little privacy now to do our shopping in peace. Thank you so much.' The crowd took a few more photos and then dispersed.

'Oh Christophe, you are so adorable. Still so adorable.' she said as they wandered off arm in arm.

Christophe laughed, then became serious. 'I'm looking for Julia, She's gone missing.'

'Oh?'

'Yes. Don't suppose you've seen her?'

'Sorry I haven't. Have you asked up at the chateau?

She and Simon seem to get along very well.'

Christophe froze and unconsciously removed his arm from hers.

'Ah,' she said, standing back to look at his face. 'Don't worry. If I do see her, I'll tell her you got sick of waiting for her so I stole you.'

She put her arm back through his and stared at their reflection in the shop window.

'Look how beautiful we look together, Christophe.'

Twenty-Five

CHRISTOPHE LEFT SOPHIE AT the entrance to the chateau and trailed listlessly around in the snow. He'd got to find Julia. He looked down a narrow street that ran between the Lodgings and the car park. Nothing. He turned around and went back the way he'd come. Maybe this was one of those ridiculous situations where two people kept crossing paths in opposite directions, constantly missing each other. The village was a warren of narrow streets and it was packed with Christmas shoppers. Yes, that was probably it. And in situations like that, somebody had to stay put and wait for the other person to find them. He went back to the lodgings. Wishful thinking probably but at the moment that was all he had.

He kicked the snow from his boots and went up to their room.

'She's not come back,' said the security guard. He looked worried.

'OK, thanks.' At least someone shared his concern.

Inside the room he looked in more detail at the case boards that they'd put together with Inspector Denton.

One board in particular drew his attention, the suspects. Guillemain's name stood out in bright red capitals, with exclamation marks, fiercely underlined three times and with a skull and cross bones. It had Julia's fury stamped all over it. No, surely not? He couldn't believe Guillemain would be involved. And if he was he wouldn't have let Christophe out. No. Not possible. Julia's gut instinct was way off on that one.

He moved on to the board on motives. What if he *was* the target and what if Charlene and Petit-Jean *were* collateral damage. The second suspect list. Cassandra and Jaimie Girault were top of the list. He dialled Jacques Morell's number. If anybody knew what Jaime was up to or could find him, it would be Jacques.

'Jacques?'

'Christophe. I was expecting a call from you sooner. I hear Guillemain arrested you.'

'Yes, but he's dropped the charges.'

'It was odd. He called me about you and some insurance scam. I thought I'd got it all straight but apparently not. He's like a dog with a bone when he thinks he's onto something.'

'Yes more like a terrier chasing the scent of its own tail than a rottweiler though. Jacques, Julia is missing and somebody tried to frame me for murder.'

'Oh?'

'Yes. And …'

'You're thinking it's the Giraults?' Jacques finished the sentence.

'Do you know where they are?'

'No. The trail has gone cold. Don't even know if she's managed to slip back in the country or if he's managed to leave. What worries me is the moment I seem to get a lead, it becomes a dead end. It's as if they see me coming.'

'You think they have someone on the inside?' Christophe was still staring at the board of suspects. There was something odd on the board next to Jaimie Girault's name. He thought it was an exclamation mark. But if Julia had done it there'd have been a hell of a lot more than she'd put on Guillemain.

'I'm certain they do, but not a clue who or where to look.' said Jacques. 'Be careful Christophe. If they do have someone on the inside, we have no idea what they know. No need to remind you that you are their number one target. And a good way to get to you would be to get to Julia, first.'

'That doesn't make me feel any better,' said Christophe as he moved closer to look at the exclamation mark.

'Let me know when you find her.'

'Will do,' said Christophe. It wasn't an exclamation mark, it was a very weird tiny drawing of a bottle of red wine.

Somebody was playing psychological games. The Girault family moved their drug concentrate around in the bulk red wine containers that were used to bring in raw red grape concentrate from South America. That was how they'd been caught. Who the hell would have drawn that? Certainly not Julia nor Bernard. He could kill himself for this. He knew Julia wasn't shopping. He was listening to his gut and it was telling him something was deeply wrong. He'd never forgive himself. He should have let it all drop. If he'd listened to Julia, they'd be back in London getting ready for Christmas. He'd been so stupid. What was more important, a bloody Baudoin painting and clearing Petit-Jean's name or finding Julia. It was the story of his life, love someone and lose them due to his jealousy, his ego and his stupidity. He'd just got to find her.

The only way to find her was to find out why the paintings had been stolen and why Petit-Jean and Charlene had been killed. It was getting late, but he couldn't even think of eating. Where was she? What if she'd fallen and was lying in a ditch somewhere? What if both he and Guillemain were wrong and she'd had an accident. He couldn't sit around and do nothing.

He grabbed his coat and headed back to the Baudoin house. Maybe the answer to this was there.

***

'Are you alright?' Julia asked Simon. 'Did I just fall asleep again?'

'Yes. It must be the concussion.'

What about you?'

'My mouth is dry all the time. And my neck is sore. I think I was grabbed from behind and strangled.' He sipped a little more of the water. 'Here,' he handed her the other glass. 'At least we've got some water,' he said.

'I have such a thirst,' said Julia, gulping it. 'How long have we been here?'

'I don't know, my watch says it's past midnight. What time did we leave the lodgings? That's the last thing I remember doing. I remember you said you recognised the security guard and we went outside to talk and that's about it.'

'You don't remember what you saw?'

'He shook his head. No. Did I see something?'

'You must have because you were looking over my shoulder and you shouted, 'Oh My God.'

'So I must have seen something.' He closed his eyes and willed himself to see. 'Not something, someone, I think I saw the security guard. Didn't you see anything? I must have been attacked from the side, my neck feels as if I've been pulled.'

'Simon we have to get out of here.'

'I've looked around but I can't see any way out. This place is hewn out of solid rock and the door is cast iron. I think we must be somewhere down in the old mine workings.'

'But have you seen anyone?'

'No. Like you I was unconscious and then when I came to, I was here and you were on the other bed.

'I want to get out. We have to get out.' She sat up and tried to get off the bed, but was really wobbly on her legs. She started going dizzy and lay back down again. Her ears started ringing and she was seeing specks of light. Somewhere in the background, far away in the distance, she could hear Simon's voice.

'Something's wrong,' he said. 'I feel really faint. The water, I think we've been drugged.' Everything had gone blank. She came round for a second and saw a shadowy figure at the door, then blacked out completely.

***

Christophe reached the Baudoin house and kicked the snow away from the door so he could push it open. That was odd. He must have forgotten to lock it. It was pitch black and cold inside. He closed the door and headed for the light switch but the electricity was off, probably shorted out because of the snow. The fire was still glowing with some red embers, so he threw a couple of firelighters and small logs on to get it going again. Julia's half empty glass was still by the side of the fire. How could this have happened? How the hell could he have lost her. He'd got to do something. He couldn't just do nothing. It was torture.

Using the light on his phone, he headed over to the boxes that they'd been looking through. He was sure he'd seen some candles in there with the incense. He rifled through them and stopped. He heard a noise behind him. He waited silently and listened. Breathing. He could hear faint breathing. There was someone in the house! He swung round to see a giant shape in silhouette. He grabbed one of the fire logs ready to hit out.

'It's me, Stefan! Please, I need to talk to you.'

Christophe kept the log raised, in case Stefan tried anything.

'How did you get in here?'

'The door was open. I came to help you.'

'Where the hell have you been?'

'I had to go into hiding until the time was right. Then I heard that Julia had gone missing and I knew I had to come.'

'Do you know where she is?' Christophe raised the log threateningly.

'No. But I know she is in danger.' Stefan stood his ground.

'Why the hell did you run off?' Christophe moved nearer to him, with the log still raised.

'Because I knew Charlene would die and that they would blame me, I had a premonition, I saw it.' Again, Stefan held his ground, not at all threatened by Christophe's actions.

'Well they didn't, did they?' Christophe lowered the log. 'They blamed me! So, your premonitions don't seem to be so hot, do they?'

'I sent the key like Petit-Jean told me to.' said Stefan

moving forward. 'I thought that you would figure out what Petit-Jean wanted you to know and all would be solved.' He moved over towards the fire and warmed his hands. 'I'm sorry. I stayed away, because I was in danger. I saw someone leaving the woods that night just after Charlene called me into her caravan.'

'Who?'

'I don't know and that's why I had to stay away, because he knows I saw him.'

'Was it definitely a man?'

'Yes.'

'But you didn't recognise him?'

'No.'

'And why is Julia in danger, Stefan?'

'Maybe because they found out what Petit-Jean was doing and what the key is for.'

'But she didn't know what the key was for Stefan. She went back to get it. That's when she went missing.'

'Oh no.'

'Yes. So, what the hell is the key for Stefan?'

'It fits the music box.'

'Here light the candles,' Christophe passed him some matches. 'We are going to have to get into the music box one way or another without the key.'

'He took hold of the small hacksaw that he'd brought down to cut the padlock, and started sawing around the lock.'

Stefan sat down on the three legged stool near the fire. He looked like a giant in a tiny cottage in a Grimm's fairy tale. Christophe watched him for a second. Stefan ignored him and closed his eyes in meditation.

Christophe continued sawing. He deliberately made as much noise as possible trying to break Stefan's

315

concentration. Julia was missing because of Mystic Stefan running away from a premonition, so he was not a big fan of meditation at the moment. It was all mad.

'She doesn't mind,' said Stefan.

'What?'

'Charlene. She doesn't mind you breaking her music box.'

'Seriously, Stefan. Don't give me any of your psychic talking to the dead stuff. If you really can talk to them, then you can ask them where Julia is. You can tell me what Petit-Jean wanted me to do, who killed him, and who killed Charlene and why.'

'It doesn't work like that.'

'Of course, it doesn't.' The box clattered again as he turned it around the other way. 'That would be far too easy!'

'I mean. What you get are not words or stories. You get sort of feelings and images in your head and occasionally voices. But it's really difficult to sort out because you don't always see it chronologically nor from the same person's point of view. It depends who you are channelling.'

Christophe stopped sawing for a moment and stared at Stefan. He was very composed sitting on the stool with his back straight. The guy really did believe this stuff. He looked so so certain of his convictions. What was even more strange, Christophe was beginning to feel a little convinced himself. He hesitated. No, it was madness. He started sawing the box again.

'Well do me a bloody favour Stefan. Log in to someone with a decent obsession on the order of things, who can tell me where Julia is. Because if anything happens to her I will never forgive you.'

'I'll try.' Stefan closed his eyes again and started chanting.

Christophe turned the box over. Just a bit more and he could probably push the lock out. It began to give way and he forced it open.

'Hold the candle nearer,' he said.

Inside there was an envelope and another key, tagged with a note that read 'padlock'.

Christophe tore open the envelope. Inside the envelope was a letter and a CD.

My dear Christophe

If you are reading this it is because Charlene and I are no longer here. Stefan warned me this might happen. I tried to keep as much as I could from Charlene to protect her but if Stefan has given this to you, I have been unable to do so and she and our baby have joined me in the next life.

Over the past year I have been trying to clear my Grandfather's name. He spoke to me through Stefan and I have been trying to find the proof. That is why we came to London.

We saw your girlfriend, and we knew instantly that she is your soulmate. We only saw her briefly, but Charlene could see the way that your spirits and past lives are entwined. She could feel your shared pain in your lives. And we felt your happiness together seeing her and then seeing your home. I didn't have the guts to intrude and disturb that with old burdens that are not yours to bear. They are my demons. Please watch the webcam footage on this disc. You will see we did not steal the paintings and we meant no harm, we needed something. Everything is under the roof trap door. You'll find everything that I have amassed so far.

I am so sorry that we fell out. I know I was wild and out

of control and I know you did everything you could to help me change but what I really needed was my soulmate. I needed Charlene to help me to see my true path in life. I know I have no right to ask this, but please, carry on our work and clear our names and that of my Grandfather.

People like us do not easily recognise, nor trust our soulmates, Christophe. Sometimes we have been through many lives, always letting them slip away. Now that you have found yours, look after her and never ever let her go.

We lost each other for a while, but you have never been far from my thoughts, your beloved friend, Petit-Jean.

Christophe began to tremble. Poor Petit-Jean and Charlene. If only he had done something, been there for him. It was a tragedy of his making.

Stefan watched him, touched his hand with his and nodded understandingly. Christophe stood up abruptly. He folded the letter and put it in his pocket. Now was not the time to dwell and get emotional. He had to find Julia.

'I think I've got something,' said Stefan. 'I can see Julia, she's underground surrounded by rock, there's an iron door.' And there is someone with her.'

'Who?'

'I don't know.'

Twenty-Six

CHRISTOPHE AND STEFAN WENT back to the lodgings and up to Christophe and Julia's room.

The security guard woke up from his chair and nodded to them sleepily. He didn't even flinch at the sight of a seven foot tall guy in a multicoloured hat.

'I don't suppose by any chance she is back?' asked Christophe

'No sorry, nobody's been by. It's late. I guess everyone is tucked up in bed.'

Christophe threw his coat on a chair, told Stefan to make some coffee and switched on the computer.

Once it was booted up, he loaded the CD.

The footage was recorded using a head camera and whoever was wearing it was creeping through the corridor of his London flat. The person in front was Charlene, even though it was badly lit with only mobile phone light, you could tell by her shape and the reddish glint of her hair. Petit-Jean must have been wearing the headcam.

They pulled out a torch and shone it first on the Chapman and took a photo, then they went over to the

Baudoin and took a photo. They seemed to be comparing it to a photo that Charlene held in her hands.

They went back to the Chapman and Charlene pulled out a specimen bottle and some tweezers and a small scalpel. They zoomed in on the Chapman and looked carefully all over it, using a magnifying glass. They went over one area several times and then used scalpel and the tweezers to remove a sample from the painting.

The camera then zoomed in on a large piece of paper with a message written on it. 'Sorry Thank you for your help to clear Odilon Baudoin's name.'

'Did you know about this?' Christophe asked Stefan.

'No. The only thing I knew was that Petit-Jean was trying to clear his grandfather's name. I channelled Odilon Baudoin and he said that he was not a Nazi collaborator and he did not shoot the others.'

'Just, for argument's sake, let's say that you *were* channelling him, and I'm not saying that I believe you were, what else did he say?'

'Nothing. Just that they had to clear his name.'

'Funny isn't it, how these dead people can give you just enough information but never actually solve a case. Why do you think that is?'

'It's to do with karma and life purpose.'

Christophe raised his eyebrows doubtfully. You had to admire the guy. His beliefs were so strong, he had an answer for everything. No different to some of the biblical stories, he supposed. Millions of people believed in a virgin birth and that took a hell of a lot of faith to think that was true.

'What karma and life purpose?' asked Christophe, intrigued. He clicked the download button so the video was saved to the computer

'Sometimes there is a path we have to go down, in order to understand ourselves and what the purpose of our life is.'

'Well, Stefan. I'm telling you now, your life purpose is to find Julia as fast as you bloody well can, or go straight to hell.' He ejected the CD, put it back in the envelope and into his pocket.

Stefan handed Christophe his coffee. He kept hold of the cup for a moment to getChristophe's attention. 'No, that is *your* life purpose. That task has been given to you.'

Ouch. Christophe felt a whole tornado in his solar plexus and nearly dropped the cup. He took a deep breath and pushed it aside. He'd got to be practical.

'Let's assume that rocks and an iron door are correct. It has to be somewhere around here because the snow is too deep for them to go very far unless they are equipped with a large snow plough. Can you see anything else?'

'I don't see so much as feel,' said Stefan.

'Well are you feeling anything then?'

'It's not cold. She's sleeping a lot. They are not doing her harm. She does not feel too scared.'

'They?'

'He, or they, I can't really see or get the feel of it. It's as if she's locked in somewhere but it is not so bad.'

'Right Stefan. You know this place even better than I do. A place with rocks, like a cave or a shack that's got sides in rock or something. Think man.'

'I can't just turn it on and off like a TV.' Stefan shook his head. He was still calm but exasperated. 'I told you, I have to let them decide what to tell me.' He went over to the fireplace and sat on the floor cross legged. 'Look, just let me think quietly, please. You're blasting out so much anger and disbelief, I can't hear my spirits think.'

'OK, you think a bit more and I'll go and tell Guillemain to start searching for a place with rocks and an iron door.' He stood up then hesitated. On the other hand, Guillemain was not going to go for it, without evidence. He already thought Christophe had turned into a conspiracy theorist lunatic. If he added belief in Stefan's psychic repertoire they weren't going to get anywhere. Also, it would mean telling him he'd found Stefan. No, he needed evidence. Evidence that something was wrong. He wafted his hand in front of a meditating Stefan. 'Right, come on Mystic Stefan, we need to get on the roof and get that trap door open.'

They went out into the first light of dawn. A fresh coat of snow had covered their tracks. When they got to the Baudoin House they found new tracks that went up to the door and moved off again.

'Somebody's been here since we left.' said Christophe

Stefan bent down and touched the ground and closed his eyes.

'It's him, the one who has taken Julia,' said Stefan.

Christophe looked at Stefan, very sceptical.

'You are kidding me! What now you're a Navajo tracker too?

'No but I am descended from the giant people of the Chicasawba and we have special powers. You don't have to believe me. You don't have to believe in anything spiritual. You don't have to believe in psychic powers, but you would be a fool not to because at the moment I am the only thing you have to go on.'

Christophe opened the door and they went inside. He was right. God help him, Stefan was right. The love of his life had disappeared and he had nothing to go on. What would Julia have said, if she was there? She'd say, gut feeling, instincts, listen to them.

'Yes, said Stefan. 'Julia would tell you to follow your instincts, your gut reaction.'

'How the hell?'

Like I said, the Chicasawba giants have special powers. Also, though, about the footprints. If you want to be logical. Who else would come knocking on the door before dawn so near to Christmas?'

'A Santa Claus with a phobia about being late?' suggested Christophe.

'So, you believe in Santa Claus but you do not believe in psychics. Very interesting.'

Christophe smiled wryly. A new age psychic with a sense of humour. Although his experience of new age psychics was non-existent, they were not famous for their sense of humour.

They walked up the stairs very slowly.

'It's OK,' said Stefan. He is not still here.'

'And you know this, how?' asked Christophe.

'I can feel it, deep inside my soul, here,' said Stefan, holding his hand on his heart.

Christophe turned to give him a warning and saw the twinkle in his eye.

'Only joking.' Stefan laughed. 'The footprints were going over each other like someone waiting, then disappeared in the direction of the village square.'

Up in the bedroom, Christophe leant out of the dormer window to see how much snow there was and if it was light enough to go up there safely.

'OK. Still dangerous but I guess it's now or never. There's not enough room up there for the both of us, not when one of us is a giant.' He picked up the rope that he and Julia had prepared and wound it around his waist, tying a reef knot. 'I'll go up and you keep a damn good hold on the other end of this rope in case I fall. I'm banking on the fact that the Chicasawba giants can easily hold the weight of a 160lb male.'

'No problem.' Stefan took Christophe's hand in his. 'Can I just say that it has been a pleasure to know both you and Julia.'

'What?'

Stefan smiled. 'Don't worry. I know you will be safe and so will Julia, but me, my time is near.'

Christophe hesitated about climbing any further up. 'Stefan what the hell are you talking about?'

'I've seen it. I've seen what happens here.'

'Now you start telling me this!'

'I have seen it. That is why I hid. But then I knew I could not change what was going to happen so I came to find you.'

'For Christ sake man, then don't do this. If you think you are going to die, don't do this. Tie the rope to the door or the beam or something and get the hell out of here.'

'The beam and door will not hold your weight. They are old and rotten. Anyway Christophe, it is our destiny.'

'Dammit Stefan. What exactly happens in this scenario?'

'He comes in and hits me, but you are on the roof and you still have the file, it is safe. I don't know after that.'

'You don't know after that?'

'Well no, because I'm dead'

'Let me get this right. You can see yourself die but you can't see yourself after you are dead and you can't see who kills you.'

'No.'

'Doesn't that make you think this psychic stuff is not very useful then?'

'That's just how it is. They tell you just as much as you need to know.'

'Very convenient.'

'Shall we start now?' asked Stefan. 'You are supposed to have started by now.'

'Hang on. What happens if we just change the scenario Stefan? You face the door so he can't hit you without you seeing him and you dodge the blow.'

'If you wish.'

'If I wish? Get a bloody grip man. Even if you believe in all this stuff, you should still wish it too. You don't want to die, do you?'

'Not yet but if it is my time, it is my time.'

This is all I need, thought Christophe. In the middle of trying to find Julia and the guy tells me if I do this, he will die. So, it's save Julia, or save Mystic Stefan. Sorry Stefan.

'I'm going up now,' said Christophe. He took off his gloves. He could get a better grip on the pegs with bare hands. 'Keep a lookout and whatever you do, do not turn your back to the door.'

Christophe grabbed the first peg. It was cold and icy. He pulled himself up to reach the next one and put his foot on the bottom one. He went up very slowly one peg, one hand then one foot at a time. When he got to the top, he lay down and crawled over to the middle part of the space between the roofs. The trap door had been completely covered over with snow and had frozen. He dug the snow out with his bare hands and fumbled around for the padlock. He wiggled the key around in it until it clicked open. He removed it and used the chain to tug on the trap door. It didn't move.

'You need to hurry,' Stefan shouted from below. 'He will be here soon.'

The snow had melted around the edges of the door and then refrozen.

'It's stuck!' shouted Christophe. He pulled hard again and his hand slipped on the chain and he nearly fell backwards. He needed something to get the ice out. He took the key out of the padlock and used it to clear the groove where the door rested in the frame. He pulled again and felt it release.

'It's open,' he shouted back down to Stefan.

He shone his mobile torch down into it. There was a vertical space no bigger than a caretaker's broom cupboard.

'Try and give me some slack on the rope,' he shouted to Stefan, 'but don't let go!'

'OK,' he heard Stefan shout back as he felt the rope give a little.

He sat on the edge of the open trap door and lowered himself down into the space. He could just about stand up with his head poking out of the top and had an arm's length of space either side of him.

'I'm in!' he shouted down to Stefan.

'The file you need is red,' came the response.

Very little of the early morning light reached the inside of the space, so he used his phone to look around. Two of the sides had pinboards on and were covered with photos and documents. One other side had shelves with paints and brushes left from Odilon Baudoin's days. The final one had bags and containers of samples taped to it, similar to the one that Charlene had in the video. He couldn't see a file anywhere.

'There's no file,' he shouted down.

'Shelves, it must be on some shelves. Near paints and brushes.

Christophe searched amongst the books and paintbrushes on rows of shelves at the back of the cupboard. He found a red file.

'Found it, but it's empty.'

'Oh,' said Stefan.'

Then Christophe looked more closely at the documents and pictures that had been taped on the walls. There were old letters from the Breton Independence movement, including both Odilon Baudoin and William Chapman's membership papers. There were various pictures of bits of paintings that had been blown up large. There were several pictures of Baudoin with Yvette and Chapman and other members of the Breton School, and cut outs of articles from old newspapers.

'You have to put everything in the file' shouted Stefan.

You don't say, thought Christophe. He started to pull the first newspaper article off the wall, then stopped. If he did that, they wouldn't know how everything was related. He put it back.

'I'm going to take pictures of it *in situ* first,' he shouted to Stefan.

'OK,' said Stefan. 'But hurry please, he will be here soon!'

No pressure then, thought Christophe. Quite reassuring that mystic Stefan doesn't want to die after all, though. He really did not want that responsibility - he'd already got enough dead skeletons in cupboards that he classed as being his own fault. He took the photos quickly, then pulled everything off and put it in a file. He pulled out the specimen jars and shoved them into the pockets of his jacket, because they wouldn't fit in the file. He'd got to get out of there. If Stefan was right about his own death, they were both in trouble.

'I'm coming back down Stefan,' he shouted.

'Be careful' Stefan shouted back.

'Me be careful. What about you?'

Hang on a minute, thought Christophe, realising this was the moment that Stefan was about to be hit on the head. Stefan had said that Christophe was still on the roof with the file when he was hit. So, what if he gave him the file first, that would change the scenario again.'

'Actually, I'm going to hand you the file down, first.'

'OK,' said Stefan.

Stefan stuck his long arm out of the window and Christophe held on to a peg with one hand and reached down with his other to give him the file. As Stefan looked up to take it, he smiled and Christophe realised the enormity of his error. Stefan had had to turn around to take the file and he had his back to the door!

Christophe heard the blow to Stefan's head but slipped on the pegs as he tried to get back down too quickly. The rope jerked as he fell the length of the slack, and he was left hanging from the dormer window. The rope jerked again and he suddenly fell another couple of feet and heard another thud. His weight must have pulled the injured Stefan across the room and wedged him against the bottom of the window on the inside.

'Stefan?!' he shouted.

No reply.

Christophe swayed back and forth on the hanging rope gently. He didn't want to make Stefan's injuries worse but he had to get back in the room somehow. After a couple of sways, he got close enough to the wall to reach up and grab the bottom window ledge. Using his feet he pushed up against the wall until he managed to get high enough to push himself up onto his elbows. He launched himself through the window head first.

Stefan was lying on the floor with blood pouring out of his head. He tried gently to stem the blood, without moving his head. He knew that if blood was still coming out it meant that his heart was still beating. He called an ambulance with one hand and felt for a pulse with the other. It was faint but there. He checked Stefan's mouth and nose to make sure the airways were clear and made sure he was still breathing. Stefan was still unconscious and looking very pale. Christophe called Guillemain.

The Air Ambulance had a lot of trouble reaching the village but when it did arrive, Stefan was still unconscious but alive. Inspector Guillemain stood in the hall of the Baudoin house, shaking his head.

'OK Christophe so what have we got?'

Christophe showed Guillemain the photos on his phone. 'Petit-Jean was on to something, otherwise he wouldn't have been a target. He also gave me a video of him in my house. He was taking a sample out of the Chapman and Baudoin paintings and comparing it to a photo.'

'And the specimen bottles and envelopes?'

'Christophe dug around in his pockets and pulled them out.'

Guillemain looked them over. 'This one looks like an old bullet.' He said looking at one of the specimen jars.

'Yes and there's a casing with blood on it too', said Christophe.

'Does it say where they found it?' asked Guillemain.

'Not on the jars,' said Christophe but there might

have been something on the notes stuck to the pin boards that I put in the file. I can't read it in the photos that I took on my phone, it's too blurred.'

'And the file?'

'Gone. It all happened exactly as Stefan said it would.'

'I'll send all of the samples to forensics in Rennes urgently. They can go in the ambulance, it will be the quickest.'

'And Julia?' asked Christophe. 'There are now three people dead, Guillemain.'

'Well, not Stefan. Not yet thankfully. If what you tell me this Stefan said is true. I don't hold with any of that psychic stuff, but I do believe your girlfriend has been taken.'

'So where is she, Guillemain?'

'Again, all supposing this psychic mumbo jumbo might be coincidentally correct, the only places I can think of like that are the old rock tunnels that go from the château up to the Autumn peaks or the ones that go down into the different houses along the back of village walls or down underneath the empty moat. I suggest we start there, although we don't have many men. I'll call around some people I know but it will be a while before they get here.'

'What about the security guard we've got at the lodgings?'

'Okay get him out too, and get him to call others from the company. Anybody else you can think of?'

'I'll come, you'll need me for this,' said a loud booming voice behind them, making everyone jump to attention.

Unusual for him, thought Christophe. Somehow, he's managed to sneak in here as quietly as a mouse on mogadon.

'Heard the air ambulance,' he shouted in his booming voice.

Christophe felt like putting his fingers in his ears. General Chapman definitely had a problem with his volume controls. Must be all that noisy military action he's done, probably turned him deaf, he concluded.

'Saw it from the ramparts! Thought it was you or your girlfriend de Flaubert. Need a military man for an operation like this. I'll take it from here, Guillemain.'

Guillemain looked at Christophe in enquiry.

Christophe shrugged his shoulders. 'I don't care who is in charge, as long as we find Julia.'

'And you will need this too,' said General Chapman as he opened up a large drawing that he had under his arm. He spread it out on the table in front of them. 'When you said she was missing, I thought about it. In this snow, these tunnels are the obvious place to retreat and hide out.'

Christophe and Guillemain leant over the drawing. 'I didn't know this map existed,' said Guillemain.

'Dates back to after the war,' said General Chapman. 'I made it. Used to go down there as a child, carefully mapping it all out ready for World War III. Always knew I'd be a military man and would need it one day.'

'Brilliant,' said Christophe. Whatever he thought of Chapman, he was relieved that they now had something to work on. 'Let's get started.'

'Not so fast de Flaubert. Not all the tunnels are mapped but most of them are. Remember it was done a long time ago.'

'Okay,' said Christophe, picking up the map and turning for the door. General Chapman tapped him on the shoulder and gestured that he should take a seat.

'At ease de Flaubert, we're not ready yet. Sit and listen.' The General took the map from Christophe and spread it out again on the table. 'De Flaubert, you will reconnoitre with the security guard and start with the tunnels up to the peaks, here,' he said, pointing to a spot on the drawings. 'You'll need rope, equipment and a better flashlight. Be careful, those tunnels have caved in, in places. I will work with you Guillemain in the passageways down to the village wall and under the moat.'

'Actually, cousin Charles, I need to go and sort this evidence out for forensics.'

'What evidence?'

'Some samples that's all. I will join you when I get back.'

'That's ridiculous,' said General Chapman. A woman's life is at stake and you're fiddling around with your plastic bags. Delegate it man.'

Guillemain shook his head. 'This is an official investigation, Charles. It must be done in the proper manner. I will join you when I have everything ready,' Guillemain insisted forcefully. 'We need to approach this from two angles. The most urgent is that you look for Miss Connors. However, I need to look at all of this information that Petit-Jean collected and try and find out who is behind this.'

'And how exactly will you know where we are?' asked General Chapman. 'There'll be no phone cover down there.'

'Christophe, send me all the photos that you took, please.' said Guillemain, picking up the samples.

The air ambulance crew were bringing Stefan down on a stretcher from the top room. He had a drip in his arm and an oxygen mask on but was still unconscious.'

'Will he make it?' asked Christophe.

The paramedic shook his head. 'Can't say at this point, sorry. It's a bad blow to the head. We'll do our best.'

332

Christophe didn't know why, but he touched Stefan's arm gently, as they took him out. It was a gut reaction, maybe he was feeling the contact would help Stefan, or maybe he was taking a last opportunity to say thank you, while he was still alive.

'I'll need the CD, as well,' said Guillemain, interrupting Christophe's thoughts.

'What? Oh yes, of course.' He took it out of his pocket and handed it over.

'Cousin Charles. I suggest you mark two different coloured routes on the map and we all take pictures of them. That is how we will know how to find each other.' He followed the paramedics out.

'Should have gone into the army, Guillemain.' General Chapman shouted after him. 'Wasted in the fraud squad you are.'

What a know it all and a bully he is, Christophe thought. But my God I'm glad he's here.

Twenty-Seven

'SIMON, WAKE UP!' SAID Julia. For the first time since they'd been kidnapped, she had a clear head.

Simon groaned. 'My neck and shoulder are killing me.'

'Someone has been in here and left us food and a light. There's a piece of paper and a bottle of wine.'

'What? Why would they do that?'

Julia went over and picked up the paper. 'It seems very odd.'

'What does it say?'

'It's a screenshot of an article in today's Paris Match online.'

'What?'

'There's a picture of Christophe and Sophie, smiling and shopping together.' She read the headline out loud, 'Sophie, the darling of Hollywood is snowed in, but she's got all she wants for Christmas.'

'Let me see,' said Simon.

She handed it to him, slightly roughly. 'Unbelievable. I go missing and he's Christmas shopping with Sophie

Petrarch!' She paced up and down the room. 'I can't believe he is not looking for me.'

Simon stood up and went to hug her. 'Julia, it is almost certainly photo-shopped. Of course, he'll be looking for you.'

Julia shook her head. Would he? Of course, he would. She picked up the bottle of wine and held it nearer to the dim light to read the label.

'No!' she shouted and sat down on the bed, in shock. 'No, God no.'

'What is it?' asked Simon? 'Julia what's wrong.'

She handed him the bottle.

'Château Lacoste, mis en bouteille au château, famille Girault,' said Simon

'We've gotta get out of here,' said Julia. 'It's got to be Jaime Girault and Cassandra. We have to get out of here.'

'What? But why would Jaime Girault be involved?'

'Because Christophe was the one responsible for breaking the drug ring he was running. He's out for revenge.'

'But why kidnap us?'

'Because I recognised the security guard. He's already tried to frame Christophe for stealing the paintings and Charlene's murder but that failed. Then I recognised the security guard and he would have been found out.'

'So why keep us alive? And why the childish copy of the Paris Match article and the wine?'

'Because that is exactly the kind of thing he would do. Psychological and emotional torture is a forte of his. And believe me I know. Keeping us alive is just him stringing out his revenge.'

'Good grief! I never knew anything of this. I just thought he was a playboy who operated only just within the law and occasionally outside of it. But this? And Murder?'

'He has a sadistic side to him,' said Julia. 'He claims it is a genetic legacy from the de Sade family and he is very proud of it. He's waited a long time for this. That's why he hasn't killed us yet.'

'Well that will be his undoing, because it means we are still alive and we have a chance of getting out of here alive!' said Simon, jumping up. 'We need a plan!'

'Or,' said Julia, looking down at the picture of Christophe with Sophie. 'Maybe the reason he is biding his time, is so that he can murder us and …'

'Frame Christophe for our murder?' suggested Simon.

'Yes, because this is all about Christophe, not Charlene and Petit-Jean, not the paintings, not you and I. This is all about his hatred of Christophe.'

'Then let's get out of here,' said Simon. 'I have an idea. I will not eat or drink anything, so that I stay awake. Then when he comes back, I'll try and hit him from behind. Which way does the door open?'

'I don't know, I've never seen it open, I've always been asleep.'

'Me neither.'

'Because he only ever comes here when we're drugged and asleep.' Julia paced up and down thinking out loud. 'So, how does he know we're asleep?'

'I've no idea there doesn't seem to be a camera anywhere.'

'Maybe he just listens.' Julia went over to the door. After her initial clear head, she had started to feel the after effects of the drugs, but she knew she had to shake it off and keep awake. 'How are we getting air in here, Simon? There must be a vent or something to let air in otherwise we would have suffocated by now.'

They pulled the bed and table back away from the walls and found there was a small air brick. Julia pulled the LED off the wall, lay down on the floor and tried to look through the air brick.

'I think it might go out into a sort of corridor, or tunnel.'

'Maybe that's where he comes and listens to see if we are asleep.'

'What if we dig a space around it and pull it out? Then we can start making the hole bigger and crawl out.'

'With what, Julia?'

'I don't know, pull one of the legs off the bed. She lifted off the mattress. Or part of the metal frame, can't we just yank a piece off?'

'Looks too solid to me,' said Simon. 'These are military grade beds.'

'There's got to be something we can use.' she said, looking round desperately. Her eyes focused on the bottle and the water glasses.

'We could smash the wine bottle and use the glass shards. Or one of the water glasses, that would be better. Don't think I could stand the smell of wine here. I feel nauseous enough as it is.' She grabbed the cover off her bed. Put the glass in it and smashed it against the wall.

***

'Thank you for helping with this,' said Christophe to the security guard as he laid out the map of the tunnels on the table at the Castle Lodgings.

'What's your name?'

'Thomas.'

'Well Thomas I'm sure you're in a hurry to get back

to your family for Christmas, so the quicker we find her, the quicker we'll all be eating turkey. I hope.'

'Sort of. But we're all working, through Christmas. We're a family run business and it's a busy time. A lot of goods and cash change hands so lots of people and even companies call on us to supplement their extra security.'

'I can imagine.'

Christophe pushed the torch and a couple of marker pens into his pocket and pointed at the map of the known tunnels that GeneralChapman had given them. He had circled the area of old iron age tunnels from the base of the *lavoire*, up to the peaks. There seemed to be tons of different passageways.

'My mobile is a bit short on battery, how is yours, Thomas?'

'Fully charged.'

'OK, you get a picture of the map as a backup. We'll use mine until it runs out. We'll put marks on the walls every time we turn, just in case we get lost. Also, don't forget, Chapman said that not all of the tunnels are mapped.'

'Chapman? As in the gallery people, up at the château?'

'Yes. Do you know them?'

'No, not personally, but we did do a job for them in London - your job actually. That's why I was so sorry to hear that your wife had gone missing. She was very kind when we picked up the paintings in London.'

'You picked up the paintings?'

'Yeah, a Chapman and a Baudoin for the gallery.'

'And what did you do with them?'

'We took them to the Chapman gallery in London.'

'What? Yes, we took them to the gallery as we'd been asked to.'

'So, they got a security company from Brittany to fly over to London to pick up two paintings and deliver them a mile down the road. It doesn't make sense.'

'We were going anyway because Guillemain from the fraud squad had invited us to a lecture he was giving on art security, and we're quite new to it.'

'Do you know who ordered the pick up?'

'No. We were just given the Chapman gallery uniforms to use, the right size containers and the transport of works of art and antiquities papers and the destination.'

'Is there any way you can find out who ordered the pick-up of the paintings?'

'I can ask my aunt. She does all the company admin.'

'Can you get hold of her?' This is vital!'

Thomas clicked on his contacts and waited for an answer. Christophe carried on looking at the tunnels. He was trying to get things straight in his head, but couldn't. None of it made sense.

'She says it is just the normal Chapman Art Gallery order papers,' said Thomas.

'Whoever did this has been very clever using you, a legitimate company rather than art crooks to set this up. Is the order signed?'

'She says no, just has the gallery stamp, but she can try and trace the payment method if that helps.'

'Yes, good idea. Save your battery and ask her to get back to us as fast as she can. Come on, let's talk as we go. I've changed my mind. We are not going on the routes up to the peaks as planned, we are going to follow the same passages as Inspector Guillemain and General Chapman.'

'Why?'

'Because, whoever organised the theft of the paintings has got Julia.'

'We thought they'd been stolen after we delivered them,' said Thomas. 'And nobody even came to ask us about it.'

'Not even Inspector Guillemain, or the English Inspector Denton?'

'No, nobody.'

'And Inspector Guillemain was coincidentally in London at the same time.' said Christophe.

'Yes,' said Thomas, looking worried.

Christophe looked over at the white board where Julia's big red underlining of Guillemain's name glared at him accusingly. Thomas followed his gaze.

'Do you think the Inspector is involved?' he asked, shocked.

'I don't know, Thomas. I just don't know.'

He folded up the map and took a deep breath. How could I have been so stupid? Guillemain plays nice when I apologise to him in the Gendarmerie, and what do I do? Mr Gullible. I make the biggest mistake of my life by giving him all of the evidence that Petit-Jean had collected. And let him talk me out of trying to set up a search for Julia immediately. But, there is one thing I do still have. Thank God I downloaded the CD onto the computer.

'We don't have any time to lose,' said Christophe. ``We'll go into the tunnels from the bottom, down by the *lavoire* and make our way up towards the château.'

'What if the Inspector *is* involved?' Thomas was starting to look nervous.

'Are you armed?' asked Christophe.

'I have an arms licence but I'm not carrying today.' Thomas replied, wide eyed. He hadn't even wanted a firearm but it was a requirement for some of the jobs they did.

'What do you have?'

'Telescopic baton.' said Thomas clutching the baton attached to his belt.

'Well let's hope that'll be enough!'

'We should notify the police,' said Thomas, taking his radio out. 'It's part of my work code, to inform the police of any changes or dangerous situations.'

'I'm sure that if you know one of the main suspects is a police officer, if it ever gets to court, they'll let you off.'

'But how will we call for back-up?' said Thomas. 'We are going to need back up.'

'If you notify them, you'll give the game away and we'll lose the element of surprise. Please Thomas trust me on this.'

Thomas looked at Christophe, looked down and fiddled nervously with his mobile. He looked up again. They'd reached the entrance to the start of the *lavoire* tunnel. The heavy iron gate was already open. He really ought to call the police. His phone rang, making them both jump out of their skins.

'*Allo*,' he said and listened, nodding. He switched off and turned to Christophe.

'Payment made by the Chapman Château maintenance and management account, and signed by General Charles Chapman.'

'Hell.' said Christophe. 'Julia and Simon must have somehow been on to him.'

'She probably recognised me from the London pick-up,' said Thomas.'

'Yes. And knowing her she would have started following the lead straight away.'

'Now can I call the police?' asked Thomas.'

Christophe hesitated for a second. Was he sure? Then he looked at Thomas.

'I have to!' said Thomas

'But what if Guillemain and Chapman are working together. You know what these Breton families are like, Thomas, and they are cousins.'

Thomas could see the desperation in Christophe's eyes.

'I guess if we're in the tunnels I wouldn't have phone cover, so maybe it would be difficult to inform the Gendarmerie straight away, and that would stand up in my defence.'

'Thank you, Thomas.'

'Doesn't help with the back up though. And one telescopic baton against a police officer and a retired General that are both armed and probably good shots, are pretty crap odds.'

'Let's hope it won't come to that. Guillemain still has to get back from Rennes and even though General Chapman has a head start, he is not expecting us.'

'We'll need to be as quiet as possible,'' said Thomas. 'Better switch everything off just in case a signal does get through down there.' He swiped the screen on his mobile but Christophe grabbed his hand.

'Tell your aunt first, so somebody knows what's going on.' Come on, and keep your baton in your hand.'

'Right,' said Thomas, looking around on the ground while he waited for his aunt to answer. He shook his head. 'No reply,' He switched it off and moved over to the gate and started shaking it. Some rust fell off near the bottom corner. He bent down and grabbed the bottom of one of the rusty bars, yanked it out and gave it to Christophe.

Christophe weighed it up in his hands and nodded.

'Good job man. Odds looking much better, now.' he said, patting Thomas on the back. 'Also, I forgot to mention that General Chapman is a bit deaf, so that's a bonus.'

'Great. May the odds forever be in our favour,' said Thomas wryly and they crept into the dark tunnel.

Twenty-Eight

JULIA HAD A PIECE of the cover wrapped around her hand, but even so the glass shard had cut into her when she applied pressure on it to dig away the cement. She was about a quarter of the way around the edge now.

'Julia stop.' said Simon. Look at your hand. 'This isn't going to work.'

She moved back from the corner of the wall to wipe the sweat and dust from her face.

'If I can get more than half of the edge out, we could try and smash it with the bottle or kick it out,' she said. 'Here you have a go for a moment.' She handed him the shard. 'Lord I'm thirsty but I'm not going to drink anything, it's bound to be drugged.'

Simon lay down on the floor and sighed. He started scraping and then stopped.

'What if he hears us? What if he comes back to listen? He'll see the hole we've made.'

'But what else can we do?' said Julia. She watched Simon delicately scraping away with hardly any pressure.

'Here, give it back to me,' she said. 'No point in both

of us getting bloody hands.'

She lay down flat again on the floor to get underneath the bottom of the brick. She started scratching then stopped.

'Can you hear that?'

'What? Said Simon.

He lay down flat next to her and listened.

'Footsteps,' she said.

'They are getting nearer,' he whispered. 'Get on the bed and pretend to be asleep. I'll try and get him as he comes in.'

Julia lay down trying to slow her breathing as if she was asleep. The steps stopped outside the door and then there was the sound of a key in the lock. Simon picked up the bottle of wine and hid it behind his back. The door opened inwards and he hit the assailant hard on the back of his head as he entered.

Charles Chapman fell to the ground unconscious, a gun in his hand.

'Christ!' said Simon. It's my father!'

'What? But why?'

'I don't know,' said Simon. 'What the hell is he doing here?'

There were further footsteps and Yvette rushed into the room.

'Simon, what have you done?' She bent down to see if Charles was still alive.

Simon bent down too, checked his father's pulse and took the gun from him.'

'He was the one who was keeping us here, he must have organised the theft of the paintings and killed Charlene and Petit-Jean.' said Simon.

'Did he Simon?'

'You know he did, Yvette.'

'Simon, this has gone far enough!'

'What do you mean? Asked Julia.

'She doesn't mean anything,' said Simon. 'She's senile. Old people make things up and imagine things. Especially when they are in shock.' Yvette stared at him, shaking her head. 'I'm telling you Yvette. Father must have known about the switching of the paintings. He knew Petit-Jean and Charlene had the evidence and he was going to expose the fraud, so he killed them.'

'What switching of the paintings?' asked Julia.

'It was Baudoin who was the real genius. My Grandfather was nothing more than an amateur. So, they…' he pointed at Yvette '… her and my grandfather saw an opportunity. Baudoin rarely signed his canvases so Chapman signed them as his, and my grandfather and Yvette made a fortune out of it. This bitter old woman played along with it so that she could overcome the stigma of being married to a traitor and live the high life in luxury.'

'Is that true?' Asked Julia, already knowing the answer. The photo she'd seen, their Baudoin being at Odilon Baudoin's feet, but the Chapman being on the canvas in the process of being painted by Odilon Baudoin.

'And Petit-Jean found out!' said Julia. 'But murder?' She looked at Yvette horrified. 'Your own grandson.

Yvette shook her head. Her cold demeanour had changed to one of deep sadness and the tears had begun to fall.

'No. I believed Petit-Jean had an accident, and that Charlene had committed suicide like everyone else.' she said, bitterly.

'How did you know she didn't?' Asked Julia.

'I didn't. Until I found out after the autopsy that she had been pregnant Then I realised that if she carried out Petit-Jean's wishes and exposed us there would be a huge scandal, the Chapman's would lose everything and her baby would rightly inherit the Chapman fortune and that is why they killed her.'

'You went along with it for long enough old woman.'

'And I would have left it to Petit-Jean in the end. I would have told him in the end. I would never have resorted to murder!'

'Your father killed Charlene for that?' said Julia

'No!' said Yvette. 'He didn't. Charles did not know!'

'Shut up! You bitter old hag,' said Simon. He turned to Julia. 'I didn't agree with my father, I didn't want any part in the murders and that is why he locked me in here with you. He's the one that had the key.'

'Except that that is not true is it?' said a voice behind them.

Inspector Guillemain walked in. 'It may surprise you to know that Stefan is now conscious and has identified you as the person that hit him on the head at the Baudoin house last night.'

'But Simon has been locked up here with me,' said Julia.

'So, you see Stefan has it all wrong, it was obviously my father,' said Simon.

'Has Mr Chapman been with you all the time, Miss Connors?'

'Well yes,' said Julia

'And have you been fully conscious all the time?'

'Well no we were drugged.'

'Are you sure both of you were drugged?'

Suddenly Simon grabbed Julia and held Chapman's gun to her head.

'Move back Guillemain. I take Julia and leave or I shoot her, make your choice.'

'Simon that's enough!' said Yvette. 'Don't do this. There has been enough lies, death and destruction in our lives. Stop! For God's sake stop!'

'You tell me! Well let me tell you something. You deserve everything you've ever got, you selfish bitter bitch. Do you know what Petit-Jean had found? He'd realised that it wasn't Odilon Baudoin who was the traitor, that it was my grandfather and he was going to expose it all.'

Yvette gasped in horror.

'Yes, your beloved Odilon tried to stop my Grandfather giving the panels to the Nazis. It was him that shot Guillemain and the others. He confessed to me on his death bed and told me to tell you.'

'And you didn't!'

'And ruin my career and our lives. You didn't deserve to know. You did everything you could to selfishly live a good life, and you didn't even have faith in the man you supposedly loved.'

'Put the gun down Simon,' said Guillemain and let Miss Connors go.

'Ah, you see therein lies the problem. I've had a considerable amount of help from someone. It was his idea for me to lock myself in here with her. He's going to be very angry with me if I let her go.'

'Girault!' said Julia, feeling sick.

Simon caressed Julia's mouth with the gun barrel. 'Shhh, calm down Julia. Otherwise I may have to hand you over to him straight away.'

'Why, why would you do that?'

'Well when Christophe started looking into the murders it all got difficult. Then he was released and it all calmed down but you went and recognised the security guard and were working it all out, so you left us no alternative. He should be here fairly soon. Just in time to wound me slightly, leaving me as the hero who uncovered the fraud and murder that my father had organised with his accomplice Girault, who took you hostage. Never to be found again.

'You're crazy,' said Julia.

'It would all have been fine, if you hadn't come down here, Yvette. And you too Guillemain.'

'Now, then what to do with you all.'

'I'm guessing nobody else knows you're here,' he looked at each of them in turn and saw Guillemain flinch. 'Ah, someone else knows. Christophe I imagine.' He turned Julia around to face him, keeping the gun to her head. 'Don't get your hopes up. You know Girault and his extremely clever sister always have a back up plan.' He turned her around again to face the others. He pushed her forwards towards General Chapman. 'Take the map from him.'

Julia picked up the map. He quickly glanced down at it, still keeping the gun to her head.

'What marks are written on the yellow line?'

'Err, nothing. Just *lavoire* at the bottom.'

'And the green line?'

'Dungeon and peaks'

'So if you, cousin, and my father are here, that must mean Christophe is heading up to the peaks.'

Guillemain remained silent.

'True or not?' he shouted, forcing the gun against Julia's head so hard that it hurt.

Still Guillemain said nothing.

'Seriously cousin, you want to be a hero? Is there anyone else looking in the tunnels?'

Guillemain saw the terror in Julia's eyes. 'No,' he said quietly.

'Well it doesn't matter because we've got a few opportune cave-ins planned. These tunnels are terribly dangerous.' He moved the gun and pushed it into Julia's back hard, making her move forward.

'Let's go.'

Julia started to struggle. 'You're mad!'

He hit her across the side of the head with the gun.

'Stop it, Julia. Behave and you might still have a choice. I don't have to give you to Girault straight away. I could even hide you from him if you are nice to me.'

'I'd rather you shoot me. You're a lunatic.'

'Well you can blame him for that!' Simon kicked his father in the head. 'His sergeant major tactics are what have made me what I am. He didn't know of course. He couldn't know. My Grandfather kept it from him all these years because if he knew he would have done the right thing with his ridiculous oaths of military honour and country.' General Chapman moaned and Simon kicked him again. He manoeuvred Julia towards the door, keeping the gun against her head.

'Go over to the bed,' he said to Guillemain. 'You too Yvette.'

'You two can shout all you like but there is no one to hear you. These tunnels are full of dead ends and once they cave in you are all doomed.'

'Simon, don't,' pleaded Julia. 'Don't do this, surely they don't deserve this?'

'Cousin Guillemain probably doesn't but my father

and Yvette do. Serves them right for giving me such a hellish up-bringing.'

'Then let me stay too!' said Julia. 'Lock me in with them too. I'd rather die than leave with you!'

'Tut tut. You don't really mean that Julia. Not after all the times that I've saved you.' he said sarcastically. 'And, of course this is going to break Christophe's heart, which really is the icing on the cake. Now let's go!'

'You are completely mad!'

He pulled Julia through the door and out into the tunnel, and kicked the door shut. The key was still in the lock. He continued to hold the gun to her head.

'Lock it!' he said.

He manoeuvred her a little further along the tunnel and pushed her down on the floor near the airbrick.

'Unbutton your shirt and take it off,' he said.

Julia fumbled with the shirt. She could still feel the gun muzzle on the back of her head.

'Now stuff it into the holes in the air brick to block it. Don't want them being able to breathe and trying to break out.

'Simon, For God's sake!'

'Just do it.' He put his free hand in his pocket and pulled out a small two way radio.'

'These are excellent. Modern technology that works underground.' He pushed her face down on the floor and held the radio next to her and pressed the button.

'Say hello nicely to Mr Girault.'

Julia shook her head.

He took the radio back and pressed the button with his free hand.

'Sorry, Jaimie, she doesn't want to talk to you.'

She didn't hear the reply.

'Of course you can have her, as long as you stick to your side of the bargain.'

Silence for a moment.

'We need two cave-ins. One in the main tunnel at the first turning after the *lavoire* and the other up at the Peaks entrance. You can do that immediately. Give us ten mins to get clear before you do the lavoire end.'

'Yes I'm sure he's up there.'

He put the radio back in his pocket. 'That's super, everything organised and sorted out tidily. It's a shame really, my father would be quite impressed with my military organisational skills if only he wasn't going to die.'

'You can't be serious. You can't honestly believe you are going to get away with this.'

'Oh, I do, Julia. I do. You and I are going to lie low in a lovely little place I know and then, I guess I'm going to have to hand you over to your friend Girault.'

Julia leapt up in a fury, not caring that he had a gun in his hand.

'You bastard, you evil, nasty piece of work!' She started hitting him with her fists and screaming.

He tried to grab her hands but she was like a wild animal in a trap that was willing to bite its own leg off to get away. He pointed the gun down and shot her in the foot. The sound of the shot was deafening as it echoed around the tunnels.

'That's enough!'

Julia screamed out in pain.

'Wow. You really do hate him don't you! He said you did.'

Julia rolled around on the floor holding her foot. Her eyes were smarting with the pain and anger. She turned to glare at him. Out of the corner of her eye she saw two shadows behind Simon. One was moving quietly towards him, holding the other back. It couldn't be Girault's men, they wouldn't have crept along, they'd have walked straight up to him. She quickly looked down so that Simon didn't see her face. She had to keep him distracted. Her foot was killing her but she had to keep calm. She held her hand to it and tried to focus on her hand that was not painful and not her foot. It was a technique she'd been taught at PTSD classes.

'Why, Simon?' she asked, her voice calm, almost friendly. 'Why would you get involved with him?'

Her reaction put him his off his guard. This was the Julia that liked him. He relaxed a little.

'Well we have a lot in common. He heard about the Chapman and Baudoin going missing and Guillemain arresting Christophe for insurance fraud, so he kindly rang to congratulate me. Then we got chatting and he was very sympathetic when rather annoyingly Christophe was released. He helped me devise a better plan. I have to say it was all going very well and then the security guard thing. I knocked you out for a while so I could think. That's when the Giraults came up with their back up plans.' He shook his head sadly. 'I didn't like it but ...Well it was your own fault. You had to go and recognise the security guard.'

'Tough shit,' said Julia as Thomas brought his baton down on the back of Simon's head.

Twenty-Nine

A LARGE CROWD OF local people and journalists had gathered in the Spring sunshine in front of the Baudoin House. A ribbon sectioned off the front and a TV crew was interviewing Sophie Petrarch and Inspector Guillemain, the new Mayor of Pont Carnac. Guillemain handed the scissors to Sophie to cut the ribbon. She hesitated for a second.

'There have been many people involved in the creation of this museum. People who have done far more than I.' She gestured to Julia to join her. Julia hobbled over with the help of Christophe and a stick. Although her foot had been pinned it still pained her to walk sometimes and she certainly wasn't back on the running track yet.

'I think you should do this Julia,' she said, smiling. 'I'm only here to get them publicity really.'

'Shall we do it together?' suggested Julia.

'Good idea.'

They held the scissors together and cut it.

'We now declare the Odilon Baudoin memorial museum open.' said Sophie.

Everybody moved off to the Café Breton for a celebratory drink and Inspector Denton went over to chat to Christophe.

'How wonderful this is, congratulations Mr de Flaubert.' He said, shaking Christophe's hand warmly. 'It is a wonderful thing you have done, getting the painter pardoned and creating the museum.'

'Thank you, Inspector Denton, it was the right thing to do I feel.'

'Ah yes. Isn't that the accusation Miss Connors always throws at you? Always doing the right thing!'

Christophe smiled. 'I suppose I don't know any other way of being.'

'Well I have a 'doing the right thing' conundrum for you I'm afraid.'

'Oh?'

'Yes. Inspector Guillemain and I went over the whole case thoroughly numerous times. We needed to ensure that the claim that Baudoin painted what were known as Chapmans was in fact correct. We had to set up a new committee for verification of the Baudoins and it has been a busy time cataloguing everything.'

'I can imagine.'

'And then there was the re-opening of the murder of the other two Breton School artists, Andre Guillemain and Pierre Audren, and the pardoning of Odilon Baudoin.'

'It is incredible that you managed to do all of that so quickly.'

'All credit to Petit-Jean Baudoin, he had done a very thorough job. The big break-through was the cartridge case that Petit-Jean and Charlene found under the floorboards. It matched the fingerprints of William Chapman from his identity card that was held in the archives. And of course, the bullet from the panelling with Andre Guillemain's blood, matching the cartridge case. The Baudoin family turned out to be very fortunate in the end.

Christophe looked across at Yvette who had aged suddenly after the terrible ordeal. She no longer walked and rarely spoke to people. She had been moved into a local care home, a sad and lonely figure.

Inspector Denton followed his gaze. 'Yes, for Madame Yvette, it is a terrible tragedy is it not?'

Christophe shook his head sadly. 'Yes, how can she ever forgive herself?'

'Well on a happier note. You will be pleased to hear that both Petit-Jean and his grandfather Odilon Baudoin are to be given the Medal of French Gratitude, posthumously.'

'That is wonderful news,' said Christophe.

'What is?' asked Julia, hobbling over.

'Petit-Jean and his grandfather are to be honoured.'

'Oh. I'm so glad! Now can you rid yourself of the guilt Christophe?'

'Almost, ninety-nine per cent.' He smiled at her. 'What is this conundrum, that you mentioned Inspector Denton?'

'Ah yes. Well, we took the hair from the sample box and it matched the hair in the brushes. A couple of those brushes also had skin cells attached so we could run the DNA, and it corresponded to that of Yvette Baudoin, as was expected.

'Yes, Baudoin used to make brushes from her hair.'

'And it also matched Petit-Jean Baudoin's DNA obviously.'

'Yes, of course.'

'Well, this is very tricky. That DNA also matched another person.'

'Oh?'

'Yes. It matched a research student working at Rennes University. It is commonplace for any person who works with DNA samples to have their own DNA catalogued in case of contamination. It is fairly conclusive, the student is Petit-Jean Baudoin's daughter.'

'Hum,' said Christophe.

'Yes, your God daughter, and Madame Yvette's great grand-daughter. As such, she is the rightful owner of the Chapmans or as we now know, Baudoin paintings.'

'Ah.'

'But then, I think you already knew that.'

Julia smiled at Christophe. 'The secret that you and Petit-Jean kept so safely, that was not yours to tell.'

'Inspector Guillemain and I have decided that we shall leave you to decide what is the right thing to do.'

Christophe glanced over at Bernard and Rochelle who were laughing at something Francoise was saying. Francoise put her arm around her father, shaking her head in mock despair.

'As you say, Inspector Denton. A conundrum.'

THE END

Printed in Great Britain
by Amazon